Acts of Faith

Also by Patricia Wynn

The Blue Satan Mystery Series:
  The Birth of Blue Satan
  The Spider's Touch
  The Motive from the Deed
  A Killing Frost

The Parson's Pleasure

Sophie's Halloo

Lord Tom

Jack on the Box

Mistletoe and Mischief

The Bumblebroth

A Country Affair

The Christmas Spirit

A Pair of Rogues

Capturing Annie

Acts of Faith

Patricia Wynn

PEMBERLEY PRESS
CORONA DEL MAR

PEMBERLEY PRESS
436 Begonia Avenue
Corona del Mar, CA 92625
www.pemberleypress.com

Jacket design by Kat & Dog Studios
Cover art: Hoogstreten, Samuel van (1627-1678). A View through a House. 1662. Dyrham Park, Gloucestershire, Great Britain. With permission from: National Trust Photo Library / Art Resource, NY.

Library of Congress Cataloging-in-Publication Data

Wynn, Patricia.
    Acts of Faith / Patricia Wynn.
        pages cm. -- (Blue Satan Mystery series ; 5)
    ISBN 978-1-935421-07-8 (first edition hardcover : alk. paper) 1. Brigands and robbers--Fiction. 2. Great Britain--History--George I, 1714-1727--Fiction. 3. Yorkshire (England)--Fiction. 4. Mystery fiction. 5. Historical fiction. I. Title.
    PS3573.Y6217A66 2014
    813'.54--dc23

                                                    2014011525

℘

This book is dedicated to my *beau-fils*
Ryan Moore

Who does me the compliment of reading my books
and takes very good care of my beloved daughter.

Acknowledgements

When I began this mystery series, there were no useful websites for research on England in 1715. Over the past fourteen years, the number and quality of resources has grown to the extent that on-site research is truly not needed. While I will never let that stop me from enjoying trips to the places I write about, and I will always treasure my trip to Coxwold, Thirsk, Byland Abbey, and every spot I saw in Yorkshire, the historical information I used came mostly from my own library of books and online scholarly sites.

For my research on Yorkshire in the early 18th century, I am greatly indebted to the *Borthwick Papers,* from the University of York, Borthwick Institute for Archives, for their valuable publications on church history. Specific parish information came from the amazing *Genuki* website for English and Irish genealogy, and *British History Online.* More local color was supplied by the site for *British Listed Buildings* and Nikolaus Pevsner's *Yorkshire, the North Riding.* For information on the history of Yorkshire agriculture, I was fortunate to find the non-profit *Internet Archive,* which is entirely supported by donations and grants. Although, if I mangled my Yorkshire dialogue, I sincerely apologize, I patched it together with the aid of the dictionary at www. Yorkshire-dialect.org and books, *The Little Book of Yorkshire,* compiled by Arnold Kellett, and *Yorkshire-English,* compiled by Edward Johnson. Anyone can now learn the steps of a minuet or other archaic dance by visiting the YouTube videos from *Dancilla.* I enjoyed the pictures and descriptions of Hawnby Hill posted by hikers about their treks. Lastly, I revisited the roads I drove and the fields I passed in the North Riding many times on *Google Earth,* and it was endlessly distracting each time to be in Yorkshire again.

My thanks, also, to the staff at the Angel in Grantham, the oldest surviving inn on the Great North Road, for showing me *La Chambre le Roi,* used by Kings John, Richard III, and Charles I, and to the George Hotel at Stamford, for providing me with a historical anecdote relevant to my plot. My apologies for moving its date a bit to suit me.

A very special thank you to my friend Molly Kelly for being such a great travelling companion on our adventures in Gloucester, the Cottswolds, and Yorkshire, for letting me set the itinerary, and for showing me Lacock. Lastly, my everlasting gratitude to the National Trust for preserving so much of England's past for us to enjoy. Their properties Dyrham Park, Chastleton House, Hamm House, Nunnington Hall, East Riddlesden Hall, and Fountains Abbey and Studley Royal provided models for the houses and gardens imagined for this book.

The verses used in this book have been taken from *Gulliver's Travels* by Jonathan Swift, published in 1726, which satirizes the political and religious conflicts of early Georgian England.

Historical Background

In the 16th century, a political and religious reform movement shook the foundations of Europe. Although today we tend to attribute it to a desire to reject the canon of the Catholic Church and to bring the Christian faith closer to original scriptures, it was first and foremost a rebellion against the international papal state. The Reformers, as they considered themselves, wanted to free themselves from the abuses that had developed over the course of centuries from the secular and political involvement of the medieval Church in civil life. They seized upon small differences in doctrine to justify the overthrow of the Pope's authority. By the mid-1500s, the nations of the Netherlands, England and Scotland, plus regions of Scandinavia, Germany, and Switzerland, had permanently seceded from the Pope's realm, each developing its own particular brand of Christianity.

Henry VIII's Church of England altered fewer points of doctrine than the others. It was not, then, a Protestant church, but over centuries, it adopted many of the reforms of Protestantism.

The anti-Catholicism that followed Bloody Mary's rule and the exaltation of the martyrs she had burned at the stake remained a factor in English civil and social life for centuries. The Gunpowder Plot, a failed assassination attempt by a group of Catholics on James I of England and VI of Scotland in 1605, and the "Popish Plot," a fictitious conspiracy invented by Titus Oates in 1678, sealed the public perception of Catholics as potential traitors. Catholics were blamed for every civic misfortune, including the Great Plague of London. The monument to the Great Fire of London in 1666 attributes the cause of the inferno to "Popish frenzy."

In 1698, Parliament passed "An Act for the further preventing the Growth of Popery," only one of several penal laws against Catholics, designed to render them too weak in number and resources to be able to revolt. Calvinists, Lutherans, Anabaptists and Quakers, all who questioned state authority over religious beliefs, were labelled "Dissenters" and briefly considered threats, but as long as they did not conspire to overthrow the government, their religious practices were tolerated.

In August, 1714, George of Hanover ascended the throne of Great Britain, invited by Parliament to succeed Queen Anne, the last of the Stuart monarchs. More than fifty Roman Catholics stood between Anne and George in the line of succession, including the only son of King James II, the Pretender, James Francis Edward Stuart; however, when Queen Anne, a member of the reformed church, had failed to produce an heir, in 1701, a Whig-dominated Parliament passed the Act of Settlement to disqualify any Roman Catholic for the throne. Again, it was because Roman Catholics acknowledged a superior power to the monarch—the Pope—not because of differences in doctrine, that this action was taken.

In 1715, the Pretender and conspirators in England, Scotland and Ireland staged a rebellion. His adherents naturally included many Catholics, but also Church of England Tories who believed in the divine right of kings.

By the summer of 1716, when this story opens, the Jacobite Rebellion, known later as "the Fifteen," had been thoroughly quelled. King George had beat the rebels, in part, by importing mercenaries from Europe. Feeling secure on his throne for the first time since his coronation, George persuaded Parliament to grant him permission to visit Hanover, his home, which he would do periodically throughout his reign. He left his son, George Augustus (later George II), to rule in his stead with limited powers.

He left an England in which the number of aristocratic families still practicing Roman Catholicism in Yorkshire, as elsewhere in the kingdom, had seriously been reduced, victims of the laws designed to stamp them out.

*W*hich two mighty Powers have, as I was going to tell you, been engaged in the most obstinate War for six and thirty moons past. It began upon the following Occasion. It is allowed on all Hands that the primitive Way of breaking Eggs before we eat them, was upon the larger End; But his present Majesty's Grand-father, while he was a Boy, going to eat an Egg, and breaking it according to the ancient Practice, happened to cut one of his Fingers. Whereupon the Emperor his Father, published an Edict, commanding all his Subjects, upon great Penalties, to break the smaller End of their Eggs.

A Voyage to Lilliput
by Lemuel Gulliver

*D*uring the Course of these Troubles, the Emperors of Blefuscu did frequently expostulate by their Ambassadors, accusing us of making a Schism in Religion, by offending against a fundamental Doctrine of our great Prophet Lustrog, in the fifty-fourth Chapter of the Brundrecal, (which is their Alcoran.) This, however, is thought to be a meer Strain upon the Text: For the Words are these; That all true Believers shall break their Eggs at the convenient End; and which is the convenient End, seems, in my humble Opinion, to be left to every Man's Conscience . . .

CHAPTER I

London, July, 1716

It was a quarter to four in the morning when Mrs. Hester Kean, trailed by two liveried footmen, arrived on foot at the Black Swan in Holborn. At the entrance to the inn yard, illuminated by a hanging lamp, Hester paused to take note of the activity in the street. Already at this hour, people were bustling with the tasks of opening their houses or setting up shop before the daily business generated by the Inns of Chancery clustered nearby. Hawkers had awakened to ply their trades, and servants emptied chamber pots, swept entries, and rushed to market before the streets filled with pedestrians and horses. Directly across Holborn, the Bell and the Black Bull vied for custom, but the Black Swan was the only inn in London that offered stagecoach service to the City of York.

Will, one of Lord Hawkhurst's footmen, carried Hester's portmanteau through the entrance to the inn yard, where the coach stood waiting for passengers, and handed it to the coachman to be lodged in the basket on the rear. Her trunks, with the clothing she would need for a long visit and gifts for her cousins, had been sent ahead by carrier. With luck, they would arrive soon after Hester. The one change of gown in her bag would have to suffice until they did.

The second footman, John, toted a basket of food put up by the cook for Hester's journey. Four o'clock was too early for the inn to supply breakfast to travellers, even the ones who had lodged there overnight.

"Here you are, mistress," John said, anxiously presenting his burden to her. "God give you a safe journey."

Returned from seeing her bag carefully stowed, Will echoed the sentiment in an equally fearful voice, "Take care of yourself, Mrs. Kean. We'll all pray for your safety." Leaning forward and lowering his voice to a reassuring note, he said, "The coachman looks like he knows his business."

Indeed, Hester thought, casting an eye over the driver for the initial stage, he did look capable. With a worn pair of jack boots up over his knees, sturdy gloves, and a broad-brimmed felt hat with a high crown, he looked every inch the reliable coachman, checking and rechecking the horses' harness as they stood swishing their tails in the pre-dawn light. In spite of the warm summer weather, he had hung a large cape over his shoulders, prepared for any inclement weather they might encounter on the road.

Assuming a bravery she did not feel, Hester smiled and thanked both footmen for their good wishes, while trying to still the nervous stomach that had kept her awake most of the night. It was useless to fear for her life over the four days it would take the stagecoach to reach York—"if God permits," as the advertisement read. The hazards of the road were too numerous and real to dismiss, but as the dire possibilities were too many to foresee, it was best to deal with each if and when it came. Aside from the usual problems of deep mud and broken axles, and the perpetual threat of highwaymen, other dangers had recently been thrust on her mind.

Only a few weeks ago in the Strand, some drunken officers of the Guard had attacked the carriage of the Earl and Countess of Bristol. The assault had been especially frightening because Lady Bristol was heavy with child. Before he had left for Hanover, King George had ordered a court martial for those involved, but if an episode of that nature could happen on the streets of London, Hester wondered what might happen on the open road. Whenever large numbers of men were assembled, there was sure to be violence, and the army had been doubled in the past year to put down the Jacobite rebellion in the North.

Reports of rioting in Norfolk, Gloucestershire, Shropshire, and even Yorkshire, too, had reached her ears. Although the King had garrisoned the houses of known Jacobites, she wondered how much his new security measures would provoke others working in secret. There would be no newssheets in Yorkshire to inform them of any disturbance in the country. They would have to rely upon letters sent from London, and any news they did receive would already be a week old.

It did no good to concern oneself with things that could not be helped, so Hester tried not to think how much she would miss the daily newssheets. She did mutter a prayer that the carriage would not overturn in a river, as the York coach had done just a few years ago, drowning most of its passengers; but beyond that one prayer she cautioned herself to be patient, the better to deal with whatever adventure or misadventure the journey might bring.

She felt the pocket beneath her skirt to assure herself that her purse was still there. She had been told that in addition to the fare she would need seven shillings to tip the coachmen and to pay for their drinks on the stops.

Will and John insisted on waiting to wave her off, though it was apparent that not all the passengers had arrived. As long as they had purchased tickets in advance, the coach would await their pleasure. She could only hope they would not be too late. As reluctant as Hester was to enter the box that would be her virtual cage for four days—at the very least from five in the morning till nine at night—if she wanted a good spot, it behooved her to take her seat. Already three of her fellow travellers, all men, had claimed theirs. She doubted that any of them would relinquish his superior place, even to a lady.

After paying the coachman what remained of her fare—earnest money having been paid to reserve the place—she accepted his help into the coach. She chose the remaining window seat, though it meant sitting with her back to the horses. This was preferable to a center seat, in case she wished to sleep. Besides, she was used to facing the rear in a coach, since her aunt and her cousins always claimed the better spots. As waiting woman to her cousin Isabella, Countess of Hawkhurst,

Hester must always defer to the comfort of her employers.

As she settled her basket upon her lap, two of the passengers tipped their hats. The third, sitting across from her, merely nodded and said, "I bid thee good day."

This manner of address confirmed the impression she had got from the plainness of his clothes and his hair, which hung limply by his face, that he was a Quaker. Her other two companions consisted of a pale, thin-featured clergyman, in black cassock, plain white neckcloth, and low-crowned hat, and a robust country gentleman in an open coat, woolen waistcoat, breeches, and jack boots up over his knees.

When the Quaker had greeted her, the clergyman had pursed his lips in distaste. Hester's father, an Anglican clergyman, now deceased, had had no patience with the "Friends" as they called themselves, but she had always found them exceptionally honest and hardworking. Their unconventional beliefs did not particularly offend her. Of course, she had never been witness to the extreme antics of certain members of their sect; but such demonstrations as they had made in the past for the most part had ended before she was born. She hoped the clergyman's obvious dislike would not lead to any unpleasantness on the road.

She was about to offer each of the men something from her basket of food when a flurry of activity in the yard announced the arrival of another passenger. A raised male voice with a trace of a foreign accent asked if this was indeed the coach to York. The ostler answered him curtly. Then, a debate with the coachman over the passenger's baggage ensued.

Peering through the small window, Hester saw the coachman and another man struggling with a large portmanteau trunk. This was followed by a thump that rocked the vehicle as the trunk presumably made its way into the basket.

In a few moments, the face of a young gentleman appeared at the door. He glanced at his fellow passengers and, receiving a glare from the Quaker, cast an anxious look about for a friendlier face. Hester and the clergyman both, who shared the backward-facing bench, nodded and smiled at him encouragingly, so removing his braided and cockaded hat, he squeezed himself through the door and set himself down between them.

Hester supposed it was the gentleman's clothing that had drawn the Quaker's frown, for though not overly rich in adornment, it displayed the unmistakable imprint of France. Like the others, Hester had elected to wear older garments, which could easily be ruined on a journey of this length. The men wore dark colours—the Quaker in plain drab—with heavy boots or sturdy shoes in case it became necessary to tramp through deep mud. The new gentleman, whom she estimated to be a few years younger than herself, wore a modest amount of lace at his neck and cuffs. His *habit à la française,* though of a cloth designed for riding, was elegantly fitted and braided. The only concessions he had made to the rigours of the road were his high-topped boots and a tied wig, though it was thickly covered with a fine white powder in the latest fashion.

The clergyman gazed upon these signs of nobility with favour. Inclining his head politely, he inquired of the young gentleman whither he was bound.

Before he received an answer, the door flew open again to admit their last travelling companion, who peered in with a severe, officious air. With no choice of seats remaining, he stepped over the legs of the country gentleman and sat between him and the Quaker.

After bidding this newcomer good day, the clergyman repeated his question to the young gentleman.

"To Yorkshire," the young man replied. He darted a wary look at the others before fixing his gaze on the hat in his lap.

"Then we shall be companions for the entire journey, for I, too, am bound for York."

When the young man declined to elaborate, the clergyman appeared to realize that a slight towards the other passengers could have been implied. With a condescending smile, he asked how far he and the young gentleman could expect to enjoy the others' company.

"I be bound for Yorkshire, too," the Quaker stated, "though I don't get down till Thirsk."

The young man's head jerked up, as if he would have spoken, but apparently thinking better of it, he lowered it again.

When solicited, the last man to take his seat gave his name as Foxcroft and volunteered that he was heading into Yorkshire on the King's business. This statement was greeted with curiosity by the country gentleman and a polite nod from the clergyman, but the Quaker eyed him askance. The young gentleman shifted in his seat. Hester noticed that the knuckles gripping the hat in his lap had turned white.

The country gentleman, who gave his name as Woodson, said that he would ride with them as far as Doncaster, from which town he would hire a horse to take him home to Moorends. "And happy I shall be to get home, I assure you, for I have been in the metropolis for nigh on two months."

"And what about you, mistress?" he inquired kindly of Hester with the hint of a bow.

"I am heading to Yorkshire as well, on a visit to my family."

"On a happy occasion, I hope?"

Regardless of her expectations, Hester replied in the affirmative, since there was nothing in the reason for her visit—neither illness nor death—which could politely be characterized as unhappy. Then, while the clergyman loudly congratulated himself on a pleasant set of companions, she reflected that, now that she was used to the idea, she was not particularly sorry to be undertaking the trip.

There was no denying that the news of her impending journey had come as a shock. She had just begun to settle into the lodgings her cousins, Harrowby, the Earl of Hawkhurst and Isabella, his countess, had rented in Royal Tunbridge Wells, when her plans for the summer months had been overset.

Their establishment at the popular resort had been delayed for a number of reasons. First had come the celebration of King George's birthday near the end of May, when the whole Court had turned out in finery to see the illuminations and bonfires at St. James's. Then the King had appointed the eighth of June as a day of solemn thanksgiving to God for putting down the "late, unnatural rebellion." Prayers and sermons had been offered up in every church, the kingdom's standards displayed, bells rung, and the guns of the Tower fired as the evening had concluded with bonfires, illuminations, and further demonstrations of public joy.

Harrowby had been detained in Parliament for a few more weeks, while the King urged the passage of a number of acts designed to secure his kingdom before he left to visit his Electorate of Hanover. With the rebellion only recently put down, Parliament had taken measures to protect his reign from every possible source of unrest.

Finally, near the end of June, King George had granted Parliament a recess until the seventh of August, instructing all members to return to their "respective countries" in full confidence that they would use their "best Endeavours to secure the Peace of the Kingdom, and to discourage and suppress all manner of Disorders; since," as he assured them, "as the first Scene of the late Rebellion was opened and ushered in by Tumults and Riots," his enemies would be "restless and unwearied in their endeavours to renew the Rebellion and to subvert the Religion, Laws and Liberties of their Country."

With little more than six weeks in which to secure the loyalty of his countrymen in Kent *and* to divert himself, Harrowby had elected to spend the greater part of it frolicking in Royal Tunbridge Wells. If his mother-in-law, Mrs. Mayfield, Hester's aunt, had been consulted, she would have opted for the Bath, where the stakes at cards were much higher. At the Bath, however, the rules of decorum were reputed to be so strict that Isabella feared there would be a restraint on flirting. And, chastened by a recent experience in which he had fallen under the influence of a mistress, Harrowby was ready to humour his wife.

Before King George took ship for Hanover, however, in order for Harrowby to fulfill his duty as a peer, the family had set off first for Rotherham Abbey, his country seat in Kent. It had been Mrs. Mayfield's intention to send Hester there in May to supervise the move of Harrowby's heir, George Lord Rennington and his wet nurse; but by the time the spring rains had ceased and the roads were passable, Harrowby and Isabella had become so attached to their son that they had been loath to part with him. They had put off his removal until they could journey down with him. Hester was gratified by this proof of their affection, since it was due in no small part to her efforts that they had overcome their initial indifference to their child.

It was, therefore, not until the last week of June that they finally travelled down, the baby, his wet nurse, Isabella's maid, and Harrowby's valet in the ancient travelling coach, and Harrowby, Isabella, Hester, and Mrs. Mayfield in a handsome new vehicle purchased to accommodate the growing family. Even in the beauty of summer, however, the country could not hold Harrowby's or Isabella's interest for long. After less than a fortnight of tending to business, the earl ordered up his carriage again, and bidding cheerful goodbyes to their son, they headed for the fashionable resort of Royal Tunbridge Wells where they would meet with their friends and be amused without the oppressive rules of Court.

Harrowby had purposely taken a house with too few rooms for his household in order to rid himself of his mother-in-law for the summer. He had decided that Mrs. Mayfield should return to Yorkshire to visit her son Dudley and his new wife Pamela, and to see to her other children who dwelt in their care. For months, Mrs. Mayfield had been hinting that her daughter Mary, the next of her children ready to leave the nursery, would soon be old enough to marry. She wished to bring Mary to Court to arrange an advantageous match. Since Dudley did not have the money to provide his sister with an attractive dowry, Mrs. Mayfield had wheedled and nagged until Harrowby had promised to settle sufficient funds on Mary to help her nab a noble husband.

Mrs. Mayfield's journey into Yorkshire had been delayed when she begged to accompany her "precious Rennington" into Kent to help Isabella see that all was properly set up in the nursery, when in reality that task would fall to Hester. Harrowby and Isabella were so ignorant about the running of their household that they failed to recognize Mrs. Mayfield's ploy. Hester could only bite her tongue and postpone the pleasure of seeing the last of her aunt for a few more weeks.

During their brief stay at Rotherham Abbey, Mrs. Mayfield's behaviour was surprisingly good. Hester suspected that her aunt still entertained hopes of a reprieve from impending exile. The lodgings at the Wells, however, did not begin to approximate the size and comfort of Harrowby's mansion in Piccadilly, so into Yorkshire she must go. Hester was grateful for any plan that would free her from her aunt's hostility for at least two months. Selfish and greedy, Mrs. Mayfield neglected no opportunity to take advantage of her daughter's position .

as a countess, and she resented Hester, not only for her attempts to protect the Hawkhurst fortune from her extravagance, but also for the influence she had on Isabella.

Isabella had been too much indulged. She was not very bright, but she was generous in her own way and capable of fondness, if not selfless love. Fortunately, she was attached to Hester, or Hester believed her aunt would have found a way to banish her from Hawkhurst House.

With the prospect of a few months' freedom from her aunt's jealousy, Hester turned her thoughts to self-improvement. She needed to steel herself from the sorrow of a recent and deep disappointment. In love with Gideon Fitzsimmons, the outlawed Viscount St. Mars, she had finally faced the probability that he would never offer her marriage. His situation in England was hopeless. As long as the Crown suspected him of murder, he could never be restored to the title he should hold as Earl of Hawkhurst, which Parliament had stripped from him and awarded to Harrowby. But in France, where he owned a considerable property, he could live in the open. He could make an advantageous marriage and be a member of the Regent's court. The last time Hester had seen him, he had declared his plan to smuggle himself into France with no mention of returning. She could not blame him for choosing freedom over life as an outlaw, but the fact that he had not asked her to accompany him or even to wait for his return had forced her to accept the end to foolish dreams.

She had almost succumbed to a different proposal of marriage, which would have solved the greatest of her problems, except for the dispiriting truth that neither she nor the gentleman who had proposed to her had been in love. To accept him, knowing this, had seemed to her to be committing a great wrong.

If only one did not feel so apart! She had learned that being surrounded by people she did not love could be far more painful than being alone.

It had taken all her fortitude to conceal this episode from her family, to hide her sadness, to devote herself to her duties, and not to dwell on things that could never be. Her greatest solace had been playing with Georgie. She already missed his infant smiles, the warm feeling of holding a baby in her arms, but the allure of a pleasant change of scenery was difficult to resist.

She found Royal Tunbridge Wells delightful with its wide, shaded walks, its shops, a bowling green, pure air, and rustic charm. Every day, if the weather was clear, the ladies and gentlemen strolled the pantiles of the Upper Walk, took the waters of Lord Muskerry's spring, and made merry in the evenings. Their daily routine was enlivened by games of bowls and horse-races on the downs. Harrowby and Isabella soon forgot their son in the promise of assemblies and parties, gaming and balls, made even more entertaining by the informality of the setting.

For the first few mornings they was there, dressed in *déshabille,* Hester accompanied Isabella and her mother to the Wells to take the recommended dose of water. At nine o'clock, they returned to their lodgings to dress. Then at ten, while Isabella and Mrs. Mayfield put finishing touches on their finery before strolling the Walks, and Harrowby set off for conversation at the coffee house, Hester attended church to pray for patience until her aunt left for Yorkshire at the end of the week.

The Church of King Charles the Martyr had been built by subscription as an assembly room and chapel for the visitors to the Wells. As the popularity of the spa had grown, the church building had been doubled in size to accommodate a greater number of worshippers. The result was an unusual square shape with an upper story of pews on two facing sides.

The interior with its dark wooden pews and cream-coloured walls was brightly lit by tall arched windows, which let in the summer light and warmth. The glory of the church was its plaster ceiling, sculpted in circles and domes. In the short time Hester had to herself every day at this hour, she bathed in the peaceful surroundings and prayed for the strength to live out her life in service to a family she could never respect.

She could tolerate Isabella, for whom she had a sort of motherly affection. When she thought, however, of being treated like a servant by her aunt for the remainder of her days, she had to question her decision to pass up the only offer of marriage she was ever likely to receive.

On the fourth day of their stay at the Wells, after the service was over, she returned to their lodgings in Mr. Ashenhurst's house to find the household in an uproar. She could hear Mrs. Mayfield's shrieks all the way down the path to the street.

A maid anxiously greeted Hester with the news that the tooth-drawer had been summoned, Mrs. Mayfield having been struck suddenly with an intolerable pain in her jaw. According to the maid, she had been crying out for Hester this half hour or more.

With a sigh, but with a twinge of sympathy, Hester quickly put her things away and followed the maid upstairs to the chamber she had been sharing with her aunt the past few days. There she found Mrs. Mayfield propped up in bed, vigorously resisting the tooth-drawer's attempts to rid her of one of her few remaining teeth. He loomed over her, brandishing a fearsome instrument, his voice raised in an effort to be heard over her screams.

"Now, now, my lady," he shouted, wincing from a slap that caught him on the chin, "I can see that you have been through this many times before. You know how much better you will feel once the offending tooth is out."

"It's not my tooth, you bloodthirsty leech! The pain was in my neck and now it's moved into my chest." In this moment she caught sight of Hester and, bursting into a wail, reached out a trembling hand. "Oh, Hester, thank God you have come! You must make this horrid man leave! I know when I have a rotten tooth and this one is not!"

The fear on her face was unquestionably real. Hester hurried to the bed and clasped her aunt's outstretched hand. "Indeed, sir, if my aunt insists that her tooth is not the source of her pain, it would seem useless to remove it."

"Do you suppose I do not know my own business, mistress? Do you think me a fool? Why, all that is needed is one glance in her mouth to see how severely it's rotted. She'd be better off to let me draw all the teeth she has, so her false ones can take a better hold."

There was some sense in what he said. Mrs. Mayfield's teeth were a constant source of complaint. Hester had been sent on countless errands to purchase every tooth powder and mastic touted in the news-sheets, but none had been of any help. One look at her aunt's livid face, however, informed Hester that she would never give her consent, and Hester would pay—and pay dearly—if she did not take her side.

"Nevertheless," Hester said to the tooth-drawer, "I see no reason to put her through the agony of an extraction when her present trouble may be due to something else. I thank you for coming, but I must ask you to leave."

Furious now, the tooth-drawer jammed his instruments into his leather bag, fretting and fuming. "I will go," he said, taking up the bag, "but you'll be calling me again soon enough, I make no doubt. And perhaps I shall not be so quick to come another time." He donned his hat with a vicious shove and stormed from the room.

"Oh, Hester, my dear, thank goodness you were come in time. I had such palpitations, I do not know how long I could have fought him off." This was said in such a weak voice that Hester grew genuinely concerned. Her aunt never called her "my dear." Such uncharacteristic behaviour increased her alarm.

"Perhaps we should call for a physician."

"Yes, I'm afraid you must. I am not at all well."

"I shall do so directly. But where is Isabella?"

Mrs. Mayfield gave her a startled look. "Why, she has gone for her morning walk."

"Does she not know of your pain?"

"Yes, but I told her to run along. I knew you would be returning shortly. It was that fool of a housekeeper who called for the tooth-drawer, and all because I put a hand to my cheek, I suppose. But do you go and find a physician, and have some tea and pastries sent up. And don't dawdle!"

Mrs. Mayfield sounded more like her irritable self. If that was how she had addressed Isabella, Hester could hardly blame her cousin for leaving the house. The truth, however, was that Isabella was no more a nurse than her mother was and fled the scene whenever the faintest sign of illness appeared. Always robust herself, she had no understanding of symptoms and no patience with weakness.

Well, Hester had prayed for patience, and the brief show of gratitude on Mrs. Mayfield's part had been her reward. If her aunt would only continue in that pleasant vein, Hester could much more easily reconcile herself to wait upon her.

She went out into the street and made several inquiries before sending a note to a Dr. Brett, who soon came. He took her aunt's pulse and declared it to be slightly elevated. Although there was no fever, he could not like the feverish gleam in her eyes.

Mrs. Mayfield fidgeted in the bed, as she bemoaned the unlucky timing of her attack. "For you must know, Doctor, that I am under the greatest need to be well before Thursday next, for I am taking the York coach."

"My dear lady!" The doctor was patently shocked. "I am not at all certain that an activity of that nature would be wise. If you were to travel in a private conveyance, I should be more sanguine, but the public carrier?"

"Indeed, just thinking of the risks gives me palpitations. Not that I believe that to be the only cause, of course," she added, sitting up suddenly as if she would snatch back her words.

A suspicion entered Hester mind, and she frowned. Her aunt darted a look at her, then gave a moan and fell backwards onto her pillows.

Dr. Brett took her pulse again, this time reporting that it was erratic. "Clearly something is affecting your heart. I shall give you a sedative now and come back later to see how you are getting on, but I should reconsider that journey, if I were you."

"Thank you, Doctor." Mrs. Mayfield submitted meekly to being sedated, only telling Hester to be sure to relay the doctor's findings to Isabella and Harrowby as soon as they returned.

As Hester escorted Dr. Brett from the bedchamber, he spoke to her in a grave voice. "Is it true that your aunt intends to undertake such a journey?"

Hester had begun to doubt her aunt's intentions, but it was too early to speculate aloud. "It is true that she has planned to take the stagecoach."

The doctor tsked. "I cannot believe his lordship would wish to subject his mother-in-law to such an ordeal. Perhaps I should speak to him or to his lady myself?" The notion of advising the Earl of Hawkhurst on the health of a member of his family appeared to gratify him.

As Hester certainly did not wish to be the one to tell Harrowby that his mother-in-law might be too unwell to leave, she invited Dr. Brett to return after dinner to speak to them both.

This he did, and after reexamining his patient and finding her quite agitated, and reportedly suffering from mysterious pains that ranged from her head to her toes, he diagnosed a nervous complaint and pre-scribed her a long course of the local waters. Hester, who was with her aunt when she received this advice, noted a triumphant gleam in Mrs. Mayfield's eyes. It was quickly countered by a dolorous sigh and a piti-able lament that she would not be seeing her precious children.

"And who is to prepare Mary to come to town, I do not know, for Dudley's wife has never stirred outside Yorkshire. And wealthy as her papa may be, there's nothing so improving to a girl as a sojourn in London. I fear my poor Mary will seem the veriest country mouse when she arrives."

The doctor was sufficiently moved by her concern to state that if Lord Hawkhurst could send her in his private coach, providing she broke her journey often, he might be prevailed upon to withdraw his objections to the trip.

Mrs. Mayfield barely managed a civil reply, but she clenched her teeth and emitting a few moans said she doubted she could rise from her bed any time the next week. And, besides, she could never so im-pose on her "dear Hawkhurst" as to deprive him of his vehicle for a whole fortnight.

"No," she said, shaking her head with a brave smile, "I must not go. I succumb to your advice, Doctor. Besides, I have thought of a plan which will do just as well. Hester can go in my place."

Dr. Brett seemed relieved that he would not be losing his noble pa-tient, or the next best thing in a nobleman's mother-in-law. He beamed at Hester and congratulated her on her youth and excellent health.

When he informed the earl and his wife of his diagnosis, Har-rowby closed his eyes and groaned. Then, a thought occurred to him and he asked with a hopeful look, "I don't suppose she's on her death-bed, is she?"

Isabella gasped. "Mama might die?"

Dr. Brett responded gravely, "No, my lady. I do not think we need fear that. At least, not yet."

Harrowby's face fell. He sighed. "I didn't think so. But you are certain she is too sick to travel?"

"Oh, Mama must not attempt it!" Isabella cried. "Why, she cannot abide being shut up in a carriage. She says it gives her the worst sort of headache."

Dr. Brett agreed. "I greatly fear it, my lord. I should not like to risk my professional reputation by giving her my leave to go."

"Oh, you wouldn't, eh? Then, where shall I put her for the next two months? Just tell me that if you will. If she has to share a bedchamber with Mrs. Kean, we shall never hear the end of her complaints."

Isabella was nonplussed, but the doctor proved eager to relieve them of this worry. "I believe Mrs. Mayfield came up with a solution to that problem herself by suggesting that her niece go to Yorkshire in her place."

Isabella brightened. "Yes, Hester can go! Now we can be merry again and not give the matter another thought."

Harrowby was not so certain that a summer with Mrs. Mayfield would be as merry as one without her, but at least the problem of the bedchamber had been resolved.

The very next day, Hester found herself on the way to London, where she packed and made arrangements for a much longer trip. It had been too much to expect that Harrowby or Isabella would see through Mrs. Mayfield's pretence. She had out-manoeuvred her niece and fooled the others, perhaps having concocted her scheme weeks ago.

But there was no use dwelling on her aunt's chicanery. By the time Hester boarded the York coach, she had become reconciled to the trip, and except for the rigours of the journey, she would not regret a visit to the North Riding where she had been raised.

She would have been happier if she were not to stay with her cousin Dudley, who had inherited most of his mother's bad qualities and was boorish to boot. But Mary was Hester's favourite cousin. It might be amusing to prepare her for a London visit.

At least she would be in the country, surrounded by scenery she loved and away from London, where everything reminded her of St. Mars and what she greatly feared had been their final farewell.

She only hoped the journey would not be strained by the tension she felt developing among the passengers in the coach.

Immediately all the Troops gave a Shout between Terror and Surprize; for the Sun shone clear, and the Reflexion dazzled their Eyes, as I waved the Scymiter to and fro in my Hand.

CHAPTER II

The evening after Hester boarded the York coach, Gideon Fitzsimmons, the outlawed Viscount St. Mars, reined his horse outside a hedge inn in the County of Kent and slid his eyes over the dismal sight. The timbers that girded the roof still sagged, and its thatch was so thin he could spy some of the rafters through it. In spite of the inn's ragged appearance, however, Gideon was grateful to be home.

Not that this miserable inn deep in the Weald was home, but it had been the first refuge he had found after being declared outlaw, and it had proven to be a useful hide-out on more than one occasion.

A tow-headed boy eagerly ran out to greet him. Dismounting, Gideon tossed the boy his reins and instructed him to return the hack to the Mermaid Inn at Rye.

"Has Tom arrived?" he asked, giving the boy enough coin to defray the cost of the journey, plus a handsome tip.

"Yessir. He's been waitin' for ye these three days or more." On a wistful note he added, "He didn't bring that mare of yours, though."

Gideon grinned and tossed him another penny to salve his disappointment, pleased to hear news of his faithful groom. He had sent a letter to London advising Tom of his imminent return before finding passage aboard a smugglers' vessel in France. It had taken a few days for the captain of the sloop to feel safe enough to leave Calais, but since the great thaw of the winter ice and the end to the rebellion, the traffic in the Channel had been so heavy that there were too many boats crossing to and from the Continent for his Majesty's men to board them all. For once, the journey had been blessedly uneventful.

Giving the boy a playful cuff on the head, Gideon left him to his work and made his way to the door. It opened into the public room, furnished with a few rough tables and stools before an open hearth. In spite of the warm summer day, a fire had been lit. It filled the air with smoke and rendered the room unpleasantly close. The turnspit dog trotting in his wheel was panting from the excessive heat, but the smell of roasting beef meant that Gideon would soon be recompensed for the discomfort.

At first glance, the room seemed empty, except for the innkeeper Lade, a lanky, bad-tempered wretch, who slouched behind his bar, muttering sullenly into a pint of ale. At the sound of the door, he looked up, stopped his muttering, and growled, "Wull, I'll cap downright. Look 'oo's turned up. Come to tip me my earnest, I'll warrant."

The scrape of a chair made Gideon turn towards the corner as the man who was sitting there leapt to his feet.

"My—sir! Welcome home, sir." Tom took two steps forward and bowed, a broad smile bathing his features.

Gideon could not resist returning the grin. "It's good to be here. And to see you looking so well, Tom. Marriage must suit you."

An inevitable flush filled Tom's cheeks. "It does that, my—sir."

"So it's 'my' sir, is it?" Lade sneered. "Just plain 'sir' ain't good enough fer ye?"

The truth was that Tom, who had served Gideon since he was a boy, still found it hard not to address him as "my lord", especially when his emotions were aroused. But he knew how crucial it was to preserve the secret of his master's identity. If Lade ever tumbled to the fact that Gideon was the Viscount St. Mars—a man with a reward of a thousand pounds on his head—he would instantly give up the retainer Gideon paid him to use his rooms in favour of the greater sum.

"An' I h'an't fergot that ye stole me wench from me neither," Lade complained.

Tom turned to Lade with gritted teeth. "I've told you before, you thievin' louse! I won't have you talkin' about my wife."

Tom's wife Katy had been released from gaol at the same time as Lade with no option but to serve as his waiting wench or starve. Occasionally, he had made her entertain his lustier customers, too. Branded as a thief, she would never have been accepted back into the respectable trade her parents had practiced, but she had brought her considerable talent with a needle to Gideon's service, making all his clothes and disguises. In due time, Tom had become convinced of her worth. His attraction to her had never been in question, and it was easy to see from the happiness on his face that he was more than satisfied with his new situation.

Now he glared at Lade with balled fists. Lade cackled with glee, until Gideon said, in a voice that brooked no argument, "Enough, Lade! Do not think for one minute that I'll protect you from Tom. If you persist in insulting his wife, he has every right to call you to account. And I warn you that, in addition to possessing a strong pair of fists, he is very adept with a whip."

The innkeeper glowered. "I was jus' havin' a bit of fun wif 'im, is all." His tone turned wheedling. "You wouldn't wanna raise a cloud wif me, would ye? Tell me if 'is Majesty's man got clean away? Him what I helped ye wif."

"No, I won't smoke a pipe with you, but I would gladly drink a mug of ale."

"Shall I see to your horse, sir?" Tom asked, with a curt glance at Lade.

"No, the boy will take it back to Rye. Is my room ready, Tom?"

Tom nodded.

"Then let me finish here before I take my dinner upstairs."

As impatient as Gideon was to hear Tom's news, it was important to remain in Lade's good graces. This was, after all, Lade's house. He might be glad for the money Gideon paid him, but if his dignity were sufficiently offended, in a fit of temper he might decide that Gideon's patronage was more trouble than it was worth. Then, he might see how much he could get by interesting the local authorities in a gentleman who needed a place to hide.

Fortunately, he believed that Gideon was a Jacobite spy, or a member of his own criminal fraternity, or both. Gideon had been able to use these assumptions to his advantage, for Lade fancied himself a loyal Jacobite. Exactly from where his allegiance to the Pretender had sprung, Gideon had never bothered to learn. He suspected it had arisen merely from Lade's resentment of authority, in which case, if James Stuart ever obtained the crown, Lade would curse him just as bitterly as he did German George. Nevertheless, his sentiments were useful, so Gideon played on Lade's fantasy that he was a brave soldier in the Stuart cause.

At Gideon's request Lade had recently harboured an escaped Jacobite rebel until Gideon could smuggle the man into France. There might be others they could help, so now was not the time to burn one's boats.

As Tom left the room, Lade drew Gideon a frothy mug, and without invitation, plopped himself down on the stool across from him. For the next half hour, Gideon fed Lade a few insignificant details of their escape and assured him that their friend had arrived in France safe and sound. He let Lade believe that they both had spent the ensuing weeks conspiring with "the King over the water," in whose name they drank several toasts. But Gideon had never joined the flood of exiles and escaped prisoners who had recently increased the Pretender's retinue. He did not tell his drunken host that he had largely passed the last three months at his own estate of St. Mars, tending to his land and his personal business. The days of Gideon's involvement with the Stuart cause had been brief. He had no intention of resuming his connection with James, who had neither the strength nor the temperament to rule. By now, even the French had deserted him, though James's adherents in France still intrigued. They would never give up the cause, even though James himself had retreated, first to Avignon and recently, Gideon had heard, to Urbino, where it was expected he would fight in the Pope's army under his French title of Chevalier de St. George. With their financial support from the French cut off, many of his followers had been forced to seek their fortunes similarly in Toulon, Marseilles, Italy, and beyond.

After enduring a final toast and a few choruses of a Jacobite song, Gideon bade his host good night, wearied by the need to maintain the pretence and grateful to escape. He bounded up the stairs to learn whatever Tom could tell him. He found his table laid and his dinner nearly cooled. The chamber was much too warm to light a fire, but Gideon would be content with the food as it was. It was English, it was simple, and it was hearty. He enjoyed a good French meal with its tasty sauces as much as anyone, but it was always a pleasure to come home to beef and pudding.

Tom refused to dine with his master, believing it an insult to his lord's dignity, but he would take a chair on Gideon's orders. He had just sat down when between bites Gideon asked about the fate of the other Jacobite prisoners.

Tom eyed him warily, fearing, perhaps, that Gideon planned to help them all escape. "There's been twenty-four more tried and condemned, but only four of them put to death. They do say as how Lord Widdrington is to be transported to the Carolinas, and Mr. Charles Radcliffe's hanging has twice been stayed."

"Yes, I read about the mob that surrounded his coach when he was taken for arraignment. It sounded as if they nearly pulled him free. I wish I had been there to see it. On the order of some twenty thousand people I heard."

Tom nodded, eager to report something positive. "They say, too, as how King George may fear another risin' if Mr. Radcliffe is hanged."

Radcliffe's brother, the Earl of Derwentwater, James's childhood playmate, had met his death so nobly and at such an early age, proudly proclaiming loyalty to his cousin James from the scaffold, that a great deal of sympathy had been aroused. Thoughtfully chewing his food, Gideon hoped George could be brought to see that executing Derwentwater's younger brother and the remainder of the rebels would make him even less popular than he already was.

"I read about the assault on Read's Mug House—five men arrested and hanged for that."

"Aye, but the streets've been quiet since. The Lord Mayor's come down hard on the idle and the vagrants. People know his Majesty means business."

Gideon wiped his mouth with a serviette. "What else can you tell me?"

The month of June, according to Tom, had seen a continuation of the trials for treason that had led to Gideon's last escapade. Day by day, the newssheets in London had reported more arrests, and with rare exceptions all who were tried were condemned. A few of the peers, however, and even some of the commoners who had spent months locked in the Tower had brought their *habeus corpus* and had been released on bail with money supplied by their friends in Parliament. Gideon was relieved to hear the name of Sir William Wyndham among them, but aggrieved to learn that Lord Landsdown had been detained. He knew that the baron had corresponded with the Pretender, as had so many Tory peers, but that he had never involved himself in the rebellion. These men had been Gideon's father's friends, but he would not fool himself that he could save them.

Noting the change in his mood, Tom hastened to give him better news. More of the rebels had escaped from gaol, Brigadier MacIntosh and Thomas Forster, among them. Gideon knew the two represented only a fraction of those taken, but he was pleased by the information, nevertheless.

Now, with a rising tension in his stomach, he posed the question he had long wanted to ask, "And what of Mrs. Kean? Have you seen or heard anything from her?"

"No, my lord. If she'd written, I would have posted her letter on to you."

Gideon spoke lightly to conceal his disappointment. "Then we must conclude that all is well. I don't suppose you have gone to see if the family is at the Abbey?"

Tom shook his head.

"Well, they ought to be down this time of year. I shall ride over tomorrow night and see for myself."

The next day was long, and not merely because the sun set so late. Throughout his journey to France and back, Gideon had brooded over a misunderstanding that seemed to exist between himself and Mrs. Kean. No matter how much he had cudgeled his brain, he still could not understand why she had pulled away from him. He could think of nothing he had done to offend her. Still, he had the feeling that he had failed her in some way. He had to discover what it was. If she would only tell him, he would do anything in his power to set it right. He had not wished to leave for France with their relationship in peril, but having rescued a Jacobite from gaol, he had felt responsible for seeing him safely through the dangerous crossing. Surely a few months' delay was not too long to mend the tear in their friendship?

Setting out at dusk on two hired horses, he and Tom rode the fifteen miles to Hawkhurst, where they waited until midnight before approaching Rotherham Abbey. The vast estate had been his father's country seat, the place that should have been Gideon's home.

When they arrived, the house appeared to be dark. Rotherham Abbey had been built out of stones recovered from a Cistercian abbey dissolved by Henry VIII. Traces of its old buildings remained in partial walls and heaps of stones just a hundred yards below the Jacobean house. The mansion loomed above the old abbey ruins, covered now by two hundred years of wild growth. Leaving Tom outside the ruins as lookout, Gideon felt his way through the tangle of vines that concealed the entrance to an underground passage leading into the house. Groping in the dark, he located the entrance, and after taking a few minutes to light the simple lanthorn he had brought, he entered the cool, dank tunnel.

This had originally been the passage between the abbot's house and his church, so its floor was paved with stones. The walls held back the soil, but a strong earthy scent filled Gideon's nostrils as he made his way along it. Beneath his fingers the stones felt cool and damp.

Gideon's heart beat rapidly with the anticipation of finding Mrs. Kean in her bed. She had been assigned the small chamber behind whose wall the other end of this passage was concealed. As a bedchamber, it was scarcely more than a closet, insignificant in appearance except for the ornately-carved paneling adorning one wall, built purposely to hide a door that could take either a persecuted priest or an escaping royalist to safety. The secret of the passage had always been kept by the earl and his heir, but, lacking an heir, Gideon had entrusted the knowledge of it to Tom and Mrs. Kean. Although embarrassed by his first foray into her bedchamber, Mrs. Kean had said nothing to discourage him from using it again.

The passage seemed interminably long, but once he reached the base of the steps leading up inside the wall, he paused for a moment in doubt. If Mrs. Kean were truly angry with him, how might she respond to this invasion of her chamber? Then, reminding himself that she had never greeted him with anything but friendship, he climbed the twisted staircase and felt for the latch. The spring released with just a slight click, and he slowly pushed the door ajar.

The chamber was dark, but so it should be at this hour, whether or not she was in bed. The air was still, but he fancied he detected traces of her unique perfume. He held up his torch and whispered her name, but no response issued from the bed. Making his way across the small chamber and parting the bed curtains, he saw not only that the bed was empty, but that the small table next to it was shrouded in a holland cover, attesting to the fact that the family was not residence.

Disappointment pressed heavily on his chest. Unwilling to resign himself to the evidence, he searched the garderobe and looked inside the chest at the foot of the bed. They held nothing but coverlets. He sat down on the trunk and tried to imagine where Mrs. Kean could be.

The possibilities—if not endless—were too numerous for a quick answer. If the family had followed the Court, they could be at Kensington, Windsor, or Hampton Court. It was even possible that they had remained in London. He doubted they would stay there in the heat of summer. Much more likely that they would go to the Bath or Royal Tunbridge Wells, but it would be too hard to discover where they had gone without returning to London and making inquiries at Hawkhurst House.

With a determined sigh, he stood, ready to retrace his steps. Then he heard a slight noise, as if someone had given the door a nudge.

Gideon froze, prepared to extinguish his lanthorn. Then, he heard more sounds—scratching, a snuffling noise, a whine. With a smile he crossed to the door that linked this small room with the antechamber to the chapel gallery and opened it. As he had expected, outside he found his father's lurcher who, recognizing him, at once went into a frenzy, whining, licking at his hands, and beating Gideon's legs with his long thin tail, while wriggling ecstatically against him.

"Hush, Argos!" Gideon whispered, petting the dog, which was so tall he hardly had to bend. He pulled Argos into the bedchamber by his thick brass collar. "Hush, or you'll give me away."

With the door closed, Gideon indulged the dog with a hard ruffling of his fur while Argos's tongue lolled out of his mouth. In truth, Gideon indulged himself as well, for it was cheering to receive an enthusiastic welcome, if only from a dog. Then, when Argos had calmed down a bit, Gideon said, "Time for me to leave and for you to return to whatever it is you do."

As he stepped to the door to open it, the dog stared after him. Then, he lowered himself into a seated position near the bed. Gideon glanced back, gave a muted whistle, and patted the side of his leg, whispering for the dog to come.

Argos shifted miserably on his haunches and whined. He was clever enough to know he was about to be ushered from the room.

Gideon heaved an impatient sigh. "C'mon, boy. I have to leave now."

The dog's face sobered. He licked his chops, swallowed, and closed his mouth, but refused to budge. In his eyes, Gideon saw a shadow of his own loneliness.

"You miss my father, boy, don't you? God knows that idiot cousin of mine was never fond of dogs."

Gideon recalled that the first time he had sneaked into the house, prowling as far as his father's rooms. Argos had followed him back to this door, where Gideon had promptly disappeared, leaving the dog alone as his father had done.

"I can't take you with me," Gideon said, his voice full of regret, but the dog refused to come.

Would anyone miss Argos? Certainly the servant who fed him would note his absence. His father's priest and Gideon's old tutor, the Reverend Mr. Bramwell, might eventually notice that the dog was gone, but Gideon doubted the priest would disturb himself to search for a missing dog.

"Very well." He gave the dog a stern look. "But mind, you shall have to keep up! I doubt you've been coursing at all this past year. And God only knows what Tom will say when he sees you."

The change in his tone was all the encouragement the dog needed. He bounded in joy, wagging his tail, his tongue once again hanging from his long, narrow jaw.

Gideon crossed to the hidden door and opened it. "Just don't knock me down the stairs." He had no need to look back to know that the dog was on his heels, but in the interest of prudence, he motioned for Argos to precede him down the flight of steps before closing the door in the paneling securely behind him.

When they eventually emerged in the ruins in the dark, the dog—startled by the tangle of vines—suddenly burst through them. Tom ducked as if he had seen a ghost and sputtered an oath. Then, when he was enveloped in a frenzy of canine affection, he whispered angrily, "What foolishness is this, Master Gideon? What will we do with a coursing hound?" He was not so hard-hearted, however, as to resist petting the dog.

"I know it was foolish, but you should have seen the look he gave me. I tried to leave him, but he insisted he would be no trouble."

Tom snorted. Then, he said, "Well, let's hope they don't have you up for stealing a dog now, too."

Gideon laughed as he took up the reins to his horse and mounted. Argos was galloping about in a great circle, exuberant at last to be reunited with his family.

"And Mrs. Kean?" Tom asked, once he was mounted, too.

His question squeezed the weight in Gideon's chest. "Not there. There's no sign of the family."

"Where do you suppose they've gone?"

Gideon shrugged. "I'll have to send Katy to Hawkhurst House to ferret out their whereabouts. But on the chance they've gone to Royal Tunbridge Wells, we'll nose about there on our way back to London."

As they headed back to Lade's inn to spend the remaining hours of the night, the disappointment Gideon had felt on seeing that Mrs. Kean was not in her chamber continued to squeeze his heart. He had so desperately hoped to see her. It would be hard to be patient while he discovered where she was.

He gained comfort from the sight of Argos trotting happily alongside his horse. No need to worry that the dog would tire. It had been bred from a greyhound and a collie to course all the day long.

The trip had not been wasted, after all.

℘

A few days later, Gideon's cousin Harrowby, Lord Hawkhurst set out in his coach for Hampton Court to pay a visit to the Prince and Princess of Wales. He believed it prudent to stay abreast of Court gossip, as well as informed of who was currently in favour and who was not. Just before the King had left, he had stripped the Duke of Argyll of his post as commander of the forces in North Britain, in spite of Argyll's success in putting down the rebellion. Someone close to the King had convinced him that the Duke had not pursued the rebels diligently enough, suggesting a dangerous sympathy for the Scots. So, perhaps fearing the Duke's popularity with his troops, King George had not wished to entrust so much power to the leader of the Campbell clan.

It was more likely, however, that the King mistrusted Argyll's relationship with the Prince of Wales. Harrowby had heard that the King's ministers, Townsend and Walpole, worried that Argyll would conspire against them with the backing of the Prince. They had pled with the King not to go to Hanover; but one of the first things George had done upon taking the throne was insist that Parliament remove the clause in the Act of Settlement requiring Parliament's permission for the ruler to absent himself from the kingdom.

The decisions George had taken before leaving had nearly provoked a crisis. Though the King had entrusted his heir with the oversight of the kingdom in his absence, there was no love lost between monarch and son. Consequently, George had placed legal restrictions on the power the Prince could wield. He had refused to name his son as Regent. The Prince had reacted with indignation, then fury when the King had removed Argyll from his position as the Prince's Groom of the Stole. Only the King's threat to bring his brother Ernst August to England to oversee the kingdom in his stead had brought the Prince of Wales to heel. The effect of their quarrel had been so unsettling to the Court that Harrowby wished to make certain that his house would always be on the correct side of any royal spat.

Isabella had chosen to remain at the Wells with her mother. She was having too much fun flirting to join Harrowby on another uncomfortable journey. Her mother, too ill to travel north, had miraculously found the strength—now that Hester was safely on her way to York—to take her customary seat at the card tables.

Harrowby could not complain about any journey that removed him from Mrs. Mayfield's company. The route he had chosen was pleasant enough, taking him by Penshurst Place and from there, via Horley and Leigh to Epsom where the races were held, and so onto Kingston-upon-Thames and Hampton Court. He did not anticipate any trouble, as the coach would not be crossing any heaths where highwaymen were known to prey. This was fortunate as some of his servants had been left behind in London. He felt sufficiently protected by his coachman, his groom and just two outriders.

It came as a surprise then, as they were rolling along a narrow stretch of road near Chiddingstone, hemmed in by thick hedges and beneath a thick canopy of trees, when the coach lurched to a sudden halt. Before Harrowby could put his head out the window to ask what business was toward, his coachman called back, "There's a great branch fallen in the road, my lord!"

"Then, move it, you fools! And be quick!"

The coachman had already issued the order to the two outriders, who squeezed their horses past the carriage and dismounted to deal with the offending limb. Harrowby settled himself back on the seat cushions to wait, grumbling about the poor roads and farmers who neglected their duty to keep them maintained.

A jolt rocked the coach, as if second branch had fallen hard on the roof, jerking Harrowby out of his seat. Shouts from the men reached him as, startled, the horses bolted, then reared, still blocked by the branch. The abrupt changes in direction knocked Harrowby back onto the seat, then down to the floor. He strove for balance as the carriage swung back and forth, its leather straps protesting with loud creaks. He heard the coachman calling to his animals as he struggled with the reins. Gripping the seat with both hands, Harrowby was too scared of tipping to cry out.

Before the carriage stopped swaying, the muzzle of a pistol appeared through the open window. The figure of a man in a blue satin cape leapt down from the roof.

In a chilling voice, which silenced Harrowby's servants, he called out to the guards, "I have a pistol directed at your master's head. No one will be hurt if you throw down your arms and leave me to my work."

A series of heavy thuds as their guns hit the ground informed Harrowby that his men had obeyed.

His heart was hammering, but rage clogged his throat. "You . . . again!" he blustered. "How dare you, you knave!"

"Yes, it is I again, my lord, at your service." The figure Harrowby recognized as the highwayman Blue Satan flung open the carriage door and stood facing him, a jubilant grin on his lips. The upper half of his face was concealed by a black mask. A tricorn hat was pulled low over his brow, and the blue satin cape Harrowby had secretly coveted clung to a pair of broad shoulders. "I must ask you to step down, please."

Harrowby was so incensed that for once he forgot to be afraid. "And if I do not, sir?"

"Then, regrettably, I shall be forced to shoot you."

The voice was soft, but it contained a menace Harrowby did not recall from their first encounter. A note of suppressed fury—though the man had not raised his voice—sent a chill of caution down Harrowby's spine.

He scrambled out of the coach without benefit of the step, which perhaps was the reason his knees buckled.

Blue Satan had the gall to address him in a conversational tone. "You travel alone, I see. Where are you headed, my lord.?"

"Not that it's any business of yours, but I am on my way to Court, where I shall see to it that his Highness doubles the reward his Majesty put on your head!"

Blue Satan flashed an impudent grin. "You flatter me, sir."

"I do nothing of the kind! I shall not rest until I see you hanging from a gibbet."

The scoundrel nodded, as if gratified. "Well, now that that is clear, perhaps I might relieve you of your valuables. Your purse, please, as well as that handsome ring you are wearing."

Harrowby's rage rendered him too stiff to respond. The nerve of the blackguard, to take the Hawkhurst signet ring!

"Please make haste, my lord, before my patience wears thin."

One of the outriders took a step forward, but the coachman grabbed his sleeve. He whispered loudly, "There's too much risk to my lord."

At the movement, Blue Satan raised his pistol again and placed the muzzle between Harrowby's eyes. "Your coachman is very wise, my lord. He is a credit to your household, for without his prudence you would now be dead." He jerked the barrel of his weapon to indicate Harrowby's pocket. "The purse and the ring." This time there was no "please."

Afraid to provoke the villain, Harrowby dug into his coat pocket and drew out a thick leather pouch. He tossed it to the highwayman, who easily caught it. He hesitated over the ring, but another jerk of the pistol, made him wrench it off his finger. It soon followed the pouch.

"That should be reasonably adequate for now," Blue Satan said, for all the world as if the money were in payment of a debt. "You may return to your carriage and carry on with your journey."

He moved to the front of the coach where the servants had dropped their guns, the groom's big blunderbuss and a pair of side arms. Sweeping them away with his foot to move them out of the men's reach, he invited them to resume their places. As Harrowby returned to his seat, Blue Satan kept them all covered with his pistol until they had cleared the branch from the road and remounted. Then, he cheerfully waved them off.

As the Hawkhurst coach and horses rolled out of sight, Tom emerged from a thicket, leading their two horses. The large dog trotted by his side. Argos greeted Gideon exuberantly, as if he had not seen him for a week.

"Do something with those guns," Gideon said to Tom, while stripping off his mask and cape. He rolled them into a flattened ball and shoved them into a pocket Katy had fashioned in his saddle blanket.

"Do you want to keep them?" Tom bent to pick up the blunderbuss.

"No. Hide them. If we run into a hue and cry, it will better if they are not found on us."

"And what about them things you stole off Master Harrowby?" Tom snorted, as he shook balls and powder out of the loaded small arms. "D'you think those won't land you in Newgate?"

"I never stole them!" Gideon said righteously. "That ring belongs to me and so does the money."

"You and I know that, but a magistrate won't never believe it."

Gideon opened the purse and extracted more than half the coins and notes—still a considerable amount. The rest he tossed into the bushes with the pouch. "There. If we are searched, they'll not find the sum Harrowby is missing. The last thing anyone will suspect is that a highwayman would throw money away."

"And your father's signet?" Tom hurled the guns one at a time after the pouch, breaking twigs and leaves as they fell to the ground.

Gideon tightened his jaw. "The ring stays with me."

His firmness silenced Tom, while Gideon altered his disguise, adding a long black periwig and a touch of shoe blacking to his brows. As soon as Tom had checked his appearance and nodded his approval, the two mounted swiftly and set their horses towards Sevenoaks and the road to London.

They did not speak again until they had outrun a possible hue and cry, though it was unlikely one would be raised for a single crime. Once they had ridden far enough to feel safe, they settled their horses into a sustainable trot.

As soon as they arrived in London, Gideon would send a message to Mrs. Kean at Hawkhurst House. He had sent Tom into Royal Tunbridge Wells with instructions to search for her on the Walks. Tom had observed the strollers from a distance, but though he had soon spotted Isabella and her mother, he had not seen any sign of Mrs. Kean. He had followed the ladies back to their lodgings and struck up a chat with a servant in the street, who mentioned that "the other young lady" had returned to London. The same servant, who enjoyed a good gossip, had informed him that his lordship planned to leave that morning to pay a visit to the Prince and Princess of Wales at Hampton Court.

Gideon could not understand why Mrs. Kean had been sent away, but he was exhilarated by the news that she would be free of her family. It would have been hard to meet her in a village, where everyone was at leisure and she would be surrounded day and night by people who knew him. The plan to hold up Harrowby's carriage—sternly opposed by Tom—had come to him in a moment of restless spirits.

If he was to be hanged for a highwayman, then it seemed about time he stole something. And he could think of no more deserving victim than his cousin Harrowby.

Harrowby had wronged him. Until recently, Gideon had not realized how much. Today's adventure would not settle the score between them, but finally Gideon had taken back a bit of what was his.

*A*ll Crimes against the State are punished here with the utmost Severity; but if the Person accused make his Innocence plainly to appear upon his Tryal, the Accuser is immediately put to an ignominious Death; and out of his Goods or Lands, the innocent Person is quadruply recompensed for the Loss of his Time, for the Danger he underwent, for the Hardship of his Imprisonment, and for all the Charges he hath been at in making his Defence.

CHAPTER III

After the passengers had finally settled in their seats and the coach had left London behind, Hester offered to share the contents of her basket with her companions. A few politely declined, not wishing to deprive her of her food. The young gentleman next to her refused at first, but when his eyes kept wandering hungrily to the plum cake, she begged him to accept a piece, saying, "I recollect that when my brother and his friends were your age, they could eat their weight in cakes everyday and still dispose of more."

Her teasing smile removed any hint of a rebuke for his stare. He returned it briefly, still with a nervous air, but accepting the cake, thanked her in as few words as possible.

There their conversation would have ended if, encouraged by his youthful hunger, she had not persisted. "Will you be visiting family in Yorkshire like me?"

The innocent question threw him into a panic. His glance darted back and forth between the other passengers, while he made a show of needing to swallow his mouthful before replying. Then, when he did, it was merely to cough and nod before returning his gaze to his lap.

Startled by such extreme shyness, Hester turned her head to study the scenery they passed. She would not pursue the young man if conversation was painful to him. Unfortunately, his reticence to speak had attracted the notice of Mr. Foxcroft seated directly across from him, the man who had announced that he was travelling on the King's business. He eyed the young man suspiciously, as if contemplating further questions.

He opened his mouth to speak, but feeling protective, Hester forestalled his questions by asking one herself. "You said you were travelling on the King's business, sir. May we know what nature of business it is?"

Reluctantly, he turned towards her, tearing his gaze away from the young man. "Yes, mistress. I have been appointed King's Commissioner to carry out a recent act of Parliament, to examine the estates of traitors and papist recusants in the North Riding of Yorkshire."

Hester felt the young man beside her tense. She believed she had stumbled upon his reason for remaining silent. If he was a Roman Catholic, then it was possible he was travelling illegally. Even if he did have permission from the authorities to travel, his journey could be made difficult if his religion were known.

She expressed an interest in the Commissioner's task, hoping by drawing him out to give the young man a moment to recover his sangfroid. Soon, he took advantage of the opportunity their conversation afforded him to fold his arms, lean his head back, and pretend to sleep.

The Commissioner expounded on his duty, which was to examine the estates in question for the purpose of raising money from them for the use of the public. Since the days of William and Mary, Roman Catholics had been burdened with special taxes and their rights to inherit land had been curtailed. Whenever Jacobites had rebelled, the Crown had inhibited Catholics' ability to assist a rebellion by taking away their horses and their arms.

Fortunately, as the Commissioner spoke, the other passengers were drawn into the conversation. One subject led to another. Not until then did Hester feel the tension in her neighbour's body ease.

They were passing through flat, uninspiring scenery, which she recalled from the journey she had made to London with her aunt and Isabella. Had that been only less than two years ago? How much had happened to them in those two years.

Isabella had quickly become the toast of the Whigs in London. Among her suitors had been a duke, the handsome Viscount St. Mars, and his cousin Harrowby Fitzsimmons, then merely a baronet. Though Mrs. Mayfield had prayed for the duke to propose, it soon had become clear that without a large fortune and a higher rank, Isabella would never become a duchess. Then St. Mars had been accused of murder, and by the time Harrowby had stepped into his shoes as the new Earl of Hawkhurst, Mrs. Mayfield's trap had been set. Harrowby had been tricked into a clandestine wedding. St. Mars had gone into hiding, but his friendship with Hester had quickly grown, as first he had come to terms with Isabella's defection and then had worked to solve the mystery of his father's killing.

The Jacobite rebellion had embroiled them with agents of espionage. Now that the rebellion was resolved, Hester expected her life would settle into a tedious pattern, much like the scenery she saw through her window. As her spirits began to sink, her eyelids drooped, and despite the constant bumps and lurches of the coach, she dozed.

The first day of their journey passed without serious incident. The coachman diverged once from the turnpike road near Ware to escape paying the toll, but as they lost no time in the divergence, no one complained. They baited at Stevenage, where the gentlemen insisted on paying for Hester's dinner. Since it was the usual custom for gentlemen to treat the female passengers, she did not long resist their offer. Their food had barely arrived, however, before the coachman said they must resume their journey, so after swallowing as much as they could shove down their throats in five minutes, they took their places again. The coachman pushed all the way to St. Neot's before stopping to let them sleep.

Descending from the vehicle just before dark, hot and dusty and sore from bracing herself against the jostling motion of the coach, Hester tipped the coachman of the first stage, who would soon make the return journey to London. She remembered to spare a penny for the post-boy, too.

Throughout the long day, the young gentleman had kept silent.

This would not be an effective way for him to escape notice, Hester knew, so she resolved to do something about it on the morrow. For now, she was grateful to learn that she was to have a bed all to herself, as there were no other female travellers at the inn with whom to share it.

The morning came soon, when she was roused by the innkeeper's wife before dawn and had to hurry down to join the men in the coach. They were allowed a brief stop to break their fast at the Bell at Stilton, where Hester sampled the local cheese and found it a bit too rich for her taste. From there the coach pressed on to Stamford, a prosperous town built entirely of stone and widely regarded as the finest sight on the road between Edinburgh and London. They planned to dine at the George Inn, where Hester had stayed two years ago with Isabella and her aunt on their way to Court.

The inn was an ancient hostelry, particularly known for its respectability. So it came as a shock to find it with broken windows and the marks of battering on the door. Even Lord Burghley's coat of arms carved in the stone lintel had been marred. A small army of glaziers, plasterers and stone masons were working to repair the damage which must only recently have occurred. When the coach let the passengers down, the landlord, Mr. Wildman, came out to greet them with the evident wish of allaying their concerns. He assured them that all the usual comforts would be found inside. Upon being pressed by the gentlemen, however, he was forced to comment upon what had occurred.

"A most shameful incident accounts for the damage you see, but as it was not the fault of anyone employed by the inn, I pray you will disregard it." When this statement failed to satisfy their curiosity, he reluctantly explained that one of the dragoons stationed in the town to suppress the local Jacobites had murdered Mr. Bolton, a man who had rented the tap just west of the inn.

"It is the only act of violence ever known to shame this house." Mr. Wildman wrung his hands. "But I'm afraid Mr. Bolton's sympathies were well-known. He and his friends were kneeling to drink to the memory of her former Majesty, Queen Anne, when the soldier, taking umbrage I suppose, cut him down with his sword. Poor Mr. Bolton was instantly killed. Then, before we knew what had happened, an innumerable rabble surrounded the inn, armed with all sorts of makeshift weapons, breaking windows and threatening to demolish the house entirely unless the soldier was handed to them. The villain escaped out the back gate, but the mob kept on with its destruction until a constable managed to convince them that the dragoon was no longer within."

At this point, the coachman reminded them that he wished to make many miles before nightfall, which recalled Mr. Wildman to his duties. He bustled them inside for a quick meal, which they ate in silence, sobered by the tale he had told them.

The violence he had related was just the sort of incident Hester had feared to meet with on the road. Saddened by any death, she could only be grateful that the murder had not occurred when she was there to see it. The dragoons had been stationed in Stamford because the sympathies of the local populace were strongly Jacobite. The defeat of the rebels in the North must have vanquished any hope of a Stuart restoration, but as Hester returned to the coach, rushed by the coachman, she thought she saw traces of bitterness on the faces she passed.

The coachman's wish to put many miles behind them was not to be fulfilled. Not far out of Stamford, it started to drizzle, and soon the rain fell with such force as to threaten to bog them down.

Before such a possibility could occur, the coachman begged the passengers to descend to lighten the load upon the wheels. This prompted a chorus of groans and sighs, but no one questioned his judgement. No one wished to risk being stuck in the mud and required to help push the coach out. They hastily donned their hats, coats, and capes. The coachman opened the doors, and the passengers prepared to descend. The Quaker stepped down first on Hester's side. Mr. Woodson and the clergyman exited through the opposite door, which was next to their seats. When the young gentleman would have followed them, Hester stopped him by placing a hand on his arm and asking if he would help her to alight. The Commissioner, who had paused as if to offer his assistance, frowned, but gestured for the younger man and Hester to proceed.

Before stepping down into the mud, Hester pulled her riding hood over her head and took a firm hold on the young man's arm. When she had descended, instead of relinquishing it, she asked if he would lend her his support as they walked. He could hardly refuse. His manners were sufficiently polite that he agreed with scarcely a hint of wishing to do otherwise.

For the next little while all their faculties were dedicated to finding the driest possible path for their feet. The others were similarly occupied as they picked their way over the deep pools in the road and endeavoured not to lose their footing. Their progress was hindered by the rain which fell in torrents, drenching them all within minutes. As water soaked through her woolen cloak, Hester felt like swearing. Then her foot slipped.

Saved from a messy fall by her escort's quick catch, she could only laugh.

Her laughter broke through the young man's shyness, and he chuckled. "If I fall, I shall try not to pull you down with me," he said haltingly. He clearly was not French because his words carried no accent, but there was something about his speech that suggested he was not accustomed to speaking English.

"That is a very handsome offer," Hester replied, "as long as I shall not be expected to catch you, for I am certain I could not."

He chuckled again, then glanced past her to the coach which had pulled ahead. The horses were knee deep in mud, but the lightening of the coach seemed to have worked, for its wheels were turning, even as they lurched from deep rut to deep rut. There was no way to tell how much longer they would have to walk.

Their fellow passengers trailed the coach at a safe distance to keep from being splattered with mud. They moved in three separate groups, the Quaker and the Commissioner each alone, and Mr. Woodson and the clergyman assisting each other. All appeared too busy negotiating the road to notice what the others were doing.

The young man stepped over a particularly wide puddle then turned to help Hester leap across it. Fearing their conversation had come to an end, Hester spoke loudly to make herself heard over the pounding rain, "If we are to drown together, it seems only fitting that we should know each other's names. I am Hester Kean, and I am on my way to visit my cousins near Coxwold."

She had phrased her introduction in this manner with the hope of eliciting at least as much information from him. She was surprised when he gave her a startled look.

"What is your cousins' name?"

"Mayfield. My cousin is Dudley Mayfield, and his sisters and brothers live with him. Their mother was supposed to make the journey instead but fell ill at the last moment."

He frowned as if in concentration, while streams of water cascaded off his hat. "The name Mayfield sounds familiar to me."

"Do you know Coxwold?"

"Yes. At least, I know of it. It has been many years since I was there."

"You have not told me your name," Hester reminded him, shielding her eyes with one hand.

He bit his lower lip and threw a glance over his shoulder at the other passengers, but they were too far away to hear. Still, he mumbled, "My name is Charles Fenwick. I am en route to my father's house."

She could barely hear him over the clatter of the rain. "Is it near Coxwold?"

"Yes."

"Then I daresay my cousins and your father will know each other."

"It is possible." He turned his head away, evidently not wishing to divulge more.

Hester decided she would have to be satisfied with this much for now. They had plenty of hours before them in which to become better acquainted.

As they continued to pick their way in the wake of the vehicle, the rainfall eased. After another half-mile or so, the coach reached higher ground, and the coachman waited for the passengers to catch up. They doffed their wet coats and shook out their hats. Their boots and shoes were covered in mud, and the hem of Hester's dress was thoroughly dirtied.

From there their progress was necessarily so slow that they barely reached Grantham before dark. The mood in the coach was far from congenial. The only benefit from the rain was that it had taken their minds off the violence they had heard about in Stamford. Wet and exhausted, they exchanged no further conversation during the remainder of that day's stage. As soon as they arrived at the Angel, an imposing inn with a handsome facade, they retired to their rooms to dry their clothes. Here, they were not so fortunate in their accommodations as yesterday, for the inclement weather had driven many travellers to seek refuge. Several had been delayed by the lack of sufficient post-horses in the town. Hester found that she was to share a bed with an elderly woman, who glared at her as if the inconvenience were all Hester's fault.

They dined in a room on the first floor which contained a massive ancient fireplace, where a huge haunch of beef roasted slowly on a spit. In one corner, a small spiral staircase led to a lookout from which approaching dignitaries might be spied as they entered the town. The room boasted three oriel windows overlooking the High Street, but no moonlight shone through the glass on this cloudy night. The walls were paneled in ancient oak, which rendered the room even darker. The mullions and ceilings above the windows were elaborately carved in stone, exuding a venerable air. Indeed, the waiter proudly informed Hester that five English kings had supped in this room, including King John of Magna Carta fame.

As exhausted as she was, Hester could not pay the room the tribute it deserved. Given the lateness of the hour, the passengers quickly disposed of their meal and sought whatever sleep their cramped quarters would allow.

The woman who shared Hester's bed snored loudly all night. Hester had barely managed to fall asleep, it seemed, when the maid awakened her with the news that the King's Commissioner had insisted on setting off earlier than scheduled that morning. He had given instructions for all the passengers to be rousted from their beds.

Throwing off sleep with an effort, Hester rose and fumbled for her belongings, trying not to disturb her touchy bedfellow. She dressed in the dark and felt her way downstairs to the yard. It must have been within the Commissioner's authority to advance the time of their departure, for when Hester reached the coach, she found the rest of her companions already seated inside.

Such an early start on empty stomachs was conducive to neither conversation nor good spirits. The passengers dozed as best they could, until the coachman stopped along the road for a quick mug of beer. There the travellers grabbed whatever they could in the way of breakfast, while the coachman downed his drink. Then off they set on the road to Newark.

When, a few hours later, the coach pulled in to Newark, Hester noticed that, instead of following the rest of the passengers into the White Hart where they would dine, Mr. Foxcroft remained in the yard and pulled one of the ostlers aside. Her sense of foreboding was confirmed when, just as they had finished their meal and were ready to leave, a wardman, accompanied by Mr. Foxcroft, entered the yard from beneath a projecting gallery of windows and called to them to halt.

The passengers stopped in their tracks, looking at one another in mystification. As the two men approached, Mr. Foxcroft touched the wardman on the arm and spoke in a low tone, indicating Mr. Fenwick with a nod.

"You, sir!" The wardman called out, pointing his staff at Mr. Fenwick. "You'd best come with me."

"Me? Why?" Mr. Fenwick's face turned white. Then, as outrage overcame his fear, red bloomed on his cheeks. "What have I done?"

The wardman looked anxiously at Mr. Foxcroft, who nodded his head in encouragement. He turned back to the young man. "The magistrate will need to see your travel warrant."

The others, who had stayed rooted to their places by curiosity, warily regarded the young man, who defiantly stood his ground.

"Why must he? And I repeat, what have I done to merit such treatment?"

Faced with a question it was beyond his ken to answer, the wardman again looked to Mr. Foxcroft for guidance. The Commissioner gazed sternly back, as if insisting that he do his duty.

The wardman's tone was not quite so confident when he replied, "Well, according to this gentleman here, you could be a papist. And if that's so, then you shouldn't be travelling on the stage."

Standing next to Mr. Fenwick, Hester felt anger and fear emanating from him as he rounded on the Commissioner. "I do have permission to travel. I am going home, to my father's house in Yorkshire." He reached inside his coat for a shagreen pocket-book and, removing an official-looking paper, tried to hand it to the wardman.

The wardman recoiled, as if the paper might burn him. "No, that'll never do! You'd best save it for the magistrate."

"But, if you take me to a magistrate, the coach will be delayed." As Mr. Fenwick said this, he glanced round at his fellow passengers, who returned his gaze, their eyes filling with dismay.

"Now, wait one moment, young man." The clergyman, who had tried to befriend him earlier, spoke in an offended tone. "You cannot expect us to wait until this business is resolved."

Mr. Woodson ruefully agreed. "Sorry, Fenwick, but the parson is right. The journey's long enough, without we're made to stop another night."

"Then, if I accompany you," Mr. Fenwick said to the wardman, "I shall lose my place in the coach. And who can say when there will be another seat available?"

"That is none of our concern," Mr. Foxcroft said. "You should have thought of that before stepping into this coach. It is plain to me that you have returned from a lengthy sojourn in France, where I suspect you attended a papist school!"

The clergyman gasped and stared at poor Mr. Fenwick as if he'd been bitten by a viper.

So many Roman Catholics had sent their children to be educated in France by priests that a law had been passed, making the practice illegal. If the Commissioner's accusation was true, it would explain why Mr. Fenwick had been so reluctant to divulge any personal information to his fellow passengers.

Degrees of shock appeared on every face. Even Hester felt a bit uneasy, uncertain how to deal with the situation.

Mr. Fenwick blanched. "You have no proof of that, sir, and where I have travelled from is none of your business." He turned to the wardman. "Please, can you not simply read the warrant? I assure you that all is in order."

At these confident words, some of the tension among his fellow passengers eased. "Indeed," the clergyman said, "if the young man's warrant is in order, you cannot detain him."

"Aye. Have a quick look at his papers, and let us be on our way." Mr. Woodson glowered at the Commissioner, whose fault this was.

By this time, a crowd had gathered about them. People weighed in on either side. Hester's sympathies were fully on Mr. Fenwick's. When the impasse continued, and it became increasingly clear that the Commissioner would not budge, a fact occurred to Hester which might tip the scales in the young gentleman's favour.

Speaking loudly enough to be heard by those most concerned, she said, "Of course, if you mean to arrest Mr. Fenwick, his accuser will need to remain behind as well."

Her impartial tone made Mr. Fenwick stare at her in hurt surprise. Then, as she returned his gaze with a guileless expression, understanding lit his eyes, and he refrained from comment.

The wardman frowned in thought before addressing his next remark to Mr. Foxcroft. "The lady has the right of it, sir. I can't ask the constable to make an arrest without you come along as witness."

Mr. Foxcroft, to whom this fact had obviously not occurred, was briefly struck speechless before asserting that the wardman had a duty to his town.

"And if I am not mistaken," Hester added in a pensive tone, "if the gentleman's papers do prove to be in order, the person who brings the false charges will also be required to bear the cost of prosecution."

As soon as he absorbed her statement, the wardman turned to glare at Mr. Foxcroft. "Either you come along o' me, sir, and make your accusation, or I'll have to let this gentleman go. It's not up to me to challenge his rights."

The scales had been tipped. A general murmur of approval and nods all around made Mr. Foxcroft gnash his teeth in anger. He threw up his hands and, turning his back to them all, ordered the coachman to gather his passengers to leave.

With a shaky sigh, Mr. Fenwick gave Hester a grateful look and offered an arm to help her back into the coach. Grinning, Mr. Woodson tipped his hat. The clergyman muttered as he resumed his place inside, and after taking his seat, the Quaker folded his arms and glared at them all in disapproval.

Now, Hester realized, they must endure two more days, trapped in the vehicle together, while Mr. Foxcroft stewed in hostile silence.

It was due entirely to Mr. Woodson's good nature, and to the clergyman's and Hester's polite manners, that the remaining two days passed tolerably. Fortunately, the going became easier the nearer they came to Doncaster. The road here was relatively smooth, the ground so firm that according to Mr. Woodson, it never needed repair. At the realization that he, the only truly congenial traveller among them, would part from them at Doncaster, the whole company seemed to heave a regretful sigh.

The northern town, where he took his leave, bustled with the knitting industry and boasted several good inns. Their coachman drove them to the post-house, whose host, in addition to being their landlord, was also the town's postmaster and its mayor. He was so prosperous, they were told, that he even kept a pack of hounds. Here, in Doncaster, the travellers must spend two nights, the next day being Sunday, which obliged them to rest.

In the morning Hester attended service at the minster and spent the next few hours visiting the town's ancient buildings. She saw nothing here to suggest the sort of disturbance they had heard of in Stamford. She napped in the afternoon and in the evening did her best to avoid her fellow passengers, of whom by now she was thoroughly sick. She only glimpsed Mr. Fenwick once and assumed that he, too, was doing his best to avoid them. The resentment and hostility between him and Mr. Foxworth had been so palpable that at times the younger man had chosen to walk beside the vehicle rather than have to gaze upon the disapproving visage across from him. The forced idleness, however, at least afforded Hester a chance to catch up on her sleep. By Monday, she was eager for an early start.

The final leg of their journey was spent largely in silence. Conversation languished to an occasional remark upon the points of interest they passed. Since the scenery was rural and only the rare horseman overtook them, there was not much to discuss. For Hester's benefit, the clergyman pointed out the ruins of the old Roman road, which appeared now and then, giving her something to search for.

It was with great relief that she first caught a glimpse of York Minster's towers in the distance, but it was many hours more before they reached it. Their approach into the city of York was along a long, straight causeway, part of the old Roman road, and the tall stone towers of the minster could be seen from many miles away. Fortunately, it had not rained too much here recently, and the rivers were all contained within their banks. After what seemed an interminable day, they finally crossed the bridge over the Ouse with its elegant arch, the finest in all of Great Britain, and passed through Micklegate Bar into the ancient walled city of York. From there, just one more turn brought them into Coney Street, where they pulled into the yard of the Black Swan Inn an hour before dusk.

Mr. Fenwick handed Hester down from the vehicle. The other two men followed in their wake. Mr. Foxworth took off down the street in a rapid stride without bothering to take leave of his companions. The clergyman and the Quaker paused long enough to make a civil goodbye. Hester wished them both a safe journey on the morrow, for both would be continuing onto Thirsk. At one of their stops that morning Mr. Fenwick had informed her, too, that he would ride on to Thirsk and, there, hire a horse and secure the services of a guide to conduct him to his father's house. Tonight he would put up at the Black Swan, as would she, but Hester bid him *adieu,* as well, for she did not intend to rise early enough on the morrow to do so.

As all the formalities were now accomplished, she looked about for a familiar face. With no serious mishaps to delay the coach longer than the projected number of days, she expected to find her cousin Dudley awaiting her in the town. He could not be sure of the exact hour of her arrival, however. The last thing she expected was that he would drag his heels outside the inn keeping watch for the stage. So, when there was so sign of him, after tipping the last coachman and post-boy, she followed Mr. Fenwick inside.

She was shown to a pleasant room where at last she could refresh herself after her long journey. The maid brought her a pitcher of warm water, and she washed her face and hands and brushed the worst of the dust from her hair. She changed into the cleanest of her gowns and put the other out to be brushed and aired overnight before going downstairs to see what could be had in the way of a light supper.

She was nearly finished with her repast when two strangers entered the room, led by the innkeeper. The gentleman was big and loud. The young lady, who must be his daughter, judging by the likeness in their features, had a buoyant, affected manner. Both had small, narrowly placed eyes, full lips, and the hint of a double chin.

With a nod in Hester's direction, the innkeeper whispered something in the gentleman's ear. The gentleman did not wait for the innkeeper's introduction but, crossing the room towards her, waved him off and greeted her, saying, "Ah, Mrs. Kean, at last we find you! You would not countenance the trouble we have had to do so!"

Startled by this address from a stranger, Hester said, "Indeed, I am sorry to have caused you any inconvenience, sir, but I am afraid you have the advantage of me."

The young lady rapped her father on the arm and laughingly said, "If that is not just like you, Papa! Why, here is Mrs. Kean, just off the stage, and you forget to introduce yourself. I am your cousin Pamela, Mrs. Dudley Mayfield, and this silly gentleman is my father, Sir Ralph Wetherby. We are come to escort you to our house."

The situation now made clear, Hester smiled and thanked them for coming to fetch her.

"My apologies for meeting you like this," she said, indicating her tousled hair and crumpled gown. "I was expecting to see Dudley and did not know that he had burdened you with the task."

"Isn't that just like a man! For you must know he wished to go to Malton to see a horse."

Hester was sufficiently acquainted with her cousin's affinity for horses, especially racing horses, not to be surprised, and only mildly offended by his neglect. If she had not saved Dudley from a charge of murder on a recent occasion, she would not have given his choice any thought, but it seemed the least he could have done was escort her to his home. She put this notion behind her, though, aware that he might be uncomfortable to meet her for fear it would remind them both of the incident.

After suitably expressing her gratitude to Dudley's wife and father-in-law, she invited them to join her at table. They had already supped, country hours being earlier than those kept in town, but they agreed to take refreshment and to keep her company while she ate.

"Are you stopping here?" she asked, once they had been seated and their host had taken their order.

"No, we put up at the Angel," Sir Ralph said. "It's much the best hostelry in York. And once you have eaten, we will move your belongings there."

Taken aback, Hester said, "That is very kind, but I have already taken a chamber here. It is perfectly satisfactory."

"Nonsense! We cannot have a cousin of ours sleeping at the inn that serves the stage!"

"I assure you that my room is clean and aired. Besides which, I have sent out my gown to be cleaned. It would be impossible for me to change lodgings at this late hour."

Sir Ralph was not convinced. "You can bring the rest of your things, and we can make arrangements for the gown to be carried to the Angel later. It will be no bother."

Perceiving that Sir Ralph was accustomed to having his own way, Hester replied as politely yet as firmly as she could. "It may not be too much bother for the inn, though I doubt the innkeeper will be pleased. He will surely regret the loss of a guest. It will be something of a bother for me, however, as I have unpacked my bag, and after being rattled in the coach for four of the past five days, I must plead fatigue. As grateful as I am to you both, I can scarcely keep my eyes open now."

At this point Pamela interceded, since it appeared that her father would persist. "Of course, Mrs. Kean is fatigued! You must not ask her to move, Papa. We can just as easily collect her in the morning."

Still at a loss to understand, he finally agreed, merely saying that he found it strange that anyone would prefer the Black Swan to the Angel.

Suppressing her annoyance, Hester did not waste her breath trying to make her sentiments any clearer. Sir Ralph did not appear to be offended by her decision, merely nonplussed. Searching for a way to change the subject, she was relieved to see Mr. Fenwick enter the room.

Spying her seated in company, he merely bowed in acknowledgement before taking a table alone.

Sir Ralph spun his head to see whom she had noticed, then turned back to ask, "One of your fellow passengers?"

"Yes, a Mr. Fenwick. We travelled down together. He says his father's house is not too far from Coxwold."

The words were scarcely out of her mouth before Sir Ralph exclaimed, "Fenwick! Why, he is a near neighbour of ours! A friend and a neighbour of many years." He turned in his chair and called out to the younger man, "Here, Fenwick! You must join us!" He stood and beckoned to the innkeeper. "Here, fellow! Carry that young gentleman's stool over here."

Mr. Fenwick blanched at being summoned by a gentleman he plainly did not recognize, He shot Hester a panicked glance. Feeling a flush of chagrin steal across her cheeks, Hester could do nothing but return his gaze with a wry lift of her brows.

Sir Ralph stood to take the young man's hand while Mr. Fenwick eyed him with misgiving. "I . . . am sorry, sir, but . . . I am afraid I do not recall . . . ."

Sir Ralph gave a hearty laugh, the very picture of rural bonhomie. "There's nothing to be sorry for, boy. I know your father. Well, well," he said, looking Mr. Fenwick over with approval. "It's a long time since I last saw you . . . Charles, isn't it? I wonder why your father didn't tell me you would be on the London coach?"

At the sound of his Christian name, the young man visibly relaxed. "Perhaps because he was unable to, sir. He had no way of knowing which coach to meet. I wrote to him only a fortnight ago to advise him that I would be coming home before securing passage on the stage."

"Ah, that will be the reason. Well, set yourself down. You will want a bite and a mug of ale, I daresay."

"A glass of wine, sir, instead, if you do not object."

Sir Ralph started to protest. Then a thought occurred to him. "Yes . . . yes, of course. Well, you must know that in Yorkshire we receive shipments of good claret directly from France. They come right up the

Ouse here. I doubt you will find any better in London town."

Mr. Fenwick thanked him. He must be relieved, Hester thought, to find himself among friends after so many uncomfortable days. He threw her a quizzical look, however, which told her he still did not know the identity of the gentleman who had accosted him.

Hester did her best to overcome the awkwardness by presenting him to Pamela and explaining her relationship to Pamela and her father. "In fact," she said to assist him further, "Sir Ralph and I have only met this evening. I was expecting my cousin Dudley to fetch me, but Sir Ralph and his daughter were kind enough to come in his stead."

"Is your father coming to fetch you later?" Sir Ralph asked.

"No, as I said, he did not know which coach to meet. Besides, the difficulty of travelling—" he stopped, perhaps conscious of saying more than he wished. Not only would it be difficult for his father to obtain the necessary permit to travel, even just to make the short journey to York, he would also have to employ his one horse, which would make the undertaking imprudent at best.

"Yes, yes," Sir Ralph said, shaking his head, "shameful business! Not on your father's part—you mustn't misunderstand me—but the Crown's. What can they be thinking to abuse honest citizens so? Well, you must ride up with us. We shall be very glad of your company."

The invitation took Mr. Fenwick by surprise. "I should very much like to but, you see, I am already booked on the coach for Thirsk tomorrow. From there I will use a guide to find the way to my father's house."

"But that is nonsense!" Sir Ralph protested. "The coach will take you farther than required and another day at least, when if you come with us, you will be at home tomorrow in time for dinner."

Mr. Fenwick opened his mouth, but Sir Ralph said, "No, I insist! I shall be very happy to hire you a horse. And you needn't fear it will be a jade. You must remember that the very best horses on earth are to be found in Yorkshire, even the hacks at our inns. You shall ride up with us and surprise your family, and let that be an end to it."

Faced with this persistent generosity, Mr. Fenwick could do little but accept. Even Hester could think of no reason why he should not.

Pamela asked them both how their journey had passed, and after exchanging a look with Hester, Mr. Fenwick admitted that there had been unpleasant aspects to it. Sir Ralph asked a few probing questions and without too much resistance, the young man unburdened himself enough to describe the scene in Newark when the King's Commissioner had tried to have him arrested. His listeners gazed in horror, then with admiring approval when he told them how Hester had come to his rescue. Relating it now, he was able to laugh, but Sir Ralph shook his head gravely.

"What a fright for you, dear boy! I daresay your father will be most upset to hear it. And you say this Commissioner is here to examine the households of Catholic recusants?"

Mr. Fenwick turned sober, recalling the shame and frustration he had been made to feel. "Yes, Foxworth swore that he would be visiting our house. I fear he plans to do us mischief."

Sir Ralph patted his arm. "There's nothing for you to worry about. Your father has complied with all the laws. This Foxworth will find nothing amiss, though it has cost your father in many ways. His neighbours do what they can for him, I assure you." He gave Mr. Fenwick a wink.

Clueless as to what the wink could mean, Mr. Fenwick merely thanked him for any kindness to his father.

While listening to these exchanges, Pamela had been fidgeting. Clearly she was bored. At the first opportunity she changed the subject to one she had been eager to broach. "Your trunks have not yet arrived," she said to Hester. "I declare, I am longing to see the gowns you have brought from London!" As she said this, she eyed Hester's rumpled dress with a certain misgiving.

"I hope they arrive soon. I should hate for your neighbours to meet me in my travelling clothes."

"Did you pack the gowns Dudley's mama promised to send?"

"Yes, of course. They are Isabella's castoffs for Mary."

Pamela's eyes bugged with anticipation. "I should like to have my dressmaker make patterns from them."

Sir Ralph joked about how the ladies must always be thinking of fashion, but added that his daughter should always have the best.

Hester endured as much of their jollity as she could, before begging to be excused to get some sleep. She hoped to be better able to tolerate such feeble conversation on the morrow. It would not, after all, be very different from the sort of talk that prevailed at Hawkhurst House. At least on the long ride she would have some intelligent company in the form of Mr. Fenwick, who in spite of his reserve, seemed an amiable young man.

*F*or which Reason they will never allow, that a Child is under any Obligation to his Father for begetting him, or to his Mother for bringing him into the World; which, considering the Miseries of human life, was neither a Benefit in itself, nor intended so by his Parents, whose Thoughts in their Love encounters were otherwise employed. Upon these, and the like Reasonings, their Opinion is, that Parents are the last of all others to be trusted with the Education of their own Children; And therefore they have in every Town publick Nurseries, where all Parents, except Cottagers and Labourers, are obliged to send their Infants of both Sexes to be reared and educated when they come to the age of twenty Moons; at which Time they are supposed to have some Rudiments of Docility.

CHAPTER IV

They agreed not to set out the next morning until after they had broken their fast. If Hester had not had her hosts to consider, she would have taken advantage of being in York to visit York Minster. After the confinement of the past several days, a brisk walk would have been agreeable. Pamela had completed her shopping, however, and Hester could not ask her to wait, so she was dressed, fed, and ready to leave the inn by nine o'clock.

Never a confident horsewoman, she was anxious over whether the hired mount would be too spirited for her to manage, but the horse they brought her was staid enough. Sir Ralph apologized for putting her on such a slug, but sitting atop its broad, flat back, Hester assured him that the beast's paces suited her perfectly. He found this hard to believe, but since Hester's father had been too poor to keep a stable, she had grown up walking or riding in carts more often than not. She did not tell Sir Ralph this, as it would have sunk her in her new cousins' estimation, they obviously being as wild about horses as Dudley.

In spite of Hester's initial skittishness, it was pleasant to be on horseback after being shut up in a carriage. The day proved fine, and their progress was much faster than it would have been on the stage. It seemed to her they fairly skimmed over the hills, though she knew

St. Mars would laugh to hear her describe such a sedate ride in that manner.

But, she reminded herself, she must not always be imagining what St. Mars would say. She must take advantage of this journey to forget him.

She was aided by Pamela who, as soon as they started out, attached herself to Hester's side and pummeled her with questions about London, King George's Court, the new French fashions, and especially about Lord and Lady Hawkhurst. She had plainly never been satisfied with the details of their household that Dudley had been willing to supply.

Recalling what a disaster Dudley's visit to London had been the preceding year, Hester was not surprised, but if Pamela's reason for marrying Dudley was his connection to an earl, she must be frustrated by his reticence.

"Did your father never think of taking you to Court?" Now that Hester had met Sir Ralph, she found it hard to understand why Pamela had never been to London.

"No." Pamela sighed. "And I should still like to go, but Papa says it would be a great waste when one can find anything one wants here in Yorkshire."

"Certainly a great deal of money is wasted there." Hester tried to soothe Pamela's feelings, for it was unlikely that Dudley would ever take her. She would have liked to ask how Pamela had come to marry an oaf like her cousin, but their acquaintance was too recent for her to be so inquisitive.

"We attend the York assizes, though. And I daresay we enjoy as many amusements there as one would in London." Raising her chin, Pamela looked prepared for Hester to contradict her, but Hester would never be so impolite, no matter how ridiculous the statement was. If Pamela could derive consolation by deceiving herself, she would be the last to spoil it.

Her dignity restored, Pamela prated on about the neighbours eager to meet Hester. Behind them, Sir Ralph kept up a flow of conversation with Charles—as Hester had begun to think of him—occasionally calling out to his daughter to steer her in the proper direction.

Their journey took them through the village of Shipton, where Sir Ralph insisted on a brief divergence to see a house being built for a local family by Sir John Vanbrugh. Sir Ralph explained that it had replaced an Elizabethan house, and the interior was reputed to be very grand. It proved to be a noble red brick structure, too large to visit in their limited time, but he promised to bring them back to see it during Hester's stay in Yorkshire. He talked about the improvements he had made to his own house of Yearsley Park, and hoped she would call upon him as soon as possible so that he might show her about.

"The man I employed used nothing but the best. All the latest fashions."

From Shipton they rode cross-country at times, passing by green field after field, some with grazing cows, some with horses and sheep. A good half were in tillage and deeply furrowed. Wherever the crop was wheat, it stood waist high. Fields of rape spread yellow in the sun. They passed farmers, mending and replanting their hedges with hawthorn and holly, and staking them with hazel and other wood. Hester was sorry she had arrived too late to see the mayflower in bloom, but wild carrot—Devil's Oatmeal, as it was called in Yorkshire—spread under the hedges like bishop's lace. Soon the moors would be awash with purple heather. Being here in the summer, in her native country, filled her with a strange mixture of melancholy and contentment. The air itself, so sweet with freshly cut grass, acted like balm to her spirits.

Sir Ralph's intention was to escort the ladies to Beckwith Manor, the Mayfields' country seat, before guiding Charles to his father's house, Oulston Hall.

By the time they arrived at Beckwith it was dinner time. Hester was looking forward not only to a meal, but to a rest from the saddle. As they reached the gate, however, a servant, who had been posted as lookout, ran out of his cottage to tell them that they were urgently wanted up at the manor.

"Is anything wrong?" Pamela asked, but the servant could not say.

Sir Ralph circled his horse to confer with Charles. "We had best see what this is about before riding on." He begged forgiveness for the delay.

"But, of course." Charles offered to wait at the gate, but both Pamela and Sir Ralph urged him to follow them to the house for refreshment.

In a few more minutes, they pulled up their horses in front of a grey stone Jacobean house, built in the shape of a square around a small central courtyard. A groom hurried from the stable to help Pamela down from her horse, and Charles, who had quickly dismounted, assisted Hester to alight. Her feet had barely touched down, when her cousin Mary, looking more mature than Hester had last seen her, came running out of the door, distress etched deeply across her face. A spaniel followed on her heels, barking at the sight of strangers.

As Mary reached them, she shushed it angrily, before turning to Pamela. "Oh, Pam! Sir Ralph . . . Hester!" Her voice quivered, and she looked on the verge of tears. "The most disturbing thing has happened!"

"What is it, girl? Whatever it is, nothing can be so bad that you should forget to greet your guests civilly." Sir Ralph indicated poor Charles who hung back, loath to intrude.

Instead of apologizing, Mary stamped her foot, tears springing from her eyes. "It is, too, that bad!" She must have felt Charles's alarmed gaze, for she made a colossal effort to contain her emotions. "I am sorry, sir, but the news I have to relate is of the worst possible kind, for a neighbour of ours has been killed."

As Hester put an arm about her cousin, Pamela exclaimed, "Who? Who was it, Mary?"

"Mr. Fenwick. They say he's been murdered!"

The next hour was one of the worst in Hester's experience. The moment the name Fenwick passed Mary's lips, they all gasped in shock. Their eyes flew as one to the young gentleman, who stared at Mary as if paralyzed. He put a hand to his head and moaned.

Mary turned a questioning gaze on Hester, but it was clear from the alarm on her face that she had guessed.

"This is Mr. Charles Fenwick," Hester explained in a low voice, "I believe the gentleman you just spoke of was his father."

A hand flew to Mary's mouth. "Oh, I am sorry! I did not know."

Hester hushed her, giving her waist a squeeze to convey that it had not been her fault. Releasing Mary, then, she transferred her attention to her young travelling companion, still too stunned by the terrible news to move. Since both Pamela and Sir Ralph seemed to be at a loss for words, and stood mutely gaping at him, Hester suggested, "Perhaps we should take Mr. Fenwick indoors and offer him a glass of brandy."

Sir Ralph snapped out of his reverie to second the notion. "Aye, a glass of brandy will be the very thing. See that your servant brings one up, Pammy. There's a good girl." He took Charles by the arm and urged him in through the door to the porch.

Mary and Hester followed them into the screens passage, then through the ancient hall, its dark wood paneling decked with mounted antlers, rows of pikestaffs and halberds, and the Mayfield family tree. At the opposite end, they passed into a small parlour where Sir Ralph pressed the younger man to sit, while Pamela issued orders to a manservant waiting in the hall.

Before she did anything else, Hester removed her hat, covered in dust from the ride. Then she went to Charles's side and took one of his hands between hers.

Cradling it, she conveyed her sympathy in words, which, though conventional, were sincerely felt. That he should have travelled so far to be greeted with such appalling news seemed to her the utmost misfortune, for though he had never admitted to attending school in France, it was evident that he had been away from his father's house for a number of years.

Hester coaxed him to speak, aware that conversation would help to dispel the shock. She asked how long it had been since he had last seen his father.

He drew his brows together, as if to answer even a simple question cost him great effort. "I have not seen any of my family in the past ten years, except my younger brother, who left home with me." He looked up to meet her gaze. Reassured by the sympathy he read in her face, he said, "We were both sent to school in France. My brother resides there still."

This confirmed Hester's suspicions. If she were not mistaken, his brother had been sent to France for a different sort of education. Assuming Charles had been raised as his father's heir, his younger brother might very well have been raised to become a priest. That was often the way with Catholic families, but there was nowhere in England where a boy could receive such instruction in the Roman faith. Neither could he now travel home to Yorkshire except in disguise, for the risk of being discovered to be a priest was much too great after the recent rebellion.

Soon, the brandy arrived on a tray, and Sir Ralph poured the younger man a glass. "We might all like to have one," he told the servant. "I know I do. Mrs. Kean?" he asked, when Pamela forgot her duty as hostess.

"Thank you. I should prefer a dish of tea," she told the servant, "but if you do not have it, brandy will do."

By this time, the spirits had revived Charles to the extent that he could ask Mary, "You said that my father was murdered? Who did it, and how? Why?"

His confusion was pitiable. When Hester reflected on how young he must have been when he left home, she realized how alien everything here must feel. To be greeted with this news must seem like a nightmare, not real.

Mary had been staring at their young guest with a mixture of nervous anguish and curiosity, but she bestirred herself to answer him gently, "I am afraid there is very little I can tell you. A servant from your father's house rode over last night to tell us that he was found in a wood and that he had been shot. Apparently, he set out early yesterday morning on his normal ride. An hour later, his horse returned without him. The servants searched for him and found him in a little wood quite far from the house, which perhaps is the reason no one heard the shot."

"But who would do this?" Charles was completely at a loss.

"I do not think anyone knows. A poacher, perhaps, or a deserter from the army? Many troops have passed through Yorkshire on their way into Scotland or Leicestershire. And there have been riots in the towns. I am sorry to be the bearer of such dreadful news."

Sir Ralph tsked and shook his head. "Yes, a dreadful business.

Make no doubt, it will turn out to be a deserter. I had not thought of that myself, but I see what sense that makes."

"None of it makes any sense to me." The young man rubbed his forehead. "But I am so fatigued from the journey, I can hardly think straight."

"Yes, and I'm sure we're all famished." Pamela at last recalled her duties. "Mr. Fenwick . . . Papa, will you dine with us."

On being called upon to answer, Charles shook his head as if to awaken himself, but his voice still sounded dazed. "If your father does not mind, I should prefer to ride home as soon as possible. I must see my mother and my sisters . . . ."

"Of course, you must," Hester said, with a look at Sir Ralph.

His face had drawn into a frown. "Naturally, my boy . . . though I should think a bite of food . . . ."

Hester stared pointedly at him and gave her head a little shake, which prevented him from completing his sentence.

"Well . . . yes . . . of course. I suppose you must excuse us, Pammy. I daresay I can stop off for a bite on my way back. Shouldn't be gone longer than half an hour."

Poor Charles stood to go. Mechanically he followed Sir Ralph back through the hall and the screens passage, which separated the hall from Dudley's bedchamber in the front and the kitchen and pantries towards the back. Hester escorted them as far as the front porch, where a groom waited with their horses, and bid Charles goodbye, expressing her wish that he would advise them if there was anything they could do to help. She—and Pamela she presumed—would call on his mother at the first opportunity.

After their horses disappeared around the corner of the house, she rejoined her cousins in the parlour, where she found them in the midst of a row.

"You needn't have blurted it out!" Pamela was saying. "I was never so mortified in all my life!"

"How was I to know who he was? If you had presented him to me, as you should, I would never have made such a terrible mistake."

"Well, how was I to guess that the neighbour you was speaking of was going to be the poor boy's papa?"

As Hester stepped into the room, she hastened to intervene. "Yes, the timing was most unfortunate, but these things occur when one is upset. Nobody is blaming you, Mary, least of all poor Charles Fenwick. He had to be told, after all, and better he should find out here than at home."

She sat on a settee covered in a rather moth-eaten velours d'Utrecht and patted the place beside her. "Now, come tell us everything you know."

"No, wait!" Pamela put up her hand. "Do not say another word until we have sat to dinner. I meant it when I said I was famished. Mary, show Hester up to her room so she can refresh herself. Then, both of you hurry back down so we can hear all about it."

They obeyed, Hester because she truly wished for a moment to freshen up, and Mary because she could not wait to escape her sister-in-law.

They ascended the west staircase and wended their way to Mary's bedchamber. "Pamela told me to put you in my chamber," Mary said. "I shall have to sleep with Clarissa."

A sullen note had entered her voice. Hester remembered her cousin Clarissa as the least likeable of her aunt's children. "I do not wish to oust you from your room. Would you rather sleep in here with me?"

Mary's face brightened at once. "Are you sure you would not mind?" When Hester said she would be happy to share with her, Mary added, "Then will you please tell Pamela it was your idea and not mine? If I do it, she'll accuse me of not being a gracious hostess, but Clarissa kicks, and I think she only pretends to be asleep when she does it."

Hester assured her that she would not allow her to be blamed for the change in arrangements, but she pled for a few moments alone in which to recover from her journey. In a much more cheerful frame of mind, Mary left her to her own devices.

Inside Mary's bedchamber, Hester took a moment first to glance round. She noticed little change in Mary's room since her last visit, nearly two years ago. A small attempt to brighten the chamber with flowers had been made for her sake, but the rug on the floor and the bed curtains were as worn as the last time she had seen them. The same sense of neglect was apparent on the tapestries hanging in the stairwell

and the frayed carpets on the landings. If Pamela had brought a sub-
stantial dowry to the family, it was clear that Dudley had not used it
to refurbish his house. Hester wondered how much of the money had
gone into paying off his gambling debts and how much into horses.

She found her portmanteau and her few things set out by the maid.
In spite of her hunger, she took the time to change into the gown that
had been brushed at the inn in York. It was not necessary to change on
such a rushed occasion, but she was heartily sick of the dress in which
she had spent most of the past five days.

She poured fresh water from a pitcher into a basin and splashed
it over her face. Pulling a brush through her hair, she thought about
poor Charles Fenwick and wondered how he would be received by
his mother and sisters. After so many years, they would scarcely know
him—or he them—but he struck Hester as a thoughtful young man
whose support would be welcome in a crisis. Her heart ached, for he
would have to assume his father's duties without ever receiving the
benefit of his instruction. There was not much she could do to assist
him, but perhaps Sir Ralph would be willing to take him in hand.
He seemed to regard Charles's family kindly, in spite of their being
papists.

When hunger pangs overcame her desire for solitude, Hester
placed a fresh white cap upon her head. Then she felt a bit readier to
face Pamela and the rest of the family.

When she joined the others in the Great Parlour where a board
had been set, she found that Dudley had just returned. Fresh off his
horse, with his neckcloth askew, he entered the room with a pair of
hunting dogs at his heels. Ordering them back into the hall and tossing his riding-crop aside, he removed his felt hat and stuffed it under
his arm. He greeted Hester with a nervous kiss and, avoiding her direct
gaze, said he was sure they were all very glad to see her. With a gruff
gesture, he begged her to take a chair at the table where Mary and
Pamela were already seated.

"Are any of the children going to join us?" Hester asked as she took
her seat.

"Lud, no!" Dudley spoke with relief. "They get their grub in the
nursery. It's bad enough that we have to put up with Mary now, with-

out the little ones join us."

"I shall go up to see them after dinner," Hester said, while Mary stuck out her tongue at her brother.

Hester pretended to ignore the lapse in manners, but Pamela said, "There she goes! I tell you, Mary, you must not behave like a hoyden if you expect to catch a husband. What will your cousin Hester think of you! I doubt the ladies at Court carry on like that."

"Generally speaking, they do not," Hester said, giving Mary a teasing smile to dull her sister-in-law's barb.

Mary did not return the smile. She seemed to have grown sullen over the past two years. Hester was afraid that Dudley's new wife had not improved the relations between Dudley and his family or apparently raised the tone in the house. Of them all, it was Mary who had always had the most sense, so the sooner she could be removed from her brother's influence, the better it would be for her.

Two manservants entered with their food, and nothing more was said about Mary's behaviour while the food was passed round.

Then, Hester recalled that Dudley knew nothing of the day's events and, wishing to change the subject, asked Mary to tell him about Mr. Fenwick. She was pleased to see the girl comply without any of the relish a young lady with a taste for being the center of attention would show.

Dudley was suitably shocked. "Old Fenwick murdered, you say! Now who would do that?"

With a sad look, Mary shrugged. "The servant told me that no one knows. When neither you nor Pamela was here, I didn't quite know what I should do."

"Nothing you or anyone else could have done." Dudley frowned, pausing with a bite of roast goose on the way to his mouth. "Still . . . shot you say? It won't be a poacher then."

Hester told him about the murder they had heard of in Stamford. "Are any troops quartered nearby?"

"No, and I haven't heard of any deserters passing through, or any other trouble, which I'm sure we would if any were about."

"How was Mr. Fenwick regarded by the neighbours?" she asked.

Dudley raised his brows. "Well, he's a papist, if that's what you mean. Keeps—I mean, kept mostly to himself. Tried to keep quiet so's the authorities would forget he was there. Sent his daughters to that papist convent in York." He chewed pensively then added, "The vicar had him up before the Archdeaconry court a few months back for not paying his Easter offering."

"Oh, dear." Sighing, Hester told him about the incident in Newark when the King's Commissioner had tried to have Charles Fenwick arrested.

Mary expressed immediate sympathy, but Dudley protested that the Commissioner was only doing his job. "How was he to know that Fenwick wasn't a damned Jacobite on his way to join the rebellion?"

"In the stagecoach? And with the rebels already defeated?" Hester gave him a dubious look. "If this were a few months ago, perhaps such a suspicion would have been justified. What I witnessed, however, seemed more like the viciousness of an over-zealous official than a reasonable concern. It made for a very uncomfortable journey, I assure you."

While the servants took away their plates and served the second course, she told them how she had been squeezed between a Roman Catholic, a Quaker, an Anglican clergyman, and the King's Commissioner with only a country squire to share the burden of making civil conversation.

"Poor Hester!" Mary laughed, taking a portion of the marinated fish a servant held out to her.

Helping himself to a plump partridge, Dudley snorted. "Better you than me!"

Peering at a dish of jellies, Pamela sighed. "And how hard it must have been to recall you were leaving the gaiety of Royal Tunbridge Wells behind you."

"It was a bit difficult to leave the Wells, which is charming, but I am very glad to be in Yorkshire, after all."

"And how did you leave the dear countess? And Dudley's mama?"

Dudley's snort was muffled by a mouthful of food. "With Isabella flirting with every gentleman in sight, and m'mother wagerin' all of Hawkhurst's fortune away, I'll warrant."

"For shame, my dearest! How can you speak of your sister and your dear mama in that manner?"

"'Tis only the truth," Mary muttered, gazing down at her plate.

Hester ignored their comments to answer Pamela. "I left them very well, thank you. There was an unfortunate episode with my aunt's health, which is why I am here with you now, but I wrote you of that before leaving the Wells. Did you receive my letter?"

"Yes, it was brought round three days ago. And very concerned we all were, I assure you. Tell me, how does dear Mama get on now?"

"Oh, she's fully recovered," Hester said cheerfully. Another snort from Dudley and an angry look from Mary told her that they were wise to their mother's tricks. It was fine for Dudley who had his new wife and his estate to occupy him, but what about Mary, who might naturally expect a mother to care enough to visit her from time to time, no matter how much she dreaded the journey?

Deaf to their thoughts, Pamela asked, "When might we have the privilege of a visit from Lord and Lady Hawkhurst?"

"Humph! If you're waiting for that, my girl, you'll wait until the Ouse runs dry." Dudley said.

"Perhaps if you wrote to your sister and told her how honoured I would be—"

"If you think for one moment that Bella will leave her beaus for you, you don't know her, as I've told you before!"

Pamela assumed a mulish expression and would have chastised him, but Mary said irritably, "Indeed, he speaks no more than the truth. Now that Isabella has caught an earl, she cares nothing for us."

Hester tried to make peace. "In fairness to your sister, it is not entirely that. While it is true that she is unlikely to visit, the reason is rather that she finds the country so dull, she avoids going even into Kent to Rotherham Abbey. She is so much a fixture at Court that I'm certain his Highness the Prince of Wales would be very loath to let her go. I am certain she would much rather you visited her at Hawkhurst House. She loves nothing better than introducing her family and friends to the pleasures she enjoys." Hester turned to Mary. "Indeed, she is looking forward to your visit."

Mary's lips twitched in stubborn disbelief, but she said no more as she finished her gooseberry tart.

Pamela gave Dudley a lowering look. "Then it will be up to us to pay them the visit."

"Not me!" he retorted, with a bilious pout. "I've already been to Court, and all it got me was a pack of troubles! Missed most of that summer's races, besides. I'll not be dragged on that fool's errand again."

From the glares they exchanged, Hester could see that this argument was not a new one. It was not up to her to settle a quarrel between husband and wife, but at last she had an answer as to why Pamela, with an acceptable fortune, should have accepted Dudley's offer of marriage.

A countess as sister-in-law would surely have been an inducement to a lady who wished to go to Court.

After dinner, Hester visited the nursery with Mary to see her aunt's other children. Clarissa, twelve, was the most like her mother, tyrannizing her younger brothers and scheming when slyness would get her more than an ill-tempered fit. She fawned over Hester, petting her and plying her with questions designed to secure a treat or leave from her nursemaid. When Hester tried to give equal attention to her brothers, ten, nine, and seven, or the youngest, a girl of six, she pouted and flounced about the room, wreaking havoc on everyone's feelings.

The children's nursemaid was an oppressed, drab creature, who clearly had no other choice in life but to play keeper to this menagerie. She did well to feed them, wash them, and prevent them from injuring each other. Their education was sorely neglected, their mother having no respect for learning beyond how to make an advantageous match. Dudley, Isabella, and Mary, at least, had had the benefit of a governess as long as their father had been alive, but unless someone took the younger ones in hand and soon, Hester would not give their futures much chance.

After promising to visit them again and to take them out for a walk—one at a time, she stressed—she made her escape to Mary's chamber for a long-desired rest. She could tell that Mary would have loved to pour out her discontent to a sympathetic ear, but she was enough like her father to recognize that Hester was exhausted and that better opportunities would arise.

In the evening, Pamela monopolized the conversation with more questions about the King, the Prince and Princess of Wales, and the new French fashions. Hester tried her best to satisfy Pamela's curiosity without arousing her envy, but it was plain that she begrudged Mary the opportunity that she had been denied. Dudley left them to their chatter, after promising Hester some good sport if she ever wished to ride out.

Later, tucked up in bed for the night, Mary did pour out her bitterness to her cousin. She complained that Pamela treated her with jealousy and resentment and that Dudley never took her part. Underneath it all, Hester sensed a deep hurt for the lack of interest Mrs. Mayfield had taken in her or the other children. It had been, "Isabella, this" and "my Isabella that," for all of Mary's life, and now that Isabella was a countess, it seemed that her mother had forgotten all about them.

Hester had little to say in Mrs. Mayfield's defence, so she did not try. The only solace she could offer was how assiduously Mrs. Mayfield had nagged Harrowby until he had consented to give Mary a dowry so she could make a good match. She did not have the heart to tell the girl how viciously her mother would bully her into accepting one of her suitors. Whether they pleased her or disgusted her would make no difference to Mrs. Mayfield.

She did not need to warn her, however, for Mary soon demonstrated that she knew her mother at least that well. "What if I do not meet a gentleman I care for? Will Lord Hawkhurst take my part?"

Since Harrowby's willingness to help her would depend entirely upon his mood, Hester could only say that she would do her utmost to influence him in Mary's favour, should the need arise. "But it will help a great deal if you give him no reason to regret his generosity. He is not always on the best of terms with your mother, so if you can manage not to offend him, he may be inclined to champion you, if only to remind her who is lord in his house. I do not mean that you should quarrel with her, however, for if there is one thing no gentleman likes, it is to be subjected to quarrels at home."

Mary soberly listened to her advice, and with a relic of the good sense she had once possessed, promised Hester that she would do her best to make Lord Hawkhurst glad that he had agreed to be her patron.

Finally, Hester managed to sleep after promising Mary that she would see to it that she got her share of amusement in preparing for her visit to London.

*A*s the News of my Arrival spread through the Kingdom, it brought prodigious Numbers of rich, idle, and curious People to see me; so that the Villages were almost emptied, and great Neglect of Tillage and Household Affairs must have ensued, if his Imperial Majesty had not provided by several Proclamations and Orders of State against this Inconveniency. He directed that those, who had already beheld me, should return home, and not presume to come within fifty Yards of my House, without License from Court; whereby the Secretaries of States got considerable Fees.

CHAPTER V

Fortunately, Hester's trunks arrived the next morning, so she had a fresh gown to wear when they were visited by the neighbours who came not only to see Dudley's cousin from London, but also to satisfy their curiosity about the murder.

The first to arrive was the curate of the parish and his wife, who were received downstairs in the Great Parlour, whose windows looked out over the formal garden. The Reverend Mr. Ward wore a permanent look of discontent, which seemed to have rubbed off on his wife over the course of their marriage. His comportment, dress, and demeanour would have suited a Puritan better than an Anglican, Hester thought. Their manners were civil, but no one would have called them warm. Their visit would clearly have been inspired only by duty if not for the opportunity the murder of Mr. Fenwick had afforded them to expound on the sins of idolatry.

After solemnly welcoming Hester to the parish, Mr. Ward expressed a hope that he might see her in church on Sunday.

Hester assured him that it would give her great pleasure to attend, adding that her father had held the curacy of Hawnby for many years.

He raised an eyebrow. "Hawnby? Now let me see. The Reverend

Mr. Kean, I take it, as you are a spinster? The name is not unfamiliar to me, although we would not have crossed paths since my former parish was to the south. Lord Fauconberg granted me the living in Coxwold only this past year."

She could see his mind working when he mused, "Rather spread for a parish, Hawnby. Similar in size to mine, but without nearly as many parishioners, I should say."

Hester confirmed that indeed it was smaller in those terms, which seemed to give the Reverend Mr. Ward considerable satisfaction. He looked better pleased with her, indeed, much happier than when they had first been introduced.

The knowledge that she was the daughter of a clergyman had raised her in his esteem, and it afforded him license to expound upon his parish and express his unhappiness with the presence of Roman Catholics in it.

"It is a matter of great concern to me, as you can imagine." He dolefully shook his head. "Of particular concern during the recent rebellion, of course, although we have not as many recusant families here as in my former church. Monitoring the activities of the papists in my parish is a duty I take quite seriously. They were the greatest source of sedition in the rebellion, but I could proudly relate to his Majesty's men that due to my diligence, none of the recusants in Coxwold became involved in the conspiracy—although, I am afraid I was obliged to report the late Mr. Fenwick on more than one occasion for his transgressions."

"Yes, my cousin informed me of his failure to pay the Easter offering."

Mr. Ward sighed. "That was certainly deplorable, as was his excuse that the double taxation he had been placed under made it difficult for him to comply. He refused to concede that those taxes were necessary to pay for the burden recusancy places on the kingdom. But his worst offences occurred a few years before my tenancy. He was once called before the court for holding a papist school in his house! Of course, I have done all I could to counteract the pernicious influence of such men in the area. We are very fortunate to have a charity school in Coxwold, which should give me the means to keep the children of the poor from the influence of popery, were it not for the interference of men like Fenwick. Papist families have been known to take these children into their homes and make converts of them, you must know."

The hostility with which he spoke of the Roman Catholics in his parish distressed Hester when she thought of poor Charles Fenwick and the problems he would have to face. It would be useless to argue with Mr. Ward, however, who was not alone in his conviction that recusants, especially Catholics, would do anything to pervert his parishioners. Archbishop Sharp, who had held the archbishopric of York until his death two years ago, had firmly believed they were the greatest threat to the Anglican Church.

Hawnby had not been a center of Roman Catholicism, so Hester could not truly say that they were wrong, but if none of the families in Coxwold parish had taken up arms against King George, then surely they did not deserve to be harassed and punished.

Throughout her conversation with the curate, Pamela had been entertaining Mrs. Ward, or attempting to entertain her with descriptions of the gowns Hester had unpacked that morning, most of which were Isabella's older garments to be altered for Mary. Talk of the kind of finery she would never be able to possess had only increased Mrs. Ward's discontent. She could barely conceal a tendency to glare at Hester for the worldly vanity she was likely to encourage in the neighbourhood.

She could not vent her spleen upon her host's family, so she found another direction for it. "I heard you speaking of Mr. Fenwick," she said. "I cannot say I was surprised to hear that he had been murdered."

"Really?" Hester asked, dismayed. "Was he so universally disliked? I never met him, of course."

"Humph! I cannot speak to the generality of feelings towards him, but the Lord will wreak His vengeance on the ungodly."

"I cannot believe He would use a murderer as His tool." Hester smiled with false sweetness, before turning back to Mr. Ward and raising her eyebrows in query.

He frowned at his wife, who had placed him in an untenable position. "Perhaps, my wife has allowed her Christian zeal to trip up her tongue. Of course, the Lord does not condone murder, but neither does He tolerate a refusal to worship Him according to the laws of the land. I pointed this out to Mr. Fenwick on numerous occasions, but he would never listen to reason."

Realizing that it would be useless to enter a debate on the Lord's expectations or wishes, Hester abandoned the subject to ask, "Have you called on his widow yet?"

He bristled. "Naturally, I did my duty, only to discover that Fenwick is to be buried in a family chapel, which some popish priest has no doubt consecrated."

"So you will not be officiating at his funeral?"

"No, I shall not!"

"Do you know when his interment is to take place?"

He pursed his lips in anger. "I am not privy to that information."

As the Fenwicks were clearly devout Roman Catholics, Mr. Fenwick would likely be buried with the aid of a Catholic priest, which meant that none of the Protestant gentlemen in the neighbourhood would be invited to attend. She had merely asked in order to know when it might be convenient for his family to receive a visit of condolence, but seeing that she would get no sympathetic information from Mr. Ward, she turned the conversation to something less controversial.

Not knowing when Hester's trunks would arrive, Pamela had not planned a dinner to present her to the neighbours, but now she invited the Wards to a party in their cousin's honour, saying, "Let us make it for Tuesday next."

The Wards accepted and soon took their leave, Pamela having made it clear that she must immediately get to work sending out her other invitations.

Before she could start on them, however, another visitor appeared. Mrs. Mynchon was the wife of the justice of peace, who lived on the neighbouring estate. She was a plump, cheerful lady whom Hester had met on her previous stay.

After greetings were exchanged and the usual questions concerning the rigours of her trip addressed, the talk naturally turned to the heinous crime that had been perpetrated in their small community.

"I have never been more shocked in my life," Mrs. Mynchon declared, taking the high-backed chair a servant had placed for her. "And what possible reason can there be for such violence? It's not as if the poor family hasn't suffered enough."

When Hester gave her a questioning look, she explained, "Oh, it's all this business about being a papist. If you saw Oulston Hall now, you would not believe that the Fenwicks were once one of the grandest families in the area. Their circumstances have been so reduced—those restrictions on their movements and their property and all those punishing taxes—forced to sell off land to avoid them. Why now, I daresay, they've hardly two sticks left to rub together."

Pamela murmured something unintelligible, but it was clear that her sympathy for the Fenwicks' straitened circumstances was not nearly as deep as their visitor's. In contrast, Mary looked stricken. The laws against papists would not have been a topic of conversation in the nursery.

Hester gave a sympathetic response before informing their visitor that she had ridden on the stage with Charles Fenwick and had found him to be a pleasant young gentleman.

At the mention of his name, Mrs. Mynchon perked up. "And a blessing it is that he should arrive at such a time, for I do not know what his mother would do without him. I met him yesterday when I paid them a visit. He has grown into a handsome-featured young man, and his manners are very pretty, too. He pretended to remember me, though he was very young when he was sent off, and he could not have glimpsed me more than once or twice before that."

"Were you not on frequent visiting terms with the Fenwicks?"

With a sudden change in her demeanour, Mrs. Mynchon gave an uncharacteristically subdued response. "We were . . . but of late, less so."

When Hester hesitated over her next remark, Mrs. Mynchon added, "But we have ever been on very good terms . . . Mrs. Fenwick and I."

It would have been rude for Hester to pose the obvious question—whether the relations between Mr. Fenwick and Mr. Mynchon had not been quite as amiable—so she said instead, "I know nothing about the deceased Mr. Fenwick, other than his religion. What can you tell me about him?"

Mrs. Mynchon blew out her cheeks as if she found it hard to phrase an appropriate answer. "I hardly know what to say," she admitted. "I suppose it is because being a papist governed so much of his life. He could not afford to engage in many of the activities the other gentlemen in the area did, and we never saw them in church, of course. Then, so many of the Roman Catholic families have sold up and moved away that their circle has grown smaller. I don't want to speak ill of the dead, but I can tell you that he had grown bitter over the years and he seemed worse since the rebellion."

"Did he take any part in it?"

Mrs. Mynchon looked alarmed. "Lud, no! I should not like to give that impression. I believe it was just that men of his faith came under suspicion again, and the laws against them were more strictly enforced. After living amongst us peacefully for so many years, it must have been hard to be suspected of misdoing."

Hester sighed. "Yes, so it must have been." And now Charles Fenwick must take up his burden with even fewer resources, she thought, but believing the conversation had turned too gloomy, she changed the subject.

"I have not enquired after your husband. How is Mr. Mynchon?"

Very ready to move to another topic, Mrs. Mynchon gave a laugh. "He is the same as he ever was. Busy with his work and his collections."

"His collections?"

"Oh, my yes! Did you not know? He is a great collector of curiosities. If you like, please come to see them. It gives him a great deal of pleasure to show them off."

Hester replied honestly that nothing would please her more. She had always been fascinated by the strange things in nature, but aside from the occasional monster exhibited at an inn in London, such opportunities rarely came her way. She had never had the privilege of seeing a virtuoso's collection.

The fact that her aunt had never mentioned Mr. Mynchon's rarities did not surprise her, for her aunt would not have the least interest in science or in anything with the slightest hint of being unfashionable.

She promised Mrs. Mynchon that she and Mary, at least, would pay her husband a visit at the earliest opportunity. Pamela begged off for the reason that she had been treated to Mr. Mynchon's curiosities more than once, but she invited the couple to the dinner she was planning in honour of Hester's arrival.

Mrs. Mynchon accepted with alacrity. Soon she took herself off, which allowed Pamela to get back to her planning.

"I have been longing to give a party this age, but Dudley always comes up with an excuse for why I should not. I tell him that we cannot expect to hold our heads up in society if we do not provide entertainment for our neighbours. He will not be able to refuse me if you are here."

Hester laughed. "I am happy to be of use. Just tell me what I can do to help."

A gleam came into Pamela's eyes. "I have not purchased a new gown since we wed." This was not particularly unexpected, since she and Dudley had been married for less than a year. Nevertheless, she appeared to feel ill-used when she said, "Perhaps there will be something amongst the gowns you brought for Mary that will do better for me."

Hester had not anticipated this request, but she could say, "I am fairly certain there will be. If you would like to look them over tomorrow, I can help with any alterations." As Pamela was much the same height as Isabella, and only slightly less buxom, there should be ample time before the dinner party to alter one dress and still have the opportunity for a visit of condolence to Mrs. Fenwick.

Pamela was so eager to obtain one of Isabella's gowns that she was ready to try them on immediately. When Mary quite naturally bristled, Hester reminded Pamela of the notes she needed to write to the neighbours or there would "be no occasion for which to have the dress."

By late afternoon, Pamela had her invitations written, sealed, and dispatched to the neighbours' houses in the hands of servant. Clarissa had managed to wheedle permission from her nursemaid to have tea with her older sisters and Hester. Although Pamela was displeased, she consented, finding it easier to give in on this one occasion than to deal with the tantrum that would ensue if she did not.

Besides, she had a treat to anticipate. With a contented smile, she told Hester how much she was looking forward to seeing Isabella's gowns and informed her that she had asked her dressmaker to attend them in the morning. Swallowing a sip of tea, Hester asked if they should not first visit Oulston Hall to offer their sympathy to Mrs. Fenwick.

Pamela's smile quickly faded, but she conceded that perhaps they should.

"And I shall go with you," Mary said eagerly.

"Me, too!" Clarissa insisted.

"Nonsense!" Pamela snapped. "I can think of nothing more inappropriate. We are not talking of a trip to the seaside, you know."

Clarissa pouted and begged. Mary's expression threatened mutiny, but catching the warning on Hester's face, she refrained from protest.

"Of course, you may not go, Clarissa," Hester said. "You would find it terribly tedious. The family will be in mourning, and there will be no treats. If you are very good to Nurse, however, I shall take you into the village later this week."

Ignoring Clarissa's whine, Hester added, "On the other hand, I think Mary should go. She will wish to repeat her apology to Mr. Charles Fenwick, for I doubt he was sentient enough to hear it. Moreover, if the purpose of my coming here is to prepare her for a stay in London, then we must expose her to as many situations as local society has to offer, whether happy occasions or sad."

Pamela could not object to these arguments, and Clarissa was sufficiently pacified by Hester's promise to cease nagging until she had stuffed three cakes into her mouth, whereupon she was led back to the nursery in angry tears.

It was moments like these, Hester reflected, when she felt much older than her twenty-one years.

A note was sent round to the dressmaker, postponing her attendance until late afternoon, and in the morning the ladies set out to visit the widow in a new carriage. Pamela proudly informed Hester that it was a wedding gift from her papa, who had wanted to insure that his daughter travelled in style.

The journey was only a matter of a few miles. It could better have been accomplished on horseback, for they were bumped unmercifully about on the rutted lanes. Hester was surprised that she had never heard of the Fenwicks before, but in truth, she had spent just a few hectic weeks at Beckwith Manor on her earlier visit, and the whole time had been taken up with preparations for Isabella's life at Court. Too, Mrs. Mayfield had not been eager to expose her beautiful daughter to the local swains. She had had a much grander plan for Isabella's prospects than marriage to a country squire.

Their first sight of Oulston Hall revealed it to be only slightly more ancient than Dudley's house. Though similar in style, it was clearly more neglected. It was shaped in the letter E, with a truncated middle wing where the central porch led into the screens passage. The length of the house appeared to be no more than one room deep.

Aside from the failure to enlarge the house as the change in architectural fashion demanded, other signs of penury were evident in the crumbling garden walls and the ill-repaired stonework over the porch door. The customs of mourning were being observed, however; all the windows and the door were draped in black. There was no sign of hired mutes, but this was a custom less practiced in the country than the city.

When the coach carrying Hester and the others drove up to the front door, only one servant appeared to take the horses' heads. Pamela's coachman was obliged to hand the young ladies down. The Fenwicks' groom cast them a suspicious look, then turned away and ignored them.

Hester's knock on the door raised another manservant, similarly wary, who morosely admitted them to the house after demanding to know their business. He led them through the screens passage and left them standing in the hall while he went in search of his mistress. The hall was paved in light stone squares. Its paneling was of dark oak, and the room's only sources of light were two mullioned windows on the wall across from a wide stone hearth. In the place where the family's collection of weapons should have hung, the walls were bare.

Soon, instead of the servant, Charles entered the room and, though pale, greeted them with something akin to relief. "It is good of you to come. My mother will be grateful for the kind attention. If you will come with me, I shall show you to her bedchamber."

"Is she ill?" Pamela asked, hanging back.

"No, just taken to bed in her bereavement. My father's death has hit her very hard. If I had not returned just now, I hate to think how much more difficult things would be for her."

"Mr. Fenwick." Mary spoke up before his mother could be added to her audience. "I must apologize most sincerely to you for blurting out my news in such an inconsiderate manner."

He turned to look at her, and for the first time appeared to see her. Something he saw in her eyes made him flush. "Not at all," he said. "It was obvious how distressed you were by the news of my father's death. I can only be grateful for your sentiment. My father did not always meet with such kindness, I understand."

Turning, with no elaboration on this remark, he led them through a parlour to a dark, narrow staircase at the north end of the house. From the first floor landing, it was just a few steps through two small closets, past the door to another chamber, before they reached Mrs. Fenwick's bedchamber. Charles knocked gently on the door before opening it and announcing to his mother that she had three visitors.

This room, like the others Hester had glimpsed was furnished in heavy pieces made of oak, indicating, as well as anything could, the reduced fortunes of the family. It was plain to Hester that not one table or chair had been purchased for many decades at least. There were no lighter pieces in walnut, no japanned chests, and not one piece of the china that had been popular now for decades.

The day was so warm that the bed curtains had been left open. The woman lying in it appeared drained by care, but as Pamela led Hester and Mary into the room, Mrs. Fenwick raised her head and gave them all a sharp glance. Her lips thinned in resentment. She did not look at all glad to see them.

"Mother, you must know your neighbour Mrs. Mayfield and her sister-in-law, Mrs. Mary Mayfield. And this lady," he said, indicating Hester, "is the one I told you about, Mrs. Hester Kean, who was so kind to me on my journey home."

"Yes, I know her," she said, nodding curtly to Pamela. "Sir Ralph Wetherby's girl, but I haven't met Mrs. Mary." She looked the girl over critically, then turned to Hester and greeted her with the first smile they had seen. "Charles has told me how you routed the King's Commissioner who would have had him locked up in gaol. I am grateful to you, Mrs. Kean. How I would have coped if word had reached me of his imprisonment, I do not know, especially as his father had just—" Her lips trembled and she broke off, fading back onto her pillow.

As the daughter of a clergyman, Hester was much more accomplished than the other two ladies when it came to visiting the bereaved. She crossed to the bed and taking Mrs. Fenwick's hand in hers expressed her sympathy for the loss of her husband. The widow speechlessly thanked her with a squeeze of her hand.

Released from their paralysis, Pamela and Mary each took a brief turn at the widow's bedside before retreating to the wall near the door. While they were making their speeches, Hester took a surreptitious look about the room. The walls were bare of ornamentation except for a crucifix facing the bed. Beneath it stood a table with a candle in a holder. A thin pillow on the floor in front of it indicated that this was where Mrs. Fenwick knelt to say her prayers.

There was only one place for visitors to sit, so Charles proposed giving the ladies a dish of something in the parlour downstairs.

"Mary, why don't you go with Pamela, and I shall stay with Mrs. Fenwick for a few moments if it will not tire her?"

With a brief nod Mrs. Fenwick indicated her willingness for Hester to stay. The plan seemed to suit everyone, but only Pamela betrayed relief on escaping the room. Mary's regretful glance showed how affected she had been by the sight of Charles's mother in her grief. Hester was glad to see that being surrounded by the selfishness and hypocrisy in her mother's house had not deprived the girl of human kindness.

She seated herself in the chair that Charles had drawn up by the bed.

"It is kind of you to stay," Mrs. Fenwick said, once the others had gone, "but you must not think me neglected. I have sent for my daughters, who will be here soon, and Charles is a great comfort to me."

"He is a very fine young man. You must be proud of him."

"Yes, as was his father. The reports we received of Charles were always good. To think that my husband was taken from us before he had a chance to see him again . . . ." The rigid control with which Mrs. Fenwick had conducted herself slipped.

Hester clasped her hand. Words could not convey her sympathy in such a painful situation.

When the widow had collected herself again, Hester asked, "Have they captured the person who did it?"

Mrs. Fenwick shook her head. "We've asked the neighbours, but no one has seen any strangers about." Anger flashed in her eyes, and the bitterness Mrs. Mynchon had spoken of showed in the lines of her face. "If we had more servants, we could have raised a hue and cry, but with the double taxation and the penalties, we live in a very reduced state, as you must have observed."

"Would your neighbours not lend you their servants and horses?"

"I cannot complain of them," the widow said, if reluctantly. "If Sir Ralph had been at home, I daresay he would have rallied his."

"My cousin Dudley?"

Mrs. Fenwick gave her a glance then let her gaze drift. Choosing her words carefully so as not to offend, she said, "I believe he would, under the circumstances, if he, too, had not been away. But you must understand that their willingness was not the problem. With only one horse—the only one we are allowed to keep—it was hours before we found Mr. Fenwick and could send word to anyone.

"The poor horse was frightened, too. It ran back to the barn, shaking, and was in no fit state to ride. Our servants set out on foot to locate my husband. They would have taken the dogs, but they had gone with Mr. Fenwick and did not leave his body to come home. Then, once he was located, they had to fetch the horse and make a litter to carry him up to the house. By the time this was done, too much time had elapsed. Whoever had perpetrated such an evil deed would have been long gone before I thought of summoning the neighbours, and then I had to send a servant to inform the local magistrate."

Hester could not imagine the restriction of having only one horse when one lived so far from one's neighbours. Before moving to London, she had lived in a village near the church, just a few steps from help. To be so far from assistance in such a crisis must have been terribly upsetting. The government's restrictions on Catholics were not merely cruel, they could be foolish and dangerous.

But if they were intended to drive popery from England, they were succeeding. The taxes alone were such a burden that many families had lost their estates. Every year, fewer recusants had been listed in her father's parish, and she assumed the same was true in most.

Sensing that Mrs. Fenwick would not welcome her comments on this point, at least not today, she said instead, "My cousin Dudley informed me that no strangers have been reported in the area. If that be the case, can you think of anyone who might have wished to harm your husband?"

Before Mrs. Fenwick could answer, they were interrupted by the manservant who entered and stood quietly waiting for his presence to be acknowledged.

"What is it, Joseph?"

He jerked his head towards the door. "You have a visitor, mistress—Mr. Moreland."

With a quick glance at Hester, Mrs. Fenwick said, "Please tell him that I will see him shortly. Tell him that a neighbour is with me." The news of the visitor seemed to have disturbed her for her cheeks had turned pale.

As the servant stepped out, as silently as he had entered, she asked, "You were saying?" Her hands moved anxiously over the coverlets.

Judging the moment to be inappropriate to repeat her question, Hester said, "Nothing that cannot wait. I should not keep you from your other guest. Shall I join the others downstairs?"

Mrs. Fenwick's face closed and she gave her head a little nod. Pleading a headache, she thanked Hester again for her kindness to Charles, before begging her to send him up.

Dismissed, Hester made her way back to the staircase. In the antechamber just before the landing, she crossed paths with a stranger, who took a step backwards and bowed. This was undoubtedly Mrs. Fenwick's new visitor, a thin gentleman with a prominent brow and deep-set eyes. Although he watched Hester carefully until she disappeared through the door, he said nothing in the way of a greeting. The encounter gave her an unsettled feeling, for there was something disturbing in the visitor's gaze. She could not put her finger on it—perhaps the cold way he had stared at her—but as she was unlikely to encounter him again, she shook the feeling off. She only hoped he would not distress Mrs. Fenwick, who had enough to worry about.

Hester found her way down the dark stairs and into the parlour, where she discovered that Charles and Mary had struck up a shy conversation. Mary had never seemed particularly shy, but neither was she accustomed to the company of handsome young men. Her innocence did her no disservice, for her smile was genuine and her eyes sparkled. She really was a very pretty girl, Hester reflected, when she was not sulking. Once she was properly dressed and out in society, she was likely to be captivating.

For a young man who had passed so many years in France, Charles did not seem to be put off by Mary's lack of polish. But, perhaps, attending a school run by Catholic priests, he had been as sheltered as she had been.

As soon as Hester entered the room, Pamela stood and announced that they must be on their way. Mary's face fell, but recalling the purpose of their visit, she did not quarrel. Hester would have liked to learn more about Mr. Fenwick and the details surrounding his death, but she was not at home in London, and too much of a stranger here for any inquiry on her part to be of much use.

She did have the feeling that Mrs. Fenwick could have mentioned at least one person who might have harmed her husband, but whether she would ever trust Hester enough to name him was another matter.

Hester informed Charles that his mother had asked him to attend her. Before they parted from him, Mary prevailed upon her sister-in-law to invite him to visit them whenever he felt able to leave his mother's side. Pamela did this with an appearance of good grace, but Hester sensed she would rather not have been obliged to comply.

In the carriage, she confirmed Hester's suspicions by scolding Mary for her pertness, saying that it was not for her to invite people to her brother's house.

"It's my house, too," Mary said with a pout. "And I did not invite him. I asked you to do it."

"It is not yours. It is Dudley's, and mine as his wife, as well you know. You have no right to the house at all."

Although patently true, this was a callous thing to say, Beckwith Manor being the only home Mary had ever known. But it was unlikely she would ever have any rights over a house. Women seldom did.

Regardless of that immutable fact, Hester hoped Pamela would indulge Mary in her request. "Do you have any objection to receiving Charles Fenwick?" she asked. "I am sure Mary meant only to show kindness to a grieving neighbour. It cannot be easy for a young gentleman to discover that he is the sole comfort and support of a mother and sisters he hardly knows. The burden of his new responsibilities will be hard to assume, and the mood of that house will be gloomy for months. It would be charitable to provide him with an occasional escape."

She kept her tone as light as possible when delivering this speech, hoping to persuade rather than push Dudley's wife into offering Charles her hospitality. Fortunately, Pamela's awe for Court and anyone who had visited it on a regular basis made her listen to Hester's pronouncements with a respect she would undoubtedly abandon once she had visited London on her own. She granted that it would be the charitable thing to do, but repeated that, in future, Mary should ask permission before inviting anyone to the house.

At home again at Beckwith Manor, the ladies spent the afternoon with Pamela's dressmaker, fitting the gowns Hester had brought. One of the benefits of serving Isabella as waiting woman was that Hester inherited many of the clothes Isabella grew tired of, or that she discovered after buying did not really suit her. Having borne her first child earlier in the year, Isabella had outgrown several of her best gowns, and although some could be altered, those that could not be made to flatter her had been discarded and replaced with others in the latest fashions from France.

With more subdued colouring than her cousin's and without her golden locks, Hester had often found that Isabella's palette did not become her. She had packed a great many in these colours, hoping they would suit Mary. She was slimmer than Isabella, and fortunately looked to advantage in the golds and yellows favoured by her sister.

What Hester had not foreseen was Pamela's envy. Even with her mantua-maker there to draw patterns of the gowns, the beauty of the extravagant fabrics was something that could not be duplicated with the selection of cloth she would find in York. She expressed her admiration for one gown so often that Hester had to take the hint. Fortunately, the cut of the dress was a bit too worldly for a girl fresh out of the nursery, so Hester persuaded Mary to relinquish it to her sister-in-law. Since it was by far the most splendid of the lot, Pamela was appeased, and the session ended in harmony, with enough needlework for the ladies to keep them busy for weeks.

They were grateful for the employment, for it rained over the next few days. The only thing that drew them from the house was the church service on Sunday. Monday morning dawned clear at last. In the belief that it was best to discharge unpleasant chores as soon as possible, Hester kept her promise to Clarissa and took her for a morning walk. The girl's conversation proved to be even more tedious than Pamela's. All she wished to hear was of the gentlemen at Court and whether Hester had any beaus. Unlike Mary, Clarissa had developed a sort of worship for her sister Isabella and, often repeating her mother's extravagant praise of her favourite child, expressed a wish to be just like her. "But instead of settling for an earl," she declared, "I shall be a duchess, and then won't Mary die of envy!"

Fortunately, taking a walk over the same lanes she had often trod with her nursemaid could not entertain Clarissa for long, especially when Hester gave damping responses to her more selfish comments. After just an hour, Clarissa was easily persuaded to return to the house with sweetmeats as an inducement.

They entered the house by the door to the kitchen garden. Hester left the girl in charge of Cook, who promised to return her to the nursemaid as soon as she had eaten her fill. Cook was a bit distracted, though, for a visitor had come and Pamela had called for refreshments to be sent into the Great Parlour.

Assuming the visitor was a neighbour come to pay a call on the cousin from Town, Hester first went to her room to freshen her face and hair and change her gown. Then, coming back downstairs and moving towards the hall, she was surprised to see a greyhound dog, lying at the door to the porch, evidently having been instructed by its master tò stay. When she entered the screens passage, the dog perked up its ears, thumped its long, thin tail on the wooden floor, and gave a friendly whine. Though it fidgeted and squirmed, begging for attention, it remained obediently rooted to the spot. It bore a strong resemblance to Argos, Lord Hawkhurst's dog, except that it did not wear such a mournful air.

Hester could never see a greyhound without being reminded of Rotherham Abbey. Without warning, her thoughts flew to St. Mars, and a pang struck deep inside her heart.

For weeks, she had tried to ignore the dull ache constricting her chest, but a morning spent like this one, in the company of the worst her family had to offer in the way of selflessness and intelligence, had made her vulnerable. At moments like these, it was hard not to miss St. Mars even more than usual. She had to pause inside the hall to compose herself. Then, resisting the urge to retreat to her bedchamber for a good cry, she directed her steps to the Great Parlour to see who their visitor was.

As she neared the room, the murmur of voices reached her, followed by the trill of Pamela's laughter. Expecting to see a neighbour she had not yet met, she walked in and came to an abrupt halt as a gentleman stood up from his chair. His fair hair was tied back in a queue with a black ribbon, and as he faced her, his blue eyes danced.

For the next few moments, all her senses were blurred. Her heart beat like the pounding of an anvil, and she thought she might faint. The buzzing of a hundred bees hummed loudly in her ears. Her vision dimmed, and she moved her lips, but no words came.

"Ah, here is Hester now." Pamela's high voice, cheerier than Hester had ever heard it, brought her back from the brink of oblivion. "Sir Robert, may I present my husband's cousin, Mrs. Hester Kean? But, perhaps you already have met at Hawkhurst House?"

As St. Mars stepped forward to meet her, a warning flickered in his eyes. He bowed over Hester's hand, saying "No, we have never met, though I have often heard his lordship speak of you with the greatest affection and respect." Turning again to Pamela, he explained, "I have never had the privilege of visiting Lord Hawkhurst at home. We frequent the same coffee house, and when he overheard me mention to a friend that I was coming into Yorkshire to purchase an estate, he insisted I call upon you here."

By now, Hester's faintness had been replaced with an elation so forceful, she feared she would burst into laughter or tears. As she curtsied and murmured an unintelligible greeting, her lips trembled with joy. She did not dare look into St. Mars's eyes or the glow in her own would have given them both away.

As it was, Pamela detected something odd in her manner, for she tittered and said, "It is rare for us to receive gentlemen from London, but Hester will say there is nothing to boast about when we do, for I daresay she encounters more than a dozen amusing courtiers every day."

Hester had collected herself enough to respond composedly to Pamela's jealous barb. "A dozen gentlemen, perhaps, but not many I would call amusing . . . with no disrespect to my cousin's friends, of course."

St. Mars bowed low over her hand again. "With two such enchanting ladies here, I must endeavour to impress." He included Pamela in this statement, but his eyes spoke otherwise. The happiness Hester saw in them when he gazed at her—mixed with a small measure of relief, as if he had been uncertain of her welcome—filled her heart to overflowing.

It took real effort to pretend she did not know him, but if she had managed to hide her love from him for more than a year, she ought to be able to hide it from Pamela. "I am sorry to have interrupted your visit. Shall we sit?" She led him back to the chairs which the footman had grouped into a circle, saying, "You said something about purchasing an estate?"

"Yes." As St. Mars took a chair beside hers, he continued, "For some time, I have thought of purchasing more land, and the tales I have heard of this part of Yorkshire and the grand new houses being erected here, the more curious I have been to see it. I shall put up at the inn in Thirsk and search for a suitable property."

Pamela tsked. "You must move to the inn at Coxwold. You will be much closer to us then."

His hesitation was too brief for anyone but Hester to detect. "I shall inquire, but for the moment I am comfortable enough."

Pamela persisted. "Whatever you do, you must visit us often and tell us what you have found." A happy notion occurred to her. "And you must come to dinner tomorrow, for we have invited several neighbours to meet Hester. A new gentleman is always a welcome addition."

St. Mars gave Hester a quick glance, but she did not respond to his unspoken question. There was no one coming who was likely to recognize him. "I shall not cause you any inconvenience?"

"No, far from it. You will complete our numbers, and save me the necessity of inviting the curate's assistant. My sister-in-law Mary will be dining with us. She is but fifteen, but she will be entering society soon, and I had forgot to include her in my numbers."

"Then I accept with pleasure."

Hester did venture one question. "How did you find us, Sir Robert?"

"That was no trouble. I knew that Mr. Mayfield's estate was situated near Coxwold, so I had only to ask the way from the village. I have passed this way before on a journey further north."

The heavy tread of boots on the wooden floor announced the arrival of Dudley, who strode rapidly into the room, trailed by his dogs. Without pausing to see if he interrupted, he demanded, "Who is the owner of that splendid mare?"

Chuckling, St. Mars rose to his feet. "She is mine."

Dudley looked him over with profound approval. "That is one of the finest pieces of horseflesh I've ever seen! And I know a bit about horses. How much would you take for her?"

"Sorry, but she's not for sale."

"Really, Dudley!" Pamela exclaimed. "Have you no manners at all? Storming in here without so much as a how d'ye do?"

She might as well have not spoken, for he continued, "You must give me a chance to match her against the best in my stable."

"Willingly." St. Mars nodded. "I've not had much opportunity to test her paces, but the course must be flat. I'll not risk her legs over ditches."

"What must you think of us, Sir Robert?" In a desperate move to regain his attention, Pamela appealed to her guest. "You cannot be accustomed to such ragged country manners as these!"

He laughed. "Manners will always take second place when two sportsmen are together, but I shall be happy to present myself to your husband." He made Dudley a proper bow and said, "Sir Robert Mavors, at your service."

Dudley threw his wife a scowl, as if to say she was wasting his time, but he responded with a brief bow. "Dudley Mayfield—but you must already know that or you'd not be here. Did you get a chance to see my nags? I can take you to see them now."

"You will not," Pamela said in her frostiest voice, "for we are due to dine with Papa."

"Demn! That's right! Well, we'll do it another day. Where are you putting up?"

"Sir Robert is stopping at the inn in Thirsk, but I have invited him to dine with us here tomorrow." Before Dudley could press a tour of his stable on St. Mars, she said, "I know Papa would welcome you to dine at Yearsley Park today, if you are not already bespoken. There is no one so hospitable as my Papa."

Dudley's expression had gone from elation to disappointment, but it brightened again. "That's true, y'know. I'll give him that. Very open-handed Sir Ralph is. Why don't you come along with us. He'll want a chance to cast an eye on that mare of yours, but be ready to name your price! He's a hard man to refuse."

St. Mars did not waste any breath responding to this, but after being assured that the invitation was sincerely meant, he accepted with grace.

Throughout this exchange, he had avoided Hester's gaze, but as they prepared to leave for Yearsley Park, he gestured for Pamela and Dudley to lead the way from the room. As Hester followed them, he took hold of her arm to whisper, "When we can meet?"

As dazed as she felt, her brain had been puzzling over the same question. She answered in a low voice, "I can breakfast early and start walking towards the village. Shall I meet you in the lane at nine o'clock?"

He gave a subtle nod before following Dudley and Pamela into the hall, where Dudley stopped to demand his attention again. Hester was not surprised when Dudley suggested they ride, leaving the ladies to follow in the coach.

Pamela tossed her husband a resentful look, but bit her tongue. With a toss of her head, she told Hester, "I shall meet you and Mary down here in ten minutes. Please be ready, for it would be rude of me, indeed, to arrive at my father's house later than my guest."

As she disappeared towards the stairs, Hester's eyes followed the gentlemen as they entered the screens passage. She saw the dog leap up with ill-concealed relief as soon as St. Mars appeared. Only then did she realize that the lurcher must indeed be Argos. The first emotion to hit her was incredulity, but this was followed by a gurgle of laughter. Who else but St. Mars would have the audacity to take a dog from under Harrowby's nose? She tried to recall whether Dudley had ever visited Rotherham Abbey, but could not. Even if he had, she doubted if he had given Argos more than a passing glance. He certainly would not remember him well enough to recognize Lord Hawkhurst's dog.

As she turned to go upstairs, she only hoped her own expression on seeing St. Mars had not been as besotted as the dog's.

At the same time, the Emperor had a great Desire that I should see the Magnificence of his Palace . . .

CHAPTER VI

The carriage ride to Yearsley Park, no more than a mile, could not be accomplished quickly enough to suit Pamela. She scolded Mary for having kept them waiting, though the girl had followed Hester downstairs but a minute later.

It was abundantly clear to Hester that as long as Pamela and Dudley were about, she would have little opportunity to speak with St. Mars. The two would be in constant competition for his attention. The thrill of a newcomer to their circle, one with both the address to please a lady and, for Dudley, a splendid horse, was a rare occurrence. If Dudley did not claim him for some shooting or a race, Pamela was certain to want him for her drawing room. They would have to be very discreet to manage a private meeting, but just the knowledge that he had come to find her, no matter how brief his visit turned out to be, elated her so that she could hardly contain her spirits.

He came . . . he came for me . . . kept circling inside her head. She was wondering how she would manage to conceal her joy a moment longer when Yearsley Park came into view. The house was an impressive sight, nestled at the bottom of a low hill and approached by a curving avenue of majestic trees, with extensive formal gardens visible beyond. The stone that had been used in its construction was a lovely golden colour, unlike most of the other local manors, which had been built of locally quarried grey stone.

It was attractive enough that Hester could vent her pent-up emotion in an effusion of compliments, which Pamela received with an air of complacency. She had undoubtedly heard much praise of her father's house, for Yearsley Park had evidently been rebuilt within the past ten years and, judging by the number of glazed windows that Hester could see from the coach, no expense had been spared.

Unsurprisingly, Dudley and St. Mars had arrived long before Pamela's carriage rolled to a stop in front of the door. This apparently had disturbed Sir Ralph not one whit, as Hester saw when he came out to greet her and her companions. "Thank you, my dears, for the pleasant increase to our company. I was telling Sir Robert that he did me great honour in coming, and that I shall expect to see him every day he feels like riding over to take his potluck with me."

After seeing them safely down, he ushered the ladies into a hall with a black and white marble floor, where an impressive collection of arms adorned the walls. Two fashionable painted wood cut-out figures, one of a peddler and the other of a female servant with a broom, stood in front of the fireplace, which boasted a colourful marble surround. St. Mars must have ordered Argos to sit and wait for him here in the reception hall, for the dog, lying in a corner, raised his head in greeting before morosely settling back down on the floor. A footman offered to divest the ladies of their light wraps. Then Sir Ralph hastened them into an adjoining hall, where they found Dudley expounding to St. Mars on the quality of the shooting he would experience in these parts.

After exchanging a brief greeting with St. Mars, which stretched her smile almost beyond bearing, Hester looked about her at the room on whose dark paneling large portraits had been hung. A set of hood-backed chairs with red velvet seats stood placed against the walls.

"Ah, I see you are admiring the old hall." Sir Ralph came over to join her. "This is the only room I preserved from the former house, with one important improvement which you have undoubtedly noticed."

Hester looked about her again but was unable to guess what his improvement might be, a fact she was eventually forced to admit.

The look on Sir Ralph's face revealed his acute disappointment. Tapping the toe of one shoe on the floor and gazing down at the boards, he said, "Flemish oak. I had a sprung floor built for dancing. I shall host you to a ball while you are here."

Hester redeemed herself by expressing sincere admiration for the floors, which, indeed, were very beautiful. She supposed, she had become so accustomed to fine buildings that nothing Sir Ralph could show her was likely to amaze, but if his vanity demanded praise, she was perfectly willing to provide it.

His pride in his house was obvious as he showed them all into yet another hall which gave onto the formal gardens. The walls of this room were hung in embossed leather, dark but painted with bunches of fruit in vivid colours. In the middle of the room, a table had been laid for dinner. As he invited them to sit, Sir Ralph apologized for the scant company they found, assuring them that they would rarely find themselves seated with such a small party at his table.

"I promise to do better by you both," he said to Hester and St. Mars, "but I have not been visited much these past few days. It's very unusual for a day to go by without more company."

"Perhaps the neighbours are reluctant to ride out until the murderer is caught," Pamela volunteered.

"Murderer?" St. Mars cast Hester a startled glance.

With a grave "tsk," Sir Ralph answered for his daughter, "Yes, a neighbour was shot taking a ride about his estate. But I cannot believe that will happen to anyone else. Whoever did it, whether a deserter or a poacher, must have fled."

"Are you certain that's who it was?"

Sir Ralph seemed ready to nod, but Hester said, "We cannot really be certain. The gentleman was a Roman Catholic, and it appears there was some local resentment against him."

"Some, yes, of course! But not so much as you might think, coming from London with all the dust-ups that occur there. Here in Yorkshire, neighbours are cordial, no matter what their religion. I daresay Fenwick was welcomed in every house."

"Forgive me, Sir Ralph. I was repeating what the Reverend Mr.

Ward said when he called yesterday. He complained about Mr. Fenwick's failure to pay his Easter offering and seemed to regret the presence of Roman Catholics in his parish."

Sir Ralph waved that off. "That is church business and of little concern to the rest of us. Fenwick was well-enough liked. Kept to himself a bit, but then he couldn't entertain much, could he? Not with all the taxes he had to pay."

He looked about at his guests. "But let's not spoil our dinner with talk of death and taxes! Let's talk about when we shall have our ball."

The subject of the murder was allowed to drop. St. Mars merely raised a brow in Hester's direction, letting her know that he expected to hear all the details from her, before he turned to reply to Pamela's question about whether or not he enjoyed dancing.

At the mention of a ball, Hester's heart had given a leap. Twice before, she had attended a ball where St. Mars was present, but on neither occasion had they managed to dance together. If Sir Ralph's could only take place very soon, she saw nothing this time that should prevent them from taking the floor together, but St. Mars would not remain for long in his current disguise. She would not let herself anticipate a treat that was unlikely to happen.

Still, just being in the same room with him, seeing his face across the table and hearing his beloved voice had her heart strumming as if it would burst from the vibrations. She had the feeling of a current running between them. Every stirring of his seemed to pull her as if they were floating on the same wave. If his body inclined to the right, her own felt a tug in the same direction, as if unwilling to lengthen the distance between them by even so much as an inch. She tried to break this feeling of being tied to him before it could be noticed by the group by encouraging Sir Ralph to tell her more about the work that had been done to his house.

He obliged at her great length. His droning made it even more difficult to concentrate, but when Dudley changed the subject, Sir Ralph promised to take Hester and St. Mars on a tour of the house the instant they finished their meal. She doubted this would afford her a chance to speak privately to St. Mars, but still, the prospect of walking beside him sent a thrill down her spine.

Neither Dudley nor Pamela wished to be dragged on a tour they must have been subjected to many times. Though neither was happy to see their new acquaintance carried off, they seemed prepared for the attention Sir Ralph exacted of his guests, for neither sulked when Sir Ralph proposed the treat. Pamela said that she would await them in the withdrawing room and Dudley informed St. Mars that he would meet him in the stables when their tour was done. Only Mary accompanied them, probably, Hester guessed, to avoid keeping Pamela company.

After prompting them to admire two paintings of turkeys, geese and shelduck by the same Dutch artist on the nearest wall, Sir Ralph led them from the East Hall into a small parlour hung with portraits of his relations and friends. They paused just long enough for him to name his friends, an influential list of Yorkshire landowners, before turning into an adjoining parlour, hung in gilt leather like the East Hall. This, he explained, was where the family assembled every Sunday before church.

Hester gratified him by asking where he had obtained the wall-hangings, while St. Mars peered more closely at the embossing. As long as Mary stood between them, Hester did not dare cast her eyes at St. Mars, but when Sir Ralph led them back out of the room, St. Mars politely stepped aside to allow the ladies to precede him. Hester hung back long enough to give him the smile she had been reserving and to murmur, "My lord, your audacity knows no bounds!"

The sparkle in his eyes teased her. "Did you think I would allow you to spend a peaceful summer without me?"

That was as much conversation as they were allowed before Sir Ralph instructed them to follow him back into the Great Hall, where they were invited to examine his "pedigree." A chart with his coat of arms adorning the top traced his ancestors back over more than two centuries. He drew their attention to a distant connection with Henry V before finally leading them onto a handsome staircase built of walnut. It led from a space next to the entrance hall, its wainscot painted white. All the while they climbed, he talked. He gestured to a large painting by another well-known Dutch artist on the wall of the landing and paused for their praise.

This time, St. Mars gave him the satisfaction he sought, speaking eloquently about the painter.

"Ah, it would appear that you have made a tour of the Continent, Sir Robert. Am I correct?"

"Yes, with my tutor. I developed a great admiration for the Flemish and Dutch painters."

"Um . . . yes, excellent . . . well, come along this way to the State Apartments. No doubt you'll find more to your liking. The place is full of Dutch things. Nothing but the best for Yearsley Park!"

When he turned his back to lead them, St. Mars raised a comical brow that nearly made Hester laugh. She sent him a quelling frown, but she could not control her smile.

The suite of rooms through which they next passed was magnificent enough to extract genuine exclamations from Hester. Starting with an antechamber, then a great bedchamber with two splendid closets beyond, they rivaled many similar apartments she had seen. The walls of the antechamber had been painted to resemble marble in the shape of ancient Greek columns decorated in gilt and porphyry. The bedchamber was furnished with an immense state bed, curtained in embroidered red and gold velvet and crowned with an elaborate canopy in red silk with gold fringe. The room was hung with Flemish tapestry, its floor covered with a splendid Turkey carpet. The four closets beyond contained a variety of treasures, ranging from a japanned table to clouded silk hangings.

There was certainly much to admire. The only thing that puzzled Hester was why Sir Ralph had spent so much money on state apartments when he was not a courtier. It was very unlikely that King George would visit a provincial gentleman, no matter how wealthy, who never appeared at Court. She hoped Sir Ralph would not be disappointed if his splendid apartments were never used. But, perhaps, he believed that his new relationship with the Earl and Countess of Hawkhurst would remedy any neglect of his own.

The last set of rooms they visited on the ground floor included Sir Ralph's library. Hester complimented him sincerely on such a fine number of books.

"Yes, a gentleman must have a good collection of books. I'm not one much for reading, mind, but I did not wish to put up my library without them."

Taken aback by this confession, she could only agree. "Yes, the room would certainly not be half so pleasant without them."

The tour now finished, he clapped his hands and rubbed them together, evidently pleased with their praise of his house. "Now, you shall see the stables. Since it is such a fine day, I'll take you by way of the garden."

Once again he led, and after Mary followed, Hester hung back to exchange a few words with St. Mars. "If we pretend to have been delayed by the appreciation of a painting, I have a notion we shall be forgiven."

He barely managed to stifle a laugh. "Oh? Is that what you think?" His low voice hummed with suppressed delight.

Ignoring his question, she asked, "What possessed you to come here in this guise, my lord?"

"Why, how else was I to see you? And I might have known that you would arrange for someone to be murdered, so that we should have something to discuss."

She gave him a disapproving look, but in truth she had been too pleased by the first part of his answer to scold. "The murder was none of my doing, and very sad for poor Mr. Charles Fenwick, a young gentleman who rode on the stagecoach with me."

"Do I have reason to be jealous?"

A flush erupted through her body. "You are being absurd! But I know how you love to tease. Mr. Fenwick is younger than I and a papist."

"The latter I had gathered from the conversation at dinner, but the former is a relief. Now that the prospect of any rivalry has been dismissed, do you intend for us to assist him?"

Hester was unable to respond to his question for Sir Ralph's heavy footfall alerted her to his return. With a shrug to indicate that she was not certain what she and St. Mars could do about the murder, she picked up her skirts and turned to join their host, apologizing for keeping him waiting. "But we both were enthralled by the magnificence of your writing table, Sir Ralph."

Not at all displeased, he told her where he had bought it and named all the woods used in its ornate veneer. Then they turned their steps towards the garden.

As in the house, expense had not been stinted here. The terrace had been laid out with a formal garden near the house and walks leading off from it in three directions. Directly ahead, beyond the parterre and a fishpond, Sir Ralph pointed out the yew maze, which had stood on the site since Tudor times.

"It is not so large as the one at Hampton Court, but I daresay there are not many of this size. My father did not see fit to keep it up, but when I came into my inheritance twenty years ago, I had the whole thing replanted with a thousand new trees. The servants keep it in perfect trim, and it amuses my guests, especially the younger ones. You shall have to try to find your way through it." He turned to pinch Mary's cheek. "This young lady must know her way to the center by now. She has spent enough days searching for it."

Mary's grimace revealed that the pinch was not to her liking, but she politely subjected herself to it before turning to Hester. "Yes, it is great fun! You shall have to try it, Hester."

"I shall be very happy to, but now I think we should join Dudley in the stables. He has been waiting to show St—Sir Robert your horses, Sir Ralph."

Sir Ralph clapped St. Mars on the shoulder. "And I want to see this mare my son-in-law has been bending my ear about."

They followed him down a gravel path to a gate cut through a wing of the house. On the other side stood an impressive block which housed, in addition to the stables, the buttery and the brew house on the ground floor with servants' rooms above. A pair of small terriers greeted them with frantic barks and followed them, tails wagging, as they crossed the yard.

Entering the stable, Sir Ralph called in a lively voice to his son-in-law. They found Dudley leaning over the door to a stall from which angry snorts were issuing. He turned to greet them, envy writ large across his face. "If she don't cap owt, I don't know what does!" Excitement had caused him to lapse into Yorkshire. "Are you certain you can't be persuaded to part with her?"

"Not for all the fortune in the world."

"Ah, that is just what a gentleman says when he's driving for a better price," Sir Ralph assured his son-in-law. "Let me set eyes on this paragon."

Dudley reluctantly moved to make room for his father-in-law at the door to the stall. Resentment turned down the corners of his mouth.

By now, Hester was not surprised to see St. Mars's beloved Penny, an exquisite copper mare, stamping impatiently on the flagstone floor. Catching sight of St. Mars, she whinnied a greeting, though when she spotted Hester, she threw her what seemed to be a jealous look.

"A very pretty piece, indeed. Come now, sir, you must name your price."

"I am sorry, Sir Ralph, but truly she is not for sale. Can you imagine that I would part with her?"

Their host laughed. "Do you mean to say that you did not bring her here for just that purpose, sir? When everyone about here knows that I must always have the best?"

St. Mars's laugh was polite, but tinged with incredulity. "No, I swear most assuredly that I did not. Even if I had heard of your reputation—and I have not been in your country long enough to hear stories of its inhabitants—nothing could ever persuade me to part with her."

Dudley smirked to see his father-in-law denied. "Well, if she were mine, I shouldn't let her go either, not as long as she could still run."

Hester felt St. Mars stiffen beside her, but he responded with restraint. "Mr. Mayfield understands, I see. Is there nothing you possess, Sir Ralph, which you would refuse to sell at all cost?"

His question took the older man aback. He blustered before saying, "Naturally! But I have yet to meet another man who can say as much."

St. Mars smiled. "Then I shall be happy to be the first." He turned his head to peer towards the other stalls. "I should very much like to see your horses, sir. And I shall promise to make you no offers. I came into Yorkshire in search of land, not horses."

This last was said in such a joking fashion as to rob the words of sting. With a shrug of incomprehension, Sir Ralph left off bargaining and prepared to take him on a tour of the stalls. Just then, however, a groom appeared, leading two more saddled horses, and accompanied by two gentlemen on foot. One was Charles Fenwick and the other the unnamed visitor Hester had encountered at Oulston Hall.

Sir Ralph greeted Charles with a show of warmth, perhaps to hide a feeling of relief. It had been obvious that St. Mars's refusal to sell Penny to him had caused him some embarrassment. He seemed even more delighted than usual to welcome the newcomer, whom Charles nervously introduced as Mr. Moreland, a cousin from Durham. Sir Ralph beamed at the addition to his party, even going so far as to ask St. Mars and Hester if he had not told them how rare it was to find him without more guests. He completed the introductions, presenting Charles to Dudley, the two never having met. Dudley made an awkward comment about not having seen Charles since he was still in skirts.

Mary greeted Charles with a shy smile, which he returned before, casting a guilty glance at his companion, he schooled his features into a more serious look.

Seen in the brighter light, Mr. Moreland's face was even harsher than Hester had first perceived. In a guarded manner, he expressed his thanks to their host, clearly not engaged by Sir Ralph's ebullience. When Sir Ralph invited the two men to join them on the rest of the tour and gave Mr. Moreland a friendly clap upon the back, the latter flinched as if the touch had offended his dignity. His lips pressed into a thin line and his nostrils flared disapprovingly.

"Are you a student of horseflesh, Moreland?" Sir Ralph guided them past Penny's stall on the way to his own horses.

"Not particularly, sir. As long as a horse gets me safely from one place to the next, I am satisfied."

This answer did not please Dudley, who sneered. "Then I take it you are not a sporting gentleman?"

Mr. Moreland gave Dudley a long, measuring look, but did not favour him with a reply.

At this point, Hester thought she should excuse Mary and herself from what was fast becoming a gentlemen's party. This she did, adding, "We should go in search of Pamela now. She will be wondering what has become of us."

With a regretful look at Charles, which he studiously ignored, Mary accompanied her back through the gardens and into the house. They found Pamela in the leather-paneled room, fuming over the loss of her guest.

"Your brother had no right to take Sir Robert from me. I met him first. But gentlemen always take what they want with no consideration for anyone else."

It amused Hester to think of St. Mars as a prize to be quarreled over, but she agreed. "Yes, it is in their natures, I am afraid. They will persist in their sports, but Dudley will not be able to monopolize him tomorrow at dinner. You will seat him beside you, of course."

This reminder gave Mary an idea, but having been chastised once for issuing Charles an invitation, she restrained her tone when she said, "Mr. Charles Fenwick has just brought a relation to meet Sir Ralph. Would you wish to invite them as well?"

Pamela's ears perked up, but then she sighed, remembering. "Mr. Fenwick will not be able to come for he is in mourning. We must assume that the same applies to his relations. I daresay it's just as well, for then we should have too many gentlemen, and I am not of a mind to include the Lindsay girls simply to balance the party."

Mary could not dispute her logic, but it was plain from her disappointed expression that she was fast developing an attraction to Charles Fenwick. If he were not a confirmed Roman Catholic, Hester would see no reason to discourage her, even if the match would not satisfy Mrs. Mayfield's inflated ambitions for her daughter. Given the religious differences, however, it was unlikely that either family would approve of a match between them. The guilt she had noted on Charles's face suggested that he was aware of how strongly his family would object if he were to pursue a relationship outside his faith. Their acquaintance was much too short to fear anything of the sort, however, so Hester dismissed the issue from her mind, reflecting that Charles's mourning would keep him from going out much in society.

Advising Pamela that the horses were likely to occupy the gentlemen for the remainder of the afternoon, she eventually persuaded her to go home by directing her thoughts to the morrow. It had been a relief to Hester to escape the other gentlemen. By tomorrow she hoped she would be better prepared to conceal her intimacy with St. Mars. His arrival had taken her too unawares for her to be sanguine about her behaviour today. Fortunately, her cousins were too self-absorbed to notice any oddness in her manner, but it would be impossible to repress St. Mars's audacity—or her reaction to it— if he took it into his mind to tease her. If, after a few days, her relatives noticed any particularity between them, Hester told herself, they could put it down to flirtation.

∅

The following morning, at the inn in Thirsk, Gideon arose with the sun. He had wakened at four and had found it impossible to return to sleep, as eager as he was for the day to start.

Knowing he would not be served breakfast at such an early hour, he dressed and first paid a visit to the stable to tell Tom to have Penny fed and saddled by eight o'clock. Tom had waited for him in Thirsk all the previous day and had stabled her on Gideon's return, anxiously looking her over for signs of stress. He had insisted on sleeping with her in the stable, too, distrusting the ostler with his precious charge. He grumbled when he heard that Gideon would be riding out all day again, but promised to have her ready to ride in time.

By seven o'clock, Gideon managed to coax a venison pasty and a tankard of beer out of his host. The beer in Yorkshire was twice as strong as in the South and made him regret his lack of sleep, but since he had ten miles to ride in order to reach Beckwith Manor before nine, he did not dare give into the temptation to rest his head on the pillow, even if only for a few minutes.

When the long-awaited moment of departure finally came, he commanded Argos to stay with Tom, mounted his horse, and rode off.

Unfortunately, a rain had fallen in the night, so the lanes were full of puddles. When he gave Penny leave to run, she tossed up so much mud that Gideon feared Mrs. Kean would be forced to disappoint him. It would be difficult to justify a walk on a morning like this if anyone in the family challenged her. All he could do was keep their appointment and pray that she could do the same, but concern that he might not get to see her nagged him all the long miles from Thirsk.

Even with the mud to slow her pace, Penny made short work of ten miles. Arriving fifteen minutes before the appointed time, Gideon avoided the village of Coxwold and rode on past the gate to Beckwith Manor, where he walked his horse up and down the lane to cool her down. If not for the overnight rain, it would have been a lovely morning for a rendezvous. The oaks and ashes had put out fresh summer leaves, adding light green to a rainbow of summer colours. Birds greeted him with their songs. A linnet with rich chestnut feathers on his back flew in undulating swoops over the field to Gideon's right. A tit perched in the hedge in front of him, flashing its long tail. The call of a wagtail floated out of the tall grass.

He noticed all this as he tried to be patient before checking his pocket watch for the fourth time. Then, judging that if Mrs. Kean was able to come, she would have started by now, he turned his horse and steered it past the gate again.

In a moment, he spied the top of a lady's cap appearing over the hill in front of him. Cresting the small rise between them, he saw Mrs. Kean, with raised skirts, picking her way cautiously over the puddles. The clop of Penny's hooves must have reached her ears, for she raised her skirts higher, preparing to step into the grass lining the lane to avoid the splashes from the approaching horse.

He called out softly, "If you promise not to run away, I shall promise not to cover you in mud."

She turned and flashed him a glorious smile. He reined Penny to a stop. The horse was tired from her gallop and did not resist the pull on her reins, but still, he halted her a safe distance from Mrs. Kean. Penny did have her moods.

"I had expected you to come from the opposite direction," she said, betraying a slight nervousness.

"I arrived a bit early. I was afraid you might not be able to walk out in this mud." He was grinning like a fool, but he was so happy to see her, he could not help it.

"I was careful not to be seen on my way out of the house, but if we are to meet again, this might not be the best place."

He gave her a warning look. "You are undoubtedly about to suggest that we meet in a church, but I refuse to be kept indoors when the weather is so warm. You will have to think of a different way of curbing my behaviour."

She laughed and a blush spread up her cheeks. How easy it was to tease her! And how much he loved doing it! Tearing his eyes away from her face, he dismounted, anticipation thrumming in his limbs.

For once, Penny allowed herself to be led like a docile child as Gideon stepped over to Mrs. Kean. She extended her hand and started to curtsy, but before she could, he took her by the shoulders and kissed her slowly first on one cheek, then the other.

"I am so happy to see you, dearest friend." Huskiness clogged his throat.

"And I, you, my lord."

She smiled up at him then. He searched her eyes, but found no sign of the trouble that had seemed to lie between them before he had left for France. They were lit with the same joy he felt.

He swallowed hard. "I had the devil of a time finding you. What possessed you to leave for Yorkshire without so much as a note?"

She lowered her eyes and pulled away, embarrassed but still smiling. "I believed you to be in France. Besides, I had not expected to travel here."

He felt there was something she was still not telling him, but did not press. Whatever it was, it no longer posed a barrier between them.

He offered her his arm, and they strolled slowly down the lane minding the puddles. "Tell me why you did come here then."

She related a story of how Mrs. Mayfield had tricked Harrowby with her palpitations, doing it with such good humour that he had to smile. Gideon knew he should be angry with the woman for the way she had misused her niece, but since the result had landed them together, far away from her, he could only be glad.

Guiding Mrs. Kean around a deep rut in the lane, he explained how he had traced her from Rotherham Abbey to the Wells and beyond. She rewarded his ingenuity with a smile.

"How long do you plan to stop here?" she asked.

Startled, he said, "Why as long as you do! Surely, you did not believe my story of searching for an estate?"

"No, but—" her look was incredulous—"how can you possibly stay?"

"What else would you have me do? The last time I consulted my appointments book, I didn't see any pressing engagements."

She rewarded his jest with one of her wry looks. "My lord, that is quite beside the point as you know. You must have realized that if you came into Yorkshire on a priceless horse, you would attract too much attention."

"Ah . . . now I see your objection, but I could not in conscience leave Penny behind. She missed me when I was in France. Besides, as you must have seen yesterday, with her as a topic of conversation, less attention will be focused on me."

"But what if you are found out?"

"I do not expect that to occur, but if it does, then we shall both have to flee to France."

She blinked. He waited for a greater reaction, but she refused to respond to the bait. "Do you not have any acquaintance hereabouts?"

"Only one—Viscount Fauconberg. That is the reason I did not put up at the inn in Coxwold. Even I consider that too much of a risk." Newburgh Priory, the seat of the Belasyse family and the Viscount Fauconberg, was at Coxwold. The inn stood not far from its gate, and his lordship, as its landlord, would expect to be informed of any gentleman stopping at the house.

"I believe Lord Fauconberg is travelling abroad. Would you like me to inquire?"

"If that is likely, I can risk inquiring about it myself. It would be much better if I could put up in Coxwold instead of Thirsk. Tom will not be happy with me if I demand too much of Penny, so I should eventually be forced to resort to hacks. That assumes that I can see you every day, of course."

Her lips spread in a shy smile, but she gave him a saucy look. "You will be very lucky if Pamela does not claim you for every meal. She considers you a great personal discovery. You must not be surprised if she and Dudley wage a battle over you."

"Egad! Shall I have to pay court to her?"

"Yes, I am afraid you will."

He sighed. "Well, I shall do it if it means that you and I can meet occasionally without sitting in a freezing pew or standing in the middle of a puddle. I suppose I shall have to entertain your cousin Dudley, too?"

"Most certainly. He will drag you to the races and markets—wherever horses are to be found."

He brightened. "Things could be worse. I have nothing against horses."

"I thought you were supposed to be searching for an estate." She gave him another wry look.

"Yes, but I shall be expected to want to know something of local society. Whenever you are free to meet me, I can plead an appointment to visit a house."

Her look turned wistful. "I wish it were that simple. I am supposed to prepare Mary for Court—not that I mind being with Mary. She is the best of my cousins. But my visit is a novelty for the family, including the younger children, so I am rather in demand."

"Then we shall compete for their attention. I'll wager that by the end of your visit, I'll be as popular as you."

She laughed. "That is not a fair contest. Bachelors are always preferable to spinsters."

"Oh, but that depends very much on the spinster and the bachelor. And in our case, I prefer you."

She turned her face away, but not before he saw her bite her lip to keep from dimpling.

He wanted to keep teasing her, but the hard fact was that they were standing in a sea of mud. She had been forced to relinquish his arm to keep her skirts from dragging in it.

With a sigh, he suggested they turn back. "I'll ride straight to the inn in Coxwold. If Fauconberg does prove to be away, I'll send a message to Tom telling him to convey my things from Thirsk. I won't worry about Lady Fauconberg, for I've never met her, and she is not likely to take any interest in a plain 'Sir Robert' putting up in the village. I assume they do not mix much with the local gentry?"

"Not to my knowledge. Sir Ralph seems to be the local squire, and he never goes to Court."

"What can you tell me about Charles Fenwick and his family?"

She gave a sympathetic shrug. "Only that he just returned to Yorkshire after being educated in France. And that now he must assume responsibility for his mother and a pair of sisters with very little in the way of resources. We paid a call on the widow a few days ago, and it was obvious from the furnishing of their house that their fortunes have seriously declined. The extra taxes over the years must have been a considerable burden."

"Which was why they were enacted, of course. If we cannot force people to convert, we shall simply starve them out." Gideon frowned. "It all seems pointless to me, unless . . . Have you seen anything to suggest that his father was involved in the rebellion?"

"Nothing at all, but I do not know them well enough to say for certain. No one I have spoken to about Mr. Fenwick seems to believe he was involved. The general opinion is that a deserter from the army may have come across him accidentally and killed him. When we came through Stamford, we were told of a murder that had taken place just a week or two before. A dragoon killed a local man who was known to have Jacobite sympathies."

"You think a similar thing may have occurred here?"

"It is possible, I suppose. I am not sure about this visitor of theirs, though—Mr. Moreland." She shuddered. "There is something about him. I do not know what, but he gives me the impression of having taken a dislike to us all."

He nodded. "A strangely taciturn gentleman, I agree. It was not clear to me why he and young Fenwick came to call upon Sir Ralph, as unsociable as Moreland is."

"Perhaps Charles wished to make him known to the neighbour who was such a good friend to his father."

Gideon considered and shook his head. "It did not feel that way to me. I think Moreland initiated the visit. He made the boy nervous."

Her eyes widened. "Yes, I sensed that, too. In Charles's case it may simply be that, since he has not lived with his family for the past ten years, he may hardly know Mr. Moreland and is shy with a stranger. But Mr. Moreland's arrival disturbed Mrs. Fenwick, too. She grew agitated the moment his name was announced."

"They may be frightened of him for some reason."

She frowned in thought. "There was something in their behaviour that suggested fear to me, but also guilt. Yesterday, I thought it might be because of Mary, but I had forgotten about Mrs. Fenwick's reaction."

"What about Mary?"

She flushed and shook her head. "It was silly of me, but before our meeting yesterday, Charles had seemed quite taken with Mary. Then yesterday, he appeared to be avoiding her. I thought it could be because Mr. Moreland is Roman Catholic, too, and would not approve of the boy's forming an attachment to a girl who is not."

"That could be." He grinned at her as they reached the gate and paused. "Have you a mind to play matchmaker?"

She looked horrified. "And have my family blame me for a *mésalliance?* My aunt would never forgive me."

He twisted his mouth. "I don't suppose it would change her manner towards you very much, as abominable as it is."

She laughed and shivered comically. "Oh, do not underestimate my aunt. She can always find a way to make her displeasure felt." She glanced over her shoulder at the gate. "I must be getting back to the house." She tilted her head and smiled. "But we shall see you this afternoon?"

He took her hand and kissed it. "I shall count the minutes."

She giggled and turned up the drive, saying. "You had better save your pretty speeches for Pamela or you shall be quite worn out."

Gideon watched her walk away, thinking of all the words he had been saving for her and not had the chance to say. Then he mounted Penny and set off for Coxwold.

The ride was considerably less than three miles, but as he neared Coxwold, he realized he was hungry. He rode past the low stone wall of Newburgh Priory and glanced up the lane to the house, before continuing along his path until the village came into view. The slightly rising lane carried him past a row of stone cottages and the charity school, solidly built of honey-coloured stone. The sign of the Fauconberg Arms appeared on his right, but he rode past the inn to see the village church farther up the hill. St. Michael's Church, on his left, in gold and brown was distinguished by a rare octagonal tower. Beyond it, past the gravestones in the yard, the prospect of green fields, bordered by curving and intersecting hedges under a soft blue sky, was fine enough to make him stop and gaze. Following the road farther, he reached a small timber-framed house before, with a click of his tongue, he turned Penny and guided her back to the inn.

The inn itself was a neat stone house of one block with a tiled roof and what appeared to be a well-fitted stable to the side. As Gideon pulled Penny to a stop, two young ostlers ambled out in clogs to take her reins. He gave them explicit instructions about rubbing her down, but their expressions were so blank, he could not be certain they understood him. When he asked the younger of the two if he had understood, the boy gawked at him in total silence.

The older boy answered with a snigger, "Nay, maisther, 'e's as gaumless as a gooise nicked i' t' 'eead, 'e is!"

Since this provoked a punch from the younger lad, Gideon assumed that his English had been the difficulty, not the boy's wits. He cautioned them to take care with Penny, for she would gladly bite them if given a chance. Then he made his way into the inn.

Seated inside on a stool, he ordered a heavy meal and waited until the innkeeper returned with his food to ask casually if Lord Fauconberg was to be found at home. The innkeeper was glad for the opportunity to chat about his lord and informed Gideon that his lordship was gone to the Continent for his health. Gideon let the man rattle on, comprehending no more than two of every five words of the broad Yorkshire, until he was reasonably assured that the viscount would not be coming home in the next few months.

Later, when he had finished eating, he inquired whether a room was available for a stay of several weeks. While asking this, he extracted a jingling purse from his deep coat pocket, ostensibly to pay for his meal. With his eye on the purse the innkeeper, Mr. Sadler, answered quite readily that he did have a "chamer" and offered to show it to

Gideon directly.

On their way upstairs, they met a gentleman coming down. Gideon halted when he recognized Mr. Moreland.

Surprise widened Moreland's eyes, before he cloaked his expression beneath heavy lids. Gideon's initial impression that the man was not very glad to see him altered slightly when Moreland cordially bid him good day and paused for a chat.

"I did not know you were stopping here," he said on an inquisitive note.

"I wasn't—not until this moment at least. My servant is still in Thirsk with my bags. Mrs. Mayfield recommended this inn, and since I am finding the local society congenial, I've decided to centre my search for a property here."

"I see. Well, since it seems we are to occupy the same house, why don't you join me in the taproom for a glass after you have seen your chamber?"

Curious about the change in the man's manner, Gideon agreed. He followed Mr. Sadler up the stairs and down a short corridor to a room at the end. When the innkeeper opened the door and moved aside, Gideon ducked his head to avoid the low lintel and stepped in. His examination of the sheets confirmed that they had been well-aired. The room was small but clean with a washing-stand, two low oak stools, and a chest. He entered into negotiations to secure it exclusively for himself, with lodgings for Tom and stabling for his horse. As a matter of course he haggled for a few minutes, for a Yorkshireman would never respect a man who did not. When Mr. Sadler finally held firm with the statement, "Ther's nowt good that's cheap!" it was clear that a deal had been reached. Gideon requested paper and ink to scribble a message for Tom, and Mr. Sadler promised to send a boy immediately with it to Thirsk.

With nothing else to do, then, until his dinner engagement, Gideon joined Moreland in the taproom downstairs, where the drawer soon obliged them with tankards of ale. Gideon had just drunk a glass with his meal and did not feel the need for another so soon, so he sipped his slowly.

When Moreland asked if it was not to his liking, he replied, "On the contrary, it is very good. But the beer in Yorkshire is stronger than I am accustomed to."

"Aye, they pride themselves upon it. A Yorkshire man believes in getting his shilling's worth and in giving it. You are not from the North, sir."

"No, Kent is my home. Do you know it?"

Moreland shook his head. "I have lived in the North all my life. May I ask why you are looking to buy an estate up here, so far from home?"

Gideon had come prepared with an answer to this question. "I recently came into an inheritance, and, as I understand it, the farms in this area are more productive."

"That may be true. Perhaps, too, you have heard that there is more land here for sale?" His eyes held a particularly searching look.

Gideon was taken aback. He wondered if there was something that he, as a prospective buyer, should know about the county, something that could expose his search as a fraud. But the hint of hostility in Moreland's tone could mean that he simply resented the loss of northern land to "foreigners."

"Why should there be more land for sale in Yorkshire? I know there are some grand houses being constructed in the North Riding, but I have not heard any rumours about Yorkshire land."

Moreland studied his face intently. "Not that the Catholic families have been selling off land to pay their taxes?"

"Ah, yes, that is unfortunate, but surely that is true in every county. I did not travel into Yorkshire to take advantage of their situation. If that were my motive, I could find a papist nearer to home to rob."

For a moment it seemed that Moreland had taken offence. He stiffened, and his expression grew even sterner. Then, as the irony Gideon had intended sank in, the tension in his body eased, but his look remained wary. Choosing not to respond to Gideon's jest, he took a long draught of ale and then asked instead, "When did you say you arrived in Thirsk?"

Both the question and his manner of asking it struck Gideon as suspicious. "I do not believe I mentioned it, but I came there on Thursday. Why do you ask?"

Moreland shrugged. "I merely wondered if you had had a chance to explore the Hambledon Hills before coming to Coxwold."

Gideon explained that Lord Hawkhurst had urged him to call upon his wife's family, so he had made that visit first with the hope of receiving an introduction to local society.

"And you, sir?" he asked. "Have you visited this area before?"

"Yes, reasonably often, but then I have relations here."

"Mr. Charles Fenwick, yes. When I arrived, I was told about his father's murder—a terrible business, that. You have my deepest sympathy."

Moreland acknowledged it with a sigh and a nod. "Yes, a great tragedy for his family." His taciturnity seemed to have returned, for it was a while before he spoke again, and when he did it was to say, "No doubt we shall be seeing more of each other."

"You intend to remain in the area for some time, then?"

"Yes, as long as my cousins need me." He gave a curt nod as if to say that he had no more to add.

Gideon took this to be his dismissal. He left the beer still in his glass and excused himself to return to his room. Unless Tom made incredible haste, he would not arrive before Gideon was due at Beckwith Manor for dinner. Knowing, in any case, that he would not have time to ride back to Thirsk to change, Gideon had packed a clean suit of clothes and a periwig in his saddle bag. If he had not booked this chamber, he would have had to beg the use of a chamber at Beckwith Manor to dress. He had intended to pretend that he had been riding out all morning viewing an estate, but since Dudley would have been certain to ask him for the owner's name, it was fortunate he had no need to lie.

Retracing the steps to his chamber, he reflected that he would have to make inquiries about parcels of land if he did not want his falsehoods to be exposed.

This reminded him of the questions Moreland had asked. Getting answers to them seemed to be the only motive he had had for inviting Gideon to take a drink. All had been designed to plumb his reasons for being in the neighbourhood. Meanwhile, Moreland's answers about himself had been vague. His attitude towards the land, especially since he did not seem to have an estate in the area himself, had struck Gideon as curiously possessive. It seemed as if the man had an interest in the land here, whether or not he owned any. Perhaps he wished to acquire more land for himself, so he thought of "foreign" landholders as unwelcome competition. It was unlikely that Mr. Fenwick had left any interest in his estate to a cousin, not when he had a son, but if he had been in financial straits, perhaps he had taken a loan from Moreland, using land as surety. If that were the case, poor Charles Fenwick would have to try to wring the repayment out of his land.

It was useless to speculate without more information. The only certain thing was that for some reason, no matter what Moreland said about staying here to help his cousins, his presence did not appear to afford Charles Fenwick any relief.

*T*hey bury their Dead with their Heads directly downwards, because they hold an Opinion, that in eleven Thousand Moons they are all to rise again; in which Period, the Earth (which they conceive to be flat) will turn upside down, and by this Means they shall, at their Resurrection, be found ready standing on their Feet. The Learned among them confess the Absurdity of this Doctrine; but the Practice still continues, in Compliance to the Vulgar.

CHAPTER VII

The dinner party turned out to be much as Hester had expected. At one end of the table Pamela did her utmost to captivate St. Mars, while Hester was trapped at the opposite end with Dudley.

Conversation between the two cousins was always rather awkward, as Dudley could not be in Hester's presence without recalling the embarrassing situation he had caused during his stay in London, when his unpredictable temper had nearly landed him on the gallows. He found it hard to look her in the eye and preferred to pretend she was not there.

The man to Hester's right was the Reverend Mr. Ward, who conversed with her much as if he were giving a sermon. As Dudley had no tolerance for pious talk, he directed most of his comments to Sir Ralph, who sat on the other side of Mrs. Mynchon—fortunately an enthusiast for horseracing, who partook cheerfully in the gentlemen's conversation.

Before the guests had taken their seats, Hester had been introduced to Mrs. Mynchon's husband. Mr. Mynchon was a thin, dry man who wore a rather dyspeptic expression until Hester asked him about his curiosities. Then, he became animated until Sir Ralph, overhearing their talk, cut into their conversation to say in a rallying voice, "Do not let my dear friend bore you, Mrs. Kean. To hear Mynchon tell it, he is the greatest virtuoso and curioso who has ever lived, but I defy him to produce half the subscriptions I have collected in my album. When you visit me next, I shall show it to you. Why, the great Duke of Marlborough subscribed it himself and added a great compliment to me besides."

Hester could not blame Mr. Mynchon for the look of distaste that crossed his features. His dyspeptic look returned, leading her to suspect that it was the quality of the present company which had put it on his face. As soon as Sir Ralph turned his notice elsewhere, she did her best to overcome the offence he had caused, and when Mr. Mychon became convinced that her interest in his curiosities was genuine, he invited her to his house to see them.

Now, he was seated to Pamela's left and had either to listen to her flirting with "Sir Robert" or to entertain Mary, so he addressed himself mostly to the latter. The snippets of their conversation that reached Hester consisted of his earnest advice to Mary to take advantage of her sojourn to visit all the sights the City of London had to offer. Hester would much have preferred his dinner conversation to the options she had been given, but it would not be the first or the last tedious evening she had passed.

Pamela's *tête-à-tête* with St. Mars could not last all evening, however. When, eventually, they finished their meal, she was forced to relinquish her guest to her husband, with the real possibility that she would not see him again that evening. Hester followed Pamela from the table thinking she must not be too disappointed if Dudley kept the gentlemen drinking late into the night. She consoled herself with the news she had heard St. Mars relate to Mrs. Ward, that he had secured lodgings at the inn in Coxwold, which meant that it would be easier to see him.

The ladies retired to the Great Chamber on the first floor, which overlooked the formal garden. The walls of the room were covered in heavy Brussels tapestries, and it was furnished with a number of arm-chairs with elaborate pierced and japanned arches. The paintings on the turned legs, black with floral detailing, had once been very fashionable, but now they looked chipped and worn. The chairs were one of the last purchases made by the late Mr. Mayfield before his wife's extravagance nearly ruined him. If Isabella had not married the Earl of Hawkhurst, Hester's cousins would have suffered a dismal fate, and Hester with them.

The ladies had barely taken their seats before the talk shifted to Mary's impending removal to London.

Mrs. Mynchon beamed on the girl. "You'll have your pick of the *beaux*, I'll warrant."

Pamela bore the attention to her sister-in-law as long as she could, but once the tea was brought, she put a stop to it by asking Mary to dispense the dishes as she poured them. Then, before they could return to the subject of Mary's future, she said coyly, "I believe I have made a new conquest myself."

"And I can guess who it is." This playful remark issued from Mrs. Ward, who must have heard every word that had passed between Pamela and St. Mars.

In the middle of handing Hester a dish of tea, Mary rolled her eyes. Hiding the smile that came to her lips, Hester eagerly sipped her tea. She had developed a passion for it since she had lived in sufficient luxury to drink it daily. She believed strongly in its reputed medicinal properties, though she doubted it was an effective cure for amusement.

"A handsome gentleman with very pretty manners." Mrs. Mynchon nodded. "And you have made him your gallant, I suppose."

Pamela gave an affected laugh. "I should not say for risk of sounding boastful, but I *can* say, it will surprise me if we do not see him often here."

"You shall make your husband quite jealous!" Mrs. Ward exclaimed in a flattering way.

"Hmmph!" Pamela tossed her head. "It would serve him right an' I did. He shall see how much I am valued by a London gentleman."

While Mrs. Mynchon warned her to beware of arousing any gentleman's passion, which, she declared, could be dangerous, Hester did her best to hide another smile. St. Mars had made certain he would be welcome at Beckwith Manor at any hour of any day. The trouble was that Pamela would always be on the lookout for him. Hester allowed the other ladies to compliment Pamela on her conquest, then when the conversation lagged, asked Mrs. Mynchon if she had seen any member of the Fenwick family since they last had spoken.

The lady sobered. "No, but I have heard that his sisters arrived home yesterday. They will be a great solace to their mother."

"We called upon Mrs. Fenwick the day after your visit, so the young ladies were not yet home. I hope they can quickly become a comfort to their brother as well. I do feel that his situation is particularly awkward."

The kind lady nodded and sighed. "The poor boy finished his schooling and came home so his father could teach him about the estate. Now he must learn how to manage it on his own. They have no steward, you know—can't afford one. Sir Ralph told me today that he has taken him under his wing. Promised to teach him husbandry and the like."

"If that is not just like my papa!" Pamela sat up in her chair. "He is always so kind."

"Yes, it is very good of Sir Ralph." A distinct warmth infused Mary's voice. When the other ladies turned to regard her, she blushed and lowered her gaze.

Mrs. Ward spoke sternly. "It is no more than Sir Ralph's Christian duty to help his fellow man. That does not mean that we should take too much notice of him."

Mary flushed at her rebuke, then with a falsely sweet smile said, "Not notice Sir Ralph, Mrs. Ward? How can I not take notice of so near a relation?"

The curate's wife bristled, not fooled one whit by Mary's feigned ignorance. She would have scolded the girl for her pertness, had not Pamela, who was not as quick, said, "Foolish girl! Mrs. Ward was referring to Mr. Fenwick, not Papa. And Mrs. Ward is correct. It would not do for you to see too much of Charles Fenwick since he's a papist. You must not endanger your reputation before going to London. To do so would be fatal!"

Mrs. Ward agreed, and the two launched into a series of platitudes on virtue, obedience and prudence, ignoring Mary, who grumbled under her breath that she hardly knew the young gentleman.

With a twinkle in her eye Mrs. Mynchon turned to Hester and stated, "For all that is said in favour of virtue, I've found that it is vastly overrated." She laughed so heartily at this jest that Mary joined in, despite Mrs. Ward's outraged glare.

Mr. Ward entered the room just then with the remark that Mr. Mayfield had been kind enough to excuse him from the table, aware that he did not partake in excessive drinking.

"My papa never drinks immoderately," Pamela replied haughtily, "and my husband generally follows his good example."

If this were true, Hester reflected, then Dudley had changed a great deal. She hoped it was true, for her cousin was not a pleasant drunk. She had seen him force an argument upon a gentleman who had done nothing to provoke his wrath. She wished she had thought to remind St. Mars of this aspect of Dudley's character, and made a mental note that she must do so at the first opportunity.

Mr. Ward protested that he had meant no slight upon the other gentlemen, only to draw a distinction between the accepted behaviour among the laity and that of the clergy. Pamela accepted his apology and invited him to join them in a dish of tea without any evident enthusiasm for the addition to her party. The curate accepted as if he were duty bound, but as soon as he had drunk it down, he called on his wife to join him in bidding their hostess good night.

After they had departed, Pamela released a sigh of relief and suggested a game of cards to while away the time until the gentlemen joined them. The four who remained played at whist. In consideration of Mary who had no money of her own, they played for pennies with the intention of returning them at the end.

Although it was fairly late when the gentlemen joined them, Hester was relieved to see that Dudley was only mildly drunk and that the conversation had pleased him enough that he had not lost his good humour. Pamela hastened to order a fresh pot of hot water, which arrived so promptly, it must have been simmering on the hearth all the while. She made sure that Dudley drank two cups of strong tea before she relaxed to focus on St. Mars, which suggested she was fully aware of her husband's propensity for violence.

St. Mars used the brief respite from her flirting to join the other ladies, whose game had been broken up by the gentlemen's arrival. When he stooped over the back of Mrs. Mynchon's chair to help her to arise, his gaze sought Hester's. He raised his brows in a look she interpreted to mean that he had endured a most tedious evening. Then he stepped round to assist Hester as well and whispered in her ear, "Your cousin Dudley is the greatest blockhead I have ever met."

It was all Hester could do to smother her mirth. She turned to hide it from the others. "I can only agree with you, sir."

"Agree with him in what? What did Sir Robert say, Hester?" Pamela rushed over to claim her gallant.

"Why, only that the meal we have just enjoyed was perfectly matched by the quality of the company," St. Mars answered with great aplomb.

While Pamela accepted his remark as a compliment meant largely for her, Hester thought that St. Mars had been too severe on the cook. She had not considered the dinner half so bad.

Pamela again suggested whist, and the Mynchons and her father agreed. Hester and Mary begged to be excused, neither of them flush enough in the pocket to wager. St. Mars pled the need to retire early as he had ridden many miles that day and needed to make arrangements at his new lodgings.

"Besides," he said, "I have accepted a challenge from your husband, and we are to pit our horses against each other the day after tomorrow. Since I only brought the one horse with me, I have to ensure her a couple of good nights' rest."

Pamela pouted. "You must not run off before having another cup of tea to steady you on your ride."

"I must not keep you from your game."

"Dudley can make the fourth. I want you to help me compose a letter to my cousin the earl, to thank him for sending you to us. I am wont to write to Isabella, you know, not to him."

St. Mars raised his eyebrows and nodded. "Then I shall certainly stay a moment longer." As he turned towards the tea table, he shot Hester a look of comic alarm.

Pamela poured him another dish of tea, while exercising all her feminine wiles. Her performance would have been painful for Hester to watch, had she not seen the pleasure St. Mars's attention was giving her. As long as Pamela never learned how tedious the playacting was for him—as Hester hoped and assumed it was—then surely the pretence would do her no harm.

She and Mary settled on the only sofa in the room to discuss the next steps in her preparation for London. Besides the clothes she would need, there were dancing and music lessons to plan.

When Pamela had exhausted her tricks at the tea table, which St. Mars had done little to encourage, she led him to an escritoire. After sending a servant for paper and ink, she rallied "Sir Robert" about what she should write. "I shall tell him that you appeared at our door, and thank him for sending us such a charming new friend."

"No, you must not say that. I shall dictate the words for you to use."

"What impertinence!" She tapped him on the wrist with her fan. "As if I did not know how to compose a letter!"

"I do not doubt that you can, but this one is special."

She gazed at him sideways. "Is it indeed? Can you be boasting?"

"Not at all, I promise. You shall see."

Intrigued, she waited until her pen had been dipped before she said, "Very well, what will you have me write?"

"Just this. And you must write it precisely as I say. 'Sir Robert has arrived . . .'" He waited until she had written this and was ready for more. "'. . . and he declares himself thoroughly enchanted with the society he has found in Yorkshire.'" Since he said this with what Hester considered a leer, Pamela was pleased to accept his instruction.

He had averted the threat of exposure quite neatly, Hester thought, but she sighed to think that the summer would pass the way it had this evening. If it did, she was no more likely to spend time with St. Mars here than she had at home.

And sadly, not once during all the flirting he had done with Pamela had Dudley appeared to notice. Neither had Pamela glanced at her husband to see whether he cared. This was not due to the sophisticated manners of Court society, but to the indifference of a husband and a wife who had married for mutual worldly advantage, not an uncommon situation in a world in which most marriages were arranged.

What saddened Hester more was the complete lack of any sign from either Pamela or Dudley of a desire to find a basis for affection or to build anything greater in the way of a relationship, which might eventually lead them to contentment.

The whist game ended before St. Mars could make his escape. Mr. Mynchon left his wife, Dudley, and Sir Ralph speculating on the winners of the upcoming York races to join Hester and Mary. In a brittle manner, he asked if the young ladies would wish to visit him on the morrow to view his collection.

Hester accepted eagerly, Mary with only slightly less enthusiasm. Anything would be preferable to spending another day in Pamela's company, but Hester wanted very much to see his rarities. They discussed the hour that would be most convenient and, after checking to make sure that Pamela did not need them, accepted Mr. Mynchon's invitation to come at eleven o'clock with the expectation that they would dine afterwards with him and his wife.

As St. Mars said his goodbyes, the Mynchons took advantage of the movement towards the door to take their leave as well. St. Mars made no special gesture of farewell to Hester, but the last she saw of him through the window of the hall, he was standing by his saddled horse deep in conversation with Mr. Mynchon.

The next morning, with Hester mounted securely on a staid pony, which Dudley kept for the younger children, and Mary on her favourite mare, the two ladies rode the short distance to Mynchon Grange, a good-sized manor house built of sandstone. Like so many of the other gentry dwellings in the area, it had originally been a smaller house, built in Tudor days. The older portion now made up the west wing, and a new front had been constructed to face the south. A three-story block had been added to the original rooms to house the fashionable desire for closets—small, intimate rooms beyond the principal bed-chambers where the master of the house and his wife could invite their more favoured guests.

At the front door, the groom that had accompanied Hester and Mary took their reins to lead their horses to the stables. After being ushered into the hall, they were warmly greeted by Mrs. Mynchon, who thanked them for the excuse to make up a party.

"Will there be other guests, then?" Hester asked. She hid a slight feeling of disappointment, for the presence of gentlemen might keep her from posing questions she might wish to ask.

"Just one, and he is already with Mr. Mynchon. I am to take you to them as soon as you've been relieved of your cloaks."

"Is it anyone we know?" Hester composed her features to hide the sudden fluttering in her stomach. A recollection of St. Mars conversing with Mr. Mynchon outside last night had entered her head.

"Yes, it is your cousin's new admirer, Sir Robert. And I must say, his manners are more pleasing than I expected after watching him ogle her last night. It appears that he has an interest in rarities, too. He and my husband were discussing some things they had both seen up at Oxford, and Mr. Mynchon was so taken with Sir Robert that he begged him to join us today. I hope you do not mind."

Hester soberly assured her that they should have no objection, and after she and Mary handed their cloaks to a servant, they followed Mrs. Mynchon through a doorway leading into the west wing. Here, as they passed through Mr. Mynchon's chamber, with its great tester bed, the sound of voices came to them from a doorway beyond.

"No, you are mistaken, sir," Mr. Mynchon was saying. "The whelk is not a hermaphrodite. According to Lister, the sexual organ is as pronounced in the male as it is absent in the female. I have a rare copy of his folio on whelks, if you would care to see it."

St. Mars did not reply, undoubtedly because he had heard the floorboards creak as the ladies approached. Hester stopped at the doorway to peer into the tiny room, a square space, filled floor to ceiling with shelves, cases, and boxes, with only one opening for the door and another for a window which faced west.

They had interrupted Mr. Mynchon in the middle of earnest conversation, evidenced by the intensity of his gaze through a pair of nose spectacles. He broke off in the middle of his speech, however, to greet the ladies and invite them into his inner sanctum, exhibiting much more pleasure at meeting them here than he had at Beckwith Manor. The space was so constricted and crammed so tightly with treasures that it did not allow room for either bows or curtsies, so St. Mars inclined his head and extended his hand to welcome first Hester and then Mary into the room. The three of them moved close together to make a space for Mrs. Mynchon, but she remained in the doorway, announcing that she would let them get on with their visit and would see them when they were through. She cautioned her husband not to make them late for dinner, then disappeared back the way they had come.

Now that Hester was closer to Mr. Mynchon's cases, she saw that his rarities were organized into containers with similar objects. Silver medals were displayed in one case, while another held copper and lead. Having had little preconception about what she would see, Hester was intrigued by the variety of objects he had chosen to collect. The largest number of his shelves were covered with shells, fossils, and samples of rare and exotic woods.

With an exclamation of delight, Mary reached out with one finger towards a tall, spiral shell with alternating bands in grey and white.

"No!" Mr. Mynchon's anxious cry made her jump. "You must not touch any of the shells. You might break one and it is possible that I shouldn't be able to replace it." He hurriedly moved to stand between Mary and the shelf, as if she might decide to crush them all.

Deeply chagrinned, Mary murmured an apology and looked to Hester to see how seriously she had transgressed. When Mr. Mynchon turned to hover over his shells with a feather duster, Hester responded to Mary's silent query with a comical look. The poor girl would have done no harm to Mr. Mynchon's treasures. If Hester had been the first to reach for one of them, she would have upset him just as much. Clearly, these objects were not to be touched, and they must keep their hands to themselves.

As if to divert their attention from his most fragile objects, Mr. Mynchon ushered them to a small corner cabinet which held a number of coins. Some of these, he explained, were Roman, but a great many others were the currencies of foreign kingdoms.

"Did you collect those on your own travels?" St. Mars asked.

"Most, yes, but I have also traded some of mine for others. For example, this one came from Russia." He pointed to a roughly oval-shaped coin that looked as if it had been made by pressing a thumb into clay except that the material was plainly metal. "I have never travelled to Russia, but I bought it off a fellow who received it from King Peter when he visited the Royal Observatory at Greenwich. It is called a kopeck, and the reason for its irregular shape is because, until recently, there was no mint for coins in that country. It was made from a length of silver wire, cut to the proper weight for exchange and hammered flat. I understand that King Peter was so impressed with England's mint that he has since instituted a similar system of coinage in Russia."

"May I have a closer look?" Hester dared to ask. After a brief hesitation—during which he must have determined that there was little harm that could be done to a coin—Mr. Mynchon took the coin out of its case and handed it to her. Hester held it so that Mary and St. Mars could peer at it over her shoulder. The coin was strangely crude, not round, not even truly oval. Some marks had been carved or pressed into it. "What is this figure?"

"It looks like a rider on a horse."

"Very good, Mrs. Mary!" Mr. Mynchon exclaimed, giving her a rare smile. "That is indeed a horseman. I cannot tell you what the other markings signify, only that they are in the Russian alphabet, which is not at all like our own."

Mary and Hester exchanged wide-eyed looks, before Hester returned the coin to its owner, eager to see what else he had to show them.

The medals were not as interesting to her, except as they put features to the names of a few famous people whose portraits she had never seen. Many of the copper and lead medals were so worn that the images upon them were hard to make out in a room with so little light. The silver ones commemorated more recent kings and queens, but Hester had seen better images of them in paintings. Mary, who had never visited a house or a royal palace with portraits of English kings, queens, or generals, gazed raptly at them, exclaiming over the resemblance between Charles II and James II and how handsome Queen Anne appeared in the medal struck for her coronation. She gazed with awe at the Duke of Marlborough's image on the many medals honouring his victories at the battles of Malplaquet and Blenheim.

St Mars, who knew all these faces very well, stirred impatiently at Hester's side. Before long, a touch on her hand drew her gaze to his face. With a mischievous look, he beckoned for her to move with him to the opposite corner of the room. Hester first checked to see if their defection would be felt, but as Mr. Mynchon seemed pleased with the enthusiasm Mary was showing, she turned and joined St. Mars, who pointed to the contents of the case in front of him.

"I had a glimpse of these before you arrived. They are very fine carvings and turnings, many of which I have never seen the like."

He made room for Hester beside him, then positioned himself so he could see over her shoulder and indicate each object in turn. Among many diverse curiosities in turned work, he showed her a tiny wheel and spindle in amber, and a miniature cup turned out of a peppercorn and garnished with ivory, both so exquisite as to draw her exclamations of delight.

"And see these chains? Have you ever known such fine workmanship?" The chains in silver and gold had dozens of links, yet were each not much longer than an inch.

"How can anyone see well enough to make them? Surely it would make one go blind."

He answered with a shrug. They were standing so close, she felt his movement and suddenly her pulse skipped. When he spoke, she felt his breath stir her hair like a lover's caress. Her hands shook and warmth spread through her from her head to her toes.

He was not done teasing her, however. Standing so her skirt screened their hands from the others' view, he curled his fingers through hers. He stroked her palm so gently with his thumb that her pulse went wild. She did not dare look into his eyes for fear he would see her trembling.

This blissful torment lasted only a minute before they were joined by Mr. Mynchon and Mary, and St. Mars was forced to release her hand. Their host began telling them where he had obtained each treasure in the case.

After this, only once did Hester have the nerve to raise her gaze to St. Mars's face, when she noted a number of very satisfactory signs: raised colour in his cheeks to match her own, a distinct air of distraction, and a look of restraint, which he was doing his best to hide. He avoided her as studiously as she avoided him, displaying none of his usual audacity. When he next posed a question to their host, he had to clear his voice before speaking, as if his throat was constricted. These things convinced her that she was not the only one tortured by their nearness and the need to appear as strangers.

Eventually, after they had been shown every item in Mr. Mynchon's closet and had complimented them all, he ushered them back through his bedchamber and through another door, which had been cut through the wall at some later date. Here, they found themselves in what must have been the hall of the original Tudor house. It still had a massive stone fireplace and a flagstone floor, but here Mr. Mynchon had stored the larger objects in his collection.

"A great many of these came to me by way of my brother, who is with the East India Company. From time to time he is good enough to send me objects he knows I will like."

St. Mars moved to examine a display of weapons that covered one entire wall. "Some of these are from the Americas, surely." He indicated a few decorated wooden clubs with rounded ends.

"Yes, those are tomahawks from the American Indians. I obtained those from a sailor myself. But that square-bladed dagger next to them is from East India."

He took down a sort of sword with a wickedly curved blade and made slow, swirling motions with it in the air. "This is my favourite. It would have made short shrift of an enemy's head."

Something about the gleam in his eye when he said this gave Hester a chill. Then she reminded herself that he had looked just as avid when he had hovered over his shells.

As the gentlemen discussed various weapons, Hester and Mary amused themselves by looking at an array of strange utensils and trying to guess what their purpose was. When they could not guess, they applied to Mr. Mynchon, who, in a gratified manner, came over to explain and demonstrate. In this way, two hours passed, until Mrs. Mynchon sent a servant to tell them that dinner was ready.

They joined her at a table which had been set at one end of a cosy parlour on the ground floor, not far from the kitchen.

"I hope Mr. Mynchon hasn't exhausted you. You must be starving."

Taking their chairs, they assured her that the time had passed so pleasantly, they had not once thought of their stomachs.

"I am happy to hear it, but I hope you are not just being polite. When my husband is occupied with his rarities, he has no mind for anything else."

"That may be true, but he found us a very keen and willing audience. And now I daresay," St. Mars added, looking eagerly over the many dishes on the table, "that we shall find the appetite to do justice to your cook."

He had struck just the right note to please both of his hosts. It occurred to Hester how long it had been since she had seen him comport himself in company—at least, without a role to play. Here, he had no need to pay court to Pamela or to make friends with an oaf like Dudley, or to play the fop—as he had done on numerous occasions—in order to extract information from a murder suspect. She was pleased with the ease and the kindness of his manners.

With all that their party had seen that day, there was no shortage of topics to discuss as they conversed over an excellent meal. Apparently, St. Mars had a good memory, for he was able to pose questions about a number of objects they had seen, including the collection of wood samples Hester had noticed in Mr. Mynchon's closet, but to which she had not paid much attention.

"I have tried," Mr. Mynchon said, "to collect as many samples from trees that will not grow in England as I possibly can. It is more difficult than you may imagine, for merchants can ill afford to carry objects upon their ships that they do not plan to sell. Sometimes I come across a piece of a tree that has been cut to replace a mast or a different part of a ship. Then, when it is repaired in an English port with oak, I ask for a piece before the wood is burned or tossed."

After this topic had been thoroughly exhausted, recalling that Mr. Mynchon was a magistrate, Hester ventured to ask if there had been any apprehension in the case of Mr. Fenwick's murder.

He shook his head and frowned, laying down his fork and weaving his fingers together. "There has been no new information, I'm afraid.

At this point, unless a witness comes forward, I fear that justice may never be done." Looking back down at his plate, he picked up his fork again, saying casually, "I suppose I should have a word with his son."

At the other end of the table, Hester could feel Mrs. Mynchon sit up straighter in her chair as if on alert. "My dear . . ." she said, a note of warning in her voice.

A look of profound irritation crossed her husband's features. "You need not caution me, Mrs. Mynchon. I believe I may be trusted to conduct myself appropriately."

If Mrs. Mynchon did not exactly roll her eyes at this, she still managed to convey a high degree of skepticism in the set of her mouth. "You may have no intention of giving offence, my dear, but you must know how you get the bit between your teeth whenever there's a chance of adding to your rarities."

Stabbing his slice of beef, he scoffed, "Not much chance, I should say. Not if young Fenwick is as foolish and superstitious as his father!"

"There! What have I said? You cannot manage so much as to refer to it without insulting poor Charles. It is not his fault if he has been raised with those beliefs."

"If he has, I assure you that I shall simply walk away, though one would hope that a younger man would have a more scientific view of the world. However, I suppose," he added, despondently, "given the education he has had, that will be too much to hope."

Since by now, all three of their guests had stopped eating to gaze back and forth between them with patent curiosity, Mrs. Mynchon smiled an apology. "You may have heard that my husband had a falling out with Mr. Fenwick over an artifact that has been in his family for generations."

"We did not have a falling out, as you call it! I simply made an offer to buy it from him. You and everyone else were bemoaning how poor his family had become, and I had every reason to think that my offer would fall on welcome ears. When it did not, I merely informed him of how foolish he was."

"Yes, you berated him for not believing as you do and for keeping an object that had a sacred meaning to him."

"You have no understanding of gentlemen and business affairs! It was not a falling out, I tell you! Fenwick understood perfectly that I was merely speaking the truth."

At this, it was Mrs. Mynchon's turn to scoff. "My dear!"

When Mr. Mynchon refused to respond to her tone, but instead stabbed sullenly at a bite of beef, Hester got up the nerve to ask, "What sort of artifact was it?"

With a sideways look at her husband, Mrs. Mynchon answered, "Mr. Fenwick said it was a piece of the True Cross. Apparently, an ancestor of his brought it back from Jerusalem on one of the Crusades."

"Superstition and tomfoolery!" Mr. Mynchon grumbled into his plate. "If all the purported pieces of the True Cross were stood and nailed together, they would constitute a forest! He simply could not admit that an ancestor of his had been swindled."

"Maybe he was, or maybe he wasn't," his wife said. "It was not up to you to lecture him."

"If you do not believe it is from the True Cross," St. Mars asked, "why are you so eager to have it for your collection?"

Mr. Mynchon turned to him as if, at last, someone had asked a question sensible enough to merit a reply. "Because I am convinced that the wood itself is one of the few kinds my collection lacks. I have read that the "tell" tree, referred to in the Bible, contains a fragrant juice. It is not at all like the lime tree, as once was thought, but tall and strong nevertheless. The only place it has been seen is on the lower slopes of the hills near Jerusalem and Bethlehem, but that does not make it any more likely to be a piece of Jesus's cross. My interest in it is purely scientific, I assure you."

He spoke with the intensity of an enthusiast. It was evident that he had not accepted defeat in his attempt to obtain the precious specimen.

When Mary seemed ready to open her mouth in defence of the Fenwicks, Hester interrupted her to ask her to pass the salt cellar, giving Mary a look to warn her not to become involved in such a passionate dispute. It was not their place to explain to Mr. Mynchon the importance of the relic to Mr. Fenwick or, indeed, to his whole family. Mrs. Mynchon had already tried. To relinquish such an object would be to reject faith itself and to turn their backs on all the suffering their family had experienced since the Reformation. To Mr. Mynchon it might be just a piece of wood, a rare example to be sure, but not an object of reverence. Unless, she wondered suddenly, Mr. Mynchon's passion for his rarities had taken the place of religion in his life?

The rest of their visit passed in a more restrained humour with Mrs. Mynchon, Hester, and St. Mars doing their best to maintain a flow of conversation and avoid the touchy subject. As soon as dinner was over, they took their leave. After riding as far as the gate to Beckwith Manor with the ladies, St. Mars parted from Hester and Mary, tipping his tricorn to them before trotting off.

Hester was glad he had not seen them home, first because Pamela would be jealous when she heard that Mary and she had spent half the day in his company. Hester cautioned Mary not to mention the fact, saying they would both be subjected to an inquisition if she did. This drew a laugh from Mary, who promised not to divulge the meeting herself, but warned Hester that the inquisition was likely to be twice as bad if Mr. or Mrs. Mynchon ever revealed the secret.

The second, and far more important, reason Hester was glad St. Mars had not come was one she could not share with Mary. After a morning spent in close quarters with him and after what had passed between them, her pulse was still so agitated that she needed time alone to compose herself. Her senses were in such an elevated state, she feared that the slightest provocation from St. Mars would set her off, in which case it would not be long before someone in her family spotted the truth.

The joy she had felt on seeing him had not abated one whit. Blissful thoughts had kept her awake half the night as she contemplated what the future might bring. As long as they had been in others' company, obliged to play the role of strangers, she had not allowed her mind to drift too close to the issues that surely, in coming here, he meant to resolve. When she had lain in bed, however, with Mary sleeping quietly beside her, she had indulged in speculation over every possible outcome.

That he wanted her, she could no longer be in doubt. Her brain insisted that he loved her, too, for she could not believe her attractions were potent enough to make him lust for her else.

Only one question remained. Mistress or wife? If they could manage to see each other in private long or often enough, surely all would be made clear soon.

*T*heir Parents are suffered to see them only twice a Year; the Visit is not to last above an Hour; they are allowed to kiss the Child at Meeting and Parting; but a Professor, who always standeth by on those Occasions, will not suffer them to whisper, or use any fondling Expressions, or bring any Presents of Toys, Sweet-meats, and the like.

CHAPTER VIII

Tomorrow came. The hour appointed for the race between St. Mars and Dudley had been set for noon. All the guests at Pamela's dinner party had pledged to attend, and everyone in the area who had got word of it was certain to be there, too. Pamela was all aflutter over what to wear, until she realized that she must ride or be confined in the coach, where she would be invisible. This called for the handsomest riding habit in her wardrobe. Then the question of which gentleman she should back—for there was sure to be wagering—threw her into a state of nervous agitation. She wanted to lend her support to her new gallant, but feared for her reputation if she did not wager on her husband's success.

After being subjected to her nonsense all morning, Hester was grateful when two visitors were announced, Charles Fenwick and his sister, Mrs. Frances Fenwick.

They were shown into the Great Parlour downstairs, and Mary and Hester went down to greet them. They apologized for Pamela, who was still dressing her hair.

Frances Fenwick was a pretty girl, the same age as Mary. Her black mourning dress rendered her pale, but her manners were pleasing. True, she was shy, but this was hardly surprising in a girl who had been raised by nuns. She had been exposed to even less society than Mary and constantly looked to her brother for approval whenever she spoke.

Free of Mr. Moreland's presence, Charles behaved more as he had when Hester first met him. Starkly handsome in his new black suit, he smiled unreservedly at Mary and said he hoped that she and his sister would soon become friends.

"We shall not disturb you long." He took the chair Hester had offered. "I just wanted Frances to meet the people who have been so kind to me since my return."

Hester and Mary expressed their pleasure at the acquaintance and conveyed their sympathy to Frances on the loss of her father. Then, to divert her from her grief, as Charles surely had hoped from the visit, Hester asked, "You have other sisters, do you not?"

"One other—Margaret—but she is barely twelve. We would have brought her with us," Frances volunteered, "but Charles could only carry one of us up behind him."

Her artless remark made Charles wince. He had to be mortified by the restrictions placed upon his family. In an effort to conceal his humiliation, he sat up straighter and said, "My mother was not certain that a visit from a child would be welcome. I can bring her on another occasion, if you like."

Mary exchanged a concerned look with Hester. She was likely thinking of Clarissa and what a horror it would be to subject Margaret to her. Hurriedly, she said, "If you do not mind, I should love to visit her at Oulston Hall."

She changed the subject to ask, "Do you intend to watch the race between my brother and Sir Robert today?"

Charles replied that he had not heard of it, so she eagerly told them about it and invited them to come.

With clear regret Charles said, "I am promised to Sir Ralph. He is teaching me to be a good steward of my land." His humility when he stated this convinced Hester that he meant to be an exemplary one.

She conveyed her approval with a smile. "Well, perhaps Frances could come with us and return here for dinner. I know my cousins would welcome her visit."

She was not at all certain of this, but no harm could come from the two girls' becoming acquainted, and there was little else one could do to help Mrs. Fenwick. If Pamela objected, Hester would appeal to her Christian charity and cite Sir Ralph as example. After living with Isabella and her mother, she had become very adept at persuading selfish people to do as she wished.

Charles responded to the eager look from his sister by agreeing to the proposition. "I can collect her on my way home."

With that, he left, saying that he would inform his mother of the arrangement. Hester would have offered to send a servant round with a note, but Dudley's grooms would be busy getting ready for the race and she did not dare usurp their time.

By the time the Mayfield ladies set out for Yearsley Park, where Sir Ralph had insisted the race should be held, Mary and Frances were on their way to becoming fast friends. The three, Hester, Mary and Frances, rode in the family coach, Mary having relinquished her plan to ride in consideration of her guest.

Pamela accompanied them on a showy mare, which apparently had not been exercised that morning, for it tossed its magnificent head and shied frequently as it trotted alongside the coach. Pamela managed the horse quite well, however, being an accomplished rider.

The race course had been laid out in a low meadow enclosed by an ancient stone wall. An oval track bearing traces of many hoofprints indicated that it was often used for the purpose. Signs of fresh mowing indicated that Sir Ralph's men had been out early preparing the field. A small crowd, consisting mostly of Sir Ralph's and Dudley's tenants had gathered round the perimeter. Mary waved to all her neighbours and pointed certain ones out for Hester's benefit. Frances was acquainted with a smaller number, but spied some familiar faces in the crowd. Hester noticed the Reverend Mr. Ward and his wife sitting in a cart. Mr. Mynchon and his amiable lady were waiting comfortably on their mounts. On seeing the Mayfield coach, Mrs. Mynchon waved a greeting.

As the coach inched forward, the common spectators parted to make way. When Pamela's coachman had brought the carriage as close to the stone wall as he could, Mary proposed that they get down and stand behind it to watch the race. She and Frances scrambled out like schoolgirls, leaving Hester to be handed up to the box to sit by the coachman from which higher perch she had a superior view. She saw St. Mars and Dudley astride their prancing horses, waiting for the signal to start. St. Mars's long yellow hair was pulled into a queue at the nape of his neck and tied with a black ribbon. As he held Penny in check, he ignored the bustle of the crowd. Gazing at the splendid picture he made, Hester felt her heart swell with the knowledge of the trouble he had taken to find her.

Dudley's horse was a fine-looking grey. Bred for speed, but also for hunting, it was stronger and heavier than Penny. Hester wondered what advantage, if any, would come with its superior strength.

Pamela had trotted her horse round the other side of the meadow, closer to where the two contestants were waiting. She called out gaily to her husband who, intent upon restraining his horse, ignored her. She must have been disappointed, for St. Mars did not look up, and she could not very well call out loudly to him.

"Make way. Make way." A booming voice came from behind Hester. "Step aside, there, you fool!"

Hester turned to see both Sir Ralph and Charles pressing their horses through the small crowd, which parted hastily for them. As the last man leapt out of their way, a cheer went up for Sir Ralph for hosting the event. He nodded, accepting the tribute as no more than his due.

"Well, Mrs. Kean—" Pulling up beside Hester, he called up to her as Charles dismounted to join the girls at the wall. "Have you placed your wager yet?"

She chuckled. "Not I, sir. I'm afraid I do not know enough of horseflesh to risk any money on the outcome of a race."

"That horse of Sir Robert's will be mighty hard to beat. She's got from the Darley Arabian, if I am not much mistaken."

"Indeed?" Hester knew very well that Penny was the offspring of the famous horse. It worried her to know that Sir Ralph and other equine experts, which Yorkshire was full of, would be curious to learn the horse's provenance. Expensive horses like Penny were rare indeed.

It was natural for any gentleman to wonder how "Sir Robert" had come by such a magnificent mount.

As if Sir Ralph had read her mind, he said, "I would stake my best mare on it, but he's mighty close-lipped about her, is Sir Robert."

"Perhaps he enjoys being mysterious." Hester smiled, hoping to put him off.

"You could be right." Sir Ralph seemed pleased. "Hoping to whet our curiosity and drive up her price, I'll warrant. You mark my words, his reluctance to sell her is nothing but a sham. I'll get her in the end, just see if I don't."

Hester was at pains to act amused. She must not let him see how irritating his boasts had become.

She said, "I see you brought Mr. Fenwick with you. I am glad. The treat will do him good."

"Precisely what I told him. 'All work and no play' as the wise men say, eh, Mrs. Kean?"

"We were pleased today to meet his sister Frances." She nodded towards the girls, both of whom had greeted Charles excitedly. In anticipation of the race, they were chattering like magpies.

"Aye, she's another minx, that one. A very pretty sort of girl. Why don't you all come to dinner at my house? Where's my daughter?"

Hester pointed Pamela out to him. She was riding up and down along the far side of the enclosure, putting her mare through its paces and attracting a great deal of attention, if not precisely the kind she had wanted.

"Look at her! What's she doing? If she's not careful, she'll throw the racers off. Forgive me, Mrs. Kean. I'll just go put a flea in her ear." As he turned his horse to ride back through the gathering, he called over his shoulder, "But I will see you all at dinner. No excuses, mind."

Hester sighed. Fortunately, it would be up to Pamela to quarrel with her father if she did not wish to dine at Yearsley Park, and not to her. She turned her attention to the course, just in time to see Dudley and St. Mars bring their horses up to a line that one of Sir Ralph's labourers, she assumed, had scratched in the dirt.

The man, who had retreated to the stone wall to avoid being trampled, raised a handkerchief in the air. This gesture startled Penny, who tried to rear, but St. Mars kept her firmly reined. She had just taken a few steps backward when the man dropped the handkerchief, so Dudley's horse got off to the better start.

Then St. Mars let Penny loose, and a collective "Ah!" issued from the crowd.

She flew. Her hooves barely skimmed the ground. Before Dudley's heavier horse was half-way round the course, she caught him and drove past him with a flick of her hooves.

The horses were to make three circles of the field before a winner was declared. Dudley put the whip to his mount. It surged forward, nostrils flared, breathing so loudly that Hester thought she heard it over the pounding of the horses' hooves. Foam oozed around the bit in its mouth, as inch by inch it caught up with Penny near the end of the second circuit. From then on, the horses' noses stayed within a few inches of each other. St. Mars never raised his whip. Neither did Penny show any of the stress that Dudley's mount did. There were moments when Hester suspected that St. Mars was gently holding her back.

Then just before they reached the line marking the finish, Dudley laid into his horse with a vengeance. With an anguished heave, it threw itself across the line just a nose ahead of Penny. The crowd erupted in gasps and moans, disappointed not to have seen it beaten by the beautiful mare.

Amidst the to-do that followed, Mary, Frances, and Charles rejoined Hester at the moment the coachman handed her down. She had remained in her seat long enough to watch St. Mars ease Penny to a canter, then a trot and a walk. A familiar figure had climbed over the low wall and run, grooming cloths in hand, to rub her down. It was Tom watching out for his charge.

"I've never seen such magnificent animals!" Charles raved like the schoolboy he had recently been. If nothing else, the race had given him a brief diversion from his worries.

"Yes," Mary said, "but I wish Sir Robert had won. We shall hear nothing from Dudley but how he beat Sir Robert's horse. It is a good thing I am too young to wager or I should have lost a great deal of money on the race."

Frances looked taken aback by Mary's uncharitable remark about her brother, but she had been raised away from hers and had, perhaps, never suffered at their hands.

As the small crowd dispersed, labourers back to their chores, the gentry to their estates, Pamela trotted round to join them, disappointed and overheated. She was informing them of her father's invitation, when Dudley rode over on his grey to receive their congratulations. Charles and Frances obliged him with genuine admiration so he failed to notice how feebly his family offered theirs.

Pamela told him that they had all been asked to dine with Sir Ralph, adding that he should hurry to catch Sir Robert and invite him as well.

"Sir Robert and I have plans of our own, so you must give your father our regrets."

"But I accepted for you both!"

Her indignation raised a scowl on Dudley's face. "Do you think two sportsmen want to celebrate a race with a bunch of women and children? Haven't I told you never to presume where I shall eat my dinner? And now you want to tell Sir Robert where he must eat his, too?"

Thwarted, as she had been all morning, Pamela turned carmine red. Hester feared they were about to be treated to a domestic brawl. If St. Mars had been within hearing, Pamela would have controlled her temper, but she did not really care enough about what Charles and his sister thought.

"Then we shall see you both another time," Hester inserted cheerfully, interrupting Pamela before she could spew any of the vitriol on her lips. "Come along, Pamela. We ought not to keep your father waiting."

Slightly abashed, Dudley threw Hester a glowering look from beneath his heavy brow, but he took the opportunity she had given him to flee. With a curt "Your servant, Fenwick," he turned and trotted off.

Frances had watched this exchange with round, astonished eyes. Now she fearfully looked to see what Pamela would do next, while Mary lowered her head in shame.

Conscious of observers now, Pamela gave a kick to her horse and, with her lips bunched in fury, galloped off in the opposite direction.

Hester released a pent-up sigh. Then she assumed a cheerful mien before addressing the others. "Well, I do not know about you, but I am famished, so let us be on our way, shall we?"

The girls silently followed her into the coach, while Charles mounted his horse.

With such an example of marital bliss, Hester wondered if any of the younger ones present would ever wish to seek it for themselves.

Fortunately, by the time they had arrived at Yearsley Park, Pamela had regained her composure. Though not her usually voluble self during the meal, at least she did nothing to spoil the conversation, and by the time dinner was over, she could suggest to Mary that she take Charles and Frances to explore the maze. Mary's and Frances's delight was only briefly overshadowed by Charles's reservations. He expressed the need to return to his duties, but Sir Ralph informed him that he had other business to attend and that it would do him no harm to have a little fun. So, the three young people hurried out into the garden. Sir Ralph left Hester and Pamela to keep each other company in the small parlour adjoining the hall until the others returned.

Theirs was not a comfortable *tête-à-tête,* as Hester had to endure the furious denunciation of her cousin that Pamela had bottled up inside her. She poured out a tale of misuse and abuse that grieved Hester, though it could not surprise her. She was relieved, in fact, to learn that Dudley had never struck his wife.

"I never should have listened to my father!" Pamela fumed as she paced the room. "Never! But he assured me that it would be a good match."

"What reasons did he give?" Hester now felt she could ask.

Pamela scoffed. "He said that I should be cousin to a countess and that my younger children would be more likely to gain preferments. Then, of course, there was the Mayfield estate. Joined with ours upon his death, it would become one of the largest in Yorkshire, excepting those belonging to peers, of course. He said our eldest son might even be granted a peerage on the strength of it."

"I can easily see why Dudley wished for the match. You will inherit a considerable estate."

Pamela nodded angrily. "It is due only to my father's fortune that he tolerates me, as he has assured me frequently when drunk."

Hester could not bring herself to be truly fond of Pamela. Still, her heart did go out to her. "He should never abuse you in that manner; however, if he only says such cruel things when he is drunk, I can assure you that he abuses everyone equally when he is. I don't know why, but imbibing any sort of spirits has always turned him violent. You promise he has never attempted to harm you in any physical way?"

Pamela proudly raised her head. "He would not dare. He knows my father would cut off his allowance an' he did."

"I did not know that Sir Ralph paid him an allowance."

"Ha! Do you think Dudley could have afforded to take me without? He had mortgaged his land, and if he did not marry well, and soon, he could have lost it. My father acquired his mortgage and put him on an allowance. He dare not hurt me, or Sir Ralph could turn him and his family out."

Hester was shocked to think that the fate of Mrs. Mayfield's other children rested on the strength of this unhappy marriage. She wondered if her aunt was fully aware of the terms of Dudley's marriage settlement. He had been of age when he had entered into the agreement, so he had been under no obligation to tell her. Still, she must have had some idea of his financial plight, for she was largely responsible for the loss of her husband's fortune.

What Pamela had said explained a good deal, at least on Dudley's side. It did not explain why Sir Ralph would consign his only daughter to a loveless marriage, but many fathers cared more for the continuation of their family line than for their children. Hester wondered more why Dudley had not been made to take his wife's name as a condition of the settlement.

Nearly at a loss for words of comfort, she was not sorry at first when the footman announced a visitor—until it proved to be Mr. Moreland, who strode into the room and confronted both ladies with uncompromising suspicion.

"Mrs. Fenwick received word that her daughter Frances was to be found at Beckwith Manor. Yet when I called there, I was told not only that she was not within, but that she had been taken to witness a horse-race! Then I learned that she was here in the company of a large party."

As Pamela was in no condition to speak civilly—indeed, her temper flared upon being so rudely accosted in return for her hospitality—Hester hastened to reply. "I am sorry if Mrs. Fenwick feels that she was misled. It was my doing to invite Frances so that she and Mary could become better acquainted. And, as we were on our way to see Mary's brother pit one of his horses against a friend's, we saw no harm in taking her with us. Then Sir Ralph kindly invited us all back here for dinner.

"Now, the girls are taking a turn in the maze with Mr. Charles Fenwick."

The mention of this innocent pastime did not appease Mr. Moreland. If anything, his frown became even more foreboding. "Charles has been tempted into this misbehaviour, too? Please direct me immediately to this maze. I shall have a few words to say to him."

He made Hester feel ashamed for what had, until this minute, seemed perfectly innocent. She did not appreciate the undeserved censure. Drawing herself to her full height, she said, "I do not consider it misbehaviour for children—for they are scarcely more than that—to enjoy a harmless diversion."

His jaw clamped so tightly, it twitched. "Have you forgotten that the family is in mourning? The only reason Charles should be here is to learn something useful from Sir Ralph."

"I assure you, that was his intention. He merely escorted the girls when Sir Ralph said he would be too busy this afternoon to oblige him."

"Then, I shall escort him home where he belongs." He turned and headed for the hall, not waiting to be shown the way to the garden.

Hester called after him, "Do you have that sort of authority over Mr. Fenwick? I assumed he was his own master now."

Moreland paused and looked back over his shoulder, his eyes filled with such loathing that Hester instinctively raised a hand to her throat. He did not humour her with a reply, but turned and strode from the room.

"Lud!" Pamela exclaimed. "What a horrid man! And to think that my papa has made him welcome in this house. Well, he shall never receive an invitation to mine!"

Hester gave an involuntary shudder. There had been more than just anger in Mr. Moreland's eyes. If looks could kill, then she would have been struck down, or burned at the stake as a witch.

"I believe we should enlist your father's support before we encounter Mr. Moreland again." She took up the light shawl she had left on her chair and prepared to go outside.

"You do not mean to follow him? Why ever should you?"

Hester answered grimly, "Do not forget that Mary is with them. We cannot leave her alone to deal with his wrath. If you will send a servant to locate your father, I will see what Mr. Moreland is doing."

Waiting just long enough to be certain that Pamela had followed her instructions, she hastened through the East Hall and onto the terrace to peer over the low stone railing at the far end. She walked quickly through the formal garden. The entrance to the yew maze was just across the lower garden, which had a series of parterres with a small fish pond just beyond. A set of steps led down to it from both sides. Taking the one on the left, then directly crossing the parterres and circling the pond, she paused behind a willow tree and espied Mr. Moreland standing at the entrance to the maze with his hands clasped behind his back. If they had held a switch, she would not have been greatly surprised.

No happy voices issued from the maze, suggesting that he must already have called out to the Fenwicks and silenced any cheerful exclamations with the sternness in his voice. Provided Mary was with them, Hester supposed that she could lead them out, which after a few minutes, proved to be the case.

A very subdued group emerged from between the hedges. Charles was walking stiffly erect, with a mixture of anger and shame, but he did not challenge Mr. Moreland's gaze. Frances kept her head bowed in submission. Only Mary had the temerity to display her fury, but Hester could see she was afraid as well as perplexed by her friends' meek response to Mr. Moreland's demands. Without a word, both Charles and Frances followed him as he turned and headed back in

Hester's direction.

When he saw her, he paused momentarily in his stride. His lips, already compressed, pursed in outrage, but he said nothing more as he led them away.

Trailing behind them, Mary soon came abreast of Hester and with confusion on her face, said, "What made Mr. Moreland so angry?"

"I gather he believes we have made Charles and Frances forget their mourning."

Mary looked a bit guilty at this. "I did not intend to get them into trouble."

"It wasn't your doing." Hester clasped Mary's arm and gave it an affectionate squeeze. "I saw no harm in giving them a treat. To hear Mr. Moreland describe it, you would have thought we had lured them into a debauch."

Mary giggled, then sobered, "I do not like that man."

"Nor do I." Hester sighed. "But it is not for us to judge the Fenwicks' relations. Come, let's find Pamela and go home." She did not burden Mary with her thoughts, but she wondered why Charles would allow himself to be governed by a distant cousin. Had his father been under some sort of obligation to Moreland? The condition of his house and his land indicated that his family was facing financial ruin. Had the elder Mr. Fenwick mortgaged his estate or even part of it to a relative, in the same way Dudley had risked his?

*I*am here obliged to vindicate the Reputation of an excellent Lady, who was an innocent Sufferer upon my Account. The Treasurer took a Fancy to be jealous of his Wife, from the Malice of some evil Tongues, who informed him that her Grace had taken a violent Affection for my Person; and the Court-Scandal ran for some Time that she once came privately to my Lodging. This I solemnly declare to be a most infamous Falshood.

CHAPTER IX

Under the rules governing gentlemen's behaviour, Gideon had been obliged to entertain Dudley after their race. If he had not been concerned for the welfare of his horse, he would have preferred to ride to Beckwith Manor where he might at least have seen Mrs. Kean, but eager to get Penny back to her stable, and aware that a certain degree of reciprocity would be required if he were to continue visiting the Mayfields' house, he invited Dudley to take his meal at the inn at Coxwold.

A dinner would have been enough of a penance. Not even a shared passion for horseflesh could make Dudley a tolerable companion for long. But it was the period after the meal had concluded, when Dudley stayed to drink, that proved to be the real torment, for he managed to remain awake no matter how much he imbibed, becoming increasingly belligerent and unreasonable. Gideon had to weigh every word for its capacity to offend.

Any difference of opinion, he quickly learned, could set Dudley off. That the innkeeper was all too familiar with Dudley's vices had been apparent the moment they had arrived, for his welcome had been much less cordial than resigned. Mr. Sadler could not turn away one of the largest landowners in the area, no matter how much trouble he was known to cause. That did not mean he was grateful for the custom.

The afternoon being warm, the two lounged at the table nearest the bow-window. Day changed into evening, and twilight stretched interminably into dark as Dudley recounted a series of his most daring exploits in the saddle. Mr. Sadler lighted the candles with a wary eye on Dudley, leery of sparking his wrath. A few local men dropped in, but they, too, kept a safe distance and did not linger over their beer.

Gideon drank one glass for every three of Dudley's, amazed by the man's capacity. When, finally, he had exhausted every equine anecdote in his memory, his thoughts turned to the recent killing and he thought of extracting some information from his guest while was his tongue was loosened.

"What is your opinion of this murder?" He saw no harm in exhibiting curiosity about such an extraordinary event. Under the circumstances, it would be strange if a newcomer who wished to establish himself in the area ignored it.

Dudley directed him a blurry-eyed stare. It took a few moments for him to grasp that the subject of the past many hours had changed, and when he did, he merely gave a shrug, apparently not in the least concerned that a neighbour of his had been foully assaulted. Seeming to realize that some response was called for, however, he eventually said, "Can't make hide nor hair of it. A harmless ol' devil, Fenwick— even if he was a papist." He snorted as if he had just made a clever joke.

"Could it have had anything to do with the late rebellion? Do you think he took any part?"

The question made Dudley scoff. "Not much he could do wif one horse and one gun. Mind you . . ." he wagged a finger under Gideon's nose . . . "If he had got up to anything treasonous, our parson'd've been onto it like a lecher on a whore!"

The inappropriateness of the metaphor made Gideon grin. "A strict conformist, your parson?"

"You met 'im, didn't ye? Fellow can't abide popery. Wouldn't surprise me at'all if he didn't do away wi' ol' Fenwick himself."

Gideon frowned, not sure whether to take anything Dudley said seriously. "Would just a resentment of recusancy be motive enough for murder?"

Dudley shrugged again, plainly bored with the subject. Before he could return to the topic of the Queen's Plate at York or the Bilsdale Hunt, Gideon asked, "Can you think of anyone else who might have done it? Anyone local, that is?"

It took another few seconds for his question to sink in, but presently a storm settled over Dudley's brow, as if Gideon had thrown mud in his face. "What d'ye mean by it, eh? What th' devil're you implying?" He started to his feet, but his stool had been drawn too close to the table. The tops of his legs hit the underside of the table, knocking him back in his seat.

Surprised to have aroused such passion, Gideon hurried to soothe him. "Not a thing, dear boy! I assure you, not a blessed thing! Why, what could I have meant?"

Dudley was rubbing his bruised thighs, fortunately distracted enough by the pain to desist. He recalled the source of his offence eventually, however, for casting a wavering look about the empty room, he mumbled, "None of 's bloody business. Whassit matter anyway?"

This statement was so provocative that Gideon was tempted to follow it with a request for elucidation; but at all costs, he wanted to avoid a fight with Dudley Mayfield. If they had a serious falling out, it would be harder to visit Mrs. Kean.

"None of my business, friend. You are perfectly correct there."

With these appeasing phrases, he hoped no more than to settle Dudley's temper, but with the erratic behaviour of the truly drunk, Dudley favoured him with an approving leer. "Shrewd, my friend, very shrewd. If you want butter on your bread . . . ." He touched a finger to his nose.

Gideon could not be certain that Dudley was even speaking of the murder. What he said appeared to make no sense.

He was wondering how to extract more information from him when the sound of boots on the wooden stairs announced the entrance of Mr. Moreland. He spied Gideon and Dudley and, with a graceless expression, condescended to tip his soft felt hat, as the landlord came running from the rear of the inn to head him off.

In a low voice Mr. Sadler asked the gentleman what his pleasure would be. But Dudley had heard the footsteps and swung his body round to discover who had caused the disturbance.

"Oho!" he called with a sneer. "If t'isn't the town beau come to nose into our business!"

Moreland turned to stare at him with a mixture of haughtiness and confusion. "I beg your pardon?"

"Tak noah gaum on Maister Mayfield." The landlord spoke hastily to avert an interchange which could turn ugly. "'Appen 'e's supped a bit ower much."

"I'll 'appen you, y' knave!" Dudley surged clumsily to his feet. He teetered briefly, before lunging for the landlord with both hands raised as if to throttle him.

Reckoning that no amount of diplomacy would calm Dudley now, and heartily sick of him besides, Gideon leapt to his feet and, catching up a tankard in the same motion, brought it down on the back of Dudley's head. The glancing blow was enough to topple him in his bleary state, but not hard enough to knock him senseless. Lying on the floor, flat on his back, he rested for a few seconds, dazed, then made an effort to rise. This proved to be too much for him, for he fell back, his head hitting the floor hard with a thunk. This time, he did not fight the inevitable, but instead closed his eyes, and soon loud snores emerged from his gaping mouth.

The landlord had been standing over him, wringing his hands. Now he heaved a troubled sigh. "Well, that's fettled 'im!"

Moreland, who had witnessed the incident without so much as a blink, gazed down at Dudley with a musing expression. "Is Mayfield often prone to violence?"

"Nay . . . . it's like ah tol'ye, onnly when 'e sups ower much."

Moreland gave Sadler a searching look. "How often would that be?"

Sadler shrugged. "'E is fair threpple-throated, is Maister Dudley." He turned to Gideon. "Na then, what's t'do? 'E's like t'be madder'n a bummlekite when he weks up."

Taking this as an eventuality to be avoided at all costs, Gideon said, "It is nothing to worry us. We shall simply remind him that he slipped in the pool of beer he spilt when he jumped up from the table, and hit his head on the floor." When the landlord grinned and nodded, he said, "If you will fetch my groom, he can help you carry Mr. Mayfield to a bed, unless you'd rather he lie here all night."

"Nay, nay. Ah've got a chamer for'n." The man went in search of Tom.

Moreland had not spoken during this exchange, but continued to contemplate the snoring figure on the floor.

Gideon had had enough ale for the evening. All he wanted to do now was seek his own bed. Still, he should wait to make sure that Dudley did not regain consciousness and make more trouble for the house. Tom was strong, but Dudley was built like a bull, as well as being a bully.

"I apologize for the disturbance," he said to Moreland. "It should not take us long to put Mayfield to bed, and then Mr. Sadler can serve you."

Moreland made a dismissive gesture. "There is nothing I need. I stepped in merely to pose a question, but it can wait until morning." He paused, studying Gideon sideways with the ever-present sternness on his features. "That was quick action on your part. One would guess that you have had some experience with violence yourself."

Gideon could only laugh. "Who among us has not? We English are not known for our peaceful natures. But, if you are asking whether I've ever had occasion to use that maneuver before, then the answer is no. It is not my practice to frequent taverns with unruly gentlemen, nor am I in the habit of striking gentlemen upon the head. The occasion just called for an immediate and extraordinary measure."

A slight easing of Moreland's features suggested that he found Gideon's reply believable, even if he was not yet ready to accept it as fact. "I imagine it is not often that one encounters such unreasoning violence. I wonder if, in Mr. Mayfield's case, it is confined to when he is drunk, as the landlord said."

"I have no reason to doubt him. My acquaintance with the gentleman is of short duration, however."

"Yes, I believe you said you had not been in the area long?"

Gideon let a moment pass, during which he returned Moreland's stare with one of his own. "That is correct—since Thursday last, as

I believe I mentioned before. And you? When did you arrive in the area?"

Moreland's look of affront was almost comical. It seemed acceptable for him to pose insolent questions, but not for anyone to question him. "I came as soon as I received the news about Fenwick. We must have arrived at roughly the same time."

Heavy footsteps announced the return of the innkeeper with Tom. Letting the conversation with Moreland drop, Gideon turned to greet his groom. "Sorry to roust you from your bed, Tom, but we need a stout pair of arms."

Tom cast a quick look about the room, cautiously taking in the situation. With a hint of disgust, he regarded the spectacle of Dudley laid out on the floor. "Where do you want him put . . . , sir?"

"Our host will lead you. If Mr. Mayfield should exhibit any disturbing signs of life, call me."

"Yessir." Bending down, Tom grasped Dudley beneath the arms to lift his torso, while Mr. Sadler hefted his legs at the knees. Together they struggled through the taproom door and disappeared in the direction of the stairs, the sound of their shuffling steps growing fainter.

"That man is your groom?"

Gideon turned to Moreland and raised his brows with a look meant to discourage impertinence. He hoped that Moreland was not about to repeat his catechism about Tom. "He is."

"He seems a most devoted servant. I have had occasion to speak to him when returning my horse to the stable. He is not nearly so loquacious as most."

"Ah." As he nodded, Gideon let a smile spread slowly across his face. "I'm afraid you will have to forgive him for, you see, by nature Tom is a suspicious fellow. He believes that a person who is too inquisitive must have something nefarious in mind. I have tried to ease his fears without success, but, after all, discretion is not such a bad quality in a servant."

A tightening of Moreland's jaw proved that he understood the rebuke. He could not, however, object to the way it had been given. Stiffly, he tipped his hat to Gideon and bid him a pleasant night.

Exhausted by too much drink and the tensions of the day, Gideon sat and rested his face in both hands. In just a few more minutes, the landlord and Tom returned to the taproom to report that Dudley had never opened his eyes.

Gideon sighed. "Then I shall go to bed, too, but first I should like to check on Penny." He heaved himself off the stool. "Come, Tom. Lead the way so I don't fall down the step."

When they entered the stable, Argos dragged himself out of the bed he had made in the straw, and came wriggling over to greet him. Gideon gave the dog a good petting, then went to join Tom outside Penny's stall. He was glad to see her resting quietly. She opened her eyes and bobbed her head contentedly, then shifted her weight onto another hoof before dozing off again.

"No ill effects from the race?" Gideon asked Tom in a low voice, as he leaned against the stall door.

"None that I can see. I think she enjoyed it, my lord."

Gideon smiled. "I believe she did. I did not push her, you know."

Tom snorted. "You don't think I saw that? If you had given her a bit of leg, she could have beat Mr. Mayfield's grey."

"With room to spare. But in this situation, it would not have been wise. Mr. Mayfield is the sort who prefers his friends to lose. If I had won, he would be more likely to cut me, but now he can be magnanimous and feel good about himself. Besides, if he keeps pushing me to enter Penny in the local races, I can argue that his grey beat her and, therefore, there would be no point."

He bent down to scratch Argos behind his ears. "I shall have to come up with an excuse for not attending them myself. It is likely that someone who knows me will be there. We are not so far from Mr. Darley's land, and there will be many at the Yorkshire races who can identify Penny as one of his foals. I dare not expose her too broadly, nor myself. I may have to suffer a sudden injury, something that will keep me from riding that far."

This consideration made him recall Moreland's suspicions. "To wit, I understand that Moreland has been asking questions of you?"

While Gideon had been talking, Tom had picked Penny's bridle off a hook and, after digging in a box for a rag, had started to soap the leather. Now, a growling sound issued from his throat. "He's tried to strike up a word or two, but I haven't said nothin' to 'im, my lord."

Gideon tsked and grinned. "I gathered as much. I told him you had an ugly, suspicious nature. What sort of thing did he ask?"

Tom screwed up his mouth as he rubbed the leather. "Where you come from . . . what your business is in Yorkshire . . . when you arrived at Thirsk . . . if we stopped anywhere else . . . that sort of thing."

Gideon nodded. "The same questions he asked me. What can be his reason, I wonder? It's as if he suspects me of something."

"People can be pretty leery of foreigners, my lord."

Coming from Tom, this statement amused him, for nobody mistrusted a Frenchman half so much as Tom. In this case, however, Gideon could not disagree. "He seems to believe that I have come into Yorkshire to take advantage of the Catholics' misfortunes, but papists aren't the only people who lose their estates. Many an Anglican member of the gentry have spent their way into poverty.

"But," he said, reverting to an earlier thought, "he seems very keen to place me in the county earlier than I arrived. To accuse me of Mr. Fenwick's murder?"

Tom looked up quickly, dropping the bridle in his lap. "Why would he want to do that, my lord?"

Gideon mused, chewing on the inside of his mouth. "Either because he wishes to discover who did it, or because he killed Fenwick himself and would like to throw suspicion on someone else."

"Which is it?"

Gideon shrugged. "To answer that, I shall have to become better acquainted with him."

For the first time in their conversation, Tom looked anxious. "How long will we stop here, my lord?" Tom would not complain for himself, but he must be missing his new wife.

"As long as Mrs. Kean is here or until I'm found out, whichever comes first. Sorry, Tom, but it is my turn to bring my affairs to fruition. You've settled yours." If he had not been three sheets to the wind, Gideon might not have been so confiding, but if he was going to count on Tom's help, perhaps he should give him a reason.

He was embarrassed but not displeased to see a grin spread over his servant's face. "So, that's the way the wind blows, does it? Well . . .

can't say as I'm surprised. Katy won't be neither."

"Have I been that transparent? And here I thought I had been discreet. What do you think of my choice, Tom?"

"Mrs. Kean? No gentleman could do better, my lord."

"Think she will have me?"

Wrinkling his brow, Tom appeared to give the question serious thought. He mused so long, in fact, that Gideon began to worry. "I know I am not the prize I once was."

"If you was the Earl of Hawkhurst, would you still be after her, my lord?"

Gideon smiled. "I'd like to think I would have been clever enough to see that she is too good for me, but I don't know if I ever would have had the chance to know her. It's the one good thing that has come out of this business."

"Was it worth it?"

"Well, I shan't know that, shall I, until I know if she'll have me."

Tom must have heard the frustration in his voice for he laughed. "I do think she's a bit partial to you, my lord."

His warm smile was all the assurance Gideon needed. It filled his heart with relief and something richer. "Well, on that note then, I'll retire." He patted his leg. "Come, Argos. Time for bed." The dog heaved himself up and stretched before following him to the door.

Gideon threw back over his shoulder, "Don't let me sleep past noon, Tom."

"Never you fear, my lord. I hope you haven't forgot that tomorrow's the Lord's day?"

"Damn! So it is. Then be sure to wake me in time for the service."

If Tom had not roused him, the church bells surely would have done, but with an earlier start, Gideon was able to consume a hearty breakfast with the local small beer and get to the parish church in time for the service. He entered through the south porch and waited near the door for the Mayfield party to arrive. As parishioners shuffled past him, heads bowed, he passed the time gazing about the old church. It was Tudor with a central aisle and a wide oak ceiling with painted bosses adorning the intersections of the roof beams. The window on the north side contained stain glass that appeared to be older, as if saved from an earlier Norman church.

Gideon noted that the Stuart coat of arms had been removed from the chancel arch and nothing yet put up in its place. It would take years for every church in England to erect the arms of the House of Hanover. In many parishes the expense would not be undertaken until the parishioners were certain that George was in the kingdom to stay. In the meantime the armorial bearings of the Belasyse family proudly flanked the empty space.

The chancel was largely a repository for funerary monuments, principally those of the Belasyses, Gideon surmised. On the left stood an enormous tomb with recumbent figures painted in black, gold and red, so imposing as to be visible even from where he stood. On the right side of the nave, between the chancel wall and the rows of pews, was a curious little chapel separated from the rest of the church by a chest-high wooden wall.

Gideon was about to turn his attention to the porch when Mrs. Kean and Pamela Mayfield walked through the door, leading Mary, a younger girl who could be her sister, and a collection of servants. Pamela, who looked cross, was the first to see him. She brightened and exclaimed a greeting. This caused Mrs. Kean, who had been peering back over her shoulder, quickly to turn her head. The smile that sprang to her lips made his knees grow weak.

"You must sit in our pew," Pamela urged, as if he might resist.

Since that had been precisely his plan, he thanked her with a sweeping bow. After greeting the other ladies and receiving a flirtatious smirk from the younger girl—in whom he detected traces of Mrs. Mayfield—he followed them up the aisle to their pew in the front. The servants hung back to take their places at the back of the nave in the pews set aside for them.

There was no sign of Dudley. Still, with two guests, Mrs. Kean and Gideon, the pew was rather crowded. Gideon managed to seat himself between Pamela and Mrs. Kean, but he found himself inching closer to Mrs. Kean to avoid being pinched by the encroachment of his hostess. The day was quite warm. Little air circulated this far from the door, and his knee-length coat and full-bottomed wig soon made him perspire. He took a handkerchief out of his pocket and dabbed at his face. Eventually, Pamela noticed his discomfort and reluctantly ceded him a bit more room. Gideon was very aware of Mrs. Kean beside him, cool and possessed, with a curve of amusement on her lips.

Once Sir Ralph, Mr. and Mrs. Mynchon, and a few other parish luminaries had arrived, the service began. After the opening liturgy, the Reverend Mr. Ward preached upon the need for each parishioner to consider his duty to the kingdom, whatever his capacity. He spoke with particular emphasis when calling upon the gentry to fulfill their responsibilities to the parish, an unmistakable note of displeasure in his voice. Glancing at the gentlemen to see how they received this lecture, Gideon noted that Mr. Mynchon was the only one who nodded his head in agreement. Sir Ralph maintained a stone-like face and, of course, Dudley was not present to hear it.

Neither was Charles Fenwick, a recusant, of course—or so his father had been. It remained to see whether Charles would overcome his religious scruples to comply with the laws designed to ensure that only members of the Church of England could hold public office. They required him not only to take the oaths of supremacy and allegiance, but to deny transubstantiation—the belief that the sacramental bread and wine converted into the actual body and blood of Christ—an essential tenet of Roman Catholicism. A more recent act against occasional conformity had made it impossible for Catholics to pretend to have converted by receiving communion in an Anglican church a few times per year in order to hold a county office.

Apparently, neither Dudley nor Sir Ralph had taken up the duty of serving as a justice of the peace. In Dudley's case, it was obvious that he had no desire to let business interfere with his pleasure. It surprised Gideon more that Sir Ralph was not a J.P., especially as he did not have the distraction of visiting London as a member of Parliament; but throughout the kingdom many of the largest landowners had given up the practice when lesser landlords had been nominated to the position. Still, Gideon would have expected a gentleman like Sir Ralph, so mindful of his place in local society, to take on the responsibility.

These thoughts occupied him until the blessing was pronounced and everyone stood to leave. Pamela immediately invited him to join them at Yearsley Park for dinner, an invitation seconded by Sir Ralph when he joined them in the aisle. In the press towards the door, Gideon contrived to fall into step beside Mrs. Kean, who said under her breath, "Feeling a bit smothered, my lord?"

"Baggage!" he retorted, sneaking a squeeze of her hand.

Outside, Mr. Ward greeted his visitors with well-feigned humility, still managing to extract their compliments on his sermon with the wish that he had not exhausted their patience. Gideon expressed his intention to return for a closer look at the monuments in the chancel, which obviously pleased the curate.

"As I am certain you are aware, the finest examples were constructed to honour ancestors of my patron Lord Fauconberg."

"Yes, I understand his estate is nearby."

The younger of the two Mayfield girls, who had sidled up to Gideon, gave her head a self-important shake and broke in. "And they keep Cromwell's body in the attic!"

"Clarissa!" A step behind her, Pamela grasped the girl's arm and gave it a jerk. "How dare you speak in that insolent way to Sir Robert?"

Mr. Wade was outraged. He grew several inches taller, saying, "My dear young lady, have you never been told how unattractive it is for a girl to speak rudely to her elders? Moreover how unwise it is to discuss the intimate affairs of persons of a more elevated status than your own?"

As Pamela dragged the unrepentant girl away, Mr. Wade turned back to Gideon and said in a flustered manner, "Please pay no heed to what that chit said, Sir Robert."

Gideon assured the Reverend Mr. Wade that he had already forgotten the episode, before saying again that he would like to return for a closer inspection of the monuments. Then, because he could not pass up the chance to tease Mrs. Kean, in a voice loud enough for her to hear, he added, "I am certain that something will lure me back into the church before I leave the neighbourhood."

After escorting the ladies to their carriage, he crossed to the inn to get his horse. The landlord told him that Dudley had wakened and headed for home.

"Was he angry?"

The landlord shook his head. "'E nivver said nowt."

"Maybe he's just saving his fury for me."

"Nay. Dooan't thee fret thissen! 'E's as simple as a suckin' duck, is Maister Dudley, think on."

With these words to entertain him, Gideon went out to mount his horse, taking Argos with him.

Sir Ralph had no intention of letting his daughter monopolize his guests, so Gideon was spared a repetition of Pamela's flirting. Throughout the meal, she seemed content to interject an occasional sally into the conversation between her father and "Sir Robert", always with a teasing look aimed his way. He was thankful that Sir Ralph's presence gave him an excuse for ignoring these, for she could hardly expect him to leer back at her under her father's watchful gaze. By far the most difficult task was to make nothing but polite conversation with Mrs. Kean who sat to his right. The temptation to graze her leg with his under the table was scarcely bearable. He had to focus intently on his meal, when his appetite was raging for something far different from food.

After dinner, as the only male guest—Dudley never having appeared—he sat alone with Sir Ralph over a glass of brandy. Remembering the pretence under which he had come into Yorkshire, he asked his host whether he knew of any land in the hundred—or wapentake as it was called in Yorkshire—that might be for sale.

Sir Ralph raised his eyes to the ceiling as if considering, then, lowering them again, shook his head. "None that I have heard of."

"I heard that the lower prices for crops have recently driven rents down, too."

Sir Ralph gave him a measuring look over the rim of his glass. "That is true all over England and has been for many years."

"Yes, but surely the price of land should reflect the lower income from it. Are there no landlords so mired in debt that they are obliged to sell?"

Instead of answering him, in a rallying tone Sir Ralph asked why he should wish to put his inheritance into land at such a worrisome time instead of into something like the South Sea Company. "I hear there is more to be made there, or in mines if you can find a legitimate one in which to invest."

"Perhaps. Still, I know more about land than I do about those things."

"So do we all! But come, let's not discuss business on such a fine day. Let's join the ladies and take a turn in the garden."

Nothing loath, Gideon downed his glass, and followed Sir Ralph into the parlour with the gilt leather wallhangings, where the ladies sat over their needlework and tea. Pamela came eagerly erect and offered him a dish, which he accepted, apologizing for the interruption to their conversation.

"Nonsense!" Pamela said with a titter. "Don't you know that gentlemen are always a welcome change from ladies' conversation? It was only Mary talking anyway."

Mary flushed. "I had just proposed calling on Mrs. Fenwick tomorrow in order to make the acquaintance of her daughter Margaret. We did promise Mr. Fenwick that we should do so, did we not Hester?"

Gideon turned towards Mrs. Kean, who gave Mary a regretful look. "That was before Mr. Moreland scolded Mr. Fenwick and Frances for visiting us. If we were to encounter him on our visit, it could be awkward."

"Bullied you, did he?" Gideon asked, surprised by the spurt of anger he felt.

Mrs. Kean smiled ruefully. "Yes, I'm afraid he did. He seems to have taken us in great dislike."

"He is a stern gentleman, surely. One would guess a Puritan if the Fenwicks were not papists."

"Well," Pamela asserted, "whatever he is, he is vastly disagreeable and I, for one, have no desire ever to meet him again!"

Mary looked mulish. "I promised Mr. Fenwick that I should call upon his sister. He wants us to be friends."

Mrs. Kean looked pityingly upon the girl before casting Gideon a helpless glance. She seemed to be in a quandary.

He said, "If it is an escort you need, I shall be happy to accompany you. I have not yet seen the Fenwicks' property."

Mrs. Kean thanked him formally, but he saw that his offer had pleased her. Mary beamed. Pamela looked annoyed. She could not very well offer to go with them, having expressed her aversion to Mr. Moreland so strongly.

Sir Ralph reacted to his other statement. "There will be nothing to interest you in Fenwick's estate. The boy does not mean to sell."

Sensing offence behind the words, Gideon made him a slight bow. "I have no designs on Mr. Fenwick's property, I assure you. I am merely curious to see what his tenants have planted."

Sir Ralph's face relaxed into a jovial smile. "Nothing to do with me either way! But what say you, Mary? Have you shown our guest the maze?"

All three ladies looked pleased at the suggestion. They laid down their needles, and led Gideon outside. Sir Ralph excused himself from joining them, saying he was certain his guest would prefer to be the sole gentleman among so many pretty girls.

The weather was warm, but a pleasant breeze reached them as they strolled beside the fishpond. Gideon had been obliged to offer Pamela his arm, and she held him to a snail's pace as Mary and Hester walked arm in arm in front. When they reached the opening to the maze, however, he called out to them to wait.

As soon as he and Pamela caught up, with a private smile for Mrs. Kean, he proposed that the three fairest members of the party should try to lose him in the maze and that he, after waiting for five minutes, should try to find them.

Since he followed this proposition with a wink at Pamela, she dimpled up at him and said, "And what shall you do an' you find us?"

Gideon gave her his most ingenuous look. "Why I shall return you to Sir Ralph forthwith!"

She answered with a delighted laugh, "Well, if that is your intention, sir, you shall never catch me!" She released his arm and ran lightly into the maze with a challenging glance over her shoulder.

Mary frowned and rolled her eyes, but followed her sister in. "You shall never find me, Sir Robert!"

Gideon watched them retreat for a second, then bent his head and said to Hester in a low voice, "Turn right twice and wait for me there."

With his heart pounding in excitement, he watched her disappear into the maze. The first turn was visible from the entrance. Pamela had turned left, and so had Mary. That did not mean they would not be forced back to the right, but he should have a few moments alone with Mrs. Kean.

He did not wait the five minutes he had promised, but started just after she made the first turn. He followed quickly and soon found her standing in a small enclosed space, one of the many blind alleys that normally would force them to retreat.

Mrs. Kean looked shy and nervous. He opened his arms wide and said in a quiet voice, "Now tell me, is this not better than a church?"

She laughed, then shook her head, striving for a scolding manner. "That was truly reprehensible, my lord!"

He gave a long-suffering sigh. "Have I not paid her court enough this week?"

"Shhhh! Or they will hear us. These are not solid walls."

"Then . . ." he walked slowly towards her until their bodies were nearly touching, whispering . . . "we must make good use of the little time we have."

She gazed timorously up at him. "This cannot be wise, my lord."

He could not tell whether she feared him or simply the situation. Did she think that he would force himself on her, or that if they embraced, they would be discovered?

Though his pulse was racing and he could barely swallow for the tightness in his throat, he smiled reassuringly. "If we are discovered, I shall simply state that I found you first." He took a step backwards to allow them both to breathe. He had shocked her by turning up here unannounced. Perhaps she needed more time to decipher her own feelings.

To relieve the tension between them, he turned to the first subject he could think of. "So Moreland treated you to a tantrum, did he?"

She exhaled on a shaky breath. "Yes, he scolded Pamela and me for leading the Fenwicks astray. He was particularly hateful when he did it, too, my lord."

Gideon knitted his brows. "I cannot understand him." He told her about the scene with Dudley, his comments on Dudley's violence, and the questions he had asked both him and Tom.

"He wished to know if your cousin is ever violent when he has not been drinking."

She pressed two fingers to her forehead. "I had hoped that Dudley had learned how much his drunken fits put him at risk. It sounds as if Mr. Moreland believes that Dudley killed Mr. Fenwick."

"I have to ask . . . is it possible?"

She looked up, worry filling her eyes. "I cannot believe it. Why should he? Besides, he acted quite surprised when we told him of the murder."

"Where was he when it occurred?"

She made a helpless gesture. "They said he was at the market looking at a horse or some such thing, but I have no real way of knowing. He certainly was not drunk when I saw him at dinner." She explained that Dudley had not come to meet the coach in York, and that Sir Ralph and Pamela had had to fetch her.

Gideon could not ignore a worried feeling that gnawed at his stomach. For an instant, at the inn yesterday, he had had the feeling that Dudley might know something about Fenwick's murder. But seeing the concern in her eyes, he merely said, "It is perfectly reasonable to assume that he was after a horse. He thinks of very little else. Just because I would drop heaven and earth to collect you, an' I had the right, does not mean that Dudley would."

She twinkled back at him. "No, indeed, and I seldom let Dudley's neglect annoy me—I just wish he would not behave in a manner to make the whole family wince."

"What do you think of Moreland, other than that he's a sanctimonious bully?"

"I truly do not know. I cannot understand why Charles Fenwick obeys him—not now when he should be his own master."

"He seems very protective of the boy, but then so does Sir Ralph. You saw how he reacted when I expressed a wish to view Fenwick's estate."

"Yes, but he has undertaken to teach Charles husbandry and management. Now that his father is dead, he has no one else to learn from."

Gideon considered this fairly, then nodded. "That could explain why he sounded so defensive. I get the feeling, however, that he doesn't want to encourage me to look for a parcel of land around here. I can understand if he cares a great deal about the local people. An outsider coming in will be more likely to enclose the land, turn the tenants out, and convert it to pasturage. That's much harder to do if one has a history in the area."

"Well, he does enjoy being the 'lord of the manor' more than most."

"Nothing wrong with that—shhhh!" He had heard the soft sound of slippered feet on earth and the rustle of a woman's skirts as they brushed against the hedge.

In a moment, Pamela's whisper came floating up over the hedge between the blind alley where they were hiding and the next. "Sir Robert." She repeated his name a few times before heaving a sigh. Then the rustle of her skirt quickly retreated.

Mrs. Kean looked up at him, a clear apology in her eyes.

"Very well." He treated her to a reproachful glare. "But the next time we are cornered in a maze, I shall expect you to be in a more amorous mood."

She bit her bottom lip to keep her laughter in check. It thrilled him to see that her lips were trembling.

"I shall go in search of Pamela, but I do not mean to locate her before she wilts from the heat. You should remain right here until you can control this shockingly unmaidenly behaviour." He had to turn at that point because her shoulders had begun to shake, and he was afraid he would grab her and kiss her. He vowed to himself, however, that this would not be their last encounter in the maze. And the next one must be more successful or he would go mad with waiting.

By the time he came across Pamela, she was, indeed, wilted. He assured her that he had been terribly lost and dried his forehead with an enormous handkerchief while whining about the intolerable heat.

He made certain his demeanour was so petulant that she could read nothing of the lover in it, even if she had not been discouraged by the heat herself. He complained that no maze had ever confounded him so thoroughly, and that he had suggested the game on the basis of his success in playing it at Hampton Court.

As intended, this last statement dampened her ardour, for she had to assume that he had often flirted with other ladies as his target. He reasoned it was better for her to think of him as an unprincipled rogue than as a lover who was truly smitten. This way she could protect herself from any fantasy she might construct. It had not escaped Gideon's notice that Pamela was not in love with her husband, or he with her—a dangerous situation, which could lead a woman to seek satisfaction elsewhere. Since he did not plan to fulfill any yearnings of hers, he would not pretend to be the man who would.

After pleading a great thirst, he was easily able to persuade her that they should call out for Mary to lead them out. They found both Mary and Mrs. Kean waiting for them at the entrance. Pamela was partially mollified when Mary looked at them suspiciously, for it gave her the opportunity to smile and toss her head as if she had a secret.

Mrs. Kean had asked a servant to bring them cool drinks in the garden. After downing his and ascertaining the hour they would set out to visit the Fenwicks on the morrow, he took his leave, careful to take Pamela's hand and give her a suitably languishing look.

*M*any hundred large Volumes have been published upon this Contro-versy; But the Books of the Big-Endians have been long forbidden, and the whole Party rendred incapable by Law of holding Employments.

CHAPTER X

The next morning, contrary to Hester's expectations, Pamela did not subject her to a jealous scene when St. Mars came to fetch her and Mary, but instead, though visibly dispirited, waved them off without any fuss. Whatever had taken place in the maze between Pamela and St. Mars, the enchantment had clearly been broken.

Under the circumstances, Hester thought it a bit insensitive to ask if they could use the carriage, so she accepted the use of the pony again. She found it so easily manageable that she actually enjoyed the short ride to Oulston Hall.

Mary was an easy companion and did not rattle on when she had nothing of interest to say, so Hester's mind could wander over the meeting with St. Mars in the maze.

She berated herself for being too timid with him, for not greeting him with the abandon she felt in her dreams; but in truth, the passion she had seen in his eyes had frightened her for just a moment. She yearned to give into it, but at the same time, she had never lost control of her emotions and the prospect of doing it had sent her scurrying back into the safety of propriety.

Now she could kick herself for the missed opportunity. What would he think of her? Had she been so cold that he would never look at her in that manner again?

A small voice nagged her that he had still not spoken of love. Or of marriage. Was it usual to commit physically to a union before such things were discussed? Her knowledge of such matters was limited. The only time one ever knew that a woman had given into a man's passion before wedding him was when the consequences of that passion were all too evident. When those consequences succeeded marriage, no one ever revealed what might have been experienced before.

His evident physical feelings aside, St. Mars's manner to her was the same as it had ever been: teasing, amusing, intentionally provoking. She loved the way he behaved with her, but if his feelings had taken a more serious turn, should he not at least give her a sign? Why could he not just say if he loved her and remove her doubts? If she knew how he felt, she was sure she could respond with all the ardour he wanted, but apparently she was incapable of unconscious wantonness.

Blast the man!

They arrived and were surprised to find Charles Fenwick still at home. He greeted them with uninhibited pleasure, due to the apparent absence of Mr. Moreland. Hester asked whether she might visit Charles's mother, so while Frances took Mary upstairs to meet her sister Margaret in the nursery, Hester and St. Mars were taken through the hall with its lofty ceiling to a richly decorated parlour situated behind the dais. Although the room contained two chimneypieces, the one in the corner was obviously no longer used. All the chairs had been set about the hearth at the centre of the room. Hester imagined that the unused chimney must be the source of wicked drafts in winter.

The furnishings here had at one time been very rich. They consisted of a court cupboard with an old Turkey cupboard cloth, a draw-table with an Arras table-cloth, five chairs variously covered with stamped leather and needlework, and a half-dozen joint stools. All were made of sturdy oak—not a single piece of walnut was visible. When Hester happened to glance over at St. Mars, the look he gave her revealed that the conclusion he had drawn about the Fenwicks' circumstances was the same as hers.

Mrs. Fenwick sat in one of the chairs by the window, taking advantage of the morning light to do her needlework. She stood to curtsy and her son made the introductions. More colour was in her cheeks than the last time Hester had seen her, but she wore the same downtrodden air.

St. Mars behaved as if it were a commonplace to visit a newly bereaved widow. In a considerate, low voice, he conveyed all the proper sentiments, which Mrs. Fenwick received with perfect grace. She invited them to sit, and as they did, Charles told her that Mrs. Mary Mayfield had come to make the acquaintance of her daughter Margaret.

"And you, Sir Robert, what is your connection with the Mayfields and Mrs. Kean?" the widow asked.

St. Mars was not prepared for the question, and he stammered something about being a recent acquaintance who had merely offered to escort the young ladies.

Something in his manner must have betrayed his real reason for coming, for after an awkward pause, Charles said, "I should not be surprised that you felt an escort was needed, Mrs. Kean, not after our rude departure from Yearsley Park. I really must apologize for Mr. Moreland's manner on that occasion."

Mrs. Fenwick started in her chair, opening her mouth as if to speak. Then, with a wary glance at her guests, she closed it again, hands clasped tightly in her lap.

"Not at all," Hester assured him. "It is I who should apologize for encouraging Frances to neglect her mourning." She turned to Mrs. Fenwick and said earnestly, "It was wrong of me, and if you allow her to visit us again, I promise not to tempt her with any entertainment you would find unsuitable."

Mrs. Fenwick's tension eased. "I am truly not as strict as you must think me, Mrs. Kean. I do not begrudge my children a bit of amusement. It is just that—" She broke off, looking confused, then turned to her son for help.

"It is simply that Mr. Moreland has a different opinion about the behaviour that is proper in our situation," Charles hurried to say. "It was his strictness you witnessed, not Mama's."

Hester smiled. "Then we shall look forward to seeing Frances at Beckwith Manor again. Margaret would be perfectly welcome, too, but to be honest, my cousin Clarissa, who is closest to her age, does not possess the sort of character to put a grieving person at ease. If they are to meet, it would be better to wait until Margaret has had some time to recover from her loss."

"Mrs. Mary Mayfield has been all that is kind to Frances, Mama," Charles said, in an earnest tone.

His mother gave him a look tinged with alarm. Staring woodenly at him, she said, "I do not doubt it. Nevertheless, Frances should not be encouraged to gad endlessly about."

Since this statement issued from the woman who had so recently denied her strictness, Hester was a bit taken aback. Then she noted the disappointment on Charles's face and realized that Mrs. Fenwick's censure had been aimed at him, not at her daughter. It was one thing for Frances to have a friend who was not a papist, entirely another for Charles to admire a girl who was not a member of their faith.

This time it was St. Mars who stepped in to fill the awkward silence. Turning to Charles, he said, "I understand Sir Ralph has been giving you a bit of help with husbandry. How much of your acreage is in tillage, and how much in pasture?"

He could not have lit upon a better change of subject. Relieved of his embarrassment, Charles was happy to inform them of what he had learned about his estate. As he described his property and expounded on his plans for it, his mother looked proudly on.

Leaving the gentlemen to continue their talk, she leaned towards Hester to say quietly, "I do not know what I should have done if Charles had not come home when he did. He has taken up his father's responsibilities without a single complaint, and as we are situated, they come with considerable burdens."

"He is a very dutiful son."

"Yes, but unless he can raise his rents on the land we have, it will not be easy for him to provide for his sisters. He will have to raise dowries for them, even if they enter a convent."

"My cousin Dudley is under the same obligation, and he has even more siblings to provide for."

Mrs. Fenwick retreated. "He does not labour under the same burdens."

"No, but neither is he as diligent as Charles." She could have consoled the widow with the thought that she felt more confident of Charles's success through prudence and good management than she did of Dudley's, but she was ashamed to have said as much as she already had. Her worry for her younger cousins had led her to an indiscretion.

Mrs. Fenwick appeared to understand her. Dudley's faults must be common knowledge. All she said, however, was, "Then, let us hope that Sir Ralph can be persuaded to assist them. Mrs. Mayfield is his sole heir, so he may be persuaded to help her husband's siblings."

It was far more likely that Harrowby would be asked to do it, Hester knew, since Sir Ralph would assume that his daughter would have children who would need his help. With the way things stood between Pamela and her husband, however, Hester was not so certain that children should be expected. But she kept these thoughts to herself, merely nodding in agreement with Mrs. Fenwick.

The gentlemen's discussion was heading to a close. Judging that the proper length of a morning visit had been reached, Hester stood to make their goodbyes, saying that Mary would have to be fetched for their ride home. When Charles urged his mother to invite her to stay, to be company for his sisters, Mrs. Fenwick's hesitation made Hester say hastily, "I know Mary would love to prolong the visit, but she has a dancing lesson today."

His face fell, but he offered to ride with them part way home as their routes were similar. Before his mother could raise any objections, he went in search of Mary, and the four went outside to wait for their horses to be brought round.

As they started off, Charles gave a spur to his horse to catch Mary, whose notion of a proper pace was more like her brother's than Hester's.

St. Mars held Penny back to keep pace with Hester's pony. This would have been nearly impossible if he had not exercised her earlier that morning, but after just a few jerks of her head, she settled down, calmed by the presence of the smaller, imperturbable pony.

"I do not envy that young man's situation," St. Mars said, in a voice too low for the others to hear.

The generosity of his sentiment made Hester smile. "Not even with respect to yours, my lord?"

He looked surprised. Then, recalling his standing as an outlaw, he laughed. "Do you know? For once, I had forgot. It must be the good Yorkshire air."

She made herself be serious. "You must never grow careless, my lord. I wish I could allow you to forget it, but I dare not."

He gave her a reassuring grin before reverting to his original topic. "It will not be easy for Fenwick if his mother and Moreland are constantly expressing their disapproval."

"I do not think his mother disapproves most of what he does. She simply does not wish him to fall in love with a girl who is not a papist."

With a nod, Hester directed his attention to the pair in front. Mary had slowed her horse, and now the two young people were riding side by side, Charles's stirrup occasionally brushing Mary's skirts. They seemed in thrall.

"Ah," St. Mars said, as if only now noticing their rapport. "That would be a problem. I doubt, however, that Fenwick will be in a position to marry until he can get his estate in order, and if Mary leaves for London soon, the danger will be averted. If I know Mrs. Mayfield, she already has Mary's husband picked out."

Hester sighed. "I would not doubt it, but it does seem harsh if the two have a strong attraction."

His smile was teasing. "They would not be the first to be so disappointed. It is rare for people of rank to have any say in the selection of a spouse."

This reminded Hester of something she had wondered from time to time. "Why did your father did not arrange a marriage for you?"

"He did—to a duke's daughter—but she died of the smallpox shortly after the contract was signed. In effect, I was widowed before even laying eyes on my wife. Then, before he could arrange another, his mind was taken up with the turmoil in the government. I left to tour the Continent with my tutor and was out of the country for two years. By the end of that journey, I was of age, and my father did me the courtesy of awaiting my return before proposing a new match. He would have insisted on approving any choice of mine and was ready to cut off my allowance when he could not."

That was when, Hester knew, he had wished to propose to her cousin Isabella. For a while she had suspected St. Mars of still loving her, but for many months he had been able to speak of Isabella with no emotion other than chagrin for ever believing himself in love with such a shallow woman.

Her question answered, she said, "What do you think I should do, my lord? Should I try to keep Mary from seeing Charles Fenwick?"

"No." He seemed definite on this point. "I would not throw them together, but I would let them make their own way. Life is short, and one should seize happiness where one can find it. Do you not agree?" Though he smiled, she read something in his gaze that warmed her deep inside her core.

She could not answer plainly without appearing to ask for a proposal, so she pretended to consider the question seriously. "As long as no one is severely hurt, I suppose."

They had turned in the gate to Beckwith Manor, so she asked, "Will you be staying to dinner, my lord."

He answered wryly, "After that experience in the maze, I doubt an invitation will be forthcoming, but I should not wear out my welcome in any case. If I ride on with Fenwick, I may learn something additional about Moreland."

"What do you hope to discover?"

"The reason why Mrs. Fenwick is afraid to cross him."

Hester reined her pony to a stop and threw him a searching glance. "Did you sense that, too? I thought I could be imagining it, or perhaps that she only fears what her cousin will say if Charles spends too much time with Mary."

He furrowed his brow. "I have the feeling there is something else, but I cannot put my finger on it."

Hester agreed, and by common consent they rode on before the others noticed they had stopped.

She refrained from asking him about his encounter with Pamela in the maze. In a moment he added, "In any case, it is time I made a tour of the area to pretend to look for a suitable property. If Sir Ralph can be believed, there is nothing near Coxwold for sale, so I will have to search farther afield. If we do not meet for a few days, that will be the reason."

Though Hester would miss him, she merely nodded. The truth was that she needed to spend more time preparing Mary for Court. If she did not, especially if Pamela had lost her enthusiasm for St. Mars, she was certain to grow suspicious.

St. Mars called ahead to Charles to inform him of his intention to ride on. The two gentlemen parted from the ladies a short distance from the house so they would not be delayed by meeting either Dudley or Pamela. Mary waved them off, her sigh echoing Hester's less inaudible one.

Over the next few days, Hester tried to concentrate on Mary. At times this was difficult, for neither found it easy to keep her mind on lessons. Since Mary did not trust her mother to care about her happiness, she had doubts that her upcoming visit to Court would answer her hopes. If she had not been so eager to escape from her brother's house, Hester almost believed Mary would have refused to go.

There was still a deal of needlework to be done. Since Mary had neither her own maid nor a dresser nor the money to hire a needlewoman, she and Hester must do most of the sewing themselves. Every day they sat for long hours over their work. Mary insisted on taking a solitary ride every afternoon to clear her brain and rest her eyes. Knowing how much her riding would be restricted in London, Hester urged Pamela to allow it. The girl would be turned into a matron soon enough.

Hester had not been able to focus since St. Mars had appeared. Her initial elation on seeing him—though still quite easily aroused— had been elbowed aside by a few sober reflections. She had asked herself what his turning up in Yorkshire could mean, and the only answer that made any sense was that he loved her. There had been hints in the past that he wanted her, but never enough to tell her exactly for what. She had started as his confidant and friend, and she was not so naïve as to dismiss the importance of those roles to a man as isolated as he was. He might be infatuated, of course, in which case his feelings for her would dim. The fact remained, though, that if he had wanted a dazzling lover or even a wife, he could have stayed in France and found any number of ladies eager to fill either of those positions.

That he had chosen instead to come in search of her implied that whatever he wanted could only be satisfied by her. Hester prided herself on an ability to think with logic, but throughout her relationship with St. Mars, logic had been at war with her heart. Now, for the first time when she reasoned, her conclusions supported her long-suppressed desires.

The only questions now, it seemed, were whether St. Mars wanted her for a mistress or a wife, and whether she herself would settle for the former if he never offered marriage. No matter how much she wanted to give into him, as a clergyman's daughter she had seen too many examples of the consequences of illicit passion to wish to risk them herself.

It was a relief to all the ladies in the house when a dancing master arrived from York. He had been engaged every day for one week, the money for his hire supplied by the elder Mrs. Mayfield, since dancing instruction was one thing she could not trust Hester to provide. Pamela insisted on taking part in the lessons, too, for though she had taken some before her marriage, Monsieur d'Olier came supplied with the latest steps from the Regent's court in France. Anything that gave Pamela the illusion of the life she coveted claimed her most eager attention.

During her brief infatuation with "Sir Robert," she had stopped asking Hester questions about London, but now she resumed and could not ask enough. She wished to hear everything about the King's mistresses and the Princess's ladies-in-waiting. She became so curious about the latter, in fact, that Hester began to suspect she had set her mind on obtaining a position for herself.

Hester's instinct was to dissuade her, until she reflected that Dudley was unlikely to miss his wife. He had already received what he wanted from her—her dowry plus the allowance Sir Ralph paid him. Clearly, he devoted little time to his wife. Now that the first week of Hester's visit was past, he no longer made a pretence of taking any interest in his family. He rarely appeared at dinner, spending his days away from home in sporting pursuits and his evenings out drinking with his cronies, she assumed. Pamela was patently accustomed to this neglect for she gave no sign of regretting his company. Hester feared that Dudley had become as much a caricature of the country gentleman as the squires in Mr. Congreve's plays.

With regard to the usual obligation of marriage, as far as she could see, he had no interest in producing an heir, not with three brothers to answer the purpose.

She had no notion of how much effort, if any, Dudley put into managing his estates. When she ventured to ask Mary, the girl scoffed and said that Sir Ralph's steward had as much to do with the overseeing of them as Dudley did himself. He had indeed mortgaged his land to Sir Ralph, including its supervision.

Taking all this into account, Hester began to think that Pamela might be better off at Court. If she could obtain a place, the sinecure could only benefit her family. Of course, someone would have to act in her interest to secure it. Without any political tie to the King's advisors, a bribe would have to be paid to the King's mistress, Madame Schulenberg, now the Duchess of Kendal. Whether Sir Ralph or Harrowby would be willing to pay this was another matter.

When at last the subject was broached, Pamela's only concern about the position seemed to be whether she would be obliged to wait on the Princess during the shooting season, for she should hate to miss it.

"Do you shoot?" Hester asked. Queen Anne had been a keen devotee of the chase. Some other ladies accompanied the hunt, but this was a fact about Dudley's wife she had not known.

"Yes, my father taught me. He lacked a son, you see, so he taught me to shoot so that I might accompany him. If any gentleman was available, he preferred to go with him, but you have seen how gregarious he is. He does not like to be alone."

"Do you ever ride out with Dudley?"

"Oh, yes." She emitted an unladylike snort. "I daresay, the fact that I can ride and shoot well is the only thing he truly likes about me."

Hester did her best to deny such a dismal statement, but feared she did not sound very convinced of it herself.

෪

Gideon had found it easy to converse with Charles Fenwick, an amiable young man in need of advice from an older one. Though Gideon had never worked in the management of the Hawkhurst estates, he had managed his seigniory in France. Before the two men's routes diverged, they chatted about everything from the choosing of crops to problems with tenants.

As soon as he could introduce the subject naturally, Gideon asked whether Mr. Moreland was still visiting his family.

A curtain fell over Charles's eyes as he replied, "Yes, our cousin is still with us." Then, hurriedly, as if afraid Gideon would ask, "Today he is visiting friends in the neighbourhood."

Gideon feigned no more than a polite interest. "I wondered why I had not seen him. We are stopping at the same inn, you know."

"Yes, he mentioned seeing you there." For the first time since they had found themselves alone, Charles seemed reticent to speak.

Gideon received the impression that Charles feared he had already divulged too much. Perhaps Moreland had warned him not to be open with strangers, for during the remainder of their ride he spoke very little. Gideon reminded himself that the boy was a virtual stranger to the area and that his father's killer had still not been identified. He must be very confused about whom to trust.

After making a few inquiries in Coxwold, none of which elicited any information on estates for sale, Gideon was ready to expand his pretended search. The effort would support his declared reason for being in the area, should anyone suspect him of not being the person he professed to be. As inquisitive as Mr. Moreland was, Gideon would not have been surprised to learn that the man had attempted to verify his story.

If Gideon had truly been interested in finding a parcel of land, the sensible thing to have done would have been to ask Dudley to accompany him, but the last thing he wanted was to spend more hours in Dudley's company. He had not seen him since their drunken evening together and would have to suffer a visit soon, but if he had to absent himself from Mrs. Kean's company to maintain the fiction he had created, he would take advantage of the opportunity to escape her cousin, too.

After securing Sadler's promise to hold their rooms, he set out with Tom for York with Argos trotting alongside. A few miles down the road, the dog spied a hare and took off with a burst of speed, his back curving and stretching, his eyes fixed like an eagle's on its prey. Gideon had to call him back to avoid a charge of poaching. After a few similar episodes, Argos got the message that they were not on a hunt and settled into an easy gait for a journey.

"Didn't I say he would be a bother, my lord?" Tom said, as he trotted his horse beside Penny.

"Yes, but I knew he would be company for you when I'm away, so I overlooked the inconvenience to myself."

A moment passed before a reluctant grin spread over Tom's lips. "I wasn't born yesterday, my lord. When you took that dog, you didn't know we'd be coming north."

Gideon laughed. "No, and it wasn't you who needed a companion, but I cannot regret taking him, not when I see how happy he is."

Tom gave a "humph," but he made no further complaints about the dog.

They made a leisurely journey, stopping on the road to ask farmers if they knew of any land for sale. The men Gideon questioned stared back at him as if he had grown horns. If they made any reply, it was generally in such a thick Yorkshire that neither Tom nor he could understand, but since his questions were intended merely to create the impression of a search, Gideon simply responded with a nod and rode on.

When they had ridden a reasonable distance from Coxwold, he suspended all pretence, and they pressed on to York, skirting the village of Clinton, which was known even in London as the site of frequent horse-races. Gideon dined at a hostelry outside the city wall that did not cater to posting travellers. With no confidence in the ostlers at this kind of establishment, Tom refused to leave the horses, so Gideon ordered a meal carried out to him.

He had finished his dinner and settled his bill of fare, about to return to his horse, when he spied a familiar figure passing just outside the bow window.

It was Moreland.

Gideon moved closer to the window to watch the man's progress down the road. He had no desire to meet Moreland, but his curiosity had been raised. He considered trailing the man to discover what he was doing in York. The possibility had struck Gideon that Moreland could be a Jacobite agent, in which case his business here could have something to do with the rebellion.

Before he could disappear entirely, Gideon turned on his heel and strode to the stable, where he quickly informed Tom of his intention.

Since Tom's mouth was filled with a large bite of cheese, he was prevented from uttering much in the way of protest, but Gideon read the warning in his eyes. He assured Tom he would be back as soon as his errand bore fruit or proved worthless, and hurried out into the street.

Setting a brisk pace, he soon came within sight of his quarry, who fortunately had not deviated from this road. When he eventually did, it was to enter the walled city through a bar that took them just south of the minster. Gideon hesitated to follow, concerned about the chance that someone who knew him might see him. He was not wearing any disguise. The black wig and paint he used to walk about London was in his saddle bag, but he had not had time enough to put them on.

Moreland, however, turned before he reached the minster and, keeping roughly on a southwest course, wove in and out of the traffic plying the narrow medieval streets. His gait was purposeful, but there was nothing urgent in his manner to raise the interest of the troops quartered within the walls. Their colourful uniforms were visible in every shop and on every street. Moreland's unhurried pace helped him blend naturally with the other pedestrians. The soldiers took no more notice of him than they did of anyone else.

Moreland's path took them to the River Ouse and over the bridge. From there he continued on a street that Gideon recognized as Micklegate. Here, because of the proximity to the coaching inns, Gideon was careful to tilt the brim of his hat over one side of his face. More-land continued until he had exited the old city by way of Micklegate Bar.

Then, as he headed for a row of houses lining the main road, he gave a furtive look over his shoulder, making Gideon turn abruptly as if to head into a house. He paused and peered up at the building before him as if uncertain, while observing Moreland out the corner of his eye. Moreland's curious behaviour continued until he had knocked and been admitted to a modest house just a short way beyond the bar by a woman dressed in a plain grey gown.

There was nothing about the house to distinguish it from its neighbours except an air of genteel poverty. In spite of the warm day, its curtains onto the road were drawn.

Gideon looked for someone in the street he could ask about the owner of the house, but before he could, the door opened again and a second woman emerged and walked hastily towards him. He glanced left and right as if seeking a particular residence, but was forced to keep walking or raise her suspicions. As she passed, he raised his hat, but she kept her eyes modestly on the ground, pretending not to see him. This could have been due to modesty or—an unsettling thought—perhaps Moreland had spotted him and warned her.

In either case, Gideon had no means of discovering the owner of the house, and except for the surreptitious glances Moreland had given upon nearing it, he had no reason to suspect anything underhand about his visit. Gideon decided to return to Tom and find a place to pass the night.

As he wove his way back through the busy streets of York, careful to keep an eye out for anyone who might know him, he pondered a detail that had struck him as odd.

The second woman he had seen emerging from the house had been wearing the same grey dress as the first.

✌

After a few days of making adjustments to Isabella's gowns, Hester decided she would need a few yards of lace to trim the bodices. They revealed more of Mary's breasts than was proper in a young maiden. A strip of lace added to the top could make up for the lower necklines.

Pamela was never averse to visiting the market, so they planned a trip to Thirsk on Monday.

The Saturday before their journey, Charles paid them a brief visit. As they sat down in the Great Parlour to chat, recalling his family's limited means of transport, Hester asked if his mother or Frances would like to accompany them to Thirsk. She ignored Pamela's glare and hoped that Charles did not see it. Hester had taken the liberty because the expedition was hers and Pamela had elected to join her.

Pleased by the invitation, he promised to ask, and later that day, he sent a message by a servant, saying that although his mother must keep to her seclusion for another few weeks, she sent her thanks for the kind attention. She gave her permission for Frances to go as long as Charles accompanied her.

Hester supposed that Mrs. Fenwick wanted Charles to ensure that his sister would not be led astray by the Mayfields again. Mary was delighted by the prospect of their company, and between Hester's efforts and hers, Pamela was persuaded to accept the addition to their party with more graciousness than she felt.

On the appointed day, they dressed and broke their fast earlier than usual in order to fetch Frances in the carriage. Pamela had complained that having five passengers would make for an unpleasant trip, but when they got to Oulston Hall, they learned that it was Charles's intention to ride beside their vehicle. His decision appeased Pamela, but a few minutes later, Mary stated that she never could abide a closed vehicle and wished she had ridden her horse instead.

The distance to Thirsk was nearly ten miles. Since it had not rained the past week, the road was dry. The journey was accomplished in just an hour and a half, so in reasonably good spirits they arrived at the market town at half-past ten o'clock, and made their way to its centre. As the carriage rolled past a row of timbered and thatched cottages lining the way into town, they heard the lowing of cattle and the bleating of sheep coming from the market.

Assisted by the footman who had ridden up beside him, the coachman did his best to avoid the part of town devoted to the market for animals. He inched his way through a modest crowd of merchants and farmers to set the ladies down only a few yards from the market square. Charles offered to accompany the coachman to the inn to make sure that the horses were settled and said he would meet them in fifteen minutes in front of the market cross.

With the footman to escort them, the four ladies slowly made their way through the crowds in the dusty street. The odor of dung mixed with human sweat hung heavy in the warm summer air. Beneath these scents Hester detected the pervasive acrid smell of tanning and leather, the industry for which the town was known. Excited shouts reached them from the green where the cattle were penned. Hester cringed with distaste as the bellows of a bull in the baiting ring cut through the cacophony of the crowd. It was forbidden for any butcher to offer a bull for sale at Thirsk market unless it had first been baited by his immense dog, but the practice of baiting bulls had always struck her as cruel. Most of the men who had come to town had come to watch the spectacle, leaving their women to peruse the booths.

Before meeting Charles at the market cross, the ladies took a stroll past some of the booths to note the ones they wished to visit. When Pamela dawdled over a piece of silverwork, Mary anxiously reminded her that they must not keep Charles waiting. They found him standing near the market cross and together headed for the draper's shop.

Hester recalled this shop from a previous trip to Thirsk. It had started as a booth in the market, she had been told, but had lately been turned into a fixture. A shop of any kind was a rare amenity for a village. This one drew customers from great distances away. Since today was market day, the small house was overcrowded, making her wish they could have visited it on a different day, but they needed to search the stalls for a lacemaker's wares.

When the draper spied four ladies entering his shop, he passed the customer he was helping to his assistant and came to wait on them himself. For a while they amused themselves looking over the bundles of cloth, but since the City of York received as fine quality goods from France, Holland, and China as those found in the City of London, they were not tempted by the slightly inferior wares the draper showed them. With the money her aunt had given her, Hester bought only some material to line a mantua for Mary to be made later in London, where the silk would be purchased. Pamela bought enough linen to make a new chemise.

The footman and Charles carried the ladies' packages as they returned to the market to search for the lacemaker's stall. Hester found what she was looking for and bought two ells of what she knew to be smuggled Brussels lace, though the vendor claimed that it had been made in Bedfordshire. A ribbon seller was set up in a booth not far away, and Mary, Pamela, and Hester each came away with new ribbons. Since Frances would be in black bombazine for the better part of a year, she had no need of new finery. She only gazed longingly at the bright colours.

After their purchases were made, they repaired to the inn for dinner. After giving his name to the landlord, Charles informed the ladies that they were to be his guests. Hester worried that the expense would be imprudent, but he looked so proud to be able to treat them, she was forced to accept. After a filling, if simple, meal, they gathered up their parcels while the footman was sent to call up their carriage.

As they came into the yard, overlooked by three cross-timbered stories, each with a railed gallery, Hester noticed a man standing anxiously with his hat in his hands just beyond the entrance from the street. His air was downtrodden, but his clothes looked respectable and clean. When he caught sight of them coming out to their coach, his face lit. He dashed into the yard, right up to Charles, and grasped at his sleeve.

As Charles stared in astonishment, in heavy Yorkshire the man pleaded with him to intercede with his new master to give him back his farm. Unnerved, Charles informed the man that he must have mistaken him for someone else.

"Nay, nay! Tha' knows me, young maister, sitha!" As Charles tried to loosen the man's grip, his manner became frenzied.

Pamela shrieked and called to the footman for assistance. He shoved the last of the bundles he was carrying into the coach, and ran to wrestle with the stranger.

As they struggled, Charles shook himself loose and bustled the ladies into the carriage.

The stranger's desperate shouts were muffled by the footman's grip on his neck. As he fought, however, Hester thought she heard him say, "Wi'll get us ooan back!"

By this time, the landlord and ostlers had come running to toss the man back into the road. They freed the footman, who, seeing that the gentleman and ladies were safely inside, climbed quickly up to his place on the box.

At the last moment, Charles remembered his horse. He anxiously cried out to the ostler to tie its reins to the vehicle. As soon as this was done, the coachman showed the horses his whip and with a jerk, the coach bolted out of the yard.

Pale and shaken, Charles asked the ladies if any of them had been hurt. They denied any harm, and in a worried voice, Mary asked if he had sustained any injury. After assuring her that he was perfectly well, he said, "What possessed that man to assault me? I have never seen him in my life. He must be an escaped lunatic."

"I've seen him before." Pamela spoke with a note of disgust. "He was one of Papa's tenants, but he was turned out last week, for Papa intends to use those acres for pasturage. That's what has the man upset, I'll warrant."

Now that she knew what his problem was, Hester pitied the man whose livelihood had been taken away. "Yes, that would explain his desperation."

"Was that what he was saying? I am afraid I could not understand one word." Charles looked chagrinned, sympathetic now to the man's misfortune.

Hester smiled. "I forgot that you would not understand Yorkshire. He was asking you to help him get back his farm."

"Why would he ask me? Did he confuse me with Sir Ralph?"

"No, he would not have done that, even seeing you with Pamela." Recalling the man's other words, a puzzle overtook her thoughts. "I do not know why he approached you, but he asked you to plead with his new master on his behalf. He said that you knew him."

Taken aback, Charles looked troubled. "I cannot fathom why he would say that. How should I know any of Sir Ralph's tenants?"

"Perhaps he saw you riding over Yearsley Park with Sir Ralph."

He mused and nodded, still looking troubled. "Yes, I suppose that could be, but I do not recollect meeting him. It makes no sense that I would have any influence with Sir Ralph on the disposition of his acreage."

"When a man is desperate, he may not think clearly. Besides, as you say, he cannot really know you. Perhaps he made the mistake of believing you related to Sir Ralph in some way."

As she helped him reason it through, the colour returned to his cheeks, and by the time they reached Oulston Hall, they had put the incident behind them.

That evening, Sir Ralph rode over to invite them all to dine the next day. With no sign of Dudley, he joined the ladies in the Great Parlour for a glass of wine. While they sipped at ratafia and he indulged in a glass of canary, he teased them about the purchases they had made, saying the *beaux* in the neighbourhood would never know what hit them.

As Pamela gave him the details of their day, Hester recalled the incident in the inn yard, and, when Pamela ran out of things to say, she informed Sir Ralph about it.

The smile froze on his face. He stared, red creeping into his cheeks, before swinging round to face his daughter. "Is this true, Pammy?"

She gasped. "Oh, Lud, I forgot to tell you! It was the most unpleasant thing! He put his dirty hands on Mr. Fenwick's sleeve and would not let go until the landlord and his men prised him loose."

"We were wondering why on earth he would assault Mr. Fenwick when his grievance is with you, sir," Hester said.

Sir Ralph blustered, "The fellow must be mad! How dare he accost my daughter and her friends! As if a landlord don't have the right to dispose of his property however he likes. I shall have to inform the constable."

Hester regretted calling the incident to his attention, but if she had not, Charles was likely to have done so the next time they spoke. "I doubt he will have any occasion to speak to us again." She hoped to soothe his anger and dissuade him from taking action against the poor man.

He shook his head. "I cannot overlook this affront. I'll speak to Mynchon and see what he advises. But don't let it worry you, my dears. I'll make sure the ruffian does not come near enough to disturb you again."

In an effort to lighten the mood, he proposed a game of whist, but Pamela declined for everyone, claiming fatigue after the trip into Thirsk. Not appearing too disappointed, he extracted their promise to come see him on the morrow and left them to their rest.

It was not until Hester lay in bed and played the scene over in her head that she recalled the tenant's last words, which had sounded somewhat like a threat. In plain English, he had claimed that he—and others perhaps—would get their own back. Even with legal action, she did not believe he could succeed. The courts were unlikely to support the claim of a tenant against his landlord. Even cases between landlords were difficult to resolve and could run on in chancery for years. And as Sir Ralph had said, though it might be cruel, he had every right to put his land to whatever use he wished.

That given, she wondered why the man had made such a claim. She hoped he did not have any violence in mind.

She could think of no reason why he would be under the delusion that Charles Fenwick could help him. Perhaps he truly was unhinged. His imprudent behaviour could have been one of the reasons Sir Ralph had turned him off. Hester knew, however, that many landlords were struggling under the low price of grain and, as a consequence, that many had turned their fields into pasturage which they could more easily work themselves. If their expenses were high, as Sir Ralph's must be, they must extract every possible penny from their land. Some landowners had been fortunate enough to discover coal under their acres, but many also had been cheated by the men they had paid to mine it. Neither mining nor trade had ever been part of a gentleman's education.

Hester tried to get to sleep, telling herself that, although the incident was regrettable, they were never likely to encounter the tenant again, but the man's insistence that Charles did know him and his implied threat continued to stimulate her mind.

Though he had not called Charles by name, he had seemed convinced of his identity. She worried that the man's fixation on Charles would not abate and that he would find other ways to approach him. If he was mad, she supposed he could turn even more violent than he had been that day.

With all the troubles that the Fenwicks faced, the last thing Charles needed was an enemy.

*T*his Diversion is only practiced by those Persons, who are Candidates for great Employments, and high Favour, at Court. They are trained in this Art from their Youth, and are not always of noble Birth, or liberal Education. When a great Office is vacant, either by Death or Disgrace, (which often happens) five or six of those Candidates petition the Emperor to entertain his Majesty and the Court with a Dance on the Rope; and whoever jumps the highest without falling, succeeds in the Office.

CHAPTER XI

A few days after they had left for York, Gideon and Tom returned to Coxwold. The next morning, leaving Argos behind with Tom, Gideon rode to Beckwith Manor to call on Mrs. Kean and the Mayfields. As he was ushered through the hall, he heard the sounds of a lute coming from deeper within the house. He had hoped to find Mrs. Kean alone, but inside the Great Parlour he found her with Pamela and Mary, executing the steps of a fast-paced *courante*.

He paused at the door, gesturing to the servant to keep his presence a secret. The chairs had been moved back against the walls to provide a space in which to dance. A man with a lute sat near a window, plucking at his instrument. Gideon watched the ladies cavort until Mary, who was paired with the dancing master, spied him and, blushingly, came to a halt.

"Non, non, non, mademoiselle! Qu'est ce qui ce passe?"

Mrs. Kean and Pamela interrupted their steps to see what had upset the dancing master and, when they spotted Gideon, laughed.

"Excellent!" Pamela clapped her hands in delight. "We shall have a gentleman to practice with us."

"Egad! Do not say I've been caught." Gideon sauntered into the room. "Where is Mayfield, and why have you not enlisted him?"

"Dudley!" Pamela pouted. "If you think he would give up his amusements for me, you are sorely mistaken, sir. But," she added, tossing him a smile which he was glad to see had more reserve than she had been wont to show him, "now that you are here, we shall not allow you to escape. You shall dance for your dinner!"

Grinning, Gideon heaved an elaborate sigh. He gazed at each of the ladies in turn, until his eyes rested on Mrs. Kean. She was trying to preserve her countenance and apparently finding it difficult. His heart swelled in his chest at the thought of taking her hands in his. Feigning deep regret, he said, "If I do dance, that will leave one of you without a partner."

The dancing master took charge then, saying that he would be honoured for *monsieur* to join them. He said that he could watch the two pairs at once and correct their steps. At a Court ball, only one pair of dancers would take the floor at a time while the rest of the courtiers watched.

"Very well, but I shall not have you ladies fighting over me. I shall dance a different step with each of you. Who will be my first partner?"

He was not surprised when Pamela put herself forward. Taking her place beside him, and accepting the hand he held out, she said, "Now, you must follow Monsieur d'Olier's instructions, but I daresay, if you have danced at Court, you know all the steps."

"Not at all. It has been many months since I attended a ball, and last I did, there was no one to partner me. You would not believe it, but on that occasion the gentlemen outnumbered the ladies—a rare circumstance, indeed." He did not dare meet Mrs. Kean's eye, for on that evening, she had been disguised as a footman, so they had not been able to dance together. He did not need to witness her expression to know that she had caught his reference.

Mary was reluctant to practice in the company of a gentleman, but Mrs. Kean told her that she must take advantage of the opportunity to overcome her shyness.

After they practiced a series of *bourées, coupées,* and leaps, Monsieur d'Olier looked quite pleased with his pupils. He told Mary and Mrs. Kean to step to the side and told the lute player to set them

an *allemande*. Pamela turned to face Gideon. They clasped hands behind each other's back, and to Monsieur d'Olier's count they stepped
aside, raised up on the tips of their toes, and executed a kick. Gideon
dropped Pamela's right hand and turned her under his arm. Then they
resumed their positions and began again.

Despite the length of the piece, Gideon was amazed to discover
that he was enjoying himself. He had never had much interest in dancing. Learning it was simply expected, one of the duties of being an
aristocrat, to perform at Court for the queen's pleasure. But in this
setting, as long as he had been excluded from society, he discovered a
certain pleasure in it.

When it was Mary's turn, Monsieur d'Olier called for a *gavotte*.
She turned to face Gideon, but never having danced with a gentleman,
could not lift her eyes from the floor. As they stepped and hopped
through the simple dance, Gideon attempted to relax her by making
polite conversation.

"How are you bearing up under all the fuss?" He asked, employ-
ing the tone of a sympathetic older brother. "I remember when I was
being tutored for my first appearance at Court. Every now and then, I
would run away to escape the criticism."

Mary missed a step, provoking a remonstrance from Monsieur
d'Olier. He made them execute the step again. Then, when they resumed the dance, she seemed anxious to justify herself. "It is not that
I need to escape. I simply like a daily ride. And you mustn't think
that Hester criticizes, for she doesn't. She is very patient with me. It is
simply . . . ."

When she did not complete her thought, he gave her an understanding grin. "My dear girl, you have no need to explain anything to
me. I recall it all too well."

She rewarded him with a smile that held more relief than amusement. She would have studied her feet, then, if Monsieur d'Olier had
not reminded her of her posture. As she then stared straight ahead,
silently moving her lips with the steps, Gideon refrained from disturbing her concentration again.

Finally, it was Mrs. Kean's turn to partner him. Before Monsieur
d'Olier could give an order to the lute player, Gideon called to him,

"Come, is it not time for a minuet?"

The Frenchman looked pleased as he gestured for Mrs Kean to come forward. He asked Pamela and Mary to move back to give the dancers more room and said to Mary, "*Regardez bien, Mademoiselle* Mayfield. Ze minuet is ze most *populaire* dance at ze French court."

In the minuet the dancers seldom touched, but they approached and retreated from each other in imitation of courtship. Mrs. Kean took her place across the room from Gideon and he held her gaze with his eyes. As the light-hearted music began, they circled the room with *pas de bourré,* arms held loosely at their sides. Then, as they spiraled inward, moving ever closer, Gideon found that his throat was growing tight. Mrs. Kean's expression was guarded, but he noticed she was trembling. As the steps brought them near enough to reach out their right hands and touch, his eyes were drawn to her lips.

With their palms lightly brushing, they circled in a series of half-*coupées* and *fleurets.* Their bodies were close enough now to screen each other from the watchers' view, so they could smile without restraint. It was Mrs. Kean's beautiful smile that had first made him notice the quiet woman overshadowed by her dazzling cousin. It was not long before that smile had become the greatest solace in his troubled life. Precisely when he had started to dream of her lips, he could not recollect, but now they formed part of his every waking thought. It was all he could manage now not to kiss her.

As the dance took them apart again, he struggled to compose himself. How much longer would he have to wait? She could not ignore the fact that he loved her. And except for a natural shyness when they were alone together in the maze, she had given no sign of discouraging him. Why did it have to be so cursed difficult to get her alone!

Wishing all her family to the devil, he courted her with his eyes as they advanced and retreated repeatedly through the minuet. When the music came to a halt, Monsieur d'Olier clapped his hands in delight.

"*Bravo! Bravo! Zat is precisely how you must do it, mademoiselle. If monsieur will oblige . . . ?*"

Gideon was in too great a state of desire to continue. Taking out his handkerchief to wipe his forehead, he excused himself, pleading fatigue. "I am sorry, *monsieur, mesdames,* but I must conserve some of my energy for sport. How you ladies manage to keep this up all night is beyond me." Turning to Pamela, he asked where he might find her husband.

With a moue of disappointment, she informed him that Dudley had ridden to Yearsley Park to discuss estate business with her father. "We shall be dining there today, so if you find him, perhaps you will join us."

Gideon assured her that nothing would give him greater pleasure, before bowing himself out of the room. He was happy when a glance informed him that Mrs. Kean had not quite recovered her sangfroid. She looked nearly as shaken by their dance as he was.

Cantering up the lane that led into Yearsley Park, he did spy Dudley and his father-in-law astride their horses, heading away from the house. They perceived him and altered their course to meet him. Dudley greeted him with surprising enthusiasm, considering that the last time they had met, Gideon had knocked him unconscious with a mug.

"There you are, Mavors! I was just saying to Sir Ralph that I had not seen you about for days."

"Yes, my search took me too far away to permit a return to Cox-wold to sleep."

"Any success?" Sir Ralph asked—congenially, Gideon assumed, since if he had found any land to buy, it would not be in the area Sir Ralph considered particularly his.

"Alas, no. I am finding it hard to speak to the natives. Even if I understand them, they seem reluctant to divulge any information to a foreigner."

"Just as I expected." Sir Ralph shook his head as if he had warned Gideon of as much. He invited Gideon to look over the sheep his steward had just purchased, adding, "If you do manage to acquire some land, you should follow my lead. Best investment these days."

"I thought you advised me to put my inheritance into stocks?" Gideon softened this reminder with a laugh.

Sir Ralph's smile wavered, but he returned quickly, "I thought that might suit you better if you spend the greater part of the year in

London. But you seem to be set on land, and if it's land you want, then you cannot beat sheep for profit." Turning his horse towards the gate, he said, "Come now. Enough of this talk about money. Let's go see what my steward has found."

For the next hour or so, Gideon accompanied the two men as Sir Ralph guided them to some acreage down the lane. He showed them his improvements and praised the quality of his sheep. They returned to the house just in time to dine and presently were joined by the Mayfield ladies and Mrs. Kean.

During dinner, Gideon found the opportunity to tell them that he would like to thank them for their hospitality by treating them to a consort of music. "The musicians could perform for us at the inn in Coxwold. When I stopped in York, I saw a group of three performers advertised. If you are willing to put forth a few dates, I will be happy to make the arrangements."

His suggestion was received with great enthusiasm. Pamela, especially, was thrilled, but Sir Ralph insisted that the party would be more comfortable at Yearsley Park than at the common inn. His rooms were larger and the chairs more cushioned. Since Gideon could not deny the truth of this, he agreed, provided it was understood that he should furnish the musicians and pay for the refreshments. A few dates in the future were discussed, and he promised to send a note to York the next day to arrange for the performers to come.

They were lingering over their last course when Charles Fenwick was unexpectedly announced. He came palely into the hall, hard on the heels of the footman. Sir Ralph started to greet him with his usual geniality, but stopped when he saw the expression of distress on the young man's face.

"What it is, my boy?" With an anxious look, he started from his chair.

"You must forgive me for interrupting your dinner, but I had to come directly." Charles glanced at the company, unsure whether he should continue in front of them.

"Yes, I see. Well, let us just step into my closet, shall we? No reason for everyone to get up. Keep eating, my dears. I will not answer for the cook's temper an' you quit."

Sir Ralph quickly ushered Charles out of the hall in the direction of his chamber. The rest exchanged curious glances, Mary clearly the most concerned.

"Wonder what's got the boy in such a lather." Dudley raised his brow at Pamela, as if expecting her to explain.

"How should I know? It must be something serious for him to burst in so rudely."

Mrs. Kean seemed anxious to put a stop to any speculation. "Sir Ralph will inform us if he is at liberty to do so."

That silenced them for a moment, but eventually Pamela said, "I just think that if a person interrupts one's dinner, he ought to expect a little curiosity."

Mrs. Kean smiled back to show that she had meant no rebuke. "It is natural. I confess to a great curiosity myself. I meant only that without any information, it is useless to speculate. Sir Ralph will tell us about it soon if he may."

Gideon changed the subject by reverting to the topic of the consort. He told them that the group he planned to engage was composed of a violin, a bass viol, and a flute. "I had been thinking of a consort since I spied the notice, but the dancing today convinced me to follow my inclination."

"Dancing? Today?" Dudley asked.

With a laugh, Gideon told him how he had been lured into partnering the ladies at their dance lesson. He crafted his tale in the hope of distracting them from Charles's business. His plan worked. Only Mary did not lose her anxious look.

Before they had finished the excellent cherry tart the cook had made, Sir Ralph rejoined them. He came without Charles who, he said, had returned to his house.

"Poor boy is quite undone." Sir Ralph resumed his seat with a sigh. "The King's Commissioner is here to examine his accounts. Of course, I told him I would assist him in any way possible." He glanced round the table before lowering his eyes to the tart on his plate. "I was used to assist his papa when such things occurred. Even swore I had spotted him in church on more than one occasion, but that was years ago when my testimony was enough to answer. Wouldn't do him any good today." He sighed again, before taking a large bite of his tart.

"What does he want you to do?" Dudley asked, a tinge of outrage in his voice.

"Eh?" Sir Ralph looked up, perplexed. Then he said, "Oh, nothing. The boy don't want anything, just a bit of soothing."

"What did you tell him?" Gideon asked.

Sir Ralph chewed and shrugged. "Nothing much I could say, you know—let him think he can come to me any time with his troubles. I told him to comply with whatever the Commissioner wants. Doesn't do to get these fellows' hackles up. The sooner he gets what he came for, the sooner he'll leave."

Mrs. Kean anxiously asked. "Did he mention the Commissioner's name?" She looked as if it were important.

"Yes . . . Foster . . . Foxcroft? Something like that."

In a voice of dread, she said, "Foxcroft—that is the man who travelled with us on the York stage. He is rabidly anti-papist."

Dudley gave an amused snort. "He ought to be. That's his job. Can't say I'm enamoured with papists, myself."

"What have they ever done to you?" Mary said sharply, startling them all.

When they turned in one body to gaze at her, she flushed and lowered her head. "I just meant that they do not do any harm here. I do not see why we cannot just leave them alone."

"Well said!" Gideon spoke just as Pamela and Sir Ralph both warned her to mind her tongue.

Dudley shook his fork at her. "You had better watch that tongue of yours, miss, or they'll be accusing you of treason. Just you wait and see. You'd better not go spewing that nonsense in London or they'll lock you up. An't that right, Hester?"

Mrs. Kean awarded him a mildly scolding glance, but said gently to Mary, "Your brother exaggerates, as usual, but he is correct that it will not be prudent to express your tolerance so openly. Especially right now when the prisons in London are full of Jacobites. Once the arrests have stopped and you are married, you will have more freedom to express your views, but until then, best keep them to yourself."

After this Mary looked so miserable that Mrs. Kean asked if they might make their excuses. "We had an energetic morning with Monsieur d'Olier and could both use a rest."

"I will gladly escort you home," Gideon offered, rising, but Dudley said, "No, you won't, Mavors."

Startled and affronted, Gideon turned and gave him a haughty look.

Dudley laughed. "Sorry. I only meant that you have done enough penance with the ladies. Come with me, and we'll chase some rabbits."

Gideon forced the muscles of his face to relax. He was not accustomed to being ordered about by oafs, but Dudley believed himself his equal. It wasn't Dudley's fault that Gideon was forced to disguise his rank. "I did not bring my guns."

Dudley waved this away. "You can borrow one of Sir Ralph's." He turned to confirm this with his father-in-law, and the only thing Gideon could do without appearing churlish was to insist on returning to the inn to change his clothing.

✸

Mary was silent on the way back to Beckwith Manor. Pamela did not notice for she was excited about the upcoming consort and already planning the gown she would wear. Since Sir Ralph was a widower with no other offspring, she still acted as his hostess and would do so on this occasion.

Consorts of music were held in York during the assizes. She had attended them with her father. Hosting an evening of chamber music with hired musicians would give her the satisfaction of imitating the very best of London society.

Hester waited until that evening when they were sitting in the parlour doing needlework before bringing up the subject of the King's Commissioner.

"It cannot be comfortable for Mrs. Fenwick and her daughters to be in their house while Mr. Foxcroft is there. We should invite them here to escape the unpleasantness."

Mary, whose needle had languished more than once in her lap, rewarded Hester with a dazzling smile.

Pamela was in such a good humour that she raised little objection. "You and Mary may invite them if you like, but I shall be too busy making arrangements for the consort. We shall want to serve a light repast to our guests, so I need to discuss the menu with my father's cook."

It was agreed that Hester and Mary would ride to Oulston Hall on the morrow, immediately after their last dancing lesson, to invite the Fenwick ladies for tea.

The next day, when they arrived, the servant who admitted them wore a harried look, but he conducted them to his mistress's bedchamber. On the way there, Mary peered into every room they passed, but there was no sign of Charles. They found Mrs. Fenwick propped up in bed in a plain Indian gown, her hair covered by a veil with a widow's peak attached.

When Hester explained their errand, she regarded them both with tears in her eyes and thanked them again for their kindness. She declined the invitation for herself, explaining that she must complete the period of solitude due her late-husband, but agreed that Mr. Foxcroft's presence had distressed her girls. She gave permission for them to go.

Mary offered to go to the nursery to fetch them, and while a servant escorted her there, Hester remained with Mrs. Fenwick, who told her, "Mr. Foxcroft took possession of my husband's account books. Charles tried to get him to examine them here in his presence, but Mr. Foxcroft insisted he has the authority to take them away. There should be nothing in them that can harm us, but if the Crown wishes to raise our taxes again, there is nothing we can do.

"Poor Charles," she said. "I fear his education did not prepare him for this hostility." Bitterly, she added, "The sooner he faces our lot, the better, I suppose."

"Is Mr. Moreland still with you? Can he not advise Charles in these matters?"

A wariness came over Mrs. Fenwick's features. She averted her gaze. "I am afraid he is no longer here. He had other business and could not stop."

Noting the effect the mention of Mr. Moreland had caused, Hester changed the subject. She talked about trivial things until Mary reappeared with Frances and Margaret.

Taking their leave of Mrs. Fenwick, they went in search of their horses. While they waited for the boy to bring them round, Hester's gaze wandered over the house. Some carvings over the door to the porch amidst the worn stones and gargoyles caught her eye. She took a closer look and thought she distinguished the heads of a king and queen. Judging by the first figure's hair, the king was Charles I, which made the other his Roman Catholic queen, Henrietta Maria.

While the girls chatted, she thought about the meaning of the carvings. The Fenwick family must have been staunch royalists—not surprising when one considered how Cromwell's Puritans had attacked any semblance of the Catholic faith. The Civil War must have been the beginning of the decline in the Fenwicks' fortunes. Whether the carvings suggested a continuing commitment to the Stuart cause was impossible to say, but she was inclined to believe that their penury was such that Mr. Fenwick would not have risked the little he had left on James's claim to the throne.

On the other hand, many had risked a great deal more on the chance that they would be rewarded when a Stuart resumed the throne. Without having met the late Mr. Fenwick, it was impossible for Hester to venture a guess about either his recklessness or his loyalties.

A groom led the horses from the stable and helped them to mount. With the two Fenwick girls riding pillion, they all were conveyed back to Beckwith Manor.

∅

Eating his breakfast the next morning, Gideon asked the landlord whether Mr. Moreland was still taking a chamber in his house and learned that, although he had returned from his journey to York, he currently was not. When Gideon expressed his regret at not having the occasion to bid the gentleman farewell, Mr. Sadler informed him that Moreland visited frequently. He had friends in the area besides the Fenwicks, and made a point of seeing them, as well.

A new gentleman had taken his room, a Mr. Foxcroft who said he was travelling on the King's business. When Mr. Sadler told Gideon this, his voice lowered to a sullen growl. Not eager to meet with any official himself, Gideon asked what he knew about the man's commission, but the landlord had little to add beyond what Sir Ralph had reported. He did say that the first thing Foxcroft had done was to call at the curate's house.

Hoping to learn as much as he could about the Commissioner's mission, Gideon decided to make his promised visit to the curate. On the pretext of wishing to see the monuments in the church, he waited until the bells rang the call to Morning Prayer, then strolled across the road and took a seat in the pew for visitors.

At the close of the brief service, he approached the Reverend Mr. Ward, who had been delighted to see "Sir Robert" in attendance. He professed to have nothing urgent to keep him from showing his visitor round, so the two reentered the church and walked up the center aisle. Leading the way, Mr. Ward paused by the little altar on the right.

"You will be curious to learn the story of our Lady Chapel—an unusual feature in an Anglican church. It dates from when the church was built in the early fifteenth century." He pointed to a black slab in the aisle. "Do you see that grave? That is for Sir John Manston, who died in 1464. Although his wife's name is on the second brass, the date of her death was never inserted, so we do not know if she is buried with her husband. That would have been a hundred years before parish records of burials were kept. But there is a record that one Elizabeth Vavasour, a cousin of Lady Elizabeth's, bequeathed a silver chalice and paten and two best candlesticks to the altar of St. Mary in this church.

"Of course, only papists pray to St. Mary, so the chapel is no longer used for that purpose, but given the source and the nature of the bequest, it has always been respected."

"Cromwell's men never discovered it?"

"No, that was fortunate—" Mr. Ward headed towards the chancel again—"and ironic, when one knows that his body lies just up the road."

Gideon paused in mid-step. "The story is true then?"

The curate turned back with an eager look. "Oh, yes!" He glanced over his shoulder and lowered his voice to a whisper. "Cromwell's daughter Mary was married to the second Viscount Fauconberg. After her father's beheading, she carried his headless remains to the priory. They are said to be kept in the attic."

Gideon widened his eyes to indicate how much the story had impressed him. Looking gratified, but also a bit guilty for repeating gossip about the forebears of his patron, Mr. Ward led the way into the chancel and stopped before the oldest monument.

On the massive limestone tomb, surrounded by columns and pinnacles painted in black, gold, and red, and many armorial bearings, the recumbent figures of Sir William Belasyse and his wife Margaret were supported by the smaller effigies of their five children. Mr. Ward explained that Sir William's uncle, Dr. Anthony Belasyse, had acted as a King's Commissioner at the Dissolution and had been rewarded with the estate of Newburgh Priory.

"As an ordained priest, he never married so, therefore, he willed the estate to his nephew, as you see here."

The figures on the facing monument, dressed in black with large ruffs around their necks, carved some fifty years later, were kneeling in prayer. In keeping with the Puritan spirit of the times, it had none of the extreme ornamentation of the first.

"And here," the curate said, stepping closer to the altar rail to return to the left side, "we have the first Earl Fauconberg, Thomas, and his grandfather Henry, who died before he could inherit." The two standing figures, life-sized, had been carved in white marble. Beneath a pair of hovering cherubs, both wore the long, curled periwigs still in fashion, but Henry, who had never received the title, was dressed in Roman garb, complete with sandals and toga. His hand was held out as if to ward off the earthly crown extended by the cherubs, while his grandson Thomas, who had died this century, proudly clasped his coronet.

"It was Thomas who was married to Cromwell's daughter, was it not? I seem to recall it now."

"Yes." Mr. Ward seemed pleased with his knowledge.

"I remember the notice when she died, just a few years past."

Mr. Ward nodded. "Alas, she was in Chiswick when the death occurred, so the church was not honoured with her tomb. Still—" he sighed.

As nothing followed his sigh, Gideon took advantage of the pause to say, "The tomb of the first Belasyse put me in mind of some news I recently heard. A King's Commissioner is stopping at the inn here. Do you have any notion what his commission about?"

"As it happens, I do. Mr. Foxcroft—for that is his name—consulted me directly he came into the village." Mr. Ward, who had maintained a congenial mood throughout the tour, put on a more sober mien. "He is here in the North Riding to examine the estates of traitors and recusant papists. Naturally, he came to me for the names of the latter."

"And are there many recusants hereabouts?"

"Not what one would call many, I suppose. Not nearly as many as one finds in Ripon, for instance, but where souls are concerned, Sir Robert, there cannot be too few."

Gideon nodded gravely to concur with this pious statement. "Are there any that particularly concern you?"

Mr. Ward tilted his head to one side and gave Gideon a confiding look. "I shall not give names, but I can tell you there are certain families who try to seduce my parishioners with popery. They are not above taking in orphans to corrupt their souls. I was pleased to see that Mr. Foxcroft takes his commission very seriously. If there are any irregularities with the law, I am confident he will discover them."

"And what of the other sort? Traitors?"

The Reverend Mr. Ward was taken aback. He stammered, "It is really not my place to identify them—although, of course, if I did, it would obviously be my duty . . . ."

"You have no reason to believe that the recusants you spoke of are Jacobites?"

The curate looked rattled. "No, none that I can report." With a visible effort, he calmed himself. "There has been no unrest in this parish. If there had, I should have been told."

"No unrest, sir? But what about the murder of Mr. Fenwick? He was a recusant, or so I heard. Is it possible he was killed because someone suspected him of being a traitor?"

Mr. Ward turned pale. "I do not know what you have heard, but I never accused poor Fenwick of being a Jacobite. It is my parish duty to speak out against treason as well as popery, but I have never confused the two."

Gideon said, "Then, let us hope that no one else did, for that would be tragic."

Deciding that he had teased the curate long enough, he turned to admire the stained glass behind the altar before thanking him for the pleasant tour.

Mr. Ward walked with him as far as the porch, expressing his hope that he would see "Sir Robert" again in his church. His manner was not quite as welcoming as before.

Gideon assured him that his business in the area was not yet completed and that as long as he was stopping in Coxwold it should always be his intention to attend services here.

He did not say that it was because he wished to take advantage of every opportunity to sit beside Mrs. Kean. Somehow, he did not think that was what the curate wished to hear.

He returned to the inn, a bit less concerned about meeting the King's Commissioner, whose mission would focus his attention most intently on those who had already been convicted of treason, whose estates would be forfeit to the Crown. The recusants' estates would be examined to see if they had found a way to evade the additional taxes placed on their land. Here in the North, far away from Crown authorities, enforcement of the laws against them had probably been lax, but whenever the threat of popery arose, as it had recently with the rebellion, stricter enforcement would be imposed.

He had no doubt that Mr. Ward had set the Commissioner onto poor Charles Fenwick. Gideon was not so eager to encounter him that he was willing to visit Charles to see how he got on, but he could ask Mrs. Kean what she knew about his situation.

He had not forgotten his promise to engage the musicians for the consort, so first he went in search of Tom. Supposing him to be bored with spending his days at the inn with little or nothing to do, he sent him to York with instructions to locate the group he had read about and to hire them for Saturday next. If they were already engaged for that evening, then any other would do. Clearly, neither Sir Ralph nor his neighbours were too occupied at this time of year for there to be any difficulty about a particular evening.

Tom seemed pleased enough to have the errand. He reminded Gideon that he would have to mind his dog if he did not want Argos to get them into trouble by running down all the hares within ten miles of the village.

Gideon assured him that he and Argos could manage well enough but told him to saddle Penny before he left.

It was time he figured out a way to see Mrs. Kean alone.

*I*t is computed, that eleven Thousand Persons have, at several Times, suffered Death, rather than submit to break their Eggs at the smaller End.

CHAPTER XII

Hester had not looked forward to meeting Mr. Foxcroft again, but the next morning when she and Mary went to fetch Frances and Margaret, they arrived at Oulston Hall in time to hear the unmistakable sounds of an altercation issuing from somewhere deep inside the house. Hester paused in the hall, worrying that knowledge of their presence might add to Charles's difficulties. Among the raised voices, she recognized his, and almost certainly the other male voice was Foxcroft's.

As she and Mary stood hesitating, the sound of angry footsteps on the ancient floors came towards them. They had no time to retreat before Mr. Foxcroft came bursting into the hall with Charles on his heels.

The presence of two young ladies made the Commissioner halt in mid-stride. With barely concealed anger, he prepared to bow, but as his eyes travelled to Hester's face, a gleam of recognition lit them. With a sneer, he completed his bow and waited until the ladies had made their curtsies before saying, "Why, Mrs. Kean . . . what a surprise it is to see you here. I had not realized that you and Mr. Fenwick were so well acquainted."

She smiled courteously. "That is because we were not acquainted until we met in the coach. My cousins, the Mayfields, live within two miles of Oulston Hall, but as I had only visited them when Mr. Fenwick was a child, I had never had the pleasure of meeting him."

She could tell that Foxcroft did not entirely believe her, but he had no basis for accusing her of falsehood. She wondered how miserable a man must be to be so mistrusting of his fellow creatures.

He looked at Mary, then, and Hester made the introduction. She would have been amused by Mary's obvious distaste for Mr. Foxcroft if she had not been in charge of teaching her the ways of the polite world.

"And Mrs. Mary," Foxcroft said. "Were you acquainted with Mr. Fenwick here?"

"With Charles Fenwick, no, but I did know his father. We are on excellent terms with *all* our neighbours." The emphasis she gave this last statement was clear, even if the words were not strictly true. As a girl, Mary had had little contact with the adults in her neighbourhood, especially if they did not attend the parish church. And neither Dudley nor his mother had wasted time making friends with their neighbours unless there was something they wanted from them.

Whether her statement were true or not, Charles was grateful for Mary's support. The smile he bestowed on her was so full of warmth that the girl blushed.

"I shall be making inquiries among the other neighbours. If there is anything of significance to be learned, I am certain I shall learn it."

He started to walk past them, but Hester stopped him. "What precisely do you mean, Mr. Foxcroft? If there is anything I can assist you to discover, you have only to ask. I am at your service."

Taken aback, he turned and paused. Then he said, "You will forgive me, Mrs. Kean, if I prefer to make my inquiries elsewhere. I have not forgotten your defence of this young gentleman on the road."

Hester gave him her most innocent look. "Defence? I did nothing but remind you of the consequences of laying a charge. You had roused us all from our sleep very early that morning with the reason that your business could not be delayed another hour. If you had charged Mr. Fenwick, it was you who would have missed the coach, not me."

Purple with indignation, Mr. Foxcroft turned on his heels and left the house without remembering to bid them all good day.

"Bravo, Hester! Bravo!" Mary cheered.

"You have bested him again, Mrs. Kean!"

Hester was glad to see the smile on Charles's face, but she said ruefully, "I should never have allowed that man to provoke me, but his attitude angered me so that I lost what little sense I possess. I am terribly sorry, Charles, but I fear my rudeness will only make matters worse for you."

This sobered him, but he was too chivalrous to agree. He insisted that whatever resulted from her challenge to Foxcroft would be more than compensated for by the pleasure he had got from the look on Foxcroft's face.

He sent a servant to tell his sisters that Mary and Hester were there to take them to Beckwith Manor. While they waited for the girls to join them, Mary told Charles about the musical consort that "Sir Robert" had planned and asked whether he thought his mother would think it too frivolous an evening for Frances and him to attend.

His look turned wistful. "I am sure we both would like to come. Mama is not opposed to music. There is no tenet in the Catholic faith that labels it sinful. I shall have to ask her about Frances, but—" and here he appeared to make a great decision—"I shall be happy to accept for myself.

"But—" he looked between them—"would it not be more proper to wait for an invitation from Sir Robert? He might not wish to include us."

Hester had to remind herself not to speak too assuredly on "Sir Robert's" behalf, but thought she could say, "As Sir Robert's role will be to hire the musicians, and Sir Ralph is the actual host, I believe it safe to say that an invitation to your family will be forthcoming."

The pleasure this brought to Charles's face nearly made up for her ill-timed display with Mr. Foxcroft. There was not much in this young man's life at the moment to bring him joy. She wondered how well he remembered the father he was expected to mourn. Surely he must grieve for a father's absence, but considering how few years he had lived at home beyond his infancy, they could not have spent much time in each other's company.

A thought occurred to Hester then that sent a shiver down her spine. If Charles had arrived on the York stage just a day earlier, he surely would have been considered a suspect in his father's murder.

Frances joined them and reported that Margaret was not feeling well enough to leave home. Though she tried to say this convincingly, Hester and Mary both suspected that the girl had not enjoyed her only visit to Beckwith Manor and that Clarissa was to blame. It was a mortifying reflection, but it could not be helped. Poor Mary would always have to bear the taint of her disagreeable mother and siblings.

Charles accompanied them home and would have parted from them at the door, except that a servant informed them that both Sir Ralph and "Sir Robert" were inside. Pleading the need to speak to Sir Ralph on a matter of business, Charles followed them into the house. They found Argos lying disconsolately in the hall. Pamela, "Sir Robert," Sir Ralph, and even Dudley were seated in the Great Parlour, talking over the preparations for the consort, Pamela contentedly petting the spaniel in her lap.

Mary had barely completed her curtsy before she crossed the room to whisper something in Sir Ralph's ear. He stooped to listen with an air of amusement, then raising his head, said teasingly to Charles, "Ah, Fenwick, dear boy . . . seeing you has just put me in mind of something I should like to ask. Sir Robert and I are planning an evening of music, and of course, we would like your sister Frances and you—and your mother, of course, if she would—to attend."

Charles flushed and stammered his acceptance. While he was explaining the need to consult his mother's wishes with regard to Frances, Pamela looked daggers at Mary, whose behaviour, Hester had to admit, had been more that of a hoyden than of a member of polite society. Mary was obviously too accustomed to Sir Ralph's indulgence and had used it to gain advantage over her sister-in-law. No real harm had been done, but Hester would have to teach her not to employ such wiles in future unless she wished to be labeled a flirt.

After more details concerning the evening had been discussed, leaving only the engagement of the musicians to fix, Sir Ralph stood up to go. Charles asked for a few minutes of his time, and the two walked out together.

St. Mars remained. He told them about the difficulty he had had in obtaining news of any estate for sale. He enumerated the villages he had covered in his search and asked whether there were others they could suggest.

Dudley talked about the neighbourhood east of Easingwold and what he knew of the landowners. "Beyond that, of course, you will run into Carlisle's estates—Castle Howard. I doubt you will find anything in that direction."

St. Mars pretended to ponder this information before turning to address Hester. "Did I hear you say that you came from somewhere near here, Mrs. Kean?"

"Yes, my father was the curate of All Saints at Hawnby. It is about seven miles northwest of Helmsley."

"Do you think I might have any luck near Hawnby?"

Dudley loudly cleared his throat. "Most of that area is part of the Cavendish estate, on the edge of the moors. Don't know that you'll find much suitable."

Hester answered, as if he had not interrupted, "I do not know what land may have become available since I left there two years ago."

St. Mars gave a thoughtful nod. "Perhaps it would be worthwhile to take a ride in that direction. Would you be willing to be my guide?"

"I should love to see my old home," Hester said eagerly. "I had a friend there, a lady who taught me to speak French. She is a Huguenot who married a Yorkshireman."

"I'll tell you something better!" A thought had occurred to Dudley. "That area is not far from Bilsdale and Duncombe Park. After Buckingham died, Sir Thomas's uncle bought the Helmsley Castle estate, but Forster, Buckingham's whip, still manages the duke's pack of hounds. He invites the local gentlemen to hunt with them. It's the most splendid entertainment! You will not find anything else like it in the whole of England!"

Hester's heart sank. The notion of visiting her old village with St. Mars had filled her with a sudden yearning. Without ever having considered the possibility before, now she felt a strong desire for him to see where she had been raised, not just for the beauty of the moors, but to see for himself the modesty of her upbringing. If he saw how poor it had been in comparison to his, his feelings for her might diminish, but that would be better for them both to discover before their relationship progressed. If they did, she would know in time to save herself from the worst consequences. If they did not, the remoteness and poverty of Hawnby would tell him more about her than she could ever convey.

She could not object to Dudley's suggestion without alerting everyone to their intimacy, but St. Mars handled the problem for her.

With a disarming grin, he told Dudley, "Too late, I'm afraid. If you had mentioned that before, I might have agreed to it—it does sound splendid—but now that I've asked Mrs. Kean to be my guide, it would not be very chivalrous of me to back out. Besides, there will be plenty of occasions for me to meet Forster once I have my own estate nearby. So, the sooner I find one, the sooner I can take part in a hunt."

This made good sense, even to Dudley. His disappointment was keen, but he said, "Very well. But if you do not need me to show you round Duncombe Park, I hope you will excuse me from making the journey with you. I had rather stay and attend to business here."

St. Mars gracefully accepted this excuse, knowing perfectly well how insincere it was. He was obliged, however, to ask Pamela if she would like to accompany them. While Pamela was hesitating over her answer, Dudley, now bored, excused himself, saying he needed to check on a mare that was due to foal. He invited "Sir Robert" to join him in the stable when he was through with the ladies' business and took himself from the room.

"When do you intend to go?" Pamela asked, giving a few strokes to the spaniel's head. The journey would take them all day, and except for the opportunity to flirt with "Sir Robert," it did not offer any promise of entertainment.

St. Mars turned to Hester with a brow raised in query.

She said, "If it suits you, we could go tomorrow." Pamela had made an appointment with a milliner from York and Hester hoped her interest in clothes would take precedence over any desire to be with them.

Indeed, Pamela was perfectly willing to excuse herself on the grounds of a prior engagement; however, she recalled, "You will not wish to be alone with Sir Robert, Hester, so you had better take Mary with you."

Mary, who had taken no part in the discussion, was sunk in a reverie and emerged from it with a start on hearing the sound of her name. "Take me where?" she asked.

When Hester explained the need for her company, she seemed reluctant to go until Hester suggested that perhaps Frances or Charles would care to go with them. "The heather should be in bloom. I doubt that Charles has ever been up on the moors, or if he has, perhaps he has forgotten." Turning to St. Mars, she said, "If you would not mind, we could return by way of Byland Abbey. It is possible the ruins might interest them." The old stone walls would provide St. Mars and her a few moments of privacy, too.

Her suggestion completely altered Mary's attitude towards the journey. Springing out of her chair, she said she would try to catch Charles before he left so they would not have to send a servant after him with the invitation.

Hester had not thought to ask Pamela's permission to invite the Fenwicks, and her expression revealed her displeasure. The dog in her lap sat up and cocked his head at his mistress.

"You should not indulge her, Hester. You will spoil her. And what my mama-in-law will say when she hears how much time Mary has spent with those papists, I do not know."

St. Mars glanced curiously at her. "I thought your father was their greatest friend."

Pamela drew herself up, and, losing his comfortable seat, the spaniel jumped onto the floor. "What Sir Ralph chooses to do with his patronage has nothing to do with me. He is not the one who has to answer to Mrs. Mayfield if one of her children develops papist notions."

"No," Hester agreed, "but neither should you have to answer for their religious education. If their mother chooses to leave them in Dudley's care, it is his duty, not yours. You must not let her hold you responsible."

When Pamela did not looked appeased, she added, "If any harm should come from Mary's friendship with the Fenwicks, you can tell my aunt that it was all my fault. But Mary will be leaving for London soon, and when she gets there, her days will be so full, she will hardly have a moment to think of them." Hester said this to make peace with Pamela, but she hoped that Mary would never be so puffed up as to forget a friend she had made before she entered London society.

The mention of London, however, reminded Pamela of all the pleasures she had been denied. She turned to St. Mars and said, half-jokingly, "Tell me, Sir Robert. What do you think of the splendid notion I have had? I've a mind to get an appointment in waiting to the Princess of Wales. Do you think I should enjoy life at Court?"

St. Mars glanced at Hester before responding. He must have read her encouragement, for he said, "It is possible. Serving at Court is not an easy thing, though. You would have to be willing to stand for hours on end."

"And her Highness is a great walker," Hester added. "Some of her ladies complain that she makes them walk with her from St. James's to Kensington. She believes that the exercise is good for one's health."

Pamela waved this away. "I am a great walker myself. And standing cannot be as strenuous as riding to hunt all day. Are those the only difficulties you foresee?"

St. Mars smiled. "If neither of those prospects daunts you, I can only say that a lady with your qualities would surely be a success."

Having placated his hostess, he rose to go, asking Hester to name the hour he should call for her and Mary. After they had agreed on an early start, he bowed to both ladies, and sauntered from the room.

Pamela watched him go with something akin to suspicion on her face. When Hester asked her what was wrong, Pamela said, "I do not know, but my father said he is not so sure we should trust Sir Robert."

"Sir Ralph said that? Why?"

"He said we only have Sir Robert's word for it that Lord Hawkhurst recommended him to us. He said I should write to his lordship again and ask him to confirm Sir Robert's claim."

Suppressing her alarm, Hester said, "I was planning to write Isabella this evening. Would you like me to add a message from you?"

"No, I wish to write to her myself and see if she is willing to get a post for me."

Hester could not press the issue. Fortunately, the soonest Pamela could receive a letter in return was more than two weeks, and Isabella was such a terrible correspondent, she was unlikely to respond quickly. She was accustomed to having Hester write her letters for her.

Tomorrow she must not forget to alert St. Mars to the news that his pretence might soon be exposed.

When she remembered to raise the subject, they were riding side by side on the way to Hawnby. Despite everyone's exuberant spirits, since Hester was mounted on the pony, they were forced to ride at a sedate pace. This meant that St. Mars again had to restrain his horse. He had assured her that Penny would settle down after they had covered a few miles.

Argos loped along beside them, his tongue lolling. Mary and Charles had galloped ahead, so engrossed with each other that they had not noticed the distance increase between them and their companions. Dudley's groom had trotted ahead to keep an eye on the pair.

Hester told St. Mars that Pamela intended to write to either Isabella or Harrowby to confirm their friendship with "Sir Robert." "If she does, and they answer, you may have to disappear at a moment's notice."

He surprised her with a deep laugh. "Excellent!"

"Is it?"

"Never fear, my dear. I came armed with something that can buy me another two weeks at least. With the exchange of letters, that should give me another month as 'Sir Robert.'"

She waited for him to explain. He refused to, however, merely giving her the look of a cat who'd swallowed the cream.

"Now, why do I have the feeling that there is something you are not telling me, my lord?"

"Me? Why should you suspect me?"

She tried not to laugh in case the groom could hear. "I must beg your forgiveness, of course. How unjust of me to imagine that you might have done something outrageous!"

He pretended to consider her words fairly, before saying in a thoughtful tone, "Outrageous?" He shrugged. "Perhaps. Some might say it was illegal, but I should not agree."

Now, she was well and truly flummoxed. "Do you plan to tell me what you've done?"

Penny chose that moment to shy at a pheasant that Argos had flushed. St. Mars took the reins with both hands. "That depends on how kindly you treat me."

She laughed, but a stirring inside her raised a tremor in her voice. "I am never unkind to you, my lord."

"That, my dear, is a matter of debate. I cannot fault your loyalty, but your generosity leaves something to be desired."

Hester was finding it hard to maintain her countenance, but she would not allow him to speak of his feelings for her before he had seen the modest house that had been her home. What if he did and then regretted his words? That would be too painful to bear. Worse, what if he still expressed his desire for her, but with the intention of making her his mistress and not his wife? She would always wonder if seeing how humble her family's fortunes had been had influenced his decision.

No matter how much she loved him and how much her happiness depended on being with him, she did not think her pride would permit her to accept less than marriage. She had rather they remained friends than to debase herself. In St. Mars's world, there was little shame in being a great gentleman's mistress. As long as marriages were made to improve one's fortune, many gentlemen would turn to a mistress for love. She had no doubt that St. Mars had a great deal of affection for her, and respect as well, but even if she did not have the future of her children to consider, something very basic inside her revolted at the notion of being a man's property rather than his lawfully wedded wife, to have and to hold, for richer or poorer, in sickness and in health.

She would have to withhold any expression of affection until he knew what he wanted himself. So, suppressing a natural desire to encourage his banter, she said, "There is something else I have wanted to tell you about, my lord." She told him about the encounter with Sir Ralph's tenant in Thirsk.

"Why do you suppose he accosted Fenwick?" St. Mars allowed their former subject to drop. He had never forced his flirting on her, always accepting her hints when she wished him to stop.

She told him about her conversation with Charles and the tenant's possible motives they had discussed.

"Is it possible that Charles was lying? That he did actually know the man?"

"No." She refused to believe that Charles would lie. "Why should he?"

"I do not know, but he does have secrets. Whenever his cousin Moreland is mentioned, he becomes tight-lipped."

Without her noticing, Hester's pony had slowed. Now, he bent his head to sneak a bit of grass. She pulled on the reins and gave him a scold, while St. Mars looked on, pretending not to be amused by her poor horsemanship. After a few kicks got the pony trotting again, she asked, "Did you discover anything further about Mr. Moreland?"

"Not much," St. Mars admitted. He told her about seeing Moreland in York and following him to the house outside the walls. "The only inhabitants I saw were two ladies, wearing similar simple gowns. Not Quakerish or Puritanical, but strangely plain."

"That seems odd."

"Yes. If, as I've suspected, Moreland turns out to be a Jacobite agent, their garb would make no sense. He would be more likely to visit the houses of wealthy Jacobites who could contribute money to the cause."

"But the Fenwicks have no money, so why would he visit them?"

"Perhaps the only thing they had to offer was a cover for his activities in the area. The innkeeper said that Moreland has often stopped in Coxwold, and that the Fenwick family is not the only one he visits. I did not see him, but apparently he returned to Coxwold from York, then departed again immediately. If he is truly gone, we may never know the real nature of his relationship with the Fenwicks."

"It is plain that Charles feels freer to do as he likes when Mr. Moreland is gone. I am not so certain about his sisters."

"Even if Fenwick's mother accepts her son as the new head of the family, it is likely he will leave the raising of the girls to her. I gather she did not wish for Frances to go with us today?"

"I suppose not. Charles mumbled her excuse. But they may just have thought it would tax their horse too much to carry two riders all day."

St. Mars nodded, but his mind was clearly occupied with something else. After a short while he said, "I visited the Reverend Mr. Ward yesterday morning. I wanted to find out what I could about the King's Commissioner."

Hester looked a question at him.

"As we were talking, he expressed such animosity against papists that a thought did occur to me, which may have a connection with the tenant who accosted Charles."

"Oh?"

"I have the impression that Mr. Ward often preaches about the evils of popery. I would hesitate to suggest that he could have murdered Fenwick, but what if his preaching led someone else to do it?"

"Do you mean that a person who was overwrought, like the man we saw, might have taken it into his head to kill a papist? But why should his anger fall on Mr. Fenwick and not Sir Ralph, if it was Sir Ralph who turned him out of his home?"

"That is my point. If all he heard in church was a condemnation of papists, might his unhinged mind not seize on the notion that papists were to blame for his misfortune? Remember that the Great Fire in London was blamed on papists when there was no foundation for the accusation. The city even erected a monument blaming them."

Hester was shocked. "I do not like the notion, but there is nothing I can argue against it. The man did not seem to be mad at first. It was only when the footman tried to free Charles from his grasp that he became frantic. His last words did sound something like a threat, but when he first approached, he had removed his hat and looked anxious rather than violent."

"Perhaps I should find him and discover why he did it?"

"It would greatly ease my concern, but I do not even know the man's name."

"Sir Ralph can give it to you. See if you can get it, and let me know. I would like to find the fellow before he disappears like Moreland. Too many questions have been raised about the Fenwicks with too few answers to suit me. Something strange is going on here, and that man's behaviour just adds another facet to it."

Hester agreed. She had noticed, however, that Mary and Charles were now so far ahead as to be lost from view. Mentioning this to St. Mars, she added, "We should try to catch them, I suppose."

"If you can get that pony to gallop, I will be at your service."

Hester said ruefully, "It is not the pony's fault. Very well, I shall try not to fall off." She tapped her whip on the beast's rump and urged him into a gallop.

St. Mars called from behind her. "If you do, never fear, for I shall catch you."

He was neither obliged to catch her nor to pick her up off the ground. In a few minutes, they caught up with Mary and Charles, who had slowed their pace. Hester apologized for keeping them waiting, explaining to Charles what a miserable horsewoman she was, but he assured her that he was in no hurry.

"I should not say this," he confessed, "but it is a relief to be away from Oulston Hall. My mother and my sisters are so oppressed by grief that at times the atmosphere is intolerable." He stammered, "I do not mean that I do not feel the loss of my father, but for them, who were so close to him, it is worse."

Hester assured him she understood. "It must be very difficult to deal with their grief when at the same time you must shoulder your father's duties. If it is any help, with the passage of time their sadness will ease and your lives will become more normal. You have many years of absence to make up for, but over time you will grow more comfortable."

St. Mars brought Penny into step with Charles's horse, distracting him by asking about the progress he had made getting to know his tenants. Hester made certain from then on that she rode beside Mary instead of St. Mars. It would be irresponsible of her to let Mary spend a whole day exclusively in Charles's company, and more dangerous still for Mary or Charles to discover on what familiar terms she was with St. Mars.

They reached Hawnby by mid-morning. When Hawnby Hill came into view, Dudley's groom pointed it out, and Hester's nervousness increased. By now, surely St. Mars would have noticed the remoteness of the village. Most of England was rural, of course, but there was a wildness to her country that he would not have seen in Kent. Here, there were no prosperous yeomen of the kind he was used to. The soil was too poor and the terrain too ragged to support much more than sheep. The only great estate was Arden Hall, home of the Tancred family, and though it was handsome, surrounded by woods, and enlarged by a new south wing, it could not compare with the grandeur of houses built where the soil was more fertile. They would not pass it today in any case. Hester suppressed the vanity that prompted her to alter their route to see it.

Before they reached the beck, she called out to the groom that she would lead the party from there. With Argos bounding in great leaps through the grass, she led them west along the Rye through meadows where sheep were grazing. A row of hills sloped steeply upwards to their left, while to the right trees grew thickly along the river bank. When she spotted a well-trod path into the wood, she followed it to a narrow place in the river which was easy to ford. Argos plunged in and stood in water up to his chest to lap noisily. Hester urged her pony into the beck and let it pick its way across the small stream, then guided her companions through more trees on the opposite bank.

They emerged into a sheltered clearing occupied by a small Norman church, built of sandstone and limestone and roofed in slate. Yellow flowers grew scattered amongst the modest headstones in the yard.

Hester had no sooner brought her pony to a halt outside the south door than St. Mars pulled up at her side.

"This was your father's church?" The only inflection she heard in his voice was curiosity.

"Yes, All Saints is the church for a large parish—in reach if not number of souls. The area is sparsely inhabited, so this church must serve several villages."

The groom leapt off his horse and came forward to help her dismount, but St. Mars waved him away. "See to Mrs. Mary," he said, lowering himself from the saddle. He dropped his reins then came round and reached up to take Hester by the waist.

As her feet reached the ground, his hands lingered a bit longer than was proper. With the pretence of being virtual strangers to maintain, she did not dare meet his gaze, but the intimacy set her pulse to racing. Then Argos came beside them and shook the water out of his coat, showering them both with cold drops. Hester laughed, while St. Mars reproved him for being a hopeless reprobate.

Hester was so distracted, she failed to notice that Charles had remained on his horse until she heard Mary ask, "Charles? Are you not coming in?"

Hester turned her head to see Charles seated atop his horse a short distance away, regarding them in confusion. When he felt all their eyes on him, he asked, "Why have we stopped here?"

She realized he must never have been told that her father was a clergyman. He would simply have been informed that they were visiting her former home.

"This is the church where my father was the incumbent for many years," she explained. "I wished to see it again before riding into the village." When he did not look appeased, she added, "We shall not be stopping long. As you can see, it is quite small. You are welcome to come in with us, but if you prefer, you can wait for us here."

Looking unsettled, as if uncertain what his course of action should be, Charles indicated that he would remain with the horses. St. Mars commanded Argos to stay, and the dog plopped down in the grass beside a headstone to rest in the shade.

Mary hesitated a moment, frowning, before following Hester and St. Mars through the door. "Why won't he come in with us?" she asked, as they paused just inside to peer around.

Hester did not respond immediately. She was too overwhelmed by a surge of emotions. It felt strange to return to a place where she had spent so many years of her life. She could only be struck by how small and modest the nave appeared to her now, after less than two years at Court. The entire building might fit into the private chapel at Rotherham Abbey, but the comparison only began with size. The Rotherham Abbey chapel had been decorated in the richest style with soaring ceilings, marble pillars, gold leaf, flourishes and cherubs for ornaments. It proclaimed the owner's wealth as much as this little church attested to the poverty of the parish. All Saints was beautiful in its own way, but to an eye accustomed to such rich ornamentation, its Norman foundation and the simple additions over the centuries must seem very plain indeed.

St. Mars said nothing as he made his way past the pews to the chancel, so Hester turned to answer Mary. "I suppose that, after being educated by Roman priests, Charles feels uncomfortable in an Anglican church. He may not even know whether his priest would approve of his being here."

"But that is absurd!" Mary's words echoed in the small space, so she lowered her voice. "His father must have attended many services in Coxwold."

"Yes, but not voluntarily. Only because the law required it. Do not forget that both this church and the one in Coxwold were wrested from the Roman church. If he feels any resentment on that score, one can hardly blame him."

Mary herumphed. "That was ages ago."

"Yes, but as long as members of his faith are made to suffer for it, we cannot expect them to forget as easily as we do."

Leaving Mary to digest this, Hester turned to look for St. Mars. He had moved along to the chancel, leaving her to respond to Mary's affront. It would have seemed very odd for a stranger to show interest in the girl's concerns, so his discretion had been prudent. Now, she would see what his expression revealed when faced with the modesty of her father's parish.

As soon as Hester turned his way, however, he smiled and beckoned her by pointing to the two humble monuments—the first a tablet with a bust in an oval medallion and shield, the second another shield containing a clock face, a rose bush, a lady, and a baby in a cradle—both from early in the last century. "I assume the presentation belongs to the Tancred family," he said, as she approached.

"Actually, it does not. The manor of Hawnby has changed hands any number of times, but most recently was acquired by Lord Berkeley of Stratton in Cornwall. Lord Berkeley presented my father for the living, and I believe the patronage still rests in his hands."

"Did Lord Berkeley know your father?"

She laughed. "No. I believe his lordship's only requirement for the post was a willingness to take the oaths. When he applied to the

Archbishop of York for a recommendation, my father's name was put forward. As you may imagine, this parish was not actively sought by the more ambitious clergymen in York, but it was as much as my father could hope for."

"Why?"

She grimaced. "My father and Archbishop Sharp were at Cambridge together. Let us just say that they never got along."

His face betrayed a desire to know more, so after peering over her shoulder to make sure Mary could not hear her, she added, "I know what your opinion of my Aunt Mayfield must be, and I cannot blame you for it. Indeed—" she winced when she laughed— "I share it. But you must not think that my father shared many of her qualities. He was a learned man, and her ignorance appalled him. But he was not always as tactful or as forbearing as he should have been. In that, they were very much alike. My father often let resentment overcome his better nature, and once a slight was felt, he was unlikely to forget it."

"So his differences with the bishop were personal, not political?"

"I believe so. He did not discuss them with me, of course, but I believe they shared the same theological positions. Both supported the Act of Exclusion. My father was much more tolerant of Protestant Dissenters than he was of papists, but he did his best to bring the Dissenters in his parish back into the fold. And he was kinder to the papists than the Reverend Mr. Ward seems to be. He understood their history; he simply believed them misguided."

St. Mars smiled. "He does not sound like the implacable person you described."

"Oh, he was much more forgiving in the abstract than he was in his personal relations. There he could be as implacable as you like."

"Not with you, I hope?"

"No, but I never gave him cause to be disappointed. My brother Jeremy, though . . . ." She shook her head, knowing there was no need to elaborate.

St. Mars started to ask, "And your mother . . . " but just then Mary joined them. Again, any question about her mother would be too intimate for a stranger to ask, so instead, he said, "I am glad that you brought us here, Mrs. Kean. With all the grandeur and embellishment one sees in the new London churches, it is a pleasure to find one whose history has been so well preserved."

His words pleased her. Not only the words, but the way in which he had said them. There was no trace of condescension in his voice, when there very well could have been. A bit of the anxiety she had felt all morning lightened her shoulders.

She led her companions back outside where St. Mars assisted her to mount. Argos hoisted himself up and came over to whip St. Mars's legs with his tail, as relieved to see him as if his master had been lost.

Perhaps in penance for his refusal to enter the church, Charles insisted on helping Mary into the saddle. She was eager to forgive him, but Charles still was reserved as they rode along a path through the trees and onto a lane, Argos loping at their side.

The village of Hawnby was a quarter of a mile up the hill. As they rode to the top, a cluster of grey stone cottages came into view. Passing one, their horses disturbed a flock of geese, which flapped their wings and squawked, announcing to every one within hearing the presence of strangers.

A party of five arriving in such a small village naturally attracted a great deal of attention. Faces appeared at open doorways, but their startled expressions turned to joy as soon as they recognized Hester among the riders. A concerted flow of goodwives, old men, and a few small children—those who would not be out working in the fields— spilled out of their houses to greet her. The sea of familiar faces warmed her as she was helped to the ground. With the bobbing of curtsies and the doffing of hats, her father's former parishioners circled her, respectfully bombarding her with questions about the length of her visit, her life at Court, and whether or not she was married yet.

She was quick to deny the last, but the question raised an uncomfortable heat in her cheeks. Searching for the source of her embarrassment, the good citizens of Hawnby looked curiously at the two gentlemen accompanying her. Charles was a bit disconcerted by the unexpected attention, but after determining that he was likely too young to be engaged to Hester, they turned to stare at St. Mars.

Looking down at them, his face revealed a rare hint of self-doubt, as if he were anxious to merit their approval. It must be unsettling to find that a group of poor cottagers might not consider him worthy of a woman who had so recently lived among them, but putting on a brave front, he smiled back.

He stayed mounted with Charles and Mary until Hester had a chance to answer all the cottagers' questions. She waited until they appeared satisfied, before reaching out to greet the particular friend she was so happy to see. Mrs. Bows, looking well for her forty years, clasped her hands warmly, bringing tears to Hester's eyes.

A small village like Hawnby had offered little society for a young lady of Hester's rank. After the death of her mother and her brother Jeremy's departure for parts unknown, she had had no companion but her father. Though never much of one, in the last few years of his life, bitterness and a sense of ill-use had made him silent and morose. If not for Mrs. Bows, Hester would have felt entirely alone, but, even with the differences of culture and language between them, they had formed a true friendship based on a mutual need and an eagerness to learn. The kindness and warmth Mrs. Bows had shown Hester had been her greatest comfort.

Now, Mrs. Bows asked in her French-accented English whether Hester and her friends would honour her by taking refreshments in her house. Her right to host them was gracefully conceded by the other villagers for she was a person of some consequence in the village. Hester accepted for the whole party, so her companions dismounted to be presented to their hostess, who acknowledged them with a curtsy before leading them to the door of her house. St. Mars again commanded Argos to wait outside before bowing his head to avoid the low door lintel.

Mrs. Bows ushered them into the neat parlour, still furnished as Hester remembered, with a loom for making lace as well as enough stools for them all to be seated. While Hester explained to her friends that Mrs. Bows was the woman who had taught her French, their hostess produced dishes and a jug, which proved to contain cider. St. Mars took an appreciative sip from his dish before expressing surprise to be offered cider this far north. The cider was delicious on such a warm day and reminded Hester of the first time she had been treated with it in the same house. When they had all had a taste and St. Mars had complimented Mrs. Bows on the excellence of the brew, she replied that she had made it herself.

"We are fortunate that my husband can obtain apples when he travels on Lord Berkeley's affairs."

Hester told them that Mr. Bows was steward for the manor of Hawnby, which explained the respect with which his wife was treated by the other villagers. Even Mary knew that most villagers in Yorkshire would never have met a Frenchwoman, and indeed, would have considered her so foreign as to be suspicious at best and possibly evil.

Charles, who had spent his recent years in France, exerted himself to inquire in her language what had brought her to such an isolated place.

Her pleasure upon hearing her native tongue lit her face. After exclamations of delight on his proficiency, she explained that her family had been forced to leave France when the Edict of Nantes, which had given Protestants the right to worship freely for nearly a hundred years, was revoked by Louis XIV. "I was a child of ten at the time, *monsieur,* and it was a very frightening experience. We had to come away with scarcely any of our possessions. We settled near London and laboured hard to survive, but I was happy there to meet my husband, who brought me to Hawnby to live." She laughed. "If I had known how far it was and how cold, I might never have accepted his proposal, but he is a good man, and we have built a comfortable life here together. I do not seriously complain."

As she told her story, the young man seated next to Hester stiffened. Until that moment, she had not given a thought as to how Charles would react to Mrs. Bows. Fortunately, his manners were too polite to betray his dismay in learning that she was one of the Protestants who had been expelled from France. He must have been raised to consider them the worst sort of heretics.

Then Mrs. Bows asked him where he had learned to speak French like a native, not suspecting that as a Roman Catholic, he had been illegally educated in France.

He answered merely that he had studied French at school. Then he changed the subject to ask about her loom.

"I learned from my mother to make lace, and I make it here for the ladies at Arden House as well as for the market in Helmsley. There are not so many French lacemakers here in Yorkshire, so I find my work is more in demand than I can supply."

He congratulated her before subsiding into silence. Hester was quick to take up the conversation, inquiring after the health of her husband and others in the village she had not seen. She was afraid that Charles's discomfort could become obvious and wished to avoid any unpleasantness for her dear friend.

To maintain the pretence that he had come on their excursion to see if any land in the area was for sale, St. Mars asked Mrs. Bows if she knew of any estates nearby that might be available for purchase. She was taken aback, but after a few seconds' thought, confidently replied that the only landowners within reach of Hawnby were the Tancreds at Arden Hall and Lord Berkeley of Stratton, neither of whom had any reason to sell.

To Hester's annoyance, Charles kept fidgetting in his chair. There was so much that Hester would have told her friend—so many questions she would have asked—but little that would be appropriate in the presence of an audience. She wished she could have a day here at least, but their letters would have to suffice. As soon as the conversation languished, she explained that they must start back soon, but said she supposed they should first pay a visit to the new incumbent of the parish. She was relieved, then, to hear that he had ridden to York and was not expected back for a fortnight, freeing them from the obligation.

When Mrs. Bows informed her of the rector's absence, Charles loudly released a pent-up breath.

To cover it, Hester said quickly, "In that case, before we leave the neighbourhood, I should like to take a ride upon the moor. My companions have been very patient with my sentiment, but they deserve a treat, and there is nothing quite like the view from Hawnby Hill."

Hester and her friend took leave of each other with an embrace and tears in their eyes. Hester promised to visit, should she ever come into Yorkshire again.

As the party returned to their horses, nothing was said concerning the matters that had made Charles so uncomfortable. Even Mary preserved a silence. Mounted again, and with Argos trotting alongside, they followed Dudley's groom towards a steep, treeless hill that, while not especially high, was distinguished by a sharp, rounded peak. On their way, as they passed back through the village, Hester, who lagged behind with St. Mars, stopped outside a dwelling, larger than the rest, which recalled her deepest memories. When St. Mars pulled up beside her, she gestured to the house. "That is the parsonage, where I lived most of my life."

It had been a happy place for her as long as her mother had been alive. Hester remembered a tender woman with a soft touch and a gentle voice without whose presence the house had grown dark and cold. The suddenness of her mother's death from a fever had robbed them of her modulating influence. Mourning her deeply, the Reverend Mr. Kean had ignored the needs of his children and buried himself in his studies. It had not taken long for the anger caused by his grief to taint his relationship with Jeremy, who, not the scholar his father had expected, was bound to be a disappointment. The house had echoed with their discord, and it had fallen to Hester to try to keep the peace.

All these memories passed quickly through Hester's mind, before she turned to witness St. Mars's reaction to the humble house in front of them. If he was dismayed by the modesty of her origins, surely there would be some evidence in his countenance now—a retreat into his thoughts, a condescending smile, a curtain drawn over his gaze. She searched for signs of disenchantment, but he merely stared back with a curious look in his eyes, as if waiting for her to pose the question he saw on her face.

Then, with the ghost of a smile, he turned to face the house and, as if to examine it more closely, leaned forward and propped an elbow on the pommel of his saddle. His eyes moved slowly over the grey stone, the heavy lintels over the small windows, and the slate roof. Finally, shaking his head regretfully, he took up his reins again. "I am certain it was much more impressive when you were in residence."

Hester blurted out a laugh, releasing the tension that had tied her in knots. She tried to give him a scolding look, but felt too relieved and amused to manage better than a pout. He looked as if would have liked to kiss the pout from her lips, but a glance ahead discovered that the others were not so far ahead that one might not look back and see. With smiles on both their faces, they turned their horses and together hurried to catch up with their friends.

At the Place where the Carriage stopt, there stood an ancient Temple, esteemed to be the largest in the whole Kingdom; which having been polluted some Years before by an unnatural Murder, was, according to the Zeal of those People, looked upon as Prophane . . .

CHAPTER XIII

As they walked their horses up Hawnby Hill, they came to the final rise, which was so steep that Gideon had to peer at the ground in front of him to guide Penny up the uneven ground. Mrs. Kean's pony was sure-footed and used to the moors. It plodded straight up the slope without a misstep. Argos gamely trailed the pony, but Gideon did not take his eyes off the path until they reached the top and could bring their horses to a halt.

When he did raise his head, he saw Mrs. Kean gazing over the distance, smiling, and drinking in the view. Beneath their horses' hooves, the moor was a rolling sea of purple, stark in its beauty. In the distance, as far as the eye could see below them, light green fields and darker green woods were laid out in patches, outlined by ancient stone walls and hedgerows. To the east, another hill, longer and flatter than this, also boasted a vast purple crown of heather. Vistas like this were not to be seen in his own country of Kent. Here, the sky dominated the scene. It was easy to see why Mrs. Kean seemed buoyed by the sight, but as much as Gideon admired the scenery, he could imagine how bleak these heights must be in winter, when there was nothing to block the winds sweeping down from Scotland.

The look of contentment on Mrs. Kean's face as her eyes combed the moors might have unsettled him had he not recalled one of the first things she had said to him. She had stated that she did not miss the cold of the North. Nevertheless, it was obvious that the sight of the moors gratified her in some deeper way. If it were ever in his power, he would see that she visited the country of her birth whenever she wished. Her reluctance to part from Mrs. Bows had been palpable. Clearly their friendship had been of great importance to Mrs. Kean.

The troubled looks she had given him all morning had at last begun to make sense. She had behaved like a hostess concerned that her guest would not find the furnishings of her house sufficiently grand. This made Gideon think of Sir Ralph, who had no such concerns, but was convinced that whatever he had purchased must be the very best that money could buy. Mrs. Kean had no such pretensions, but still her manner this morning indicated that she had dreaded his reaction to the place.

Long ago, he had reached the conclusion that her father's living must have been a modest one, but aside from the evidence of her remarkable education, there was nothing astonishing in that. Gideon had always known that Mrs. Kean was poor. It explained her dependency on her cousins. One glance at the village, too, would have removed any expectation—should he have had one—of discovering a large rectory there. Nevertheless, she seemed, if not ashamed, at least to expect him to be disappointed by the modesty of her house, as if it should make any difference in the way he felt. He hoped he had reassured her, and that he would never see that doubt in her eyes again.

The groom soon reminded them that they had miles to cover before reaching Byland Abbey. He asked if they would rather take their refreshment here, but with one accord, they agreed to press on.

With the exception of Argos, who cheerfully bounded ahead, they were all more cautious upon descending, but soon found themselves back on the lanes and cattle trails that would take them south. Ever conscious of propriety, Mrs. Kean rode ahead with Mary, and Gideon fell behind with Charles. The younger man was more reserved than usual and did not respond to Gideon's attempts at conversation. Finally, as if compelled, he blurted out, "Do you know why Mrs. Kean invited me to accompany you today?"

Gideon was taken aback until he recalled that Charles considered him no greater an acquaintance of hers than he was himself. He must have thought he could ask "Sir Robert" for his opinion without causing offence.

"I believe it was Mrs. Mary's idea to include you."

When the younger man said nothing, Gideon divined the reason for his frown and offered, "She would not have known that Mrs. Kean planned to visit a Huguenot. None of us did. Not that it would have occurred to me, or perhaps to either of the ladies, that you would be made uneasy by the visit. It was natural that Mrs. Kean would wish to visit the places and friends of her youth."

Charles's frown cleared, and he stammered, "I am sorry if I have given offence. I am simply not used to being much in the company of Protestants. I could only imagine what my mother might say if she heard about our visits to the church and Mrs. Bows."

"Then, I suggest you say nothing of them to her."

Charles looked shocked. "I cannot lie to my mother, Sir Robert! I should have to do penance if I did."

Gideon laughed. "I did not advise you to lie, but could you not just say that we took refreshment in the house of one of Mrs. Kean's friends? If she asks, you can tell her that Mrs. Bows's husband works for Lord Berkeley of Stratton. You do not have to mention that she is an immigrant from France. Her name, after all, is Bows, so it will not give you away.

"If you like, you can tell her that you refused to enter the church at Hawnby. Either that will please her, or she will tell you what she thinks you should have done instead."

His teasing brought a slight flush to Charles's cheeks, but the young man looked relieved. "Yes, I shall do as you say."

Gideon left him with one last thought. "Remember, too, that unlike you, your mother has spent most her life surrounded by Anglicans and Dissenters of all kinds. I doubt that she will be shocked by your meeting a few Protestants."

Charles gave a sheepish nod, but still looked troubled. He seemed content to accompany Gideon rather than seek Mary's society.

More than an hour later, they sighted the abbey ruins in a valley just south of a chalk hill. Untilled fields gave way to small enclosures and rich bottom land before a ruined stone gate appeared in front of them. They rode beneath its damaged arch—nearly all that remained of what must have been a long stone wall—and emerged to see the former abbey church directly ahead. Grass and trees had taken root amongst its stones, creating an uneven blanket of foliage, in places so deep as to bury any sign of a structure.

From this aspect, the high walls of the church seemed to be largely intact, missing only the roof and the clerestory, but as they drew closer, they saw that nothing remained of the southern end of the abbey save room after room of foundation stones.

When Mary first saw the ruins, she gasped in amazement, but the young man riding at Gideon's side uttered a horrified, *"Mon Dieu!"* Neither of the younger members of their party had ever seen an abbey ruin, but the significance of what they now saw made a vastly different impression on each. Mary's tone was full of wonder, while Charles was plainly appalled.

Beauty still haunted the church in the stones that had not been taken to be used in the construction of other buildings. In the presbytery, a row of columns were joined by ornate arches. The one wall that remained intact graced the south transept with a row of pointed windows in its clerestory, revealing how grand the church once had been. Farthest from them, the west front, still with the tracery of a great rose window, dominated the view.

They had brought their horses to a halt while they took in the sight. Now the groom broke the silence by asking where they would like him to unload the food he had brought from Beckwith Manor.

"I believe we should take our refreshment before we explore," Mrs. Kean said. "I assume that everyone is famished?"

Mary quickly agreed. Then she turned to see if Charles seconded her opinion, but the young man's jaw was tightly clenched.

"Charles?" Mary's voice was unusually timid. "Mr. Fenwick?

"I had heard of this." His tone was a blend of outrage and sadness. "But I never imagined . . . . "

Mrs. Kean heard him and her face became shrouded in dismay. "I am so sorry, Charles. I would never have brought you here if I had known the sight would distress you. Should we go?"

When he did not respond, but continued staring moodily at the ruins, Gideon said, "Whatever occurred here, it was long ago, and Mrs. Kean is not to blame. She has nothing for which to apologize."

Startled by the irritation in his voice, Charles came to himself. When he began to stammer an apology, Gideon cut through it, saying more kindly, "Come, let us stop and eat. Nothing should ever be de-cided or discussed on an empty stomach." He dismounted and, by the time the two ladies had been helped down, Charles had joined them.

The groom found a portion of the cloister wall that was table height and covered it with a cloth. He set out bread, cheese and meat pies for Mrs. Kean to slice, as well as fruit from Sir Ralph's orchard, berries from the kitchen garden and beer in bottles from Dudley's brew house. While Argos, exhausted by the journey, found a grassy bed on which to nap, the rest of their party found smooth places on the low stone walls where they could perch. While she ate, Mary cast anxious glances at Charles, but did not dare to address him. Gideon thought he detected a hint of tears in the girl's eyes. If a member of Mary's fam-ily had sulked, she would likely have called him to account, but she was not so confident with Charles.

No one said much, since under the circumstances to speak about the buildings around them seemed tactless. Mrs. Kean tried to make trivial conversation, and Gideon helped her, but with the two young people in their party maintaining an offended silence, their efforts fell like lead weights in a pond.

Charles still looked sullen, but not even a sense of offence could rob him of the appetite stirred up by their long ride. He managed to down twice as much even as Gideon. Mrs. Kean waited until his stomach seemed to be satisfied before asking Mary if she would like to explore the ruins with her. The girl was obviously eager to distance herself from Charles's ill humour. Mrs. Kean hesitated as if weighing how successful she was likely to be if she tried to coax him out of it. Gideon doubted that any attempt to discuss the Reformation with him would do the trick, or that any of them were sufficiently equipped to explain that torturous period of history. Whatever strategy she had considered, she abandoned and, standing up, dusted off her skirt.

As the two ladies prepared to leave on their walk, she gave Gideon a pleading look, begging him to have a word with Charles. He answered her request with a twist of his lip, promising himself to challenge her on her cowardice as soon as he could get her alone.

Unaccustomed to having the role of confidant thrust upon him, he began, "Would you like to have a look round?"

Charles answered resentfully, "No. But, please do not let me detain you if you would prefer to join the ladies."

"I will, of course, if you had rather sulk alone."

Charles's head shot up, and his lips bunched in anger. "Do you expect me to rejoice at the sight of what has been done to my religion?"

"Of course not, but neither should you abuse Mrs. Kean, or Mary, for something that happened two hundred years ago."

Charles stammered, "I—I did not mean to abuse them." A flush of shame crept over his features.

Gideon knew that his reproof had been too harsh, but his irritation was due to disappointment. Once again someone had robbed him of an opportunity to spend time with Mrs. Kean. With Charles along to entertain Mary, he had counted on stealing a few moments alone with her. The abbey ruins had seemed a likely place in which to enjoy their first real embrace.

He reminded himself that Charles had been subjected to an exceptional degree of distress. To return home after several years only to learn that his father had been murdered would make anyone mistrustful. Then, with no tutoring or preparation, to be obliged to assume the responsibility for his mother and sisters would have daunted a greater man, even if his estate were not so financially encumbered.

Repressing his frustration, Gideon softened his tone. "I know it was not your intention to be rude. That's why I am giving you the hint. It was Mary who invited you, one assumes, for the pleasure of your company, and Mrs. Kean was willing to include you in the party. But even a stranger like me can see that this journey was a pilgrimage for her. She apparently fears she may never have another chance to visit her former home. And, considering what a friend she has been to you and your family, it would be unkind to spoil this one for her by demonstrating your outrage over something for which she was not responsible, no matter how just your anger may be."

Charles had listened to him with head bowed. Now, his head shot up eagerly. "You do believe it was unjust?"

Gideon threw up a hand. "I do not mean to start a religious debate. The only thing I will concede is that the dissolution of our monasteries was no more just than the French king's expulsion of the Huguenots. A great deal of injustice has been done in the name of faith, and the English are tired of it. If they were not, I doubt King George could have defeated the Pretender's men"

When Charles looked as if he would have liked to argue, Gideon added, "Even your own father, I assume, was unwilling to wage war to restore a Roman Catholic to the monarchy?"

The younger man started and turned pale. "Why do you say that? Are you suggesting that my father was a traitor?"

Gideon smiled and shook his head, "Did I not just say the opposite? The point I meant to make is that, after so many years, even with all the brutality perpetrated on both sides, isn't it better that you and Mary can be friends than that you should be at each other's throats?"

A reluctant grin was slow in coming. Charles was still not satisfied.

"I know that life is not easy for you here, and your friends are sorry for that. But since none of us caused the destruction of this place and none of our objections will bring it back, can we not enjoy the beauty that remains?"

Charles stared straight ahead. In a moment, after giving a sigh, he nodded. Together they stood and went in search of the ladies.

By the time they remounted to head for home, Charles had overcome his resentment enough to join "Sir Robert" in pointing out the various rooms of the abbey, whose foundations were still visible. Mary eagerly soaked up his words, relieved by his return to good humour. Everyone did his best to act as if the incident had never occurred. Still, when Charles was not attending, Mary cast him anxious looks, as if afraid to say anything that might offend him.

It was evident that the intimacy that had been growing between them had suffered a reverse. Mary would never be able to understand the importance the Roman Church had in Charles's life. It governed everything, from his family's straitened circumstances to the rights he had as an Englishman.

It had not been Mrs. Kean's intention to demonstrate this matter to them. If, however, Mary had not considered the differences between their religions before, she would certainly be aware of them now.

It was a rather dispirited group that made its way to Beckwith Manor. By the time the village of Cotswold appeared in the distance, even Argos was dragging. Charles rode with them as far as the lane that led to Oulston Hall, where he announced that he would leave them. Though he thanked Hester politely for including him in the excursion, his grave demeanour told her that he still was reflecting upon his experiences that day. He took leave of the others with scarcely more than a nod, leading Mary—as soon as he was out of earshot—to mutter a sound between indignation and disgust before giving her horse a kick and galloping to the stables.

With the groom still riding behind them, Hester could do nothing to express her dismay except shake her head at St. Mars. She was sorry that Mary was disappointed in Charles, but reflected it might be better for the girl to understand that the barrier between them was real. She had watched the intimacy between them grow and had not been overly concerned, but perhaps Pamela had been right to caution her. In truth, it would never do for Mary to fall in love with Charles Fenwick. Raised in a household in which religion was practiced as a legal obligation rather than a matter of faith, she was likely to find the Fenwicks' devotion to the Roman Church impossible to fathom. More tolerant than her brother and sister, Mary had defended Charles and his family. She would be hurt to discover that their tolerance might not equal her own. Hester doubted that Charles's mother would be prepared to overlook the difference in their faiths. Nor, likely, would Charles.

St. Mars's sympathetic smile did much to assuage her feelings. As they followed Mary at a more sedate pace, he walked Penny by her pony and thanked her with great propriety for allowing him to accompany her to Hawnby.

For the groom's benefit, she answered him as formally, "It is a shame you were unable to find any land to purchase. I had feared it might be difficult. If you did see anything that tempted you, however, I suggest you apply directly to Lord Berkeley. Since I'm sure he has never cast eyes on the manor, he might be willing to sell it."

St. Mars gave her a considering look. "Thank you for that idea, Mrs. Kean. If circumstances permit, I shall take it under advisement."

She felt a sudden stab of alarm. She could not tell if he was teasing her. St. Mars had a habit of presenting her with outrageous gifts, but surely even he would not purchase a whole manor with the object of pleasing her? This was a worry she could not voice, however, not even were the groom riding too far away to hear. If St. Mars was not serious about buying the manor, she must not put the notion into his head.

It was only good manners for Hester to invite "Sir Robert" in for refreshment before he took himself to the inn, and on his part to pay his respects to Dudley or Pamela, if either was at home. After they handed their reins to the groom, a servant from the house came out to inform them that Sir Ralph was in the small parlour with the mistress and wished to see them.

St. Mars gave Hester a mildly questioning look before following her indoors and through the hall, where he instructed Argos to stay. At the door to the parlour, they paused at the sight of Pamela and Sir Ralph, standing shoulder to shoulder, their expressions grim, as if about to confront them with dire news.

After one glance at their faces, Hester abandoned any conventional greeting to ask if anything were the matter.

With his lips compressed into a formidable line, and a spark of triumph in his eyes, Sir Ralph held out the letter in his hand, and said, "Yes, Mrs. Kean, I am afraid there is. It seems that Sir Robert was not referred to Pamela and her husband, as he claimed. Lord Hawkhurst writes that he has no knowledge of anyone by the name of Sir Robert Mavors."

At these words, Hester's heart leapt into her throat. She had been afraid this would happen, but not so soon. Her greatest fear was that Pamela had sent a physical description of St. Mars to Harrowby, in which case, Harrowby might have recognized his cousin. But as no constable was in evidence, at least, it appeared that St. Mars was not about to be arrested.

What confused her, however, was how quickly Pamela's letter had been answered. Harrowby must have sent a private messenger with his response.

St. Mars did not betray the least concern. He merely looked disappointed. "He claims never to have met me?"

"Yes." Sir Ralph shoved the letter into his hands. "See for yourself. I must insist that you account for your presence here, sir!"

St. Mars took the letter with a look of confusion. He took his time reading it and, when he had finished, sighed. "This is typical of all your great men." He shook his head with regret. "No matter how friendly they are in their cups, they rarely trouble themselves to remember the men with whom they have caroused."

He tsked. Hester nearly broke into a nervous giggle.

"I feared this could happen, of course," he confessed. "After years of mixing with the best society, I have learned that it is best not to place too much confidence in the memories of peers. Which is why," he added, reaching deep into his pocket, "I made certain to ask him for a letter of introduction."

He opened the leather case he had extracted and took out a folded piece of parchment, which he handed to Sir Ralph. Peering closely at it, Hester saw that it bore the Hawkhurst seal.

She could hardly restrain a gasp—not of relief, but in amazement at his audacity. How had he come by Harrowby's signet ring? Or had he ordered another one struck for himself? If the latter, it must have been nearly impossible to find a goldsmith who would make it. If the former . . . then he had been up to a mischief he had not told her about.

She recalled the hints he had given just that morning when he had teased her. No wonder he had seemed so sure of himself. Not even Sir Ralph could deny the evidence of that seal.

As he stared at it, a flush spread up his cheeks. Pamela, peering over his shoulder, bit her lip and looked guiltily up at St. Mars. "Papa?" she said, prompting him to break the seal.

He perused the letter for only a few seconds before clearing his throat. "Yes, it is as Sir Robert says." He did not meet St. Mars's eye when he added, "You must forgive me, Sir Robert, for the error."

"Not at all, sir!" St. Mars responded with great magnanimity. "It was only natural that you should wish to be certain of a stranger."

Hester was torn between a desire to laugh—it was clear he relished the role of injured party—and shame for the trick they had to play on Sir Ralph, who had been hospitable to them both. Upon hearing Sir Ralph's next remarks, however, her sense of shame waned.

"There's a good fellow. Well, we shall forget all about it. You do not blame me for writing to Lord Hawkhurst to inquire about you? I must take care of my family, you know. And as much as I enjoy good company, a man cannot be too careful about the people he admits to his house."

"Especially after a murder has been committed? Is that what you were thinking, sir?" St. Mars asked.

Sir Ralph looked blankly at him. "Yes . . . yes, of course! One cannot be too careful after a frightful incident like that. But you must not think I wished to accuse you of the crime, dear sir. Nothing could be further from my intention."

St. Mars begged him not to give the matter another thought. This request was sincere, Hester had no doubt, for if either Pamela or Sir Ralph chose to write of it to Harrowby again, St. Mars's possession of the signet ring would give him away. No matter how it had come into his hands, Hester had no doubt that Harrowby would send constables along with his next message as soon as he learned of it.

St. Mars knew this, too, for he added, "I do hope you will not mention his lordship's error to him. These great men do not like to have their faults brought to their attention, you know. They prefer to believe themselves infallible and resent having it proved that they are not—so much so, indeed, that they are likely to blame the one who enlightens them."

Both Pamela and Sir Ralph looked dismayed to think that Lord Hawkhurst could blame them for the lapse in his memory. They shook their heads and disclaimed any intention of calling the error to his attention.

"We shall put this behind us." Sir Ralph clapped his hands and rubbed them together. "Now, I'll wager you are ready for some refreshment. Pamela no doubt has a glass of something for us, eh, girl?"

Apparently, Pamela did not find it as easy to put the incident behind them, for she hesitated over a response. She had been humiliated by her father's unwarranted interference, which might have cost her the admiration of a courtier, perhaps even one who could influence her chance of winning a place at Court. Hester imagined that she could not decide whether to resent her father for this or "Sir Robert" whose forgiveness she could not entirely believe. Only time would tell if he truly bore them no grudge. Meanwhile, she did not wish to assume a position of obligation to him when his forgiveness might not be sincere.

All this Hester could read upon her features, whether Pamela were aware of her sentiments or not. St. Mars must have caught an inkling of her dilemma, too, for he spared her the necessity of prolonging an uncomfortable meeting.

With true kindness in his expression and addressing her in particular, he said, "If you will excuse me, I must return to the inn. On our journey, my horse developed a slight limp, and I would like my groom to take a look at it immediately." He made Pamela a deep bow, and when she extended her hand involuntarily, he took it and kissed it. "If you will permit, however, I shall call upon you tomorrow to discuss the plans for our musical evening."

A smile of relief brightened her features. "That would be excellent. I shall look forward to seeing you then."

He nodded before turning to Hester and bestowing the same courtesies on her with the addition of a wink, which the others could not see. He took his leave of Sir Ralph, who insisted on walking out with him to talk about the upcoming race meeting in York.

As soon as they were out of hearing, Pamela heaved an enormous sigh. "I shall never forgive Papa for embarrassing me so!"

"I'm sure his intentions were good. He may have worried that Sir Robert was becoming too intimate with your family when we could not truly know who he was."

"But he has always welcomed visitors! I do not know why he should think that this particular one might be an impostor."

"As I said, perhaps because Sir Robert has become such an integral part of our plans? Or, as Sir Robert surmised, your father was unsettled by the murder of Mr. Fenwick, and whether or not he suspected Sir Robert, felt somehow that he should be more vigilant?"

Pamela shook her head as if to clear it. "Perhaps it was for one of those reasons, but I wish he had not done it. How I am to face Sir Robert alone tomorrow, I cannot imagine."

The information that she meant to receive "Sir Robert" alone told Hester that Pamela was already overcoming her chagrin. Clearly, she did not wish to share his attention. Hester could not be surprised, for Pamela must have been jealous of her for spending the whole day in his company.

She decided it would be prudent to avoid any suspicion that a closer relationship had developed between them. "If I were you, I should simply not mention it, and Sir Robert will take the hint from you. If the children's nurse does not mind, I shall use the morning to take the younger ones for a walk into the village. It is long past time I kept my promise to them."

Pamela was delighted with her proposal. "I know they will enjoy it, but you need not give them too much of your time. Clarissa will put up a fuss, but I shall tell Mary to remain in the schoolroom with her."

"Yes—but where is Mary?" With all the to-do about "Sir Robert," Hester had forgotten that the girl had left them in an agitated state.

"I did not see her come in. She must have gone straight to her bedchamber to change. I hope she behaved herself well today."

"Yes, very well indeed. You would have been proud of her." Hester was not about to betray Mary's disappointment to Pamela. The painful feelings Mary had experienced would eventually sort themselves out. Fortunately, it was not long before they would be going to London, and the excitement of appearing at Court should drive thoughts of Charles from her head.

Then it occurred to Hester to wonder whether she herself would be returning to Court. St. Mars had followed her here on more than just a whim. She sensed he meant to declare himself. Even her vast inexperience could not keep her from knowing this. She could feel his impatience in spite of the role he played. He wished to see her alone, and now that he knew the truth about her past, her humble rank, she would no longer hold him off. The notion that at any moment he could offer her a proposition that would seal her future, be it as his wife in France or as his mistress—which might make her refuse him and commit herself forever to being a servant to her cousins—sent a wave of excitement through her. Her excitement was tempered by anxiety, but she could not seriously bring herself to doubt his goodwill.

This was not an issue that could be solved today, though, and the last thing she wanted was for Pamela to notice her distraction, so she left her to go in search of Mary.

Hester found her in their shared bedchamber. Mary had enclosed herself within the bed curtains. Hester did not disturb her at first, but set about refreshing herself at the wash-table. The maid had filled the jug with water, and it was still cool enough to feel good on her face and neck. She removed her gown and laid it across a chest to be brushed. Then, in her shift and stays, she finished washing before donning a gown more suitable for the evening.

By the time she had finished bathing, sounds of movement were issuing from the bed. Mary parted the curtains and a pinched, reddened face peered out.

"Shall I call the maid to ask for fresh water?" Hester asked her gently.

Mary's bottom lip began to quiver. "Not just yet." She swung her legs around to sit on the edge of the bed.

Since it had likely been the sympathy in her tone that had provoked Mary to tears, Hester waited until the girl broached the subject herself. She brushed her hair into a semblance of order, taking her time and letting the commonplace motion bring its own kind of comfort.

"Hester, do you think Charles would ever convert from the Roman Church?"

"No." Hester set down her brush and turned to find Mary looking pensive, but resigned. "I doubt very much that he would. He has been deeply instructed in his parents' religion, and even if his beliefs underwent a change, I suspect he would consider it a betrayal to abandon it. In any case, I should not like to ask it of him."

Mary shook her head. "And I would not wish to become as bitter as Mrs. Fenwick."

"No, poor woman, she has every reason to be bitter. Life has not been gentle to her."

Nothing more was said. Hester was relieved that Mary had the good sense to look into the future, should she ever consider converting for Charles's sake. If she had truly been in love or even deeply infatuated, she might have ignored his family's circumstances, but clearly she was not. Her feelings had merely been hurt.

"Shall I call for the maid now?"

Mary nodded and slid down from the bed.

Changing the subject, Hester said, "I do not like to be the bearer of bad news, but I must warn you that Pamela intends to ask you to entertain Clarissa tomorrow morning while I take the younger children for a walk."

Mary groaned. Under the circumstances, it was a reasonable reaction, so Hester felt safe to laugh. "I promise to keep the excursion short, and if it will help, I'll ask Cook to make her some cakes. You can mete them out to her if she manages to be good."

*T*he People so highly resented this Law, that our Histories tell us, there have been six Rebellions raised on that Account; wherein one Emperor lost his Life and another his Crown.

CHAPTER XIV

As expected, the children's nurse was delighted to have them taken off her hands. She had them dressed in their walking clothes, their hair combed, and ready to accompany Hester a quarter of an hour before the appointed time. Clarissa had been told that she must obey Mary if she wished to receive any of the seed or plum cakes Cook had miraculously produced. Though the girl still sulked, she had not enjoyed her walk with Hester so much as to prefer another like it to the promised cakes, so Hester was able to take the children away with a minimum of fuss.

The four younger Mayfields had enough vigour to make nothing of the walk of two miles to the village, even Anne, the youngest. The only real chore for Hester was keeping the three boys from harassing their sister, who was obviously the usual object of their teasing. Fortunately, the girl had a great deal of spirit. Hester was relieved to see that Anne was unlikely to be injured by her brothers, but she could not help fearing that the girl would turn out to be as foul-spirited as her mother.

They reached the village within the hour, despite all the stops along the way to pick up interesting things to throw. Anne clung to Hester's hand and peppered her with odd questions, not one of which contained any curiosity about her mother. She seemed to have little memory of either her mother or Isabella. Dudley and Pamela were the gods in her miniature world, with Clarissa and Mary just behind.

Fortunately, the distance they covered curbed some of the children's liveliness. They were willing to stand quietly to watch the blacksmith at work, and he was good enough to fashion them each a toy from an old horseshoe. Hester had come prepared with her purse and thanked him with a shilling. Then she took them to the inn and treated them to a pudding, washed down with small beer. Hester told them to keep the pudding a secret, as their nurse might disapprove of the indulgence, but as small beer was the drink they always took with breakfast, she would not object to that. The experience of eating at the inn was the real treat, since they rarely left the boundaries of the manor.

Their excitement was so palpable that Hester took pleasure in the smiles on their faces and the improvement in their manners as the morning progressed. She was almost as sorry as the children when the hour came to go home, but with the walk still ahead of them, she worried they would tire and become cross. So, she settled the bill and herded them outdoors.

As they walked along the unpaved road that passed through the village, an unkempt figure on the opposite side caught Hester's eye. The man was moving in their direction, quickly and furtively, shoulders hunched and head down. As he came nearer, Hester recognized him as the man who had accosted Charles at the inn at Thirsk. The worn condition of his clothes and thinner face were signs that his situation had not improved.

Her first instinct was to gather the children close, but the sight of his pitiable state quelled her impulse. He showed no sign of wishing to approach them. She doubted he recognized her as having been a member of Charles's party. She might have walked past him without attracting his notice, but she could not escape the feeling that there was something unjust about his plight. A niggling voice told her that he even might be able to shed light on Mr. Fenwick's murder, since he seemed convinced that Charles should be able to help him.

Grasping hold of the younger children's hands, she led them across the road. When the man paused in his tracks, surprised to find his way blocked by a lady with four children in tow, she said, "Forgive me, but are you not the man who spoke to Charles Fenwick in Thirsk?"

His wariness changed to eagerness. In broad Yorkshire, he asked if she knew "t' young maister" and if she could arrange a meeting with him.

"It is possible," she said, "but I would need to know your name and why you wish to speak to him."

He removed his felt hat and introduced himself. "John Ableson, mistress." His voice trembled and his eyes filled with tears. "Tell 'em Ah's fair brokken. Tell 'em 'is fatther nivver would o' turned us aht o' us yam."

Hester had opened her mouth to ask why he would refer to Charles's father, when, glancing past her, he gave a violent start.

With a sudden "Ey up!" he turned abruptly, colliding with a carrier who was unloading a waggon by the side of the road. Crying, "Gerr aht o' mi gate!" he pushed the man aside and hurried away.

Hester looked over her shoulder to see who had startled him and found Sir Ralph bearing down on them with a forbidding frown.

Reaching her and the children, he asked, "Did that scoundrel have the impudence to accost you?" His voice was gruff with concern. He stopped and watched as Mr. Abelson scurried round the side of a cottage and disappeared from view.

"No, it was I who stopped him," she admitted ruefully. "I did not wish to get him into trouble. I merely wondered why he had approached Charles Fenwick."

"What did he say?" Sir Ralph was red with outrage.

"Not much." She resisted the urge to apologize. "He just said something about how he had been turned out of his home."

Sir Ralph reached into his pocket for a handkerchief and wiped the perspiration from his face. "Yes." He sighed. "As I told you, I did turn him out. But he was not a good tenant, and yields being as poor as they've been, I've had to convert more of my land to grass. It's too bad, I suppose, but I must consider my own requirements first. He could just as well rent a farm on another estate."

"Yes, I see." It was not the first time Hester had heard a landowner speak of this necessity. The soil hereabouts was not the best for crops.

"But I still do not know why he should have appealed to Charles."

"Did he? Has he spoken to him?" Sir Ralph's look was intense.

"Not that I am aware. When he came up to us in Thirsk, Charles was so taken aback that I don't think he understood a word the man said. Mr. Ableson was behaving so strangely, too, that Charles just wished to get away, but if he knew of the man's condition, perhaps he would not object to taking on more help."

Sir Ralph grunted, but the anger seemed to have left him. "I doubt he would wish for Ableson's labour. The man is a sluggard and not to be trusted. That is why I had to turn him out. If I were you, I should not burden the boy with this. Fenwick has enough problems without taking on a man like Ableson."

"Yes, you are perfectly right. I shan't even mention the matter to him."

"There's a good girl. Now," he said, beaming down at the children, "shall I give you a lift home? My carriage is waiting just here at the inn."

As he gestured to it, the children clamoured for a ride. Hester would have declined, but it was evident they were growing tired. A ride in Sir Ralph's elegant coach would add a final lustre to their day.

They crossed the road, where Sir Ralph, with a festive air, gave them each a turn at sitting astride one of his carriage horses. He handed them up and down himself, laughing as he did. Hester had to admit that he knew just how to entertain children and clearly relished the activity as much as he did entertaining adults.

Soon she called an end to their merriment, reminding them that they must hurry home to their nurse, who would be expecting them. The ride was accomplished in a quarter of the time it would have taken them to walk, prompting her to thank Sir Ralph for sparing them the foot journey at the end of a long morning.

"Not at all," he assured her, handing her down. "It was provident that I saw you when I did." As he helped the children to alight, he lowered his voice and said, "You know, Mrs. Kean, I have done more thinking on it, and I do believe I shall mention this episode with Ableson to young Fenwick. Not that I think he should take him on, but to alert him in case Ableson manages to get hold of him again."

"You believe he should be warned?"

He nodded grimly. "He cannot be too careful, especially not after that business with his father."

She started. "You do not think Mr. Ableson had anything to do with that, do you?"

He smiled at her in a fatherly way. "Now, now, my dear. I did not mean to alarm you. But as I said, it pays to be prudent. Just you let me take care of this. After all, Ableson was my tenant."

Hester conceded this with a nod and, thanking him again, made her goodbye. As she followed the children into the house, however, she wondered again why Mr. Ableson had wished to speak to Charles Fenwick and had made that particular mention of Charles's father. Why would he approach Charles, a man he had never met, instead of another landowner in the region? He must have known Charles's father rather well to state that he never would have turned him out of his house. But the poor man was clearly desperate. He looked hungry, and a hungry man might say something that made no sense.

Evidently, Pamela had spent a pleasant morning, for she greeted Hester with a face wreathed in smiles. She could talk of nothing but the musical evening she and "Sir Robert" were planning. Her suspicions of him had flown with the renewal of his attentions. Far from discouraging her from seeking a place at Court—since it was his fortune that would most likely be used to pay for it—he had urged her to apply to Harrowby as soon as he returned to Hawkhurst House at the end of summer.

Hester wondered if this meant St. Mars had given up any hope of regaining his title. If that were the case, it could matter little to him if Harrowby went through his fortune by supporting every member of Isabella's family. On the other hand, perhaps he believed that Sir Ralph would be the one to fund his daughter's ambitions.

Pamela was so absorbed by "Sir Robert's" visit that she did not think to inquire about Hester's morning until they were seated together at dinner. They were eating alone, since Dudley had ridden to the market in Helmsley, and Mary had taken her meal in the nursery. This had given Pamela the liberty to speak of nothing else but the consort, but eventually even she ran out of words to express her delight with the prospect.

After asking Hester how her walk with the children had gone, she added, "I hope they behaved themselves and did not tire you?" It was clear from her tone that she expected a negative response.

"They were perfectly behaved. I quite enjoyed myself."

Pamela's eyes widened with incredulity, but she only said, "Well, I am very glad to hear it, even if you are merely being polite. I cannot think that their nursemaid has much influence over them."

"How much does Dudley concern himself with the children?"

Pamela snorted. "Dudley? Not at all. Oh, he is willing to mount them and teach them to ride, but as to their education, he leaves it entirely to me."

"What sort of instruction are they receiving?"

Taken aback, Pamela paused with her fork halfway to her mouth. "Why . . . I . . . ." After a moment's hesitation, she said, "I expect their nursemaid to instruct them in obedience and piety."

Hester placed her fork on her plate and gave Pamela a serious look. "She is hardly able to dress and feed them. I see no evidence they are being instructed." When Pamela pressed her lips into a resentful line, Hester reached out and touched her hand. "I do not mean to criticize. I just wished to know whether my aunt had provided you with any assistance, but it appears that she has not. It is not in her nature to take an interest in her children until they are of an age to marry. The trouble with that, of course, is that they will not be very marriageable if they have not received even basic instruction. The boys will have to enter a profession. Anne might be provided with a dowry, but she must learn to stitch a hem, at least.

"Would you like me to persuade my aunt to engage the Reverend Mr. Ward to tutor the boys? I cannot promise I'll succeed, but if Isabella agrees, together we might manage to get Lord Hawkhurst to pay for their instruction. Then you will only have to concern yourself with the girls, and if I can, I will see if Clarissa can be sent to a school."

Pamela inclined her head in agreement, but her posture was stiff. She had taken Hester's words as a reproof, when Hester had not intended them as such. It had simply seemed to her an opportune moment to discuss the children's situation, which bordered on neglect. This was not Pamela's fault, but her lack of interest in Dudley's siblings made it almost certain that they would be raised to be even more ignorant than Dudley, without the benefit of the land he had inherited. It was Mrs. Mayfield's duty, not Pamela's, to provide for her children, but unless Hester's aunt were prodded, she would not lift a finger to do so. The only thing Hester had wanted from Pamela was permission to approach her with their needs.

"I suppose one of us should speak to Mr. Ward to see what lessons he would be willing to undertake? Then I could give my aunt the details when I get home."

"You do it, for I may not know what to ask."

Ignoring the defensiveness in Pamela's reply, Hester agreed to speak to Mr. Ward. Then, believing it was time to change the subject, she told her about meeting her father in the village. "He came up just as I was speaking with that man who accosted Charles Fenwick in Thirsk."

Pamela looked at her in surprise. "Why should you have spoken to him?"

"I was curious. Did it not seem odd to you that he approached Charles, of all people?"

"No, I cannot say that it did. He was the only gentleman with us. He would hardly have spoken to a lady."

Hester mused for a moment. "I had not considered that, I confess. But again, today, it was Charles with whom he wished to speak. He seems to think that Charles can resolve his problems."

"Well, I fail to see how," Pamela huffed, "when he was a tenant of my father's."

"Yes, so Sir Ralph told me. He said that I should not concern myself with Mr. Ableson's welfare."

"Ableson? Is that his name?"

Hester stared at her, perplexed. "Yes, were you not in the habit of visiting your father's tenants?"

Again Pamela was offended. "Of course, I visited them. I considered it my duty. I simply did not recall the man's name. If Papa says he was his tenant, then he was."

Hester decided the subject was best dropped, but she found it even odder that Pamela would not recall a tenant's name. Since she had offended Pamela once already, however, it would be wiser to inquire elsewhere about Mr. Ableson.

She brought the conversation back to the musical evening "Sir Robert" had arranged, and in this way worked herself back into Pamela's good graces.

She did not have an early opportunity to relate the episode in Coxwold to St. Mars, for during their next few meetings, Pamela jealously guarded his attention to herself. On Sunday, he managed to sit beside Hester at Morning Prayer, but with Pamela on his other side and awake to his every movement, they could not exchange any words in private. It was difficult for Hester to focus on the service, for from the moment their eyes had met at the church door, her blood had thrummed like the strings of a harp. She did not dare look him in the face again.

When the service was over, Pamela took possession of his arm to walk outside. Hester followed with Mary. Mr. Ward greeted them just outside the porch with his usual pleasure in their attendance.

It did not take long for the church to empty, so Hester decided to take advantage of the opportunity to discover whether, provided her aunt approved, he would be willing to tutor Dudley's brothers. Telling Mary to go on without her, Hester waited for the last parishioner to be greeted before approaching Mr. Ward with her proposition. Knowing how eager the clergy usually were to augment their income, she was not surprised when he agreed. They arranged that he should write to her aunt to propose a course of study for the two oldest boys to prepare them for the church or the law and to name the remuneration he would require.

Before they parted, she thought to ask if he had known a parishioner by the name of Ableson.

A frown clouded his features. "No, Mr. Ableson and his family were never parishioners of this church. Why do you ask?"

"But you do know the name?"

"Certainly I know it. Ableson lived in a cottage on Sir Ralph's estate, but he did not attend this church."

"Was that not unusual for one of Sir Ralph's tenants?"

He pursed his lips. "Yes, unusual, but Ableson and his wife are papists. I am afraid I was never able to bring them back to the Church."

"Papists? Really? Are many of Sir Ralph's tenants papists?"

He replied in an irritable manner, "Only a few. The ones who live nearest to Mr. Fenwick's estate. I imagine that Fenwick subverted them, but they are as resistant to the truth as any who were born into the Roman Church."

"How odd!" Hester exclaimed, thinking at the same time that it was more likely that Ableson and the others had always been papists than that Mr. Fenwick had converted them. Mr. Ward was so new to the parish that he could not know everyone's history.

"My dear young lady," he said, "it is far more serious than odd! Their immortal souls have been placed in peril by submitting to idolatry. I cannot imagine why they chose such an ill-considered path, but this is the result of having papists in the parish. They are always on the lookout for weaker minds who can be persuaded to join them.

"But why did you wish to know about Ableson?" Mr. Ward asked again.

Hester saw that she would not be allowed to escape if she did not satisfy his curiosity. "I have wondered about him because he approached Mr. Charles Fenwick for assistance, and Mr. Fenwick had no idea who he was. But perhaps he believed that a fellow Roman Catholic would be more sympathetic to his plight."

"Undoubtedly." Disapproval hardened Mr. Ward's expression. "But I should advise you to have nothing more to do with him. If he truly needed help, he could come to me and the parish would assist him, but I fear his soul is too corrupted to consider the prudent course."

Hester had no desire to debate his opinion on charity, so she thanked him for the information and hurried to catch up with her family. She wondered if Sir Ralph had rented a cottage to Mr. Ableson and the others knowing full well that they were papists. If he had, it would be a further example of his forbearance. She could not believe Mr. Ward's assertion that Mr. Fenwick had converted them. It would be a strange thing, indeed, for any landowner to interfere in the spiritual life of another landowner's tenants.

Mr. Ward had spoken earlier of the way papists would take in orphans and abandoned children to raise them in the Roman Church. As far as Hester was concerned, this was a generous form of charity. If they were willing to take on the burden of raising a child, they certainly should have the right to determine in which religion the child should be instructed. But visiting another man's tenants in order to lure them into a different church was an activity she had never heard of anyone doing.

If Mr. Ward's suppositions were correct, of course, it could have given someone a motive for killing Mr. Fenwick, even Sir Ralph; but she was strongly inclined to believe that Mr. Ward had spoken out of resentment rather than reason. He had revealed his own intolerance for Roman Catholics often enough. It would not be surprising if it led him to flights of fancy.

℘

After a few days of paying court to Pamela, Gideon felt that he had done enough to overcome her suspicions. He desperately wanted to see Mrs. Kean alone, but had not been able to speak privately with her even long enough to whisper an hour or a place to meet. When his attention was not demanded by Pamela, his time was filled by Dudley or Sir Ralph, who was being even more hospitable than before to make up for accusing "Sir Robert" of fraud. They took Gideon coursing for hares, which gave Argos a chance to demonstrate his keen sight. With the hounds from Sir Ralph's kennel, they also hunted for fox.

At another time and with different company, Gideon would have enjoyed the freedom and the sport, but these diversions were only a means of measuring time until he could be alone with Mrs. Kean.

Fortunately, the day that had been chosen for the consort was approaching. He had every intention of fighting his way to her side. With the company's focus on the musicians, they ought to be able to make an assignation. With hindsight, Gideon wished he had presented himself to Dudley's family as a close acquaintance of Mrs. Kean's so that it would not seem strange if he conversed with her more. It was too late now, but he wished he had known how difficult it would be, even here, to see her alone.

※

Since the excursion to Hawnby, Mary had been quieter than usual. Though she continued her daily rides, she took them with less enthusiasm than before.

For a few days Hester left her to lick her wounds before attempting to distract her with more preparations for her journey to London. They had made good progress on altering Isabella's clothes, but there were still linens to be made, and they could plan for the caps, gloves, and other adornments that would be better bought in London.

Once Mary was at Hawkhurst House, Mrs. Dixon, their excellent housekeeper, could teach her how to manage a household, but Hester took it upon herself to improve the girl's spelling and handwriting. Isabella's writing was so bad as to appear illiterate. There was no guarantee that Mary would marry well enough to have a servant to write for her.

Her social graces were amazingly good, based on instinct, however, not instruction. Pamela's method of instructing her was by criticism, not example. Hester tried to engage Mary in rehearsing various social situations by describing to her the drawing rooms given by the Princess of Wales and the balls at Court.

Mary turned out not to be so easily distracted. Not even the reminder that she would be leaving her brother's house, never to return, succeeded in cheering her much. Hester began to worry that Mary had formed a deeper attachment to Charles Fenwick than she had suspected, but at least Mary had stopped trying to include him in all their amusements.

A note came from Frances, informing Mary that she and Margaret would soon be returning to York to school and expressing a desire to see her again before they left. The invitation agitated Mary's spirits, but unwilling to hurt Frances's feelings, she declared her intention to go. Hester's offer to accompany her was readily accepted, so the two set out late one morning for Oulston.

They had reached the house and were handing their reins to a servant when the door flew open and Mr. Mynchon stormed out. He shouted back over his shoulder, "Superstition and idolatry! I tell you again, that's all it is!" As the door slammed behind him, he continued to rant, "Of all the foolish nonsense!" before raising his head and perceiving his audience.

Instead of being taken up short, he strode angrily towards them. "Mrs. Kean, see if you cannot talk some sense into that young gentleman! I have offered him more than that cursed piece of wood is worth, but he hangs onto the foolish delusion that it is a piece of the True Cross. I told him the same thing I told his father—that they'd been gulled by a cheat—but he is every bit as stubborn as old Fenwick was! There is just no reasoning with papists. They are stubborn, self-deluding, gullible—"

The moment he paused to take a breath, Hester interrupted. "You will have to excuse me from doing anything of the sort, Mr. Mynchon. If you were unable to persuade Mr. Fenwick to sell it, even at what you know to be a fair price, then I seriously doubt that I could manage it. He obviously considers the piece of wood to be a family treasure, an object he values more than money. It is objects of that nature that families cling to in times of sorrow. I would be the last person to wish him to part with it now."

She had tried to be courteous but firm enough to put a halt to his speech. The muscles of his face twitched with a strong desire to argue, but instead of debating the issue, he turned and stamped away in search of his mount.

Hester and Mary exchanged a round-eyed look before making their way to the door, all the more uncertain now of what kind of reception to expect. Upon Hester's knock, the door was flung open with force to reveal an angry Charles. As soon as he beheld them on the threshold, however, the red in his cheeks began to subside.

"Mary—Mrs. Kean—please come in. Forgive me. I was expecting someone else."

Entering the house, Hester responded for them both, "Yes, we saw Mr. Mynchon leaving." When neither Charles nor Mary seemed to know what next to say, she added, "Mary and I have seen his collection, which is excellent. I confess, however, that his obsession with wood is one I cannot comprehend." Seeing that her attempt at levity had failed, she added more seriously, "I hope he did not distress your mother?"

"No, but only because I refused to permit him to see her. I truly believe he would have tried to browbeat her into giving him . . . what he wanted." Charles was obviously reluctant to divulge the nature of the object.

Hester did not tell him that they already knew. "I fear you are correct. I would hate to think it, but he can be quite intense in his pursuit of exotic curiosities. I should tell you that Mrs. Mynchon particularly begged him not to bother you about it. That he did not comply with her request suggests to me that he has little control over his obsessions."

Charles nodded with a sullen expression. Then remembering his manners, he ushered them inside. As he escorted them through the barren hall, he seemed more like the friend they had known than the offended party on their excursion.

"Did you see his face?" At last, Mary found the confidence to speak. "It was so flushed, he looked quite murderous!

"N-not that I know what a murderous face should look like," she stammered, aware suddenly that her choice of words had not been fortuitous.

The harm had already been done. Charles halted. His eyes widened as if a terrible thought had occurred. "Do you think . . . ?"

"No," Hester said quickly. "Surely no one is that foolish."

"But you said yourself that his obsession makes him lose control."

"But surely not to that extent! If he attached a deeper meaning to the object, as you and your family do, that would be different, but to him it is simply a piece of exotic wood. He wants it so he can complete his collection. But surely a man of his intelligence understands the triviality of a piece of wood relative to a person's life."

The firm set of Charles's lips told her he was not convinced. "If we could depend on his reason . . . ." He trailed off, then patently distressed, said, "But let us change the subject. To what do I owe the pleasure of your visit?"

Restraining the urge to persist until she had disabused him of the notion that Mr. Mynchon might have killed his father, Hester took a deep breath and told him they had come to see Frances before she returned to school.

Though still shaken, Charles looked pleased by the attention. He offered to go in search of his sister.

"If your mother would receive me, I should like to visit her while the girls talk."

Promising to convey her message to his mother, Charles bowed and left the room, leaving Hester and Mary to sit in the downstairs parlour. While they waited, Mary looked about her at the old oak chairs and the worn upholstery and sighed. There was not so much regret on her face now as pity.

Frances was the first to join them, pleased that Mary had answered her summons. She invited Mary up to her bedchamber, telling Hester that Charles and her mother would soon be down. Hester was glad to hear that Mrs. Fenwick felt able to bestir herself enough to receive visitors downstairs. She sent the two girls off, and presently, the others did appear, Mrs. Fenwick leaning on a servant's arm.

There was no new reserve in her manner to indicate that anything Charles had reported about their trip to Hawnby had earned her disapproval. Discovering whether anything about the excursion had offended her was one of the reasons Hester had wished to see her. She was relieved to have her own suspicions confirmed. She believed the offence Charles had felt was a result of his being raised in a Roman Catholic country, not of his parents' sensitivity to living amongst adherents to the English Church, an intolerance they could ill afford. If anything, Mrs. Fenwick greeted Hester with even greater cordiality than before, grateful for the friendship she and Mary had extended to her children.

Hester expressed her delight on seeing her hostess back on her feet.

"Yes, it was time to make the effort. I cannot leave poor Charles to shoulder all the burdens of this place. They must be faced."

"I am sorry you had suffer the insolence of the King's Commissioner—Mr. Foxcroft. It must have been particularly distressing to have him here at such a time. What a horrid man he is!"

"Yes, but now that he is gone, we can be thankful that his examination is behind us."

"Is he? I am glad to hear it. I suppose I should have assumed as much if Mr. Fenwick was willing to accompany us to Hawnby." Hester complimented Charles on the way he had assumed his responsibilities. Her remarks clearly pleased his mother, who expressed her gratitude for such a devoted son.

"I hope he is beginning to feel more sure of himself as a landowner."

"I believe he is. Sir Ralph's instruction has made that somewhat easier for him."

"Sir Ralph takes a certain pride in being of help to his neighbours."

"Yes, my husband was grateful to have a close neighbour he could trust. He said once that Sir Ralph had helped him find a solution to one of our financial problems."

"Oh?" The syllable was uttered merely to express a polite interest. Hester did not truly expect Mrs. Fenwick to elaborate on the details of a private matter.

"Yes, I do not know the particulars. My husband did not believe ladies capable of comprehending business transactions, and I daresay, in my case, he was correct. I only know that Sir Ralph purchased a piece of our land when the taxes on it became too great a burden for us."

This information reminded Hester of Mr. Abelson and his problems. It provided a possible answer to the issue that had exercised her curiosity. Perhaps the land that Mr. Fenwick had sold to Sir Ralph had contained Mr. Abelson's cottage. That would explain how Sir Ralph had come to have a papist for tenant.

She was about to ask Mrs. Fenwick if she knew the man's name when Frances, Mary, and Charles entered the room, chatting as if there had never been any awkwardness between them. It was plain, however, that they must take their leave, for Frances had a great many things to accomplish before her departure for York. Charles explained that he would escort her back to school himself, but said, "I will return in time to attend the consort of music at Yearsley Park."

He said this diffidently, as if uncertain whether they still wished for him to come. Hester assured him that they were all looking forward to meeting him there, before glancing at his mother to see if he had obtained her approval.

Mrs. Fenwick's smile was reserved, but in proof that she had given her permission she said, "I have decided that no harm will come of his attending a gathering of this sort, not when I know that the company will consist only of our neighbours. But I shall write Sir Robert to ask if Mr. Moreland may attend, as well. He is coming to visit, and if he accompanies Charles, then I shall have no reason to object."

Hester felt all the strangeness of this statement, but could not ask for a clarification. She thought that Charles Fenwick demonstrated great forbearance with his mother for not trusting him enough to attend a simple consort when she trusted him with all the family's business. Had they not just talked about his great sense of responsibility and how well he was comporting himself?

When Mary reacted with a startled look and turned towards him, Charles squirmed under her gaze. He ignored the obvious question, as he should, and offered to escort the ladies to their horses. As Hester and Mary took their leave, Hester made a mental note to tell Mary that she must not reveal her thoughts so clearly, no matter how reasonable they were. Being this transparent would not serve her well at Court.

*T*he Emperor had a mind one Day to entertain me with several of the Country Shows; wherein they exceed all Nations I have known, both for Dexterity and Magnificence.

CHAPTER XV

The day of the consort arrived. Pamela ordered an early dinner, so the ladies would have sufficient time to dress. She dithered over her costume until the last possible moment and even then was not satisfied. She kept asking Hester if she was certain there was nothing outmoded about her gown, the trimmings of her cap, the placement of her patches, and even her fan, which she had bought in York. Hester could honestly assure her that she was dressed in the latest fashion and that no one who had been to Court would doubt that she had appeared there many times herself.

Though this was Mary's first real venture into society, she was far easier to reassure, not being taken as much with a concern for her appearance as with anticipation of the entertainment. A certain degree of vanity was to be expected, but Hester was pleased to see that her favourite cousin had more than just vanity inside her head. She thought Mary had never looked prettier than she did in a closed gown of pale yellow silk, embroidered with red flowers, and matching mules with pointed toes. Hester wore a pale gray mantua with a long soft collar and sleeves trimmed with white lace. A pink ribbon, knotted in a bow and worn in the cleavage between her breasts provided the only touch of colour in her costume. If her Aunt Mayfield had been present, she doubted she would have had the nerve to place the bow in such a provocative place.

Her hair, as well as Mary's, was done up modestly beneath a short lace cap. As a married lady, Pamela had opted for a longer piece of lace and had schooled her tresses in curls to her shoulders.

Naturally, the fuss over her clothes caused them to leave the house a few minutes late. They hurried into the carriage, leaving Dudley to ride his horse. Hester thought that just this once he might have ridden with them, but he stoutly refused to be batted over the lanes like a tennis-ball.

All the way to Yearsley Park, Pamela fretted that she would be too late to welcome her father's guests, but they arrived just in time to greet "Sir Robert", who came early, he said, in case he could be useful.

He looked as handsome as ever in a long fair periwig that suited his colouring so much better than the black he wore with his disguises. His matching justaucorps and vest in a satin puce hugged his lean physique. The pale stockings tied over his breeches showed off his muscular calves. Hester had to be careful not to stare, though she supposed any lady could be excused for doing so.

Pamela, who had insisted for days that she must oversee every detail of the event, had left the preparations in the hands of her father's capable servants. She did not bother to check whether her orders had been carried out, but spent the few minutes before their guests arrived, keeping "Sir Robert" tied to her side in the hall. It was Hester who went upstairs to see that enough chairs had been set out in the Great Chamber and that the musicians had arrived. She found everything in order. The oriental tea-table and the massive candlestands, supported by statues of chained black slaves, had been pushed back against the wall to make room for a few rows of chairs. The chairs faced the alcove over the porch, where the three musicians stood, tuning their instruments.

The sound of carriage wheels in the drive announced the arrival of more guests, but Hester, who was not one of the hosts, stayed upstairs where she was. In a minute, St. Mars appeared in the doorway and crossed the room to take her hurriedly by the elbow. The smile, which had broken over his face as soon as he had seen her, warmed her cheeks. She wondered whether he could see the pulse beating rapidly in her throat.

"I told Pamela that I would greet the guests up here," he explained quickly. "For the moment, at least, she is trapped downstairs, but we may have only a moment before someone comes in. When and where can I see you alone? If I have to pretend I hardly know you any longer, I may go mad."

Hester saw that he was only partly joking. The earnestness in his voice caused her tongue to freeze. For a few moments, she could not think of any place she could meet him without raising Pamela's suspicions.

St. Mars tugged at her elbow. "Please. What about here, in Sir Ralph's maze?"

"Yes." She would have to think of an excuse for going to Yearsley Park without Pamela or Mary, but she must. "But how will you contrive it? What excuse can you give?"

"Leave that to me. Just tell me when."

Tomorrow was Sunday. She did not dare miss church. And the next day, Pamela's mantua maker would be at the house from morning till night to make the final alterations to Mary's gowns. "Tuesday morning," she said. "I heard Sir Ralph make plans with Dudley to visit the sheep market that day, and I shall be free. Shall we say ten o'clock?"

His grin infected her with a similar elation. "I shall meet you inside the maze at ten o'clock on Tuesday morning."

"How shall we locate each other?"

"Oh . . . excellent thought. Just take the first two right turns again and I'll be waiting in the alcove where we last met. If the spot is not secluded enough, we can move to another, but as far as I can see, the maze is hardly visited unless Sir Ralph has guests. Now, all I have to do is make up an excuse not to accompany your cousin and Sir Ralph to the sheep market."

A pair of voices floated up from the Grand Staircase, signaling an end to their *tête-à-tête*. Hester said, "I hope that nothing serious happened to Penny on our excursion. You said she had developed a limp."

He gave her a conspiratorial look. "That was just a story I invented to avoid attending the race meeting in York. The men naturally assume I will go, but that's one place I dare not show my face . . . or Penny's."

That was all he had time to say before the guests they had heard on the stairs entered the room. Anything of an intimate nature must wait until they met on Tuesday in the maze.

Letting go of Hester's arm, St. Mars turned to welcome Mr. and Mrs. Mynchon, who had just arrived. When Mr. Mynchon caught sight of St. Mars, he looked relieved, Hester supposed, to find an intelligent person with whom to converse. Exerted by her climb up the stairs, Mrs. Mychon merely waved to Hester before dropping into a chair to catch her breath. Hester went over to speak with her, content to leave the entertaining of her irascible husband to St. Mars.

Soon, the rest appeared in twos and threes: Dudley and Mary, the Reverend Mr. Ward, his wife, and their niece, visiting from Leeds, and a couple Sir Ralph had met at the assizes in York, who had ridden over from Ripon. They would spend two nights at Yearsley Park before returning to Ripon on Monday.

The last to arrive were Charles Fenwick and Mr. Moreland. Sir Ralph welcomed them with his usual exuberant courtesy. Mr. Mynchon saw them and uttered an angry huff, before taking himself to the opposite end of the room. Pamela had not been pleased to hear that Mr. Moreland was coming, but she fulfilled her role as hostess and dutifully, if coolly, accompanied them upstairs.

Perhaps aware that he was unlikely to be welcome, Mr. Moreland exerted himself to be cordial. He behaved as if he had forgotten his anger towards Hester and Mary at the maze, and for Charles's sake, Hester determined to forget it as well. She still did not understand the hostility he always seemed to feel towards them, but supposed his grief over the loss of his friend Fenwick could have put him out of sorts.

She was not obliged to converse with him after greetings were exchanged. With all the company present, St. Mars asked Pamela if the consort might begin. With her consent, St. Mars escorted her to a chair on the front row, before turning to help the other guests to their seats. With courtly attention, he conducted Mrs. Mynchon to a chair next to Pamela's, just as her father ushered the couple from Ripon to those on her other side. A look of surprise and dismay crossed her face, before good manners compelled her to hide her disappointment. St. Mars cushioned the blow by giving her a small shrug of regret. Then he promptly located Hester and with a conspiratorial glance took a chair beside her on the back row.

Sir Ralph assumed the privilege of giving the musicians the signal to commence. They struck up with a sonata by Purcell and followed this with something Hester thought might be an adaptation of a piece by Christopher Simpson, a Yorkshire musician and, therefore, a local favourite. Their playing was much better than she had expected, but nothing approaching the orchestras she had heard in London. For this audience, however, some of whom only heard music when they chose to make it themselves, the level of entertainment was highly satisfying. Sir Ralph was particularly loud with his bravos, and even Dudley seemed to appreciate the thin sounds that only three instruments could make. After taking their first bow, the musicians played on with more by Purcell, Matthew Locke and others that Hester did not recognize.

Throughout their playing, St. Mars quietly inched his chair closer to hers until the two were touching. He did not speak, and no one noticed his manoeuvre. Only Hester was aware of the heat that scorched her body when their shoulders touched. She could not reprove him for fear of attracting notice. Her only recourse was to hide the fire that burned inside her. She thought of the private meeting they had planned for Tuesday and a fearsome excitement stirred her blood.

She could have no doubt as to his intentions for the tryst. From the moment she had seen him sitting in Dudley's parlour, she had known that he had come into Yorkshire for her, not simply to stem his boredom, but to arrive at a more intimate understanding.

She still wondered whether St. Mars knew his own mind. Surely the loneliness in which he lived could have driven him to see her in a more amorous light than he ever would, had he not been outlawed. She wondered if he had considered this influence upon his feelings. At the same time, if she felt the perfect kinship between them, was it so unlikely that he felt it, too? She had decided that no other man would be able to take his place in her affections, no matter how deserving. Had he compared her to all the ladies in France who would happily be his wife or his mistress, or was that a challenge that might someday undermine any future they had together?

As the musicians took a final bow, she emerged from her reverie to find that she had not heard a single note of the last two pieces. St. Mars broke the contact between them to stand and applaud. His guests enthusiastically joined him. Hester stood with the rest, as Sir Ralph called out, "As fine a bit of playing as I've ever heard! I daresay there is nothing to surpass it in London."

Mr. Mynchon looked pained by such willful ignorance, but none of Sir Ralph's guests ventured to contradict him. Then Hester heard Pamela exclaim that as fine as the music had been, she was certain she would hear much greater music when she went to Court. As she said this, her gaze lit resentfully upon "Sir Robert," whom she obviously wished to slight in retaliation for his neglect.

As the words left her mouth, Sir Ralph turned towards her with a stunned look. He concealed his shock quickly by inviting his guests to take refreshment from the banquet set up in the Great Hall downstairs, after which he begged that they would make themselves comfortable in the East Hall.

St. Mars did his part to usher them out, offering his arm to Mrs. Mynchon. Hester hung back to let the older guests reach the table first. As she did, she heard Sir Ralph loudly whisper to his daughter, "What's this you say about going to Court?"

As Hester glanced back over her shoulder, Pamela answered with a toss of her head, "Have I not told you, Papa? I mean to apply to my sister Isabella for her help in finding me a place at Court."

Sir Ralph's face turned as red as an ember ready to burst into flame. He grasped his daughter roughly by the elbow and barely had enough grace to contain himself until Hester followed the guests out of the room.

She paused just outside the door, concerned over what Sir Ralph's objections to the scheme would be. If he worried that Pamela would expect him to pay for Madame Schulenberg's influence with the King, she wondered what Pamela would say. It was not at all certain that

Harrowby would fund her ambitions.

The musicians were still in the Great Chamber, packing away their music and their instruments, but Sir Ralph ignored them as he raised his voice in outrage. "What kind of foolishness is this? Who gave you leave to consider such a harebrained scheme?"

Pamela was startled by his reaction. Hester could hear it in her tone. "Leave? Why should I need anyone's leave? Am I not a married lady now and free to make my own decisions?"

"Yes, by God you are married! And the only job you have is to produce an heir for your husband! How do you expect to do that if you are in London and your husband is here?"

Pamela made an attempt at defiance. "Dudley already has an heir—three, in fact. He's made it abundantly clear that he has no use for me."

"And what about me? Who will be my heir, eh? Do you imagine I want to leave all this to one of old Mayfield's brats? I must have an heir of my own blood. You will give me a grandson and a few more for safe measure.

"Who planted this infamous notion in your head, anyway, eh?"

Hester cringed inwardly as Pamela told him that, though the notion had been hers, both Sir Robert and Hester had encouraged it. "They agree that I shall be a great success at Court, and who knows, but what you and even Dudley may profit from it."

"Profit from it? When you know very well that neither your husband nor I have any desire to become courtiers? I swear I shall have both their heads for this!"

"Papa, we really must join our guests, or they will think our absence odd. We can talk this over later."

"No, you will think no more on it, and that's final! Get yourself home and lure that wastrel husband of yours into your bed. If he is too lazy to do his duty, then I shall have a word with him myself."

The sound of his angry tread as he approached the door alerted Hester that she had better not be discovered listening to their conversation. She hurried down the stop few stairs. Then realizing that she would not be able to escape notice in time, she turned and slowly took a step upwards, as if returning from below.

It was hard to still her heart after being privy to such an ugly exchange, but she smiled when she spied Pamela's father moving towards her. "Oh, Sir Ralph! We had begun to wonder what was keeping you."

Struggling to regain his composure, he said gruffly, "Yes, yes, I'm coming. There's nothing wrong with the food, I hope."

"No, of course not. Everything is perfect."

At this moment, Pamela appeared in the doorway, her colour much heightened and her lips trembling. "Yes, here we are." She tried to smile, but it was evident that she was shaken.

Hester finished her trip back up to the landing. Meeting Pamela at the door to the Great Chamber, she took her arm and gave it a reassuring squeeze. "Will you be able to come down?" she whispered.

She made no attempt to conceal the fact that she had overheard their argument. Sir Ralph had already disappeared down the stairs, and it seemed more important to help Pamela overcome her hurt feelings than to pretend she had not been eavesdropping.

Pamela gave a little start and her lips formed an O. Tears shone in her eyes, before rallying, she took a handkerchief from the pocket of her skirt and dabbed them away. "Yes, just a moment more and we'll go down." Then she composed herself with head erect, and with a better attempt at a smile, preceded Hester down to the Great Hall.

She could ignore her father while seeing that their guests had been well attended, so she moved amongst them with a feverish gaiety. No one appeared to notice the change in her manner, except St. Mars who sent an arched eyebrow Hester's way. She gestured that she would tell him about it later, then made herself useful to Pamela by entertaining her more tiresome guests. As if he could read Hester's mind, after only a brief hesitation, St. Mars headed to Pamela's side to make himself agreeable.

Sir Ralph's servants had arranged a number of chairs along the walls in the East Hall. Charles Fenwick and Mr. Moreland had taken their plates to sit in a corner a slight distance from everyone else. As soon as Hester had made up her own plate and handed it to a servant, she led him to where the two gentlemen were sitting and asked if she might join them. Charles looked pleased, but directed an uncertain glance at his companion. Mr. Moreland was somewhat less than gracious, but by way of assent he inclined his head. Charles made an attempt to hide his relief. Whether his relief was due to the alleviation her company would bring to their conversation or the improvement in Mr. Moreland's manners, she could not tell, but it did not escape her notice that Charles still found his cousin's company burdensome.

Once she was settled comfortably in her chair and had relieved the servant of her plate, she began the conversation. "How fortunate that you were able to return to Oulston Hall so soon after quitting us, Mr. Moreland. Does business bring you to the neighbourhood, or are you here to provide more solace to the Fenwicks?"

"Both. I ran into Charles when he escorted his sister back to school, and he was kind enough to invite me to stop with him again. I do have some business in the area, however, so his invitation came at a provident time."

"Oh?" Hester let the word speak for her curiosity. If he wished to elaborate, he would, but it would be rude for her to inquire what his business was.

He did not volunteer anything more, so she was obliged to fill the silence. "I am sure you have found that Mr. Fenwick has taken a firm hold on his new duties. We have all been impressed by his devotion to his family and his estate."

With a shrewd look at Charles, Mr. Moreland nodded. "Yes, so it appears. He has done nothing but what one should have expected of him, however."

Hester thought he was being very stingy with his praise, but gentlemen often were. They seemed to fear that if they praised a deserving young man, the flattery would go instantly to his head and he would abandon all virtue and turn into a libertine. She gave Charles a smile that she hoped conveyed this. "Well, as I said, his neighbours think highly of his efforts. Sir Ralph cannot praise him highly enough."

The thought of Sir Ralph put her in mind of the encounter she had had with Mr. Abelson. She almost raised the subject with Charles, but this did not seem like a proper occasion to bring up a distressing topic. Besides which, she had promised to leave it to Sir Ralph to speak to Charles about their encounter.

Instead, she said, "I understand that Sir Ralph has recently felt the need to convert more of his land to pasturage. Do you think you will need to do the same, Mr. Fenwick?" She addressed him more formally in Mr. Moreland's presence, since any suggestion of an easy friendship between them seemed to irk him.

Charles sat up straighter when he answered, "No. Sir Ralph has informed me of the benefits, but it would pose too great a hardship on my tenants. I had rather keep on as my father did. As long as it is possible, of course."

Mr. Moreland did give a hint of approval then, by nodding as Charles spoke. The ghost of a smile touched his lips when he glanced at the young man. On seeing this, Charles flushed much more than he had upon hearing Hester's more effusive praise.

"Then I hope you can continue this way profitably," Hester said.

While speaking, they had nibbled at the cold meats on their plates. Hester paid a compliment to Sir Ralph's cook, and the gentlemen agreed. Their conversation continued in this desultory fashion until Sir Ralph came to join them. His boisterous attempts to engage Mr. Moreland met with no more success than Hester's. After three or four efforts had failed, he asked if Mr. Moreland would excuse Charles while he spoke with him outside for a moment. He then drew Charles away and led him to the door to the terrace, through which a few of the other guests had already disappeared.

Stuck where she was, Hester now regretted the impulse that had brought her to Mr. Moreland's side. She tried again to draw him out. "How did you find Mrs. Fenwick on your return? Is she much recovered?"

She had seen the widow herself only two days ago, so this was nothing more than a conversational gambit.

Mr. Moreland answered her readily enough. "She is better, but naturally the circumstances of her husband's death weigh heavily upon her. She is not convinced that his murderer will ever be apprehended, or that the authorities are pursuing the crime with any diligence."

"I sympathize with how she must feel. No one seems to be asking the questions that ought to be asked."

He gave her a strange, intense look. "What questions are these?

What do you know that you are not telling me, Mrs. Kean?"

Hester was taken aback. "I know nothing, I assure you. It's just that when I've inquired what progress has been made in the investigation, the answer is always that nothing new in the way of evidence has been offered."

"And whom have you questioned in this fashion?" He handed his empty plate to a passing servant, and though she had not finished hers, Hester did the same.

"Chiefly Sir Ralph and Mr. Mynchon. Sir Ralph, because I am better acquainted with him and, since he speaks frequently to his neighbours, is likely to hear more news. And Mr. Mynchon because he is a justice of the peace."

"Hah!" Mr. Moreland's mouth gave a bitter twist. "All Mr. Mynchon seems desirous of doing is distressing the family."

"You are speaking of his wish to buy one of their relics. Yes, I saw him as he was leaving Oulston Hall."

"I have to ask whether he was so keen to get the relic that he would have murdered Mr. Fenwick for it. Do you think that is possible?"

Hester was as astonished by his desire to hear her opinion as she was by the question itself, but it forced her to examine her thoughts on the subject. "His behaviour was most regrettable, of course," she said earnestly, "but I do not believe the two incidents were related. Mr. Mynchon's collection does mean a great deal to him, yes, to the point of making him intolerant of others' interests. But I believe he takes his duties as a justice of the peace more seriously than most. If anyone had information of a possible suspect for the crime, I believe he would act on it sincerely. The trouble is that no one has any idea who could have done it. There were no witnesses, and many of his neighbours were away from home. It could have been almost anyone he knew or a stranger, but whoever it was could not have a chosen a more convenient moment or a better way of committing a murder with no one around to see."

To her surprise, he listened to her with some degree of interest. She could not describe his attitude as either acceptance or respect. But clearly, he was intent on gaining whatever knowledge he could, even if it came from a lady for whom he otherwise had no patience.

He seemed sincere, but she reminded herself that his question could be a ruse. He might just as keenly wish to know what Mr. Fenwick's neighbours thought about the crime and whether he was suspected of committing it.

Hester knew that Mr. Moreland was St. Mars's prime suspect. There was certainly enough mysterious about him. Perhaps he thought that the best means of discovering whether or not he was safe would be to question an empty-headed female who would never be able to divine his purpose.

She was saved herself from further conversation with Mr. Moreland when St. Mars strolled over to join them. It seemed that he had managed to escape from Pamela.

"Mr. Moreland," he said, bowing, "your servant, sir. I was surprised to learn from our friend Sadler that you had quit us. I had not been aware that you contemplated leaving the area so soon, or I would have made a point of bidding you farewell."

Mr. Moreland made a cool response. He did not look as if he welcomed having his conversation with Hester interrupted. St. Mars did not allow this to deter him. He inquired more particularly into Mr. Moreland's movements than Hester would have dared.

While the two men talked, Hester took a look about the hall and noticed that Mary was not amongst the guests who had remained in the East Hall. Mr. Mynchon was intently examining a Delftware pyramid vase, while his wife and Pamela chatted in the corner. Dudley was fast asleep on the sofa, his chin sunk onto his chest.

Charles had failed to come back inside. The absence of both Mary and him set off an alarm inside Hester's head. If they had stepped into the maze together again, she feared a repeat of Mr. Moreland's furious performance.

As casually as she could, she excused herself from her two companions before moving unobtrusively to the door and passing onto the terrace. There she found Sir Ralph and his friends from Ripon in lively conversation. Sir Ralph was expounding upon the improvements he had made to his garden. In the distance, Hester spied the Reverend Mr. and Mrs. Ward and their niece strolling down the path between the parterres towards the central fountain, but neither Charles nor

Mary was in sight.

The need to find them before Mr. Moreland noticed their absence drove Hester down the steps towards the lower terrace surround, the view of which was hidden from the house by a row of yew trees trimmed into fantastical shapes. She prayed that the two young people had not gone into the maze, for if they had, she would not be able to locate them before Mr. Moreland's suspicions were aroused.

They were not on the northern side of the garden, but here, concealed by the yews, she could hasten along the length of the surround without being seen. The last thing she wanted was to draw anyone's attention. The fact that she had headed into the garden alone was enough to raise questions, but she hoped that Sir Ralph had been sufficiently engrossed in his favourite pastime—boasting about his mansion—that he had not seen her depart. The Wards had had their backs to her, and the guests from Ripon would never be so impolite as to express their curiosity about her movements.

She reached the bottom of the alley of trees. From here, turning right she could either head directly to the maze or go past the entrance to it to see if Charles and Mary were hidden by the trees on the opposite length of the surround. Knowing it would be hopeless to pursue them into the maze, she turned to cross the garden between the entrance to the maze and the fishpond, afraid she must be spotted by the Wards. She reached the farther row of trees, turned right behind them, and halted immediately at the sight of the pair.

Concealed from the house by the southern row of yew trees, Mary and Charles were leaning closely together. Mary stood on tiptoe, her hands resting lightly on Charles's shoulders. As Hester watched, Mary planted a tender kiss on his lips.

A warm flush infused Hester's face. She turned and hurried back around the corner, praying she had been quick enough that neither one had seen her. She retreated about twenty yards, her heart pumping, before stopping to decide what she ought to do. It would be wrong of her not to put an end to further intimacies and, yet, Mary's expression, when she had kissed Charles, had been so gentle, Hester had felt herself in the wrong to intrude.

She had interrupted Mary's sister Isabella in much more seriously compromising situations, and each time, her reaction had been the same—a strong desire to retreat, not to have to deal with the embarrassment that would be felt by everyone involved. But Isabella was married, and it was not Hester's responsibility to preserve her reputation, while Mary's mother had made it Hester's business to protect Mary's. She could not in all conscience allow the girl to damage her reputation before she had even made an appearance at Court. It would be bad enough if Mary had made up her mind to marry Charles Fenwick.

Dreading what the kiss might signify, she turned and retraced her steps. The terrace was paved, or else they might have heard her first approach. Hoping to give them enough time to break off their embrace, she called out Mary's name.

Mary called back as Hester turned the corner again to see the couple walking arm in arm towards her. She searched their faces for signs of guilt, but detected only a suggestion of melancholy. Charles looked a bit pale, to be sure, but he did not have the appearance of a young gentleman who had made a conquest.

Since neither one seemed in a mood to explain their absence, Hester continued with the pretence that she had only just arrived. "I came to fetch you because the guests will be departing soon, and Mr. Moreland will wish you to accompany him, Charles."

At this reminder, Charles did wince, but he did not seem anxious. "Yes, Mr. Moreland and I should thank Sir Robert and Sir Ralph for including us in their party and make our way home."

"If you would," Hester suggested, "could you also thank Mary's sister Pamela, for it was she who planned the refreshments."

Charles turned his head to look at her, as if only now wakening to his surroundings. "Certainly. I should have thought of that myself."

Hester smiled and took her place between them to stroll back to the house. If Mr. Moreland chanced to come upon them now, it would seem as if she had been with them all along. She kept up a flow of trivial remarks as they made their way back, and inquired of Charles if he had left Frances in good health. As he answered, she recalled a discrepancy between Mrs. Fenwick's and Mr. Moreland's accounts. Mrs. Fenwick had clearly expected his visit, yet Mr. Moreland had said that he had returned because he had met Charles by chance and Charles had invited him to Oulston Hall. The discrepancy seemed too small to be significant, which made the reason for it appear even stranger. Why should Mr. Moreland not wish it to be known that Mrs. Fenwick had been expecting him? Hester could think of no explanation that made any sense.

She kept these thoughts to herself, but she was eager to put the question to St. Mars, who might have a clue. She encouraged Charles to talk about his journey to York until they reached the end of the parterre, where they spied Mr. Moreland, standing alone on the upper terrace, gazing over the garden with a grim look.

It was a relief to Hester to know they had no need to cringe.

On seeing the three together, the furrows in Mr. Moreland's brow lifted. He did not approve of Hester, but even he would have to acknowledge that her presence constituted sufficient attendance on a young couple. As they mounted the steps, he came towards them and announced that it was time for Charles to bid their hosts good day. Charles made his bows to Hester and Mary with no appearance of a guilty conscience, and the two gentlemen walked back into the house, where all the other guests had gone.

Hester took hold of Mary's arm and turned the girl to face her. "I had to search for you before Mr. Moreland discovered you were gone and threatened another scene. I was terrified to think that you might have gone into the maze. What were you thinking?'

Mary heaved a sigh. "You needn't have worried, Hester. Even if I had been foolish enough to do it, Charles would never do anything to annoy Mr. Moreland. We only wished to have a few minutes' private speech."

Hester earnestly searched her face, but could find no evidence of secrecy. "Is there anything I should know?"

Mary twisted her lips into a wry smile. "Only that Charles and I have agreed that we should not suit."

She must have sensed Hester's relief, for she added with defiance. "I thought we might. Before our journey to Hawnby, I was meeting Charles nearly every day on my morning ride. We were very attracted to each other. We still are, I think. But neither of us is willing to change religion for the other. He asked me if I would consider it, and I had to tell him no. It was plain from the look on his face, then, that I need not bother to ask him the same question." She gave a shiver. "I could never live the way his mother and his sisters do."

Hester squeezed Mary's hands and gave her a smile. "That sounds quite reasonable. You must be a foundling."

Mary chuckled. "Now you must promise me that I shall meet even handsomer and more amiable men in London."

Hester squeezed her eyes shut. She did not wish to lie to the girl, but she could not promise she would find a husband who would make her happy. "Surely there should be one, and if not, you can always reconsider the option of conversion."

Fortunately, Mary laughed, so they were able to return to the house without a hint of the serious issue they had discussed.

The next morning, at church, Hester took a moment to thank God that she would not have to try to part Mary from a lover. She felt immeasurable relief to be spared the family scenes that would have ensued if Mary had been determined to reject her mother's dictates in order to marry a Roman Catholic. A less sensible girl might have fancied herself genuinely in love and given no thought at all to the consequences she would suffer over a lifetime of increasing penury, for barring any miraculous change in the law, that was certainly what Charles and his family faced. Hester could not help thinking that Charles's illiberal behaviour on the day of their excursion had dimmed his lustre a bit in Mary's eyes. She was enough of a Mayfield to enjoy indulging in pleasure without having to feel guilty for it. If visiting a village church, a good woman of a different faith, and a site that had been turned to ruins two centuries ago were unacceptable diversions to Charles now, Mary might wonder what more he would find impermissible as the years progressed.

Hester did not blame Charles for his current opinions for they had been nurtured by every person of authority he had known. His instruction in France, where Protestantism was nearly as great a sin as those in the Ten Commandments, would have instilled in him less tolerance for other religions than even his parents felt. She liked him immensely and applauded his fine qualities. It was entirely possible that Mary would never find as gentle or as responsible a husband, but that it was too soon to make that determination, Hester firmly believed.

With Mary's situation settled for now, she had nothing else to occupy her mind but her meeting on Tuesday with St. Mars. His behaviour towards her this morning had been exemplary. There was nothing in his manner to arouse Pamela's suspicions that they had an assignation planned. He had even abstained from crowding her in the pew, which she sometimes thought he did just to tease her.

As they emerged from the church into the summer sunshine, a flurry of activity at the inn down the road captured their attention. One of the stable lads came running towards them, searching for a certain face among the parishioners. He spied Mr. Mynchon and, darting over to him, doffed his hat and said in a voice they could all hear, "Sir! Ther's been another murther! Yond maister, 'e sed an yoa's t'come."

Gasps erupted throughout the crowd as Mr. Mynchon hastened to lead the boy back to the inn, parting the people ahead of him with a tersely uttered, "Mindroad! Mindroad!"

Hester exchanged an anxious glance with St. Mars, who excused himself from their party, saying, "I shall see what has happened and come to tell you about it directly." To Sir Ralph, he added, "I would advise you to take the ladies home."

A few shades paler than usual, Sir Ralph thanked him and gathered their party. Pamela, looking as alarmed as everyone else, saw how quickly the rest of the congregation was dispersing and nodded in agreement. "Come Hester, come Mary and Clarissa, let us hurry!"

When Clarissa opened her mouth to whine, Pamela grasped hold of her arm and nearly slapped her. "None of your impertinence, Clarissa, or I swear Nurse shall feed you nothing but bread and water for a week!"

Her carriage was only a few yards away. Sir Ralph helped them all inside. Then, promising to escort them home, he went to mount his horse.

"I wonder who it was," Pamela said, as soon as they had started off. "Now I wish we had waited to see."

Mary gave a little gasp and looked as if she might be sick. "Do you think it could be Charles?"

The same thought had occurred to Hester, but for Mary's sake, she hid her fears. "There is no reason to suspect that." She patted Mary's hand. "We'd best not speculate, or we'll only upset ourselves to no end. We will learn who it was soon enough."

"And what if it was Dudley?" Pamela said, outraged. "Why should you show more concern for that papist than for your own brother?"

At this, Mary did look ashamed. Clarissa began to wail, "If it was Dudley, what's to become of us?"

Hester knew she should feel more sympathetic than she did, but since neither Pamela nor Clarissa seemed particularly sincere, and neither had ever exhibited much affection for Dudley, she merely repeated what she had said and was grateful when Mary seconded her advice.

Pamela agreed to put a halt to speculation, only muttering that if it were Dudley who had been killed, it would serve him right for not going to church.

His excuse this morning had been a putrid cough, which had laid him in bed. Since they knew him to have been home scarcely two hours ago, Hester seriously doubted that he had managed to get himself dressed, out, and murdered in so short a time. And since there were no amusements to be had on a Sunday morning that could lure him from home, she expected to see him exactly where they had left him.

This proved to be the case, as they were informed by a servant on their arrival. Neither Pamela nor Clarissa evinced any relief at the news. Perhaps both had felt that their lives might be better, or at least more interesting, without him, which was a sad commentary on her cousin, Hester reflected.

Secure in the knowledge that none of their kin was either missing or dead, they had nothing to do but wait for "Sir Robert" to bring them news from the inn. He was with them within the quarter hour and came to join them upstairs in the Great Chamber, where they had gathered to pass the time until dinner. Sir Ralph had elected to remain at his daughter's house on the grounds that they might need more protection than just Dudley and his servants could provide.

"Sir Robert" had barely been announced when they started pelting him with questions. "Who was it?" "Have they arrested anyone?" "Did anyone witness the crime?" "Was it Charles?"

"I hope," Sir Ralph said in passionate supplication, "that we are not to expect this kind of violence again."

"Heaven forfend!" Pamela shuddered. "Do come sit, Sir Robert, and tell us all you have learned." She patted the sofa beside her.

St. Mars took the proffered seat and began, "It was not Charles Fenwick." He directed this to Mary before answering the others' questions. "It was a poor man by the name of Abelson. I gather he was once a local tenant."

The name struck Hester like a blow, not only because she had met Mr. Abelson so recently but because she had done nothing to help him. It was Sir Ralph who had prevented her from speaking to Charles to ask if he could find a place for him on his land. She turned to see Sir Ralph's reaction, expecting to find similar guilt on his countenance. His gaze flew to meet hers before the shock appeared to register. He shook his head, murmuring, "This is terrible news."

"Did you know him, Sir Ralph?" St. Mars must have seen the direction of Hester's gaze.

"Yes, I did. He was one of my tenants. I had to tell him to leave when I converted that piece of land I showed you to grass. He'd been hanging about here lately, disturbing the ladies." A worrisome thought seemed to strike him and he blurted, "I just had a conversation with young Fenwick about him yesterday. You'll recall, Mrs. Kean, I told you that I would, but with one thing and another, I had no chance until after the consort."

"Why Charles Fenwick? What did he have to do with Abelson?" St. Mars glanced back and forth between Hester and Sir Ralph, but Hester waited to see how Sir Ralph would answer.

Again, he shook his head. "No, I can't believe it of the boy. There can't have been any reason."

"What are you suggesting, Sir Ralph? That Charles Fenwick could have killed this man Abelson?"

His head jerked up. "No, of course not! Haven't I just said that I will not believe it? It will be some stranger . . . no doubt the same person who killed his father. It was only . . . but the notion is preposterous!" Despite his words, his glance and accompanying laugh were both uncertain.

"What business did they have with each other?" St. Mars asked again.

Sir Ralph shrugged. "None that I know of, but Abelson seemed to think they did. He was always on about Fenwick. Isn't that so, Mrs. Kean?"

"It seemed so, yes, on the two occasions that I saw him. Remember, Pamela? He was the man who approached Charles at the inn at Thirsk, but it was clear that Charles did not know him then."

"Yes, of course! I perfectly recall the incident! It was most upsetting."

"Then," Hester said, addressing St. Mars, "I encountered Mr. Abelson in Coxwold, and he asked if I could help him speak to Charles. He was very upset. He seemed to believe that Charles could get him out of his predicament. I was puzzled by his request, but I have since learned that Mr. Abelson was a papist. I suppose that was why he referred to Charles's father."

Sir Ralph gave a violent start. "Perhaps it was Abelson who killed old Fenwick. It's true they were both papists. There may have been some secret business between them. Papists are full of secrets, y'know." He did not add that if Charles had discovered his father's killer, he would have had a reason for revenge, but Sir Ralph's worried expression convinced Hester that the notion had occurred to him.

It was a possible scenario, Hester thought, if one were willing to cast Charles Fenwick in the role of murderer. But Abelson's words about Charles's father had not been uttered in anger. Had he not said that he would never have lost his home if old Mr. Fenwick were still alive?

"How was he killed?" she asked, when no one else spoke.

"He was shot," St. Mars answered, before pursuing his own train of thought. "If they were both papists, could there be any connection with the rebellion? Have you seen any strangers about who might be Jacobite spies?"

Hester's mind immediately flew to Mr. Moreland. She could see that St. Mars was thinking of him, too.

Before anyone could venture an opinion, Dudley entered the room in his dressing gown with his mouth stretched wide in a yawn. "What the devil's going on? Why are you in here? Where is my dinner?" His more-than-usual peevishness appeared to be due to the cold clogging his head.

While Sir Ralph enjoyed a hearty laugh at Dudley's expense, Pamela explained impatiently that they had gathered to hear the news of another murder.

This temporarily distracted Dudley from thoughts of his dinner, but when he was informed of the little they knew, he had no compassion to waste on Abelson. "From all I've heard, man's been a confounded nuisance. No wonder somebody finally lost patience with him. He should have been locked up."

Mary, disturbed by the references to Charles and his father, had been silent up until now, but she did speak up at this heartless response. "So it is fair to kill someone for being a nuisance?" she asked. "It's a wonder, then, that no one has thought fit to do away with you."

"Mary!" Pamela cried. "How dare you speak to your brother like that? I insist you apologize to him, at once!"

Not in the least distressed, Dudley sneered. "More of that impudence, my girl, and it's your back that'll need watching."

Hester moved to put a halt to this trend. "I think we have had enough talk of violence for one day without threats within the family."

"Yes, what Sir Robert must think of us, I do not know!" Pamela pursed her lips, shaking her head in shame.

"I think only that it is time I left you all in peace." He stood and made his bows to Pamela and the whole assembly.

"Oh, please do not go! We would love for you to dine with us. This talk of murder has made me quite nervous, and I should be grateful for your company."

"Don't go on my account," Dudley said. "We need to make plans for the race meeting in York. Even though my horse beat yours, I still think you should enter her."

St. Mars made his excuses, pleading another engagement. Pamela pouted, and Dudley insisted on accompanying him outside. St. Mars could not say anything private to Hester, but he managed to give her a look that said he had not forgotten their assignation on Tuesday morning, and that he expected to see her there without fail.

*A*nd from this Time began an Intrigue between his Majesty and a Junta of Ministers maliciously bent against me, which broke out in less than two Months, and had like to have ended in my utter Destruction. Of so little Weight are the greatest Services to Princes, when put into the Balance with a Refusal to gratify their Passions.

CHAPTER XVI

It took Gideon a while to shake Dudley off. In spite of his cold, he was determined not to miss the race meeting the coming week. With nothing but his own company to amuse him all morning, he was reluctant to let "Sir Robert" go and detained him just outside the stables.

Waiting for his horse to be led outside, Gideon took the opportunity to plant a seed of doubt that he would be able to attend the meeting. "I'm worried about a slight limp my mare has developed. I have not been riding her lately. My man has been putting poultices on her knee and fetlock, but as yet to no avail. I will not risk her if she doesn't come round."

"You should have Sir Ralph's groom take a look at it. He's got his own mixture, and Sir Ralph swears by it."

"If she doesn't improve over the next few days, I shall." That was the excuse he had planned to use in case he were spotted by a servant at Yearsley Park on his way to meet Mrs. Kean in the maze.

At length, he was able to escape from Dudley by reminding him that his dinner was probably being served. He mounted Tom's horse and made his way back to the inn, where Tom relieved him of the reins.

"As soon as you've brushed him down, come speak with me," Gideon told him.

He barely made it to his room before tearing off his hat and wig and tossing them on the bed. Then he sat in the lone oak chair and, with a groan, raked his fingers through his hair, ending with his elbows on his knees and his face in his hands.

If he had to see Mrs. Kean one more time without being able to touch her, he thought he might go mad. This waiting endlessly for no more than a moment alone with her had tried his patience to the limit. He did not know how much longer he would be able to restrain himself in front of her annoying relations. He would have to wait until Tuesday, but he could not stand another day of this inactivity. He would have to avoid seeing either her or her relations as long as he was in this explosive mood.

In the meantime, he must do something to occupy his brain, and since Abelson's killing suggested that Fenwick's murderer was someone who lived in the immediate vicinity, it was time to pursue his suspicions.

When Gideon heard Tom approaching his door, he collected himself. He raised his head and leaned back in his chair, determined to focus his mind on the murders.

The way Mrs. Kean had blanched when she had heard of Abelson's death told him how much the news had upset her. They had had so little chance to speak to each other that he had not even known she had discovered the man's name.

Tom knocked once, then came in and carefully closed the door before saying quietly, "My lord?"

"Have you learned anything more about this latest killing?"

Tom stood with his hands folded in front of him. "I heard they discovered the body over in a place called Snape Wood. He'd been campin' there by the look of things."

"Do you know where the place is?"

Tom shook his head, before adding, "But they said as how it wasn't far from Mr. Fenwick's estate."

Gideon blew out his breath and bit his lower lip. "Sir Ralph as much as said that he suspects Charles Fenwick of killing him."

"Mr. Fenwick?" Even Tom, who had hardly ever seen Charles, had trouble imagining him as a killer. "Why would a young gentleman do such a thing, my lord?"

"Sir Ralph provided him with a motive, too, if it was Abelson who murdered his father."

Tom mused on this and had to nod reluctantly. "I reckon it could make sense."

"If there were no other possibilities. For myself, it's Mr. Moreland who best fits my notion of a killer. I find his comings and goings very strange, and he did reappear just before Abelson's body was found."

"He is a quiet kind o' gentleman. But what would his reason be?"

Gideon abruptly slapped his legs and stood. "I do not know, but that is what I propose to discover. First, however, I shall need you to ride to Thirsk to hire me a horse."

"Another horse, my lord?" Tom asked anxiously.

"Yes, I need one that Moreland hasn't seen. It would be best if you do not bring it here. Find a place on the mill bank to tie it up, then come for me. I shall be ready to go at dark."

Tom looked pained, but resigned. He had learned not to plead with his master not to take unnecessary risks. "Yes, my lord."

Gideon grinned at him. "Good man. And tonight we'll take a little ride. I'd like to see what Mr. Moreland is doing."

Tom returned from Thirsk by seven o'clock, reporting that he had left the hired horse tied to a tree just out of sight of the inn. They had to wait until after ten o'clock for the sky to be dark enough to leave the inn unseen. Tom led his big horse Beau and Gideon followed him down to the bank where the horse, saddled and bridled, stood hobbled and grazing. Then, while Tom untied the horse, Gideon donned a short black wig to cover his fair hair. He had already applied some white paint and a few patches to his face and blackened his brows. The effect was such that nobody should recognize him unless they had the opportunity to study his face closely and at leisure. He tucked his black half-mask and blue satin cape under the saddle for further disguise in case he found an opportunity to question Moreland. Within a few minutes, Gideon was mounted and heading for Oulston Hall with

Tom on Beau beside him.

He chose a route that should avoid any encounter with either Sir Ralph or Dudley. It was not Gideon's intention to make his presence known. The best he hoped for was to observe Moreland's comings and goings, perhaps to waylay him on a dark road. He could not be sure that the man was still at Oulston Hall and did not know how he could discover this without approaching the house.

Gideon believed that the murders of Mr. Fenwick and Abelson had been committed by the same person. The news that Abelson was a papist had provided a link between the two victims and meant that a political motive had to be considered. If the deaths had anything to do with the rebellion, Gideon was convinced that Moreland was the key.

They rode to the top of a hill from which they had a clear view of Oulston Hall. Gideon dismounted, and while his horse nipped at the grass, he leaned against a tree, hoping to catch sight of some evidence that Moreland was still in residence. He had not yet figured how to lure Moreland out of the house to waylay him, but hoped to see something that would inspire an idea.

For a good half-hour or longer, Tom and he watched the house, but nothing stirred either inside or out. The windows were strangely dark except for two at the top of the house, where a faint light escaped around curtains that had been drawn. Waiting for any sign of life, Gideon used the time to study the land about the house to locate the best site for an ambush. Though hilly, the ground was too open. There were none of the deep roads and dense woods of Kent. The people must not be much plagued by highwaymen, he thought, for there was not enough cover here to make highway robbery a feasible practice. He thought he saw a place that might serve, where the road took a dip and the hedges grew quite near. He would have to get a closer look before deciding. Tom might think him completely reckless, but Gideon had no desire to rot in a Yorkshire prison while waiting for the next assizes. Not when he planned to see Mrs. Kean on Tuesday morning.

He signaled to Tom that he was ready to ride nearer to the house. They both remounted and walked their horses down the hill, sticking close to the edge of the pasture where the hedge provided shadow.

On his only visit to Oulston Hall Gideon had noticed that no dogs were kept near the house. He supposed that as poor as the Fenwicks were, they could not waste money on keeping animals that did not earn their keep, and with only one gun to the family, only Charles could hunt. The few dogs he had noticed were penned near the stable. As long as Gideon approached the house from the other side, they would not see him, and their barking should be less shrill. If they scented him, their barks would sound more as if they had caught a whiff of a fox or other pest.

The Fenwicks had an ancient tithe barn a short way from the house. Gideon steered his mount behind it and dismounted. He handed the reins to Tom and gestured to him to remain with the horses while he approached the house slowly on foot.

There was no sight or sound of men, either in the yard or in the servants' sleeping quarters over the stable. Every window was dark. He heard the whinny of a horse issuing from the stable. It was followed by a few neighs and the stamping of hooves, indicating the presence of more than just one horse. If Moreland was still here, that would account for a second horse, but Gideon's instincts told him that the noises he heard and the smells of dung and animal sweat reaching him had been produced by more than just a pair of animals.

The profound silence of the place puzzled him, until he recalled that it was Sunday and wondered if the family could be observing mass. That would be the only reason he could see for the outdoor servants to be indoors. It would also account for the fact that the only lights visible were at the top of the house, for any Roman observation would need to be conducted in the strictest secrecy. The law forbade nonjuring Dissenters and Roman Catholics from holding services in their own homes. The Popery Act put a bounty of £100 on the head of any priest convicted of saying mass. If a priest was discovered running a school, he could be imprisoned for life.

As these thoughts ran through Gideon's head, he was taken by surprise when a door at the back of the house suddenly opened. He barely had time to duck behind a shrub before a group of near three dozen people emerged. The walls of the old house had muffled the sounds of their footsteps and, since they carried no candles, he had not been alerted by any lights. They all filed quietly out of the house, passing no more than ten paces away from his hiding place. A few crossed the yard to the stable, while others left on foot in clusters of two to eight, scattering, some around the house to the lane, others through the gates into the fields.

As Gideon peered through the branches, he noted that among them were perhaps a dozen children, suggesting that whole families had come to Oulston Hall to worship. Most would be tenants and their families, but as some who had disappeared into the stables exited it with their horses, he realized that some of the Fenwicks' neighbours also had come to attend mass. Through the dark he strained to see if Moreland was one of the people leaving, but he could not make out that gentleman's form in the group.

Their going was so orderly and so completely silent, it underscored the risk they took in practicing the ritual their faith required. This was why any mass was usually conducted at the top of the house. If the authorities came to make arrests, the worshippers would have enough warning to be able to hide the evidence that a service had taken place. The plates for the host and the goblet for the wine, the crucifix, and any other implement they had used would be secreted somewhere in the paneling. Most Catholic landowners had special rooms constructed for this purpose at least, if not to hide the priests who illegally conducted the services.

While the King's Commissioner had been examining Charles's records, Gideon doubted that the family had been able to hold services, so perhaps tonight's mass was the first held here since.

As the last few people disappeared from the yard, Gideon exhaled the breath he had been holding, thankful for the black wig he had had the foresight to wear. Though the moon was pale, it still had shed enough light for the Fenwicks' guests to come and go without torches. If they had not been so intent on leaving the house without making any noise, they might have made out his form through the foliage. Gideon knew that Tom would be anxious until he made it back to the tithe barn, but thought he had better wait a few more minutes before he risked crossing the yard again.

Candles had now been lit in a few other rooms of the house. Gideon was fairly certain he knew which chamber was Mrs. Fenwick's, but he wondered if Moreland's was one of them. He would not be able to waylay Moreland tonight. Even if he had been among the people who left, it would be too late now to catch him up.

Then, as Gideon prepared to leave his hiding place, a thought entered his brain, and he cursed himself for an idiot.

The truth had been right in front of him as plain as day. How could he have been so blind that he had not read the clues? The "hold" or authority Moreland seemed to have over the Fenwicks, his disapproval of certain frivolous behaviour, his suspicion of everyone not connected with the Fenwick family, his sudden disappearance when the King's Commissioner had arrived, even the house he had visited in York. And now, the clandestine mass to which the Fenwicks' Roman Catholic neighbours had come.

Disgusted with himself and the time he had wasted suspecting Moreland of Fenwick's murder made him abandon his place of concealment with too little precaution. He was striding openly across the yard when a voice called out to him from a stable window. Gideon turned reflexively and saw the figure of a servant, leaning out an open casement. The man pivoted and, raising the alarm, vanished from the window to lead a rush downstairs.

By this time Gideon knew he had only a few seconds before all the Fenwicks' servants would be after him. He ran for the tithe barn, just as Tom rode around it, pulling the hired horse behind. They split the distance between them as three men burst from the stable armed with pitchforks and the dogs began to bark. Gideon leapt into the saddle, foregoing the use of stirrups, and grabbing the reins from Tom, lit into the horse with both heels. With his face pressed to the horse's neck, he urged it into a run. Voices cried after them as they galloped out of the yard, forced their way through a hedge, and scrambled back up the hill. They did not slow until they had achieved the crest and started down the other side. Even then, Gideon kept up a steady pace until the sign of the Fauconberg Arms came into view, when he reined his horse to a walk.

As Tom drew up beside him, Gideon said, "Phew! That was uncomfortably close!" He did his best to hide the elation the narrow escape had raised. He did not worry about being followed since the only horses left to mount a pursuit would have been the two belonging to Charles and Moreland. He had chosen an indirect path back to Coxwold, so no one who might have spotted them could report that they had ridden towards the village. Tomorrow, in daylight, if anyone attempted to track the men who had bolted from the yard at Oulston Hall, they would not be able to distinguish their hoofprints from the others in the country lane.

"What happened back there, my lord? When I saw all them people, I was sure you'd been took!"

"They nearly did run into me, but I was able to hide in time. What is more important, Tom, is now I know that Moreland did not kill Fenwick."

"How do you know? Did you speak to him?"

"No, I'm ashamed to say that the evidence was there all along. Moreland is a Roman Catholic priest. The people you saw leaving Oulston Hall had been attending a mass."

"But an't that against the law?"

"Yes. Whether it should be is another matter, but the fact remains that a Roman Catholic priest would never murder one of the faithful. Moreland may be the Fenwicks' cousin, but I doubt it. As their priest, he is the guide and comforter they trust."

"What about the queer way he behaved in York? He could still be a Jacobite, couldn't he?"

"He could, but I doubt that has anything to do with the murder. The house Moreland visited was probably the school that the Fenwick girls attend. Those women I saw dressed so plainly must have been nuns. I cannot believe the truth did not occur to me at once, but I am used to seeing nuns in France where they wear a full habit. They could never do that in England, but as long as they do not wear the trappings of a *religieuse,* the authorities cannot prove who they are."

They said no more, but stopped to tie up the hired horse on the bank and let Gideon remove his black wig. Then, while Tom hobbled the horse and made sure that water and grass were within reach, Gideon rode Beau back to the stable and unsaddled him. Leaving Beau ungroomed—for Tom would soon be along to attend to him—Gideon untied Argos from the stall where they had left him and, patting him firmly in response to his rapture, led him upstairs to his chamber.

Gideon still could not believe how stupid he had been. Perhaps if he and Mrs. Kean had had a moment to discuss their discoveries the way they usually did, one of them would have tumbled to the truth. At least tonight's adventure had eaten up part of the time he would have to wait before seeing her on Tuesday, when the solution to the murders would not be the uppermost thought in his mind.

Lying in bed later, however, he did ask himself who the murderer could be now that Moreland had been ruled out. Something strange was going on. It was impossible to separate the motives for these killings from the fact that both men were papists. By far, the most obvious reason would have been that they were someway tied up in the rebellion. But if they had been, it made no sense for them to have been killed. Anyone who suspected them of being Jacobites had only to report them to the authorities and they would have been arrested and tried.

For the first time, Gideon looked at the conundrum another way. He had been too influenced by his recent escapade with the Jacobite he had smuggled into France. With the rebellion and the ensuing arrests it was no wonder that his brain had not found it easy to think of other reasons why a gentleman might be killed, but wars and rebellions did not eliminate any of the other sins. Lust, envy, and greed would always inspire murder in the hearts of men.

He tried to think of each sin in turn to see how they might have played a role. Lust would seem to have no part, and it was hard to see how anyone could envy either Mr. Fenwick or poor displaced Abelson.

Greed then, perhaps?

But before Gideon could explore this idea, his eyelids grew heavy and he fell asleep.

In the morning, with no lead to pursue, he set out on another ostensible expedition to find an estate for sale. He did not think the pretence was still so much a necessity as he wished to put distance between himself and Dudley so the oaf could not pester him.

He and Tom rode to Thirsk to return the horse and then up into the Hambleton Hills to explore the surroundings. Argos, who had missed the previous night's adventure, loped at a steady pace beside them. The exercise helped to clear Gideon's head, but the beauty of the vistas made him wish he was seeing them with Mrs. Kean.

They returned to Coxwold as near dark as possible to be told by Mr. Sadler that "Maister Mayfield" had been round asking for "Sir Robert." Thankful for the inclination that had taken him away, Gideon fell asleep, imagining what he would say to Mrs. Kean on the morrow.

He did not sleep well. Long before the hour for breakfast, he was up and washed, anticipation thrumming through his veins.

What if she spurned him? He had not been so desperately hungry for a woman in all his life. And his hunger was more than physical, though at the moment the physical need was what pained him. He wanted to be with Hester Kean every hour of the day. He wanted to see her smile when he woke up every morning and hold her in his arms when he fell asleep at night. This was a far cry from the lust that had fooled him into believing himself in love with her cousin Isabella. That had been no more than a spell of lust, which, once broken, had vanished so completely, it was as if it had never existed. What he felt for Mrs. Kean was more profound. It was a thirst in his soul for someone who just by her presence could make him feel that his life was worth living.

He could not really believe that she would refuse him, even though it would mean leaving everything familiar behind. She did not have any strong ties to her relations, and her situation as Mrs. Mayfield's drudge was miserable. Surely, even leaving England for good would be preferable to spending her days under the thumb of that horrid woman.

He would clothe her in luxury to make up for all she lost, and knowing her as he did, he believed she would soon make a happy life for herself in France. Why else had she learned to speak French, unlike the majority of their countrymen who had the means to do so, yet never bestirred themselves to learn? Was it not a sign that living in France would one day be her fate?

Thoughts like these wound round and round his brain as he broke his fast and returned to his chamber to spruce himself up before riding to Yearsley Park.

He was giving a final twist to his neckcloth when the sound of male voices downstairs alerted him to the arrival of two men. Cautious by force of habit, he opened the door quietly and strained his ears to make out what they were saying. The only voice he could hear clearly was that of Mr. Sadler, who was protesting loudly that they had no cause to disturb his guest.

"Who laid information against him?"

Murmured words were given in response, but Sadler, perhaps meaning to warn his lodger, raised his voice again, "I doan't think Sir Robert even be about. He wer' oop early this mornin' . . ."

Gideon could not afford to listen any longer. On tiptoes, he returned to his room and barred the door. Then, leaving his possessions behind, he crossed to the window, which was already raised, and peered out to assess his options.

The window overhung the ground floor to allow for the emptying of chamber pots and bath water. The drop to the ground was no more than ten feet, but if the constables—for that was surely who had come for him—heard his boots hit the ground, they would be upon him before he could make it to the stable.

The sound of their treads on the stairs told him that now was the best chance he would have, so he hurriedly climbed out the window, dangled from the sill, and dropped as quietly as he could to the ground. Then, just as he turned to run for the stable, Tom burst through its doors, mounted on Beau and leading Penny by the bridle, with Argos bounding at her heels.

Penny was capering sideways, but saddled and ready to ride. Startled by his sudden appearance, she tried to rear, but Tom held her head firmly, as Gideon ran forward and launched himself into the saddle. Without a word, they galloped away as fast as their horses would carry them.

"Where to, my lord?" Tom called as soon as they were out of earshot.

Gideon's mind was racing. He cursed the constables, wondering how they had managed to ferret out his identity. Now that he had eluded them—they had arrived on foot—he did not fear immediate capture. He was angry and disappointed that, once again, his plans to speak privately with Mrs. Kean had been foiled.

"First to Yearsley Park," he snapped, adding bitterly, "so I can tell Mrs. Kean that I've been discovered. Then it's back to London, I suppose."

In his anguish and frustration, beneath the noise made by their galloping hooves, he barely heard Tom's protest. "But they haven't smoked you out!"

Gideon went a few more paces forward, until Tom's words finally penetrated his dejection. Then, he pulled Penny up, and turned her, sidling and prancing to face Tom, who easily reined Beau.

"What do you mean? Weren't the constables there to arrest me?"

"Yes, my lord, but they didn't know who you was. They were come for 'Sir Robert.'"

"But, why?"

Tom's face was pinched with anxiety. "I heard 'em say as how somebody's accused you of murdering Mr. Fenwick and that other man, Abelson."

Gideon was so surprised that he rocked back in his saddle. "Me?"

"Yes, my lord. I had Penny all saddled, and just nipped inside for a beer, when in they come. Sadler left me at the bar to see what they wanted, and soon as I heard what it was, I slipped outside to fetch the horses."

"That was well done, Tom." If Gideon's brain had been racing before, now it was spinning. This was a curious state of affairs, indeed. Question after question bombarded his thoughts. In a daze he steered Penny towards Yearsley Park again, saying, "We had best be moving."

ℰ

Hester, too, had risen early, had breakfasted alone and, as prettily dressed as one who was just going out for a morning walk could reasonably be, had set out with barely contained excitement for Yearsley Park. With a thirty minute journey on foot before her, she had plenty of time to grow nervous and anxious.

She knew that meeting St. Mars like this, when she was certain he had lovemaking in mind was something her father would have forbidden with all a clergyman's authority. She could not help feeling a twinge of guilt when she let her thoughts stray in that direction, but much deeper feelings were governing her now. Love was not to be refused if offered. She could not turn her back on the need that had been growing stronger and stronger inside her over the year—could it only be one year or a little longer?—since she had tumbled heels over head in love with St. Mars.

By the time she arrived at Yearsley Park, her knees were shaking. When she passed one of Sir Ralph's servants working in the park in front of the house, a gardener in the kitchen garden, and a maid, emptying a water bucket outside the service wing door, she felt the heat of embarrassment steal up into her cheeks, making it difficult to swallow.

At the entrance to the maze she paused to look out for St. Mars, but deciding it would be much worse to be seen entering the maze with him, she ducked inside. The two right turns they had agreed upon opened into the small enclosure, where to her surprise she found St. Mars pacing up and down, obviously in a state of distress.

Forgetting the nervousness that had hounded her all the way there, she said, "What is it, my lord? What has happened?"

On hearing her approach, he had sprung forward and now he took her hands in his. His features were strained, his gaze intense. "Two constables came looking for me this morning. If Tom had not been so alert, they might have caught me."

Hester gasped. "Have they discovered who you are?"

He shook his head. "No, they still believe I am Sir Robert Mavors, but the situation is almost worse. Tom heard them speaking to the innkeeper before he ran to get the horses. Thank God, he already had them saddled, or we might not have escaped. He heard the constables say that I was to be arrested for the murders of Fenwick and Abelson."

"You?" Hester was horrified. "But why? Whoever could have laid the charge against you?"

"I do not know. I heard Sadler ask, but the constables were keeping their voices low and I could not hear their response."

By now, Hester's mind was working again. "Mr. Mynchon must have sent them, but I find it hard to believe that he would suspect you of murder. I've had the impression that he likes you. Someone else must have laid the charge for him to send the constables after you. This is very suspicious, my lord."

"I agree. I cannot help thinking that the murderer must have something to do with this." By St. Mars's distracted expression, Hester could see that he was turning over different possibilities in his mind.

"Mr. Moreland, perhaps?"

His focus returned to her face. "It is possible that he accused me. On his last visit here, when he was stopping at the Fauconberg Arms, he posed a number of questions to both me and Tom. He was chiefly trying to establish when I first arrived in the area—to see if I had been around when the first murder occurred, I suppose. But my being here and having the opportunity is surely not enough to charge someone with murder? Since I had no connection with Fenwick or his family, what possible motive could I have had for killing him?"

"Would the murderer take that into consideration if his primary motive is to cover his own crime?"

He shook his head. "Moreland is not the killer. I am nearly convinced of it. I went prowling round Oulston Hall on Sunday night and saw something that made me realize who Moreland really is. He's a Roman priest."

Hester's mouth fell open. "What did you see? How did you arrive at that conclusion?"

"I saw what must have been the end of a mass. Fenwick's tenants, servants and a number of neighbours were leaving the house after being closeted indoors at the top of the house. What else could they have been doing together like that? Then all the peculiarities we both had noticed in Moreland's behaviour and in the way he relates to Charles Fenwick and his family suddenly made perfect sense when I asked myself if he could be a priest."

St. Mars told her about his realization that the women he had seen in York must be nuns at the school attended by Charles's sisters. "His authority over Mrs. Fenwick and her children, his disappearance when the Commissioner came, and the cloak of suspicion and secrecy all do make sense, do they not?"

"Yes, perfect sense. But you are convinced that he would not commit the murders? I thought you told me that Roman priests could be dangerous."

"I did, but not to fellow Roman Catholics—" he gave a little laugh—"or in the usual course of things. In the situation in which we found ourselves then, we were dealing with a desperate spy. To restore a Roman Catholic king to the throne, a priest could perhaps justify killing a person who was a serious impediment to the 'one true' faith, but the benefit to the church would have to be very high to excuse such a terrible sin.

"No," St. Mars continued, "I am convinced that Moreland is innocent and that he wants to discover Fenwick's murderer as much as we do. He may have accused me, but on what grounds, I cannot imagine. I find it hard, too, to see why he would risk calling attention to himself by bringing a charge."

"Then it very well may have been the killer who did it. Who else should we consider?"

"It would have to be someone very bold, but also someone who felt threatened. The murder of Abelson must have persuaded everyone that Fenwick's murder could not be put down to a deserter from the army or a stranger to the area. Two such chance events would seem to have near impossible odds. As soon as the murderer realized this, he must have worried that he could fall under suspicion. So he decided to throw the suspicion onto someone else."

Hester could not fault his logic, but they had both been so certain Mr. Moreland was the killer that she had stopped trying to draw a connection to anyone else. "It has to be someone who knew Mr. Fenwick and has some awareness of you. Could it be someone who simply has an uncontrollable hatred for papists?"

"Is there anyone in our acquaintance who fits that description? The Reverend Mr. Ward?"

"I have asked myself whether his resentment of the papists in his parish was as deep as that. If it is possible then I made a terrible mistake to ask him if Mr. Abelson was a member of his parish, but truthfully, I cannot see it. He does regret their presence here, but he is careful not to let his resentment lead him into expressing anything akin to hatred. To murder two men just because they were papists is the sort of act that only a madman would commit, surely."

"I'm inclined to agree."

They had been standing in the same spot in which he had greeted her, close together and grasping each other's hands. Now, as they both paused to think, St. Mars relaxed his grip. Their hands, still held, fell into a gentler clasp between them. Hester became conscious of the rougher texture of St. Mars's skin against hers, but now was not the time for amourous thoughts with St. Mars in danger.

"What about Mr. Mynchon?" Hester asked. "Did you know that he went to Oulston Hall to try to buy the Fenwicks' relic from Charles? And he was very angry when Charles refused to sell it."

"No! I thought Mrs. Mynchon had warded off that idea."

Hester gave him a rueful look. "She was not successful. Evidently, Mr. Mynchon is not to be discouraged from anything having to do with acquisitions to his collection. I'm afraid Mary made matters worse when, in front of Charles, she described Mr. Mynchon's expression as murderous. That made Charles speculate on the possibility that Mr. Mynchon had killed his father to have a better chance of obtaining the relic."

"That might have been worth considering before Abelson was killed, but Mynchon could not have the same motive for murdering him." St. Mars searched her face as he said, "What about your cousin Dudley? I understand that he was not at home when the rest of you arrived and heard about Fenwick's death."

"No, he was not, but what would Dudley's motive be?"

"He is not very fond of papists, and he reacted callously to the news of Abelson's murder."

"I would characterize his attitude towards papists as indifferent rather than passionate. He is much too lazy to hold anyone in that kind of abhorrence."

"What about his violence when he is in his cups?"

Hester sighed. "We both know the trouble his foul temper has got him into. But his violence when he's been drinking is indiscriminate.

A person would have to be right in front of him to provoke him to an assault. What are the chances again that both Mr. Fenwick and poor Mr. Abelson would find themselves in that situation? Besides, both men were shot. Dudley would have to be very drunk indeed to want to murder two men, and surely by then his aim would be too poor to hit them?"

St. Mars smiled down at her and gave her hands a gentle shake. "True." He sobered, looking pensive. "Still, I remember having the feeling, when he and I were drinking together at the inn, that he knew something about this business with Fenwick. If I could force it out of him, it might be useful."

Hester hesitated. Then she said, "At one time, I did wonder if Pamela could have killed Mr. Fenwick."

St. Mars was taken aback. "You did? Why?"

"Because she told me that she was used to hunt with her father. Sir Ralph taught her to shoot."

He still looked puzzled. "But she could not have killed Fenwick. Was she not in York to fetch you?"

Hester opened her mouth to answer, but St. Mars's head jerked up. "Sh!"

Then she heard it, footsteps coming towards them in the maze.

Before she could think what to do, St. Mars dropped her hands and grasped her by the shoulders. "You must not be discovered speaking to me. You must struggle as if I've attacked you!"

"No!" He could not be thinking clearly. If he thought she would sacrifice him for the sake of her reputation, he was terribly wrong.

The memory of coming across Mary and Charles in Sir Ralph's garden and her subsequent behaviour leapt to her mind. "We must pretend to embrace. Whoever sees us will be so embarrassed, he will turn away." If the person was just a gardener, it would not matter. If it was someone who could harm St. Mars, this might give him a minute in which to run away.

A strange little smile turned up the corners of St. Mars's lips. As the footsteps came closer, he whispered, "Are you quite certain of this, my dear Mrs. Kean?"

A thrill shot through her and she nodded.

With a slight shake of his head as if to clear it from a dream, St. Mars took her in his arms and pressed his mouth to hers.

Nothing could have prepared her for this. His lips were warm and generous and full of tenderness. He deepened his kiss, softly coaxing her to respond and parting her lips to savour her mouth, his tongue teasing her and sating her by turns. She felt all her caution slip into nothingness as she lost herself in a whirl of passion, so long denied, so longed for. Then his kisses were trailing down her neck and she moaned with the excitement aroused in her breasts and in the juncture between her legs.

His breathing came in ever louder gasps. His hands roamed all over her, her neck, her back, her arms. Then, his thumbs sought her breasts, awakening in her a need for a deeper touch. Her skirts began to rise. The air that brushed her legs felt so good as he cupped her buttocks, and she cried out with the uncontrollable pleasure of being devoured.

The sound of her own voice shocked her. She awakened to their situation and opened her eyes to find that whoever had been coming had turned away as she had planned.

All thought of anyone else, of where they were, of the world, had vanished the moment he had touched her. But she could not let him take her right here, no matter how tempted she was to give in.

She broke away to look up into his face and saw that he was as lost to passion as she had been. "My lord?"

His hands stopped moving and his gaze slowly focused.

"Are we still pretending?"

He let out a shout of laughter, but his voice shook. Then, gripping her tightly by the shoulders and lowering his head to peer directly into her eyes, he said, "Not I."

Tears clouded Hester's eyes and she smiled back at him. "Nor I, my lord."

"Gideon," he said.

"Yes . . . dear Gideon. And you shall call me Hester."

He chuckled deeply and enveloped her in his arms. "You will always be my dearest Mrs. Kean. It suits your dignity so well."

*I*ngratitude is among them a capital Crime, as we read it to have been in some other Countries: For they reason this; that whoever makes ill Returns to his Benefactor, must needs be a common Enemy to the rest of Mankind, from whom he hath received no Obligation; and therefore such a Man is not fit to live.

CHAPTER XVII

For a moment her heart sank. Then, in a low tremulous voice, he whispered into her ear, "But will you come with me to France, to St. Mars, and live with me there? Will you be my countess and my wife?"

Joy surged through her so suddenly, it impeded her ability to speak. It was a moment before she could manage, "Yes, my lord, I will."

He squeezed her tightly, burying his lips in her hair, before arousing her with a long, slow kiss. Hester felt drunk with his essence, a mixture of soap and sweat and leather. The muscles in his arms were taut about her ribs and shook with evident restraint. When they both became breathless again, he rested his forehead against hers. "I am sorry if I alarmed you. I have wanted you for so many months, it has taken every shred of my control not to grab you and kiss you in front of your cousins. That first kiss knocked my head off my shoulders, and I forgot where we were. I will do my utmost to restrain myself from now on, but you must help me hold to my promise."

Hester wondered how she was to help him when she could barely help herself, but she promised him soberly that she would. "But we must first get you safely out of this predicament."

"What predicament?" Elation filled his voice. "We shall just leap onto our horses and ride for the coast."

He sounded serious, but with St. Mars one could never tell. "And have the whole countryside raised against us? My dearest lord, how far do you think we should get? Even if we did get away, what purpose would it serve for me to be outlawed as well as you, for I should surely be named as your accomplice?"

He frowned. "I confess, that possibility had escaped me. I am not thinking clearly." He drew her hand to his lips and planted a kiss. "You shall have to think for both of us until I can duck my head in a bucket of cold water."

She felt her cheeks dimpling. She had always known St. Mars to be a passionate man, but still it was immensely gratifying to know that she could have this effect on him.

For her own part, she found that stimulation had invigorated her brain. She had never felt so bright or so alive, as if her blood were on fire.

"Before we can be free to leave, I'm afraid we must unravel this mystery. Aside from the fact that our consciences would always plague us if we did not, we can travel more securely if "Sir Robert" is never unmasked. No one doubts your identity now, but if we run, they are certain to discover your deception and the charges against you will be much worse. I am not at all confident that the consequences could not follow us into France."

"You may be right. Very well, let us think." Reluctantly, he widened the space between them. "I must be free to investigate. So I shall have to plan my movements accordingly."

The thought of his being arrested terrified her. She almost changed her mind about fleeing, but she felt they were close to uncovering the murderer, and it seemed the best solution for them both. "Where can you go to be safe?"

He mused for a moment, then said, "Strangely enough, the safest place may be Oulston Hall." When his answer made her start, he met her eyes and continued, "Yes, I am certain that is where I should go. I need to discover if it was Moreland who set the constables on me. I do not have to fear him if it was, for I can always threaten to expose him as a priest who has said a mass. I may even be able to persuade him to withdraw the charge."

"And if it was not Mr. Moreland?"

"Then I shall have to convince him that the murderer concocted the story against me. Since he must have known Abelson, he may be able to help us ascertain the person most likely to have killed them both."

"Of course. If Mr. Moreland is a priest, he would have known Mr. Abelson very well. The only thing the two victims would seem to have in common was that they were Roman Catholics. If the motive for killing them was simply malice towards their faith, however, I doubt Mr. Moreland will be much help. He suspects all of us of that."

"Has it never struck you as odd that Sir Ralph should have a papist for a tenant?"

Hester answered eagerly, "Yes, it did, but I learned from Mrs. Fenwick that Sir Ralph bought land from her husband when he could no longer afford to pay the taxes on it. I guessed that Mr. Abelson must have been a tenant on that parcel. That could account for his hope that Charles would help him to get it back."

St. Mars looked strangely at her. "Then Sir Ralph had the most obvious connection to them both. If it were not for his being in York when Fenwick was murdered, we should have to suspect him."

"But he was not in York. Neither was Pamela. That was what I was about to say when we heard someone coming."

St. Mars gripped her by the shoulders again, searching her face as she explained, "They did ride to York that day, but they were still at home when Mr. Fenwick was murdered. At least, I assume they could have been. I do not know at what hour they set out, but they had all day to get to York for the stagecoach was not due until evening."

She could see St. Mars's thoughts turning quickly. He was standing so close. The temptation to reach for his beloved face was almost overwhelming, but as much as she wanted to lose herself in his arms again, she knew they must solve this mystery, for his own safety if for no other reason.

"But Sir Ralph has always been a good friend to the Fenwicks. Mrs. Fenwick told me so herself."

St. Mars gave her a cynical look. "If there is anything that causes trouble between neighbours, it is property. Any landowner knows that. And friendship can be feigned."

Hester admitted, "I did not like it when Sir Ralph suggested that Charles might have murdered Mr. Abelson. And his assumption that Mr. Abelson could have killed Mr. Fenwick made no sense. When I spoke to Mr. Abelson, he said that Mr. Fenwick never would have turned him off his farm."

"If Sir Ralph is responsible for both killings, that could have been his first attempt to throw suspicion onto someone else."

They gazed into each other's eyes, mirroring each other's thoughts.

After a moment, Hester asked, "If it was Sir Ralph, how can we go about proving it?"

St. Mars pondered a moment longer. "We must be very careful. First, you and I are outsiders. We cannot make an accusation carelessly or we shall not be believed. Anyone local will be obliged to defend Sir Ralph in case our accusation proves false, or he may risk incurring a lifelong enemy. And, if it does turn out to be Sir Ralph, we know he's a very dangerous man. He has killed twice and will not hesitate to do so again.

"Let me see what I can do to get the charge against me dropped. Then I would like to talk to your cousin Dudley. He made a reference to Sir Ralph that makes me think he knows something."

"What can I do? And when shall we meet again? If Sir Ralph is your enemy, we cannot meet here."

He smiled and sighed, his look reluctant. "No, we do not dare." He pulled her into his arms and hugged her. "If I can get the charge dropped, I'll call for you at Beckwith Manor, and woe be unto the person who tries to prevent me. If I cannot, I'll find a way to get a message to you."

"You will not take any undue risks?"

He chuckled into her hair, which must by now look like a bird's nest. "When being arrested would make mincemeat of my plans for you? My dear Mrs. Kean, I shall be caution personified."

He did not kiss her again, but rocked with her body pressed against his, until her pulse was throbbing and she had to stifle a whimper.

Then, with a moan he broke away from her, giving his head a little shake. "I must go now, or I'll forget my good intentions." He looked into her eyes. "The next time we see each other, I hope it shall be to plan our escape."

A flutter of emotions rose up in her breast—elation, fear, guilt—she was too overcome to sort them out. Whatever he saw reflected in her gaze seemed to please him, however. "Yes, let us hope so."

"Till then . . . did I say that I love you?"

She laughed, and she had never laughed so merrily before. "No, but I inferred that you might. I made a leap of faith, but it is wonderful to hear you say it nevertheless."

"And may I infer that you love me?"

"You may infer as much as you like, but I do love you. I have loved you a long while."

"Hester!" He took a step towards her as if to envelop her again, but remembering his resolve, folded his arms in front of him. "This is intolerable!" He uttered a noise that sounded like a growl. "How can we be separated now?"

"It should not be for long. I shall find out everything I can while waiting to hear from you. I believe we are on the true path at last."

He was shaking his head. "No, please. I forbid it. This is too dangerous. Just wait until I either bring or send you word. You must promise me."

Hester struggled with her conscience. She did not wish to make him a promise that she might have to break. "I shall do nothing, unless I hear that you have been arrested. Then, I must do something."

He was sobered now, but he conceded her point with a nod. "Then you had better leave the maze first. I am not certain I have the strength to walk away from you. Do not worry, though," he added when he saw her anxious look. "Once you have left, I'll recover. This must be the way Samson felt after Delilah cut his hair."

Gideon watched her leave laughing, believing perhaps that he had been speaking in jest. But the truth was he wanted her so much that wrenching himself away from her would have taken more resolve than he had. To have her so close, nearly as defenceless against their shared passion as he was, had tested him in a way he had never been tested before. Now, if he was to avoid arrest, he would have to force his mind to his business, and ignore the glow her love had kindled in his loins or else risk that it might prove a dangerous distraction.

He took a few deep breaths until the shaking in his knees subsided. Then, quietly he followed her out of the maze.

He caught a glimpse of her outside the service wing before she disappeared round the corner of the house. Then he made his way to the stable where Tom was waiting. Unaware that Sir Ralph might pose a danger to him, Gideon had instructed him to ask Sir Ralph's man about the poultice Dudley Mayfield had mentioned, leaving it to Tom to concoct his own lies about Penny's limp.

If Gideon did not manage to have the charge of murder dropped, he would no longer need an excuse to miss the York races next week. For now, the sooner they departed from Yearsley Park the better it would be. Mrs. Kean had not said how long she thought Sir Ralph and her cousin would be away. They would not want to be at his house when he returned.

Tom was waiting outside with Argos, and obviously relieved to see him. Without a word, they mounted, saying nothing until they had cleared the gate to Yearsley Park.

"Shall I go back to the inn for your things, my lord?"

"No, we're not leaving yet. And when we do—" Gideon grinned at him—"we shall not be alone. Mrs. Kean will be riding with us." He felt just a little bit foolish, but if he did not tell someone, he might burst.

Tom looked almost as pleased as Gideon felt. "That's good news, my lord. May I take the liberty of wishing you joy?'"

"You may, but perhaps you should hold onto those wishes until we are out of this mess. We have a few matters to tend to first."

"Yes, my lord, we surely do."

On the way to Oulston Hall, Gideon told Tom what his immediate plan was. He instructed him to wait outside the gate to the Fenwick estate to watch for any sign of trouble. "You might have to contrive my escape from the law again, in which case it would be best for you to hide. If you do not see a servant departing to fetch the constables, after a half-hour or so you should be able to assume that I am safe."

"Then what do I do?"

"I'll send you a message by one of Fenwick's servants, or I'll come for you myself." Gideon commanded Argos to stay and left him with Tom outside the gate, while he made his way to the door of the old house.

A servant took Penny's reins, and Gideon gratefully noted his confident manner. In his current difficulties, he did not have the luxury to worry about his horse, but he would have been dismayed to witness a display of her histrionics.

When summoned by an indoor servant, Charles received him in a downstairs parlour. Surprised by the visit, but betraying no sign of unease, he greeted Gideon politely. "To what do I owe the honour of this visit, Sir Robert?"

Gideon gave him a rueful smile. "You may not consider it such an honour when I tell you why I am here, but I assure you, I mean you no harm. I must ask to speak with Mr. Moreland."

Taken aback by the first part of Gideon's speech, Charles was startled by the last. "Mr. Moreland?" He paused. "May I ask what the nature of your business with him is?"

"I shall be happy to tell you, but it is very important that I see him first." When Charles hesitated, he added, "Please tell me that he is still here."

Something in his voice or demeanour must have conveyed the urgency of his request for, relenting at last, Charles nodded. "You have just managed to catch him. He was about to leave, but I shall fetch him." He hesitated again. "Shall I have a servant bring you some refereshment?"

Gideon declined with a smile and a shake of his head. As Charles left the room, he released a pent-up breath. If Moreland had already left Oulston Hall, he did not know what his chances would have been. He could not know how Charles would react to the news that Gideon had been accused of his father's murder. He needed the leverage of his knowledge of Moreland's activities to insure his safety.

After a short wait, Moreland entered the room, followed closely by Charles, both wearing leery expressions. After exchanging bows, Charles invited Gideon to sit. On his way to Oulston Hall, Gideon had given some thought to the way to reveal the purpose of his visit, and he believed he had lit upon the best approach.

When, after all the gentlemen were seated, Moreland inquired as to the reason Gideon wished to see him, Gideon began, "On Sunday night, two men were spied riding away from this house."

Surprise and worry appeared briefly on both his listeners' faces. They said nothing, however, so Gideon went on, "I was one of those men and my servant was the other."

Moreland's chest swelled. "What right do you have to spy upon this house? What could you mean by it?"

Giving Charles what he hoped was a reassuring look, Gideon said, "I had some notion that you could be the person who murdered Mr. Fenwick."

The shock and affront in Moreland's expression would have been comical if so much were not at stake. Before either he or Gideon could speak, Charles cried, "No, Sir Robert, you are wrong! Mr. Moreland is the one person my family can trust."

"I know. I also know the reason for the confidence you place in him." Gideon turned back to address Moreland. "When I was here Sunday night, what I saw made me realize what I should have seen before. All the clues were there, but my suspicions had been influenced by the rebellion."

Charles's eyes widened in alarm, but Moreland merely looked scornful. "If you know who I am and have not reported me to the authorities, I suppose you are here to demand money for your silence."

This was an interpretation of his actions that Gideon had not anticipated; however, he followed Moreland's logic. Instead of the insult he might have felt, he chose to be amused. "I have no need of your money. It is your help I am after. I need to know if it was you who laid a charge of murder against me with the authorities."

His question plainly threw Moreland off guard, so much so that Gideon was convinced he had known nothing about the accusation even before Moreland answered in the negative.

"I had to check," Gideon explained. "The questions you posed to both me and my servant made it obvious that you suspected me of killing Fenwick's father, so it could have been you who accused me. If it was not, since I had already realized that you could not be the killer, it seems likely that the killer did it to throw the blame onto someone else.

"I do not know why I was chosen as scapegoat when I can prove that I was miles from here when the first murder occurred, or why you were not the target, when you could have been in the area as easily as I. For whatever reason, the murderer fears that a connection between the victims and himself will soon be made and has decided to conceal it by creating a hue and cry over me."

"Whom do you suspect?" Charles asked quickly. Moreland, who was not yet ready to clear Gideon of suspicion, said nothing.

"There is someone, but I had rather not give his name yet." He doubted Charles would be eager to accept that Sir Ralph could be the villain, not when Sir Ralph had taken such pains to ingratiate himself with the young man. "But we think that Abelson may have known or have guessed and that was the reason he was killed. It may even be why he was so anxious to speak to you."

"Abelson? That tenant?"

Ignoring Charles's question, Gideon turned to Moreland again. "Mr. Abelson was one of your parishioners, was he not?"

Moreland's eyes narrowed, but for the first time they held a glint of interest. "Yes, but, as he was turned off so suddenly, I was unable to locate him."

"From where his body was found, it's been deduced that he was living rough. He was anxious to speak to you, Fenwick, and the person he spoke to about it said that he seemed convinced that you could help him regain the tenancy of his farm."

"I know," Charles said. "On the evening of the consort, Sir Ralph took me aside and said that Mr. Abelson had accosted Mrs. Kean when she was in the village with the children."

Before he had finished speaking, Gideon was shaking his head. "That is not the story as I heard it. Mrs. Kean insists that it was she who approached Abelson. After the incident in Thirsk, when she learned who he was, she became concerned about his impoverished condition. When she tried to listen to his reason for seeking an audience with you, they were interrupted by Sir Ralph and Abelson took off running."

"Sir Ralph told me he had to turn him off the land because he was a troublemaker."

Moreland frowned at Charles. "I never knew Mr. Abelson to be troublesome. When he was your father's tenant, he was perfectly respectable . . . and very observant."

Charles looked confused and dismayed. "Then I might have been able to help him after all."

"You should not blame yourself. You were a virtual stranger to the area. You had no reason to doubt anything Sir Ralph said."

Both Gideon and Moreland observed Charles to witness his reaction to these statements. Gideon believed that Moreland had arrived at the same conclusion that he and Mrs. Kean had.

A sequence of thoughts and feelings played across Charles's features, from an initial glimmer of suspicion through disbelief, anger and offence, then back to reluctant suspicion. "You are suggesting that Sir Ralph is the person who murdered my father?"

Gideon shook his head. "I have no proof, and for the life of me I do not know why he would have done it. The only thing I can do at this juncture is point out that he is the one person who had a connection to both your father and Abelson." Gideon spoke to Moreland earnestly. "If you have information that contradicts any of this, I beg you will tell us. For instance, did either of these men, or both, involve themselves in the rebellion?"

Moreland's lips were pressed into a thin, stern line, but he gave his head a firm shake. "If they had, I should have known."

He did not say, but Gideon suspected he had regularly heard their confessions. If either man had taken part in the conspiracy for religious reasons, he would have confessed as much to his priest. It was highly improbable either would have taken part in any case unless under Moreland's direction.

As Charles had been listening to this exchange, his cheeks had grown pale. Now he said, "Before anything further is said, please let me call for refreshments. I am feeling the need for sustenance, and I assume it would not be unwelcome to you."

His guests agreed. Charles was about to step out into the hall, when Gideon recalled that Tom would be anxious to know that his master was safe.

He called after Charles, "Could you ask one of your servants to carry a message to my groom who is waiting just outside your gate? He only needs to say that all is well."

Moreland shot him a wary look, as if he feared Gideon could be sending some kind of signal.

Gideon felt a flush creeping up his neck. He grinned self-consciously. "Tom has been my servant since I was very young. He has a tendency to worry."

"He would be concerned . . . ?"

Since neither Moreland nor Charles had given any sign of wanting to report his whereabouts to the authorities, Gideon felt safe enough to say, "That I might be met with enmity in this house."

Charles reentered the room, followed soon by a manservant, carrying a type of homemade berry wine and a simple board of bread and cheese. "I have given the order for your groom to be invited up to the house. He will be made comfortable in the kitchen." As the wine was poured, still pale, Charles grimaced. "I apologize for the humble nature of the beverage. I've been told that at one time Oulston Hall had a respectable cellar, but our income will no longer stretch to either claret or cognac."

Gideon, who had neither eaten nor drunk a mouthful since early that morning, made it clear how grateful he was for the offering.

While the servant was in the room, an air of tension pervaded the space. As soon as he left, Gideon wasted no time in resuming his questions. Abandoning his previous line of inquiry, he asked Moreland, "Do you know anything about the land Mr. Fenwick sold to Sir Ralph?"

"Only that the sale was made to relieve Fenwick of the burden of taxes, and that a few Catholic families lived on the parcel."

"He did not discuss the sale with you?"

A condescending smile appeared on Moreland's face. "Parishioners' business affairs are not my concern. Mine is only their spiritual wellbeing."

"Were you not worried about possible consequences to the tenants?"

The question wiped the smile off Moreland's lips. He hesitated before answering, "I had no reason to suspect that any of them would be turned off their farms. Mr. Fenwick was very confident that Sir Ralph would keep them on."

"Did he mention why he was so confident?"

Moreland frowned. "There was something in the terms of the sale, I think. He did not say what it was, and, as he seemed considerably relieved by the arrangement, I did not ask."

"Relieved? Was that truly how he felt? There was no sense of coercion? Having to sell off part of his land did not make him bitter or angry?"

Gideon saw that his questions were having an effect on Moreland, as if he were reflecting on Fenwick's attitude about the sale and wondering why it had not seemed odd to him at the time.

"Far from it. He did not act at all bitter. He seemed relieved to the point of cheerfulness."

Gideon could not reconcile such a positive emotion with being forced to sell land. It should violate every landowner's instinct. All three men were silent while each mused over Fenwick's strange behaviour.

"There must have been something unusual about the sale," Gideon said. "Is there anything among your father's records relating to it?" he asked Charles.

Charles shook his head. "Not that I recall, except for the entry in his accounts. And the King's Commissioner, Mr. Foxcroft, found nothing irregular in them."

Frustrated, Gideon rubbed his forehead. "If something about the sale was not the reason behind the murders, then I am confounded." He raised his gaze to Charles again, "How did Sir Ralph pay your father for the land?"

"I shall have to look in the accounts. Shall I get them now?"

"No," Gideon shook his head. "But it might shed some light on the subject. Right now, I have a more pressing concern." He gave Charles a weak smile. "I do not think the constables will come searching for me here—that was one of the reasons I came here first—but if I am to pursue these matters, I must get the charges against me dropped. If I can speak to Mr. Mynchon, I have a chance of persuading him of my innocence, but if you were to come with me and speak on my behalf, that should carry more weight."

As he spoke Mr. Mynchon's name, his listeners bristled. It was Charles who spoke first, "I regret, Sir Robert, but that will not be possible."

✆

Hester walked back home on a cloud. She could not have said later how she arrived at the gate to Beckwith Manor. All she could see was St. Mars's face as he had kissed her goodbye. The only sound she heard was his voice saying that he loved her and wanted her to be his wife. Her nerves were tingling with arousal, her lips permanently stretched in a smile. For thirty minutes, she could dream of riding off with him, having his children, and spending her life as his wife in France.

Then Beckwith Manor stood before her, and she was forced to remember the danger to him if she failed to conceal her emotions. Just a little bit longer, she promised herself, just a matter of days. But somehow in those days, they must manage to unmask a killer.

A servant greeted her with the news that Pamela had asked for her. The notion that Pamela might have heard of the charge against "Sir Robert," drove her to hasten directly to Pamela's chamber.

"What took you from the house so long?" Pamela, who was sitting at her dressing table, having her hair arranged, greeted her abruptly. It was the question Hester had anticipated.

"I went out early for a walk and the morning was so delightful, I went all the way to Yearsley Park and around the gardens."

"No wonder." Pamela smirked, taking this as a compliment to her father. "Papa will be happy to hear that you enjoyed it. He is very proud of its design, you know."

"The servant said you were looking for me. Do you need me? I should go to my room and change."

"No hurry. I simply wish to talk to you about the race meeting in York. I always attend it with Papa, and you and Mary will want to come with us."

"Oh." Hester was taken aback. "I have not had any notion of going. I suppose I assumed it was only for the gentlemen."

Pamela huffed. "They would undoubtedly prefer it to be, but since the old Queen attended them, they could not dare exclude us. Many of the ladies go simply for the opportunity to shop, but several of us like to watch the races, too. Mary has been dying to see them, and I cannot think of a reason why she should not go this year."

"Yes, of course." Hester was wondering whether she would still be at Beckwith Manor next week. If St. Mars were arrested, she would have to plot his escape with Tom. She had managed to convince herself that he was safely hidden at Oulston Hall, but now that she had returned to reality, the peril he was in struck her with full force.

It was clear that Pamela had heard nothing of the accusation against him or the news of it would have been the first words out of her mouth. Hester hoped that a similar ignorance prevailed at Oulston Hall. Surely, it would not be long before someone told the constables of "Sir Robert's" frequent visits to Beckwith Manor and they came looking for him here. If they had gone to report his absence to Mr. Mynchon, he was likely to send them.

Leaving Pamela with her maid, Hester sought her bedchamber in a subdued mood. She found Mary there, dressing and looking a bit downcast. They exchanged greetings while Hester set about changing into a gown more suited to indoor activities.

Hoping to stave off any questions from Mary, for she knew she would have a harder time lying to her, Hester said, "I have just spoken with Pamela and understand that you are to attend the race meeting at York."

The enthusiasm this raised on Mary's face was scarcely more than a glimmer. "Yes, I am sure it will be splendid. Still . . ." She sighed. "I should rather move on to London. Now that I am committed to going, remaining here any longer seems pointless."

"Pamela said you were eager to attend."

"I have been, but . . . well . . . ." Mary did not complete her thought. "I am just so glad that you will be going to London with me, Hester."

A pang of guilt made Hester wince. If she disappeared with St. Mars, who would be at Hawkhurst House to defend Mary? Was her own happiness to come at the expense of her favourite cousin's? But it was not only her own happiness at stake, but that of St. Mars, whom she loved and who had been made to suffer injustice and loneliness, much of it at the hands of Hester's family.

No, her loyalties must be clear. Still, it was painful to think of hurting Mary. Once they were safely in France, she would have to write the girl a letter, explaining the choice she had made. She only hoped Mary would forgive her.

Two hours passed before a knocking at the door announced the arrival of the constables. Hester had been at pains to appear normal, as the three ladies sat and worked in one of the downstairs parlours with windows facing east and south to admit the best light for their sewing.

The knocks on the door made her jump. They fell so loudly that the ladies could hear them all the way across the house.

"Goodness!" Pamela exclaimed, putting down her needle. "Who can be raising such a dust?"

In just a few moments, a servant arrived, followed by two burly men, clutching their caps in their hands. Their eyes fearfully raked the room, as if they were afraid to discover a goblin concealed behind the furniture.

Pamela recognized them at once. Indeed, one of the men was the blacksmith who had given the children their horseshoes.

"Mr. Smith, Mr. Stamper, what is the meaning of this?"

Mr. Stamper took it upon himself to speak, but before explaining the reason for his errand, he asked, "Is Maister Mayfield abowt?"

"No, my husband is not at home. You may tell me what your business is."

When their agitated movements immediately ceased, Hester realized that the fear had been caused by the possibility of encountering Dudley.

"Wi doan't wann t'moither thee, milady. 'Tis nowt t'do wi thine. 'Tis Sir Robert Mavors wi're arter."

"Sir Robert?" Pamela exclaimed. "Why?"

In their broad Yorkshire, the constables gave her to understand that Mr. Mynchon had issued a warrant for Sir Robert's arrest."

"But that is absurd!" Pamela said indignantly.

Mary was only slightly less so. "What can Sir Robert possibly have done?"

In the face of such outrage, the two men exchanged uneasy looks. Hester remained silent, grateful for the protest the other ladies had made. She would save her own for later if it was still needed.

Mr. Smith found his courage first and blurted, "'E's wanted fer murtherin' Maister Fenwick."

"Nah, then! Geeoer!" Mr. Stamper waved his cap at the blacksmith. "Dinnen Maister Mynchon seh fer thee t'keep tha gob shoot?"

Hester understood from this that Mr. Mynchon had not wanted the news of Sir Robert's arrest bandied about. Did this mean he was still unconvinced of St. Mars's guilt? A spark of hope lit inside her. The only person she had seen Mr. Mynchon warm to was St. Mars.

Pamela had been struck speechless. Now she found her voice to utter, "But that cannot be! Sir Robert had not even arrived in this area when Mr. Fenwick was killed. Who accuses him?"

Hester held her breath for the answer, but the constables did not know. They protested that their job was only to bring the accused into Mr. Mynchon's presence and make certain he did not escape.

"Well, you may tell Mr. Mynchon from me that his accuser is wrong! I shall have a word with Mr. Mynchon myself. Meanwhile, you will not find Sir Robert here."

With mumbled apologies, the two men bowed themselves backwards to the door, where with sighs of relief they turned and hastened from the room.

At this point, Hester contributed her support for Pamela's idea of carrying her protest to Mr. Mynchon. "I cannot believe that Sir Robert had anything to do with the murders. Why, there has been no suggestion that he ever even met Mr. Fenwick. If you mean to speak to Mr. Mynchon, I shall be happy to go with you."

Now that Pamela had had a moment to reflect, however, her indignation had cooled. "I cannot believe it of him, either, but my father has entertained suspicions of Sir Robert for the past few weeks. Perhaps we should wait until he and Dudley are back from the market and consult their opinions on the matter."

Letting her frustration run away with her, Hester said, "I can tell you right now that Dudley's chief concern will be to discover what will become of Sir Robert's horse in the event that he is hanged."

It was the wrong thing to say, she could tell as soon as the words crossed her lips. Pamela drew herself up. "This is a local matter, Hester, and as such it does not regard you. I shall wait for my father's advice."

Hester realized that, if she were not careful, she would turn Pamela against St. Mars. She had blown hot and cold on him, depending on how much attention he was paying her. If she had given up her idea of becoming a waiting woman at Court, she would not have as much use for him and, long ago, she must have given up on conquering his heart.

Hester swallowed her fear for St. Mars and said calmly, "Of course. I only meant to second your resolve. It has nothing to do with me other than I hate to see anybody falsely accused."

"If Sir Robert was not about when Mr. Fenwick was killed, he ought to be able to produce a witness."

Hester took a deep breath. "That is true." She hoped that St. Mars had stayed at an inn on his way up to Yorkshire, using the name Mavors. If not, a simple letter from the innkeeper would not suffice to acquit him. Whatever occurred, he must avoid imprisonment at all cost, for there would be nothing he could do afterwards but wait for the next assizes in York. The risk to him then would be doubled, for one of the justices might have seen him before. Even if not, how long would it be before someone determined that a man by the name of Sir Robert Mavors had never existed?

That he had good Reasons to think you were a Big-Endian in your Heart; and as Treason begins in the Heart before it appears in Overt-Acts; so he accused you as a Traytor on that Account, and therefore insisted you should be put to death.

CHAPTER XVIII

Gideon was taken aback by Charles's refusal to accompany him to speak to the justice of the peace. For an instant, he was afraid that Moreland and Charles were still unconvinced of his innocence, but their reluctance to help him was soon explained when Charles related the offensive circumstances of Mr. Mynchon's visit to his house.

He tried not to let his impatience with their reason show. He must have a place where he could be safe from arrest, and Oulston Hall was his only option.

"Then, I'm afraid I shall have to impose on you for a few hours. I eluded the constables at the Fauconberg Arms, and they must be combing the area for me. I cannot believe they will come here. If I were guilty of killing of your father, this is the last place I should come. I shall have to wait until dark before approaching Mr. Mynchon on my own."

Charles consulted Moreland's opinion with a questioning look. Moreland, who had been watching Gideon silently for some time now, asked him, "Is it your intention to search for proof of Mr. Fenwick's and poor Abelson's killer?"

Gideon assured him sincerely that it was. "I cannot have this charge hanging over my head. Whether I can convince Mr. Mynchon

of my innocence or not, I do have one avenue I can pursue. I intend
to question Dudley Mayfield. I have a feeling he may know something
about Mr. Fenwick's business with Sir Ralph."

Moreland studied his face another minute. Then he gave Charles a
curt nod. "I leave the decision in your hands, my son. I must be off. It
would not be wise for me to linger any longer than I already have."

His bag was already packed. His horse had been waiting since
shortly before Gideon's arrival.

"Sir Robert, I shall take my leave of you." Then, before turning, he
added, "You have my blessing."

A smile broke out over Charles's features as he followed his priest
from the room, promising to return to Gideon once he had escorted
Mr. Moreland to his horse.

Gideon, who had stood to bid the priest goodbye, began to pace
the room. Inside, he cursed Charles's stubbornness, but as it could not
be helped, he spent the next few minutes working on a plan.

By the time Charles returned, Gideon had thought of a different request. "If you will not come with me to see Mynchon, would
you write a letter informing him that you do not believe me guilty of
murdering your father? Whoever accused me cannot possibly have any
evidence, so your testimony may be enough to clear me of suspicion.
I can send my man to the place where I stayed in Doncaster before arriving in Thirsk to bring back proof, but the trip will take him at least
two days if all goes well, and I had rather not be without him now."

Charles proved perfectly willing to agree to this, as long as he did
not have to speak to Mr. Mynchon directly. While Gideon made a trip
to the back of the house in search of Tom, Charles sat behind a small
desk and penned a letter to the effect that as he had found no evidence
of a connection between his father and Sir Robert, he felt confident of
the latter's innocence in the case of his father's killing.

"What do you intend to do next?" he asked, when Gideon reentered the room.

"I will send my groom to Mynchon's house with your letter before
I speak to him myself. Providing he does not send the constables to
lock me up, I shall look for Dudley Mayfield and see what information
I can pry from him."

"I should like to go with you when you do that," Charles said, jaw tensed. "I cannot stand by and do nothing if there is any chance of bringing my father's killer to justice."

Gideon was so used to having no one but Tom for company on his adventures that at first he was reluctant to accept Charles's offer. When he recalled the need he had felt to avenge his own father's death, however, he had to acquiesce.

"We'll have to wait until dark to look for Mayfield. There is no guarantee that we shall find him. I know a few of his haunts, and I am under the impression that he rides home after midnight most nights, but we could easily search for hours and have nothing to show for it."

His speech did not deter Charles. They agreed that Gideon's presence in the house should be kept secret from Charles's mother. "For she would only wish to know what we were up to," Charles said.

"It would be better for her sake if she is not found to have sheltered me, in case Mr. Mynchon remains unconvinced."

Gideon added that he would be comfortable in the barn and would catch a wink of sleep while they waited for nightfall. Charles promised to send some supper out for both him and Tom, and they arranged to leave the house at ten o'clock.

∅

Hester waited anxiously for word from St. Mars, afraid that at any moment they might receive news of his arrest. Late in the afternoon, after the market had closed, Sir Ralph stopped by Beckwith Manor and with Dudley at his heels came to find the ladies in the Great Parlour where Hester and Pamela were drinking tea.

Usually, after attending a horse market, Dudley was in his cheeriest mood, but this evening he was sullen. The way he avoided meeting Sir Ralph's gaze made Hester suspect they had exchanged unpleasant words on their way home. Since Sir Ralph held a mortgage on the Mayfield estate, Dudley had to submit to his father-in-law. If Sir Ralph had lectured him on his failure to produce an heir, Hester was glad she had not been present to hear that conversation.

After the gentlemen had seated themselves, and a servant had brought a fresh kettle of hot water, Hester let Pamela introduce the news that a warrant had been issued for "Sir Robert's" arrest.

Dudley issued a cry of dismay, his emotion seemingly genuine. Sir Ralph's reaction was more complex. While shaking his head in regret, he smugly stated that he had had his suspicions of the gentleman all along, which, if he were speaking truthfully, would explain his lack of surprise.

"It's a shame, of course, but it will be a relief to have the murderer discovered and punished. If I had only known, I should never have admitted him to Yearsley Park."

Hester spoke as sweetly as she could under the circumstances. "I thought your suspicions had been laid to rest when he produced the letter from Lord Hawkhurst?"

He threw her a skittish look from beneath his eyelids. "There was that, yes. It was clear, however, that he was not as closely acquainted with Lord Hawkhust as he would have had us believe at first. There was always something about him I mistrusted, and it appears that I was right."

"He has a stupendous horse," Dudley said, as if that should acquit "Sir Robert" of a great deal, even murder.

Ignoring him, Pamela said, "But is it certain? If he is the killer, then I confess that I was completely taken in."

"As was I," Hester said. "I am far from convinced. I wonder who laid the charge against him? If there were no witnesses to the crime, and Sir Robert had no connection with either victim, one must ask what evidence could possibly have been presented."

A menacing gleam appeared in Sir Ralph's eyes before he cloaked it. He gave an unconvincing laugh. "I did not know that you had read the law, Mrs. Kean. Surely, issues of this sort should be left to gentlemen."

A shiver travelled down her spine. If she had harboured any doubts about Sir Ralph's guilt, they were vanquished by this attempt to intimidate her. "Of course. Forgive me. Pamela and I had only thought that perhaps we should speak to Mr. Mynchon in Sir Robert's behalf, for his behaviour to us has always been exemplary. I trust, however, that Mr. Mynchon will be fair in his judgement. If Sir Robert is innocent,

I suspect he will be able to produce a witness who can place him far from here on the morning Mr. Fenwick was killed."

Something told her that she had said too much. A flicker of anger mixed with fear flashed in Sir Ralph's eyes. Abruptly, he stood, saying, "Enough of this talk of killers. It's time for me to head home. Thank you for the tea, my dear," he said to Pamela. He gave a curt nod to Hester and a stern look to Dudley before striding from the room.

Hester turned and said to Pamela, "Your father did not forbid us to speak to Mr. Mynchon. If you are still of a mind to go, I would like to go with you."

"Not now," Pamela said, looking troubled. "Perhaps tomorrow, but it is getting too late to pay a visit today."

It appeared that Dudley had only been waiting for his father-in-law to leave before escaping himself. Finishing his tea with one gulp, he stood and excused himself for the evening, saying, "I won't be back until late, so tell William to leave the door unlatched for me."

Pamela gave him a scathing look, but made no comment. Dudley was so seldom at home at a decent hour, it was a rare night when the door would be latched.

Hester's stomach was churning. She wanted desperately to speak to Mr. Mynchon, but as much as she believed that Sir Ralph's remarks had been made to discourage her, she could not be sure that Mr. Mynchon would not react just as badly to a lady's interference. St. Mars had told her to do nothing. She would have to trust in his ability to make things right. But she would not sleep a wink until she knew that he was safe from arrest. She would have to wait until morning and fresher news before deciding what course of action to take.

Tom returned from his errand to report that Mr. Mynchon was not at home. "His servant said he was took to York on business, but they expect him back late tonight."

Gideon cursed then mused, massaging his brow. "Well, it can't be helped. I had hoped he would read the letter in your presence so you could witness his reaction. Did you leave it with his servant?"

"Yes, my lord. He promised to deliver it the moment his master returned."

"Good man. What did you learn at the inn?" Gideon had given Tom instructions to ride past the inn to see if the constables were still there, and if not to see what Sadler reported.

"They're still there, my lord. I couldn't get anywhere near Mr. Sadler, and I didn't dare go upstairs for your things."

"No, they would be sure to stop and question you." Gideon sighed. "We shall have to wait until tomorrow morning and throw ourselves on Mynchon's mercy."

They ate some of the food Charles's servant brought out to them and fortified themselves with his home brew, while Argos happily gnawed on a bone. The wait for ten o'clock stretched long, but Gideon managed to catch a few hours of sleep before Tom waked him, announcing that soon it would be time to go.

Before Charles came out of the house to join them, Tom had saddled all three horses. Charles looked a bit skittish, but determined.

"Ready?" Gideon asked.

A look of embarrassment came over the younger man's features. "I do not have a weapon. The only gun we're allowed would be too cumbersome in the saddle."

Gideon grinned ruefully. "That makes three of us. I came away from the inn too suddenly to grab my sword. Let us hope that Dudley Mayfield is in no condition to pick a fight."

After a futile search of the few drinking establishments within a short ride of Beckwith Manor, they were forced to wait for Dudley outside his gate. The sky was clear and the moon was almost full. Together with a spectacle of stars, it lit the countryside with so much light, they could make out one another's features without the aid of torches. The night was pleasantly warm. They dismounted and tethered their horses to the gate posts. The crunches of the horses' teeth as they grazed, an occasional hoot from an owl, and the rustling of tiny nocturnal creatures were the only sounds that broke the stillness. The presence of his dog would have been welcome, but afraid Argos would give them away, Gideon had left him tied in the barn.

It was the waiting that tried Gideon most. He was not looking forward to dealing with Dudley Mayfield without any weapons, when

Dudley was certain to be armed. By now, he must have heard about the warrant for Gideon's arrest. If he accepted the charges as fact, there was no telling how he would react, especially in a drunken state. He might be as likely to think it a very good joke, but if he had one of his violent turns, Gideon would have no resources, not even a beer mug with which to hit him on the head. Gideon decided it was a good thing Charles had insisted upon coming, for reinforcements might be needed.

Thoughts of Mrs. Kean nearby in her bed made him smile. He fancied he could still taste the sweetness of her breath mingling with his. The memory of her soft, smooth skin beneath his touch still brought a tightness to his throat. He wanted nothing more than to ride to her door and take her away with him, but knew that, as usual, her decision had been right. They would have a much better chance of escaping if Fenwick's killer was caught. Besides their own interest, Gideon knew, too, that he would regret leaving Charles with no justice for his father.

There was no comfortable place to sit while they waited, so they took turns leaning against a tree. Gideon slowly paced across the lane back and forth, exchanging occasional words with Charles to soothe his anxiety.

Gideon did not know what Charles's school in France had been like. Surely, as a gentleman, he would have been taught the art of swordplay. Whether the priests had allowed the sort of fisticuffs so common among English boys was doubtful. If he had never witnessed a genuine dust-up, he might be too stunned to react.

When they had waited for over an hour, Gideon beckoned Charles and Tom to his side. "If Mayfield comes upon us suddenly, he might mistake us for robbers and either flee or fire his pistol. I think he will feel less threatened if he does not find himself confronted by three men. He and I have been on friendly terms. If I call out to identify myself, he is more likely to stop.

"The two of you should take your horses farther along the lane and tether them out of sight. Then, conceal yourselves behind those trees. As long as all goes well, there should be no need to expose your presence, but from there, you will see if I need your help."

His request made such good sense that the two men obeyed without demur. He watched as, leading their horses, they vanished up the lane into the dark. The sound made by their horses' hooves was the last sign he had of them as the stillness of the night descended once again.

Another hour later, he was leaning against the tree and fighting off the sense that tonight's efforts would be futile, when he heard the shuffling approach of a horse. A few seconds later, the figure of a rider, slouched in his saddle, took shape down the lane. It was moving ploddingly towards Gideon, with an occasional jerk of its head as the rider gave a tug on the reins. From where Gideon stood, it might have been the horse who was soused, so uneven was its gait.

With no wish to startle either Dudley or his mount, Gideon took a firm stance in the middle of the lane. The horse was nearly upon him when it halted, at which point Dudley noticed the presence of an impediment.

"You sir!" he cried in outrage. "Step aside or I shall ride you down!"

He was fumbling for the weapon at his waist, when Gideon moved round so the moon could light his features. "It is I, Sir Robert, Mayfield. I am in need of your assistance."

Dudley squinted down at him, swaying dangerously over Gideon's head. "It is you. Whaddayou mean, halting my horse in the middle of the night?"

"I've been looking for you and had no choice but to wait here. I need to ask you some questions. Would you be good enough to dismount?"

"What! Here? Why don' you come up to the house? We could have a drink."

"My thanks, but I cannot. I must speak to you in private. We could be interrupted in the house."

"By my wife, you mean. She fancies you, you know."

Gideon was not sure how to respond to this, but Dudley went on, "You can have 'er if you wann 'er. Go on! Take 'er back to Lunnon wif you. Just so long as you don' tell 'er papa I said so."

This was the opening Gideon needed. "It is about Sir Ralph that I wished to have a few words with you. Please, will you dismount?"

After a little more coaxing, he finally managed to get Dudley onto the ground, relieved that his mood was still cordial. As long as Dudley had had the advantage of looking down from his horse, Gideon had had a niggling concern that he might be trampled. Dudley seemed to be harbouring ill feelings towards his father-in-law, and it had been Gideon's reference to Sir Ralph that had finally persuaded him to descend from his horse.

He walked Dudley to the tree where he had been resting and helped him lean against its trunk.

"I need your help," he said again, once Dudley was adequately propped up. "It's about the deal between Sir Ralph and the former Mr. Fenwick for the sale of a piece of land. What do you know about it?"

With his head wavering, Dudley gave a laughing snort. "I know Sir Ralph got the best end of that bargain. He always does."

"In what way?"

Dudley glowered at him. "Whaddaya mean? I said he always gets what he wants. How do ya think he got a mortgage on my estate, huh? And forced me to marry his daughter to boot."

"Suppose you tell me," Gideon said, hoping that Dudley's account of his own dealings with Sir Ralph would shed some light on Fenwick's.

Dudley took exception to this, however. He started up, began to fall, then righted himself with Gideon's help. "None o' yer damn business! Whaddaya mean prying into my affairs?"

Gideon soothed him back down with friendly pats on the shoulder, while supporting him with the other hand. "I'm not interested in your business. It's Sir Ralph's business with the former Mr. Fenwick that concerns me. Is there anything you can tell me about it?"

Dudley gave him the same cunning grin he had at the Fauconberg Arms. "Wouldn' you just like to know?"

"Yes, I would," Gideon said, fast losing patience. "If you don't have anything of use to say about it, I'll be on my way."

"Not so fast. Not so fast." Dudley took hold of his coat with both fists. "Didn' I hear something about you and old Fenwick? You murdered 'im, didn' ya? Is that what you're up to? You wanna kill me next, is that it?"

As swiftly as a horse can kick, Dudley's temper flared. Before Gideon could protect himself, Dudley shifted both hands and wrapped them around his throat. Gideon's windpipe was immediately cut off by the pressure on the knot in his neckcloth. He grasped at Dudley's fingers and tried to pry them loose, but the other man's grip was strong and powerful, his actions fueled by fury. Gideon tried to fight his way out of Dudley's hold, striking him wherever his knee would reach. Dudley gave a grunt with each blow but never loosened his fearsome grip.

Gideon's lungs felt like bursting. His wind was running out, the light was growing dim. Had his friends not seen that he was in trouble?

A thought of Mrs. Kean made him kick out with all the life left in him, but he was already too weak to do any good. All he saw was black. His eyes were popping from his head.

A whoosh of air entered his lungs as he landed hard on the ground. Dudley's hands were gone from about his neck. His vision had not returned, but he was too feeble to care. He could do nothing but suck in huge gasps of air. It burned his throat and lungs, but every inhalation was bringing him back to life.

"Master Gideon! Are you alright? Can ye hear me?" Tom's voice penetrated his daze.

Gideon had to swallow twice, painfully, before he could croak, "Yes. I'll be all right. What happened?"

"Mr. Mayfield tried to kill ye, that's what!"

Gideon wanted to laugh, but it was much too soon. "I remember that part. How did you stop him?"

Tom's visage was becoming clearer in the moonlight. He made a gesture, halfway between a wince and a shrug. "I hit 'im over the head with a rock. 'Twas the only thing I could do, my l—sir. Me and Mr. Fenwick here tried pullin' 'im off o' ye, but we couldn't budge 'im." Now that Gideon was safe, he seemed to feel a bit guilty about striking a gentleman.

"Good thing you did." With a hand from Tom, Gideon struggled to sit up. He looked about and saw Dudley stretched out on the ground with Charles standing guard over him. "If you hadn't Tom, I think I would have been a corpse by now."

With the help of Tom's arm, he stood and, after a moment of dizziness had passed, he signaled that he was well enough to walk without assistance. He took care, however, as he crossed the few steps to where Dudley lay.

"Is he dead?" he asked, fearing for Tom if he was.

"No, his breathing is even. He's shed a great deal of blood, but I believe that is the nature of wounds to the scalp. I have never seen such savagery," Charles added, emotion thickening his voice. "I hope that you have not incurred any lasting harm."

Gideon assured him that he would recover completely in a short while, but he was beginning to feel disheartened.

"My regret is that I did not manage to get anything useful out of him. I cannot tell whether he knows anything about the deal between your father and Sir Ralph or if he simply pretended he did to impress me."

"Do you still think Sir Ralph is the killer?" Charles sounded incredulous. "After seeing what Mayfield is capable of?"

As logical as this argument was, Gideon still believed that he and Mrs. Kean had got it right. "Yes, I'm afraid I do. If you have doubts, however, perhaps we should take Mayfield to Oulston Hall and keep him until he wakes up and can speak to us in a sober state."

Charles's nod was grim. "That is what I wished to suggest. If he is bound, he cannot use violence on you again."

Gideon sighed and gingerly touched his throat. "Fortunately, I've heard that he wakens with no recollection of the havoc he's caused. But I have no objection to tying him up. Let's get him on his horse."

Tom had to do most of the lifting, but both Charles and Gideon helped. They draped Dudley's unconscious body across his saddle. He would not have a very comfortable ride, but in Gideon's opinion, he had earned every bruise he would get. By now, Dudley's head had taken enough strong blows that his brains ought to be thoroughly addled, but that might result in an improvement.

Tom insisted that Gideon ride Beau. He made sure that his master was securely on the horse's back before mounting Penny himself. It was long past their horses' bedtime, and Penny was unusually docile, but Tom would not risk the chance that she would cause Gideon a spill.

With Charles leading Dudley's horse, they walked back to Oulston Hall and deposited their burden in Charles's barn. One of his servants, who had been listening out for their return, came to help them carry Dudley inside and bind him. Gideon insisted that he and Tom would spend the night watching him, however, feeling safe enough to sleep until Dudley's outraged cries awakened them. He still nursed the small hope that Dudley would know something useful. A memory of his earlier conversation with Charles gave another direction to his thoughts.

Before Charles left them to seek his bed, Gideon said, "Tomorrow, we should take a look at your father's book of accounts. There may be a clue in there that we have missed."

℘

Morning came, and still there was no word from St. Mars. Hester was nearly beside herself with worry, but she had to conceal her concerns from both Mary and Pamela. She rose from bed early, dressed, and went downstairs to breakfast, leaving Mary in a deep sleep.

A few words exchanged with a servant informed her that Dudley had not come home last night. Remembering that St. Mars had wanted to ask him questions, she wondered what this could mean. Perhaps, Dudley had given St. Mars the information he needed to confirm their suspicions against Sir Ralph, in which case, they might be waiting to visit Mr. Mynchon this morning.

If no word came before noon, she would find it difficult to stay still. Pamela had not completely ruled out speaking to Mr. Mynchon today, but Hester had not liked the note of doubt in her voice. She was not sure she could persuade Pamela to go with her to Mynchon Grange. St. Mars had forbidden her to take any action on his behalf, but he had only been trying to protect her. Little harm could come to her simply for paying Mr. Mynchon a visit.

She waited impatiently for Pamela to make her appearance. Mary descended first, and Hester distracted herself by listing the tasks they still had to complete before leaving for London; but in truth, except for embroidering a handkerchief or two, nearly all the needlework was done.

Presently, they moved to the downstairs parlour to take advantage of the morning light. Mary talked about the race meeting, and Hester listened to her with one ear, keeping the other cocked for any sound of an arrival.

A time or two, a noise outside made her jump. On the second occasion, Mary asked her why she seemed so nervous.

Caught off guard, Hester was at pains to think of a plausible answer. She could only deny her unease and attempt to change the subject. Then a thought occurred, and she asked Mary, "Do you recall the day that Mr. Fenwick was murdered?"

Mary started. Then giving Hester a queer look, she said, "Of course. How could I forget it? Why do you ask?"

Hester shook her head as if the matter were unimportant. "I was just wondering what time Pamela left for York that day. I assume it was very early or she would have been here when the Fenwicks' servant brought you the news."

"No," Mary answered, still gazing at her with questions in her eyes. "I thought I told you that the servant did not come until evening. Pamela left with Sir Ralph around nine-thirty or ten o'clock in the morning. They ought to have been off at nine, but Sir Ralph arrived a little late. I remember because Pamela was fretting that they would not have time for all the shopping she wished to do."

Hester slowly let out a deep breath. So she and St. Mars had not been wrong. Sir Ralph could have killed Mr. Fenwick before riding to York. In all the alarm and confusion after Mr. Fenwick was found, hours had passed before anyone had been sent to report the news. When the Fenwicks' servant had ridden to Yearsley Park to inform Sir Ralph of the killing, as he surely would have before riding to Beckwith Manor, he had found Sir Ralph away on a journey to York. It would have been assumed that he had been gone all the while, and no one had considered the possibility of his being the killer. Who would, when Sir Ralph supposedly was Mr. Fenwick's friend?

"Hester? Why did you wish to know? Is it important?"

Hester tried to focus on her cousin. Raising Mary's curiosity could only put her in danger. The memory of Sir Ralph's menacing look made her suppress a shudder. "No, something simply confused me, but I must ask you never to repeat my question to anyone. Do you promise?"

Mary's frown revealed how dissatisfied she was. "Of course I'll promise, but only if you promise to explain later what is bothering you. I am no longer a child, Hester, and I know when something is wrong."

Hester assured her that she would, just before they were interrupted by Pamela's entrance. Hester gave Mary one last look of warning before turning to greet Dudley's wife.

Pamela looked dispirited this morning. She had not taken her normal pains with her toilette. She listlessly seated herself in an armchair. When asked, she replied that she had not slept well. The news about Sir Robert had depressed her.

"Then, after you have eaten breakfast, you can come with me to speak to Mr. Mynchon about it. Perhaps he has had news that will exonerate Sir Robert." He might also have learned that Sir Ralph had a motive for killing Mr. Fenwick, which would stun Pamela and upset her dreadfully, but the truth would have to be told to her eventually. There would be no easy time to hear it.

Pamela disappointed Hester, then, by saying, "How would that serve anything? Whether Sir Robert is innocent or guilty, I shall never be able to get a place at Court." Her tone became even bitterer. "You heard my father, Hester. I shall have to remain here and give my husband an heir."

Hester glanced Mary's way and saw how disturbed she was by this speech. She must have been aware of the lack of affection between her brother and his wife, but Pamela's misery and Sir Ralph's interference in his daughter's most intimate affairs must come as a shock to the girl, even with the discord she had witnessed in this house.

Hester was sorry that Pamela was so caught up in her own unhappiness that she could only think of "Sir Robert" in terms of his usefulness to herself. If she had thought for one minute that Pamela's testimony on "Sir Robert's" behalf would save St. Mars from danger, she would have been enfuriated by her self-centredness; but she had begun to realize that Pamela's praise of him would only be put down to a fawning woman's foolishness.

It would take real evidence to exonerate St. Mars, and more than just their assumptions to convince a J.P. that a gentleman known for his generous hospitality throughout the community was the killer.

As the morning progressed, glances Mary cast Hester's way from time to time suggested that she had started to put a few ideas together to arrive at suspicions of her own. Hester carefully avoided meeting her gaze. The last thing she wanted to do was to involve Mary in the business.

Finally, when the clock struck noon and there was still no message from St. Mars and no sign of Dudley, Hester could contain her impatience no longer. Saying that she felt the need to move about, she went to her chamber and changed into a walking dress and boots to go to Mynchon Grange. If necessary, she could say that she had come to visit Mrs. Mynchon, whom they had not seen in several days.

Mary met her on her way down the stairs and offered to walk with her. Hester refused her company, thanking her but saying, "I have an errand that I must make alone."

"Are you going to Mynchon Grange?"

Hester hesitated. Then, deciding that it might be best if someone knew where she had gone, she said, "Yes, but please do not tell Pamela, or it may lead to a fuss. In fact, do not tell anyone where I have gone . . . except Sir Robert or his servant, if either should come asking for me."

"Sir Robert! But—"

"I cannot answer your questions now, Mary, but I promise to as soon as I can. Just please do as I ask."

The girl reluctantly agreed, but it was plain that her brain had been puzzling over Hester's behaviour and that she was worried.

Giving her a smile of reassurance, Hester turned and exited the house.

She could have ridden the pony, but for her to take an unnecessary and solitary ride would have raised everyone's suspicions. They knew her for an enthusiastic walker, however, so her desire for exercise should not provoke any uncomfortable questions.

Mr. Mynchon's house was a few miles from Dudley's gate. She set out at her quickest pace, though haste would cover her in perspiration and dust. If St. Mars had spoken to Mr. Mynchon, they would have so much to occupy their minds that the last thing either would remark would be the state of her clothes. Her greatest fear was that St. Mars had been captured and denied the opportunity to clear himself. She could only pray that Mr. Mynchon's respect for "Sir Robert's" intelligence would have led him to hear whatever evidence St. Mars had been able to collect. If not, then her interference would be more than justified. She could not regret her decision to go.

Occupied with worry, she did not notice the scenery she passed. It was as much as she could do to remain on the correct path. A footpath led her across a few neighbouring fields before discharging her back into the lane not far from Mynchon Grange. Her impatience to know if St. Mars was safe increased with every step as she drew closer to her destination. And with impatience, her anxiety mounted. The thought that anything bad might happen to St. Mars, so close as they were to happiness together, weighed on her like a thunderous sky.

So nervous was she that when a horse appeared suddenly in front of her, emerging from Mr. Mynchon's drive, she uttered a startled cry. Her heart set up a racing pace when she saw that its rider was Sir Ralph.

"Mrs. Kean," he said, in a cordial voice which failed to conceal the note of steel underneath, "what a surprise meeting you here."

Hester could not quiet the pulse beating in her throat. Her voice trembled. "Yes, it is a surprise. What brings you here, Sir Ralph?"

He was staring down at her as if he could see right through her. "Why, the same thing that brings you, I suppose. This business of Mr. Fenwick's killer."

Hester saw that he had read her mistrust on her face. Over the past two years, she had learned to hide some of her thoughts. She knew how to disarm Isabella's pique, to persuade Harrowby with sympathetic utterances, to fool her aunt by pretending to desire the opposite of what she truly wanted. But the revulsion she felt for a murderer was not a thing she had learned to hide. He would have seen the choler and contempt she felt for him, just as she had detected his malevolence.

Still, she must make an attempt to get past him. More angry now than scared, she felt strength returning to her voice. "Is there any news about Sir Robert? We have heard nothing all morning. I have come to visit Mrs. Mynchon with the hope of hearing the gossip."

"I can spare you the need of visiting, then. Sir Robert has not yet been found. He eluded the constables at the inn. Mynchon agrees with me that his flight is tantamount to an admission of guilt."

Fear tightened Hester's chest. It was plain that Sir Ralph had come here to manipulate Mr. Mynchon's opinion of "Sir Robert." If the J.P. set up a hue and cry, St. Mars could be seriously injured, even fatally. She could not guess at his chance of receiving a fair hearing.

What had prevented St. Mars from reaching Mr. Mynchon first? She had expected him to be here long before now. Had he seen Sir Ralph coming and been forced to wait?

She forced herself to smile. "If there is no news, I would still like to see Mrs. Mynchon after walking all this way." She moved to step around his horse, but he turned it to block her. When she looked up in outrage, he was pointing a pistol at her head.

"I cannot allow that, Mrs. Kean. You should have minded your own business. We do not like outsiders meddling in our affairs."

Hester's heart leapt into her throat. Sir Ralph had shot and killed two men already. What was to stop him from murdering her here and now?

"If you fire on me, they will hear the shot at Mynchon Grange. You will not get away with murder again."

"Oh, I believe I will. I shall say that I heard the shot and rode back to see what had happened. Of course, I also spied Sir Robert riding away at great speed. Mynchon will believe me. He is greatly disappointed in Sir Robert."

Before taking aim, Sir Ralph peered in every direction to make certain there were no witnesses about. Hester had never been so afraid. She had to think of something—anything—to delay him.

She blurted, "But Sir Robert is not alone! At this moment, at least three men are with him who can prove he was not here if you try to blame him for shooting me. He knows you are guilty of the murders, and he has told them.

He turned sharply to face her. She could see her words had rattled him. He had not planned her killing in advance, for he had not known she would come. He had likely been lying in wait for "Sir Robert." The plan to kill her had been hastily devised, unlike the crimes he had already committed. Faced with a setback, he was completely at a loss.

"Tell me where he is," he demanded.

Trembling from shock, Hester gave a short laugh. "That would not be in my self-interest, Sir Ralph. Surely, *you* understand that."

Her barb did not go unremarked. But he was too upset by the check he had suffered to waste time on feeling insulted.

"I suppose you think the two of you are clever, but I have never been outwitted and I will not be now. You shall come with me until I've reckoned what to do with you. You have walked this far. You can turn and walk to Yearsley Park."

Hester had no choice but to obey. She had achieved a temporary stay, but if he started to feel desperate, she could not be certain that he would not kill her and fabricate a different lie.

She prayed that what she had said about St. Mars was true. He must at least have told Charles of his suspicions. Dudley's absence both last night and this morning suggested that St. Mars was with him, too.

Sir Ralph was unlikely to guess where "Sir Robert" had gone. It would not occur to him that the first place "Sir Robert" would go would be to the home of the person he had been accused of murdering. His mind was too twisted to think like an innocent man.

Hester stumbled down the middle of the lane with Sir Ralph mounted behind her. His horse occasionally came close enough to breathe down her neck. Its warm, moist breath sent chills down her spine. She refused to hurry. Sir Ralph could not be aware of how fast her normal pace was, not when the ladies he knew usually rode.

The shock she had suffered had weakened her knees in any case. She tripped over the deeper ruts. She could feel Sir Ralph's impatience as he was forced to hold his mount to a snail's pace.

They had not covered much distance when his anxiety erupted in a need to talk. Garrulous by nature, the silence must have unnerved him. "What led you to suspect me, Mrs. Kean? Why not Sir Robert?"

She took the opportunity to stop—anything to delay their arrival at Yearsley Park. When she faced him, she made a show of wiping her face with her handkerchief. The day was growing warm, and fear, as much as the exertion, had made her perspire.

He had halted his horse a short distance away to leave a clear aim for his pistol, which he pointed at her breast.

She made her voice sound breathless. "It was not really that difficult. You were the only person with a connection to the two victims. Mr. Abelson must have known something about Mr. Fenwick's death. You were always anxious to keep him away from Charles Fenwick."

Her suggestion that he had not been as crafty as he had thought made him angry. He kneed his horse forward, nearly trampling her. She stepped sideways and almost fell. The animal shied, too, trained to know that treading on a person was not allowed. Sir Ralph thought better of this method of putting an end to her and brought his temper under control.

Hester's pulse had started racing again. She was not sure she could make it to Yearsley Park. The inevitable reaction to danger was making her shake uncontrollably. She bent at the waist and rested her hands on her knees to quell a fit of dizziness.

"I shall give you a moment to catch your breath. Why did you choose to walk when you could have ridden?"

It was not concern for her that made him ask, she knew, but frustration at their lack of progress. She would have to find the energy to go on. The distance would normally mean nothing to her, but the thought of what awaited her at Yearsley Park had robbed her of will.

"While I am recovering my strength, perhaps you would tell me why you murdered Mr. Fenwick. I have not discovered any reason for it."

Her confession pleased him. He gave her a grim smile. "So, you do not know everything. But how could you? I made certain that no one knew of the arrangement I had with Fenwick except the two of us, not even his lady. But when he told me that Charles was coming home, I knew I would have to kill him before he told his son."

Curious, in spite of her fear, Hester righted herself. "Tell him what?"

He grinned, gratified by her ignorance. "Fenwick came to me several years ago, greatly distressed over the taxes he had to pay on his land. He knew he would not be able to raise the money to cover it all and felt forced to sell. He thought I might be interested in buying some acres from him, but truth be told, I did not have the money to hand. I was putting a great deal into my house—more than I had initially planned—but you have seen the results. There cannot be a finer house in the whole North Riding."

He spoke of his house as if its splendour justified anything, even his crimes. Hester could only gape at such delusion.

He went on, "We put our heads together and determined that we should record a sale of land between us to lower his acreage in the registers, but the sale would be a sham. The land we transferred into my name could support the tax rate I pay, and still produce income for him. I collected it, and paid it to him. He recorded the income as a payment on my debt for the land, but I had no intention of buying it.

"Fenwick was very grateful to me for taking on the work of collecting his rents. I even made a few improvements to the cottages. It would have looked strange if I had not.

Hester must have looked confused, for he continued, "Oh, at the beginning, I had no intention of killing him. The arrangement between us was genuine, as least as far as he and I were concerned. But by the time he told me Charles was coming home, I knew I would need to keep the land. And he would never have concealed our bargain from Charles, not when the boy was coming home to learn to manage the estate."

"You needed more money for Yearsley Park."

"Yes, the income from my own estate has been disappointing these past several years. I could not risk losing the house."

"But I thought you paid for Dudley's debts."

"Yes, but I picked up a great deal of acreage in the process. My worthless son-in-law will never make good on the mortgage, so Beckwith Manor is essentially mine."

There was so much Hester wished she could say, about how evil his greed was, but she knew any words from her would be useless. Sir Ralph was so persuaded of his right to everything he desired that nothing would change his mind, not when he had been willing to kill for it.

"I have let you rest long enough, Mrs. Kean. It is time to start moving again."

He held his Sword drawn in his Hand, to defend himself, if I should happen to break loose.

CHAPTER XIX

Gideon was awakened late that morning by a dog licking his face. At once, he became aware of Argos's whining and his own pounding head. His throat felt swollen and his neck was bruised. All night, the pain from being throttled had played a role in his dreams, but he had been too exhausted to wake and dispel them.

He struggled into consciousness only to discover that Dudley Mayfield was still sleeping where they had laid him in the hay. As terrible as he felt, Gideon was glad he had not been disturbed in the night, though the bright sunlight pouring into the barn told him that the day was already well-advanced.

Tom was standing over Dudley with an anxious frown. He must be concerned that he had hit the man too hard, though by any standard of fairness, Gideon thought, the blow should have been harder. Still, it would be a grave matter if Dudley had suffered serious damage. The law looked harshly on any servant who struck a landed citizen.

When Gideon pushed himself to a sitting position, a glimmer of relief lit Tom's eyes. "I didn't want to wake you, my lord. 'T'was plain to see you needed a good night's rest."

Holding Argos away with one hand, Gideon gingerly felt the bruises on his neck with the other. "It wasn't that restful, but at least I can move. What about Fenwick?" he asked.

Tom sprang to his feet and fetched a basket that had been placed near the door to the barn. "He sent out something to break your fast." He pulled out a bottle of beer and some bread and passed them to Gideon, who said, "I do not suppose he brought us any coffee."

"No, my lord, but he said he would be back in a while. Since you and Mr. Mayfield here were still asleep, he didn't see no reason to stay."

Gideon tried to eat a bite, but his throat was too sore. Even swallowing the beer caused him pain. He drank it anyway, knowing he would need some sustenance before facing the day. If he had had a dish of coffee, he could have soaked the bread in it, but it was clear that he would have to do without. He was moving more slowly than an ox pulling a plough and felt a bit like one, too, with the yoke too tight about his neck.

When he had finished eating and drinking all he could force down his throat, he stretched and got to his feet. "Let's see if we cannot encourage Mayfield to waken." Telling Tom to bring him a bucket of water, he examined Dudley's cut head. The bleeding had stopped before they had laid him on the blanket, and Gideon had been satisfied that his breathing was normal. They had not bathed his wound last night for fear that the water would restore him to consciousness. So Gideon dipped his handkerchief in the bucketful Tom drew from the well, and squeezed it over Dudley's face.

As the stream of water hit him, he started awake. The motion must have hurt his head for he groaned and closed his eyes again. Then he had no more sense than to shake it, which provoked louder groans. He cursed and, gripping his head between his hands, pried his eyes open to see who had had the effrontery to waken him.

"Sir Robert!" He made an effort to sit up and take a look round. "What—am I doing here? Where—where are we?"

"We are in Charles Fenwick's barn. We brought you here last night."

"Is he the blackguard who cudgeled me? I'll kill him if it was!"

"Who did it is not important. Someone had to stop you from throttling me."

Dudley stared at him with a mixture of wariness and guilt. Even if he did not recall what he had done, he was well aware of the sort of trouble he got into when he was drunk.

"So you say," he blustered, "but I'm the one with a great knot on my head!"

Gideon lifted his chin and pulled the neckcloth away from his neck. He did not need to have seen it to know that the bruising was evident. Dudley squinted at it and blanched. A hint of fear appeared on his face. He must be wondering what retribution "Sir Robert," a purported murderer, would demand.

While Gideon had him at a disadvantage, he said, "You ought to thank the person who stopped you or the constables would be after you now."

The mention of constables revived a memory in Dudley's brain. "Aren't they looking for you?"

"Yes, and I would like to know who set them onto me, for I was not in the area when Fenwick was killed and I can prove it. But that was not why I tried to speak to you last night. I was hoping you could tell me about Sir Ralph's purchase of some acres from Fenwick."

Dudley accepted this statement of his innocence as if "Sir Robert's" guilt had never much interested him. "Why don't you ask my damn father-in-law about that? If you want the details, he'd have them sooner than I would."

"I will confront Sir Ralph soon, but before I do, I need more information. You suggested to me that you were aware of something irregular in the business between them."

Dudley had no recollection of saying anything of the sort, but he must often have been confronted with statements he had made and forgotten. Frowning, he mused for a while, then said in a surly tone, "I don't know any of the particulars, but years ago, when the sale was made, Sir Ralph boasted that he and Fenwick had put one over on the tax collector. I don't know what they did, but it was strange how Fenwick still took an interest in that land."

"What do you mean?"

Dudley shrugged. "I know he kept visiting the tenants, and Sir Ralph never seemed to mind. If anybody took that much interest in my tenants, I would know how to set him straight!"

The information was too vague, but Gideon felt there was something in it he was missing. After Dudley assured him that that was all he had ever known about the transaction, Gideon indicated the food basket and told Dudley to help himself.

What to do now with so little to go on? All his hopes had rested on getting information from Dudley Mayfield. If Charles could not find anything queer in his father's accounts—which was likely since the King's Commissioner had just gone through them and approved them—what could Gideon offer Mynchon to support his accusation of Sir Ralph?

He rinsed his handkerchief and used it to wipe his face. Then, he re-wrapped his cravat about his neck and having seen how stained it was, twisted the ends and tucked them into his shirt. He was dusting the hay off his breeches, when Charles came in, bearing a heavy book of accounts.

"Have you found anything?" Gideon asked.

With a helpless look, Charles shook his head. "I do not know what to look for." He gestured with the book for Gideon to follow him outside, where he placed it atop a mounting block that stood between the stable and the barn. Tom followed them outside and stood watching for anyone coming up the drive, while Argos settled himself at Gideon's feet. Looking a bit sheepish and very disheveled, Dudley joined them as they studied the book.

"I found the first entry where the sale is mentioned. See here— *'Received this 18th day of February 1707/08, of Sir Ralph Wetherby, 1£ 2s 6d, being due on the mortgage of 45 acres of land. I say received by me, Francis Fenwick.'"*

"Is that all?" Gideon exclaimed. "The Commissioner did not see anything odd about such a small sum?"

"It is not all." Charles turned a page and pointed to another entry. "Look here." He turned another two pages and said, "And here. There are several instances of my father receiving similar sums, always with the notation that it is in payment for that parcel of land. Sir Ralph must have paid just a small amount towards it twice a year."

A snort of derision issued from behind them. "A small amount,

I'll say!"

Surprised, Gideon and Charles turned to learn the reason for Dudley's reaction. Feeling their eyes upon him, he looked defensively back. "The rents alone on that property would amount to more than that. That was good farm land, and it's prime grazing land now."

They must have looked reluctant to accept his word, for he tapped Gideon's shoulder with the back of his hand and said, "You saw it, Mavors. Sir Ralph showed it to you, himself. That's the land he put his new sheep on."

Raising his brow, Gideon turned to Charles and said, "I believe Mayfield is correct. This is a very small sum to pay for such good land. There must have been something irregular in their arrangement. Have you added all the payments to see what the total is?"

"Not yet, but I did discover that the payments ceased just before my father was killed. The Commissioner must have assumed that the mortgage had been paid. Or else," Charles said bitterly, "he did not care if my family had been cheated. If I had known enough to wonder, I should never have had the courage to ask Sir Ralph about it, not when it seemed that he was our father's good friend."

"Your mother trusted him, I know, but I think it's just as well that you did not suspect him. You might not be alive now, if you had."

Gideon sensed Dudley's start behind them. "You mean, Sir Ralph did the killings?"

Charles answered him grimly. "I found it difficult to believe, too, until I saw these few entries."

He opened the book to a different page, and the other two crowded around it. There, in the same hand, they saw a recording from 1709/10 which matched the first they had read in every respect, except that after the sum recorded as received of Sir Ralph Wetherby, were added the words, *'by the hand of John Abelson.'*

"He used Abelson to deliver the rent, or whatever it was." Dudley said, in a wondering tone.

Gideon pondered the entry and shook his head. "I still cannot see my way through this. It does prove a connection between the three men, though." He looked at Charles. "I am ready to go see Mynchon. He may be able to shed some light on this. If you will not come with me, will you let me borrow this book?"

Charles agreed to let him take it. "But you will return it soon?"

"As soon as I am free to do so." If anything prevented him, Charles would know where the book was. He might have to overcome his pride to ask Mynchon for it, but the exercise would not harm him.

"What about me?" Dudley asked.

Gideon did not know whether Dudley Mayfield would be a help or a hindrance, but decided that anybody's testimony in his favour would be a good thing.

"You're aware that I intend to accuse your father-in-law of two murders?"

Mayfield shrugged. "I wouldn't mind turning the scales on the old villain. He's made my life miserable enough."

There was still the testimony of the innkeeper in Doncaster to obtain, but Gideon decided to keep Tom with him for now. He could send him for a letter if Mynchon did not believe him.

With Charles's account book safely stowed in a saddlebag, Gideon, Dudley, and Tom rode east to Mynchon Grange, which lay a few miles beyond Yearsley Park. Since Beckwith Manor was only a short distance out of their way, Dudley suggested stopping at his house to freshen up. The thought of seeing Hester tempted Gideon, but no matter how badly he wished to, or how much he needed a wash, he did not dare tarry longer.

By agreement, they took a wide route around Yearsley Park, riding cross-country to improve their chances of avoiding Sir Ralph. Dudley was riding his grey, his horse and Penny well-matched as to pace. Argos ran beside them. They covered the fields and the low hills at a gallop, scattering sheep and drawing the eyes of a few labourers working the ground, with Tom following at a slight distance.

Gideon no longer cared if Dudley saw how sound Penny was. If everything could be resolved today—or within a few days, at least—he and Hester would be gone before the race meeting in York next week. If he could not persuade Mynchon of his innocence, having to invent a reason why he could not attend the races would be the very least of his worries.

They had skirted Yearsley Park when Penny tripped over a rough patch on the footpath they had been following. Gideon pulled up to see if she had been injured. He walked her a few paces under Tom's expert eye, but all seemed well. Looking at the path ahead, however, Gideon saw that the next field had been plowed and decided not to risk her legs.

He called to Dudley, who had reined his horse to wait, "From here, we will make better time on the road."

The place where they joined it was only a mile or so from Mynchon Grange. Gideon reckoned that the whole trip had taken them less than twenty minutes, but the hour was already well past noon. He hoped they would catch the J.P. at home eating his dinner. If Mynchon was not at home, Gideon would have to beg Mrs. Mynchon's permission to wait for her husband.

The road here was not much wider than a lane with a sharp bend up ahead. Gideon was riding just a horse's length ahead of Dudley—three ahead of Tom—when he rounded the corner and was brought to a sudden halt by a sight that robbed him of breath.

Mrs. Kean was limping towards him. Sir Ralph was following closely on horseback. And he had a pistol aimed at her back.

The fear on Mrs. Kean's face did something queer to Gideon. Blood surged into his head. For a moment, he thought he was going to be sick. Then rage boiled up in his veins. He had told her not to take a step until she heard from him. How could she disobey him when he had warned her of danger? Then, in a flash his rage turned against the proper target, and the only thing he knew was a desire to murder the man who had made her suffer. His eyes met hers, and relief followed by a deeper terror crossed her face.

There was no time for cleverness. Sir Ralph had spotted them in the same instant. It was too late to plan an ambush.

"What the devil!" Dudley sharply reined his gray beside Gideon. "Hester! Sir Ralph! What have you done to her?"

Tom came to a halt behind them and uttered a loud gasp. Commanded to halt, Argos emitted a low growl.

Sir Ralph ordered Mrs. Kean to stop as he reined and faced them. A brief look of triumph had crossed his face before he spotted Dudley riding behind Gideon. His expression changed to dismay, then anger, then desperation.

"She was planning to assist his escape!" He indicated "Sir Robert" with his gun. "Don't believe anything he tells you. Quick! Grasp hold of him, so I do not miss." He cocked his pistol and aimed it straight at Gideon.

Dumb from shock, Dudley's body reacted more quickly than his brain. He spurred his horse in front of Gideon's, stammering, "Wait!

His move trapped Hester in the small space between Dudley's horse and Sir Ralph's in the narrow lane. Both were tightly reined, no more than twenty feet apart, and nervously prancing. Hester sought Gideon's gaze, and relayed her sensations—fear, hope, a desperate fatigue, and dread at the thought of seeing him hurt.

He felt as if a noose were tightening around his neck, not from Dudley's throttling, but from a paralyzing terror of seeing her hurt. What if they had not taken this road? What if they had been delayed by just ten minutes? How would he have found her if Sir Ralph had managed to get her away?

"Don't do anything foolish, my lord." As if he could read Gideon's thoughts, Tom cautioned him.

Gideon struggled to think. He wanted to shield Hester with his body, but he could not get past Dudley in the lane without alarming his grey. If he moved too suddenly, Sir Ralph might fire. The horses were nervous. Any one of them might trample her in panic. Even the dog's growling might set one of them off.

Gideon's mind flailed desperately for a plan. It felt like ages, but was only seconds, before logic gave him a degree of hope. Sir Ralph would not shoot Hester because he would not have time to reload before Dudley and Gideon seized him. Gideon's pulse eased enough that he could swallow.

"Give up, Sir Ralph," he called. "No one will believe your lies now. If you had any suspicion of Mrs. Kean, you would be taking her to Mynchon Grange, not riding away from it."

"Do not listen to him, Mayfield.!" Sir Ralph reflexively turned his weapon on his son-in-law. "Remember where your loyalties belong, my boy."

Unable to see Dudley's expression, Gideon worried that Sir Ralph would manage to intimidate him. He tightened his grip on Penny's reins, ready to spur forward. It was just possible that he could attack Sir Ralph, if he knew in which direction Hester would move. Locking her gaze with his, he willed her to understand. *"À gauche,"* he called, just loud enough for her to hear, betting that neither Sir Ralph nor Dudley would comprehend the French. Then he raised his voice to Sir Ralph again. "Your actions have betrayed you as the murderer. Will killing more people conceal those crimes?"

Sir Ralph's cheeks had turned ashen. "I will not have to kill that many. Isn't that true, Dudley, my boy? Remember who holds the mortgage on Beckwith Manor. If I am obliged to kill Mrs. Kean, we shall say that Sir Robert did it."

The roar of an enraged bull made them jump. The sound had issued from Dudley's mouth. Before Gideon could stop him, Hester's cousin kicked his horse and charged at Sir Ralph. With only a second to get out of his way, Hester flung herself left, as Gideon had warned, and fell into the ditch by the side of the road.

Sir Ralph was so startled by Dudley's attack that he recoiled. His aim went wide as his pistol went off. The ball hit Dudley but he did not slow. His horse stormed into Sir Ralph's like a destrier of old, urged by the force of Dudley's rage. As Gideon spurred Penny forward, Dudley launched himself at his father-in-law, muscular arms outstretched. The two fell into the road with Dudley atop. Sir Ralph raised his hands before his face to ward off blows, but even with blood oozing from Dudley's side, he pummeled Sir Ralph with all the fury of a wounded animal.

Seeing that Dudley had the clear upper hand, Gideon leapt off his horse to pull Hester into his arms. "My darling, are you well?" He looked her over quickly from head to toe, then clasped her tightly and repeatedly kissed her hair, the only part of her his lips could reach. He did not release her for she was trembling so hard, he feared she might faint. "Are you hurt in any way?"

"No, but I have never been so afraid." She raised her head to peer up at him. Her face was paler than usual, but a trace of colour was returning to her cheeks. She shuddered one last time. "Sir Ralph is a horrible man. Gideon, he killed both those men without a bit of remorse. I feared he would do the same to me—and to you."

"Now you are safe." He hugged her again before turning to see if Dudley needed him.

Sir Ralph was sprawled on the ground. Gideon could not tell if he was conscious or, indeed, even breathing. Dudley had stopped pounding him and was standing, straddling his body. He loomed over his father-in-law while blood soaked into his shirt from a hole beneath his arm. His swaying made Gideon worry that he might be near to collapse.

Tom was a few feet away, restraining Argos, who was barking and lunging at the figure on the ground. When Gideon commanded him to hush, he gave a long, drawn-out whine, disappointed that his help was not needed.

After making sure that Hester was steady, Gideon released his grip on her shoulders, and she walked over with him to examine the injured. While she exclaimed over the grazing wound to Dudley's ribs and praised him for coming to her rescue, Gideon stooped over Sir Ralph's body. Dudley had turned his father-in-law's face into a bloodied mess which made Gideon wince. His hand involuntarily moved to his own neck, before he felt for Sir Ralph's pulse.

The man was still alive. Gideon did not know how lucky Sir Ralph would feel to have survived such a beating, especially when he learned that he would hang, but after threatening Hester, he deserved a brutal fate.

Releasing Argos to gambol around his master, Tom went to collect the horses. Gideon thanked Dudley and asked if he felt well enough to ride to Mynchon Grange to give the J.P. his statement. Evidently pleased to play the hero, for once, Dudley was eager to, so Gideon helped Hester bind his ribs with strips torn from Dudley's ruined shirt. Soon, Tom returned leading their mounts. Nervous from the sounds of conflict and the smell of blood, still they had not strayed far.

With Gideon's help, Tom hoisted Sir Ralph, still unconscious, like a sack across his horse's back, while Dudley and Hester waited. Then, with Tom at Penny's head, Gideon took Hester by the waist and threw her up behind his saddle. If Dudley noticed anything strange about this arrangement, he did not say. He was weak enough now to accept

Tom's help onto his horse with a look of thanks.

ℬ

The excitement raised at Mynchon Grange, when their wounded and disheveled party rode up to the door, was nearly as great as if James Stuart had appeared with an army. As soon as Dudley testified that his father-in-law had threatened to kill Mrs. Kean, Mr. Mynchon sent a servant to fetch the two constables from the Fauconberg Arms to place Sir Ralph under arrest.

Hester stayed with the gentlemen long enough to repeat what Sir Ralph had told her of his motive for killing Mr. Fenwick. Then she gratefully surrendered to Mrs. Mynchon, who conducted her to a bedroom and left her to a maid's ministrations. Hester's shaking had finally stopped, leaving her weak as a newborn lamb. As the maid bathed her face, the tears she had been too frightened to shed finally came, running down her cheeks in such torrents that she thought she might drown. She cried from relief, too, for she would never be able to forget the sight of Sir Ralph's pistol pointed directly at St. Mars's heart. Her own danger had seemed as nothing compared to the threat of watching him die. She had never witnessed fear on his face until today, but his eyes had revealed that his terror was for her, too.

From pure exhaustion, she fell into a deep sleep, her last thought thanking God for sparing them both.

The next morning, she was awakened by the maid who carried in a tray with a large breakfast and a pot of chocolate. Hester was appalled to discover that she had slept through the night, but was forced to admit she felt better for the rest. She had a sense of unreality, as if the events of yesterday had happened to someone else. She could not recall her dreams, but knew they had been filled with terrors of some kind.

The maid had brushed her clothes and laid them out on the chest, so as soon as she had finished her breakfast, she dressed and went in search of Mrs. Mynchon.

She found her hostess bustling about downstairs. It was clear that Mrs. Mynchon had been up and busy for hours. She examined Hester's face before declaring how glad she was to see her colour so much better. "For you were as pale as a blancmange when you walked through the door."

Hester thanked her for her kindness and her tender care, but said she ought to return to Beckwith Manor as soon as possible. By now, Pamela would have heard of her father's arrest and she would need all the support Hester could give.

Mrs. Mynchon sadly shook her head. "Yes, poor lamb. She was distraught when we carried the news to her. Sir Robert would have gone with Mr. Mayfield to do it, but as he had not been able to wash or change his clothes, me and Mr. Mynchon offered to do it. Sir Robert would have been kind to her, I know, but under the circumstances we thought the news would come better from older friends."

"So Sir Robert returned to the inn?" Hester wished she could see him. After the fright she had endured, she was still in need of the comfort only his arms could bring.

"Yes, and I shouldn't be surprised if he did not fall directly into bed, too. He had not slept much the night before. Just between you and me, Mr. Mynchon never was convinced that Sir Robert was the killer, but he has taken himself to task for letting Sir Ralph pull the wool over his eyes. You know, he never did like Sir Ralph."

Hester did not let on that this had been obvious to anyone who had ever seen them together in the same room. Mr. Mynchon's instincts about Sir Ralph had been much better than her own. She had found him full of pretension and his own importance, but his manner had struck her at best as amusing, at worst merely annoying. She had never met anyone exactly like him before, and hoped she never would again, but knew from now on she would always be wary of such a high degree of conceit.

Mrs. Mynchon offered to accompany her home and Hester gratefully accepted. In truth, she dreaded facing Pamela alone. She did not feel strong enough yet to assume the burden of Pamela's sorrow.

During their ride, however, she was heartened when Mrs. Mynchon remembered to mention that "Sir Robert" had left word for her that he would visit her today at Beckwith Manor.

"He wanted to escort you there himself, and indeed, was very concerned for your welfare, but I persuaded him that rest would do you the most good."

Hester had to turn to look out the window and pretend to be gazing at the passing scenery in order to hide the smile that came to her lips.

Her first errand on reaching Beckwith Manor was to check on Dudley's wound. She discovered, however, that after a good night's sleep, feeling hale and hearty this morning, her cousin had taken himself on a ride about his estate. This was better news than she had dared to hope for.

Turning her attention to Pamela then, Hester and Mrs. Mynchon found her tucked up in bed. When Hester gave a tentative knock on her chamber door and the two were admitted by Pamela's maid, they were greeted by eyes red from weeping and big with fear. Pamela stared at Hester as if expecting to be blamed for her father's sins.

Hester quickly crossed the room to her side, took up her hand, and let her know how much she regretted that Sir Ralph's guilt had caused her pain. Her words provoked a long bout of tears. It was quite some time before Pamela could be comforted enough to talk, but seeing that Hester had her cousin well in hand, Mrs. Mynchon whispered that she would leave them to it and quietly made her exit.

After some coaxing, Hester managed to persuade Pamela to confide in her. Besides the grief and shame of learning that her father was a murderer, she was afraid of what her future would bring. Neither mentioned the undeniable fact that Sir Ralph would be put to death for his crimes. Instead, they discussed Pamela's problems as if the sentence against him had already been carried out.

They discussed her worries at length. Yearsley Park would have to be sold, and for that Pamela had no regrets. "Papa always did love his estate more than he ever loved me."

Hester, who knew how he had sacrificed his daughter's happiness to build it, could not deny this statement.

What they did not know was how much the estate would bring. Hester had begun to suspect that Yearsley Park might be encumbered with debt. If that were true, then depending on the size of the burden,

Beckwith Manor might also be at risk. Pamela did not know what to expect from her father's will. "He said that if I gave birth to an heir, he planned to leave the lot to him, but as it is, I do not know what provisions he has made. But no matter what his will says, everything that comes to me will be Dudley's and not mine. I will have no choice but to stay."

Hester wished she could offer Pamela more comfort, but there was nothing she could say. The law was clear. Any property that came to a woman, either from wages, investment, gift, or inheritance, became her husband's upon marriage. If the sale of Yearsley Park produced a fortune, it would be Dudley's by right. Without the threat Sir Ralph had held over him, Pamela had nothing with which to bargain for better treatment.

A servant knocked and entered. "Sir Robert is downstairs, Mrs. Kean, and is asking for you."

Pamela sat up with a frenzied look. "You must make my apologies, Hester. I cannot face Sir Robert." A thought suddenly occurred to her. "Perhaps he would like to buy Papa's estate. You could ask him."

Assuring Pamela that she would, and promising to visit her again later, Hester first ran into her chamber. She did not want to keep St. Mars waiting long enough to change her clothes, so she only checked the glass to make sure that her hair was in order and to rinse her teeth.

When she descended the stairs, he was pacing in the hall. The sound of her tread on the steps made him raise his head. A smile spread over his features as he crossed the hall to meet her, and the relief she felt to see him all in one piece brought easy tears to her eyes. The shock of yesterday's events still had the power to shake her.

As she reached the next-to-last step, he did not bother to see if anyone was watching before swooping her into his arms. Alarmed, but in spite of herself thrilled, Hester felt her feet leave the floor as he swung her around. He spoke into her ear, "It is done, love. Now we can leave. When shall I come for you?"

Hester's heart was overcome. Her mind was awhirl. She wished she could stay forever wrapped in his arms, inhaling the scent of him. She pushed him an arm's length away to suggest going into the parlour where they could talk, but then she caught sight of the bruises on his neck. "You are hurt!" she exclaimed, raising a hand to touch them gently. "How did this happen?"

"That, my dear, is the handiwork of your cousin—quite literally his hands. But never mind that now. You and I have plans to make."

Hester shook her head. "I will not budge until you tell me, except to move this conversation into the parlour." Taking him by the hand, she led him from the hall.

"If it means I can kiss you, I will be very happy to go." The moment they had crossed the threshold into the smaller room, he followed up this statement by wrapping his arms around her waist and kissing her as if his life depended upon it.

Still with their lips touching, Hester drew him away from the door. She was happy to give in, but not ready yet to have their intimacy exposed. The past few days had been filled with enough drama. She did not know whether the news would throw Pamela into hysterics or Mary into sulks, but until she had recovered from the damage Sir Ralph's threats had done to her equilibrium, she could not bear to experience another scene.

St. Mars tenderly held her face between his hands while exploring her mouth. Any resolve that Hester had melted in the path of his onslaught, until finally, rising passion forced him to pull away.

Resting his forehead on hers, he paused to catch his breath before saying, "Just think that soon we'll be able to do this any time we want."

The boyish note in his voice made her laugh. "First, though, are you going to tell me what happened?"

Issuing a dramatic sigh, he related to her all that had passed after they had separated in the maze. When he got to the part in his story where Dudley assaulted him, he made light of it, but the purples and blues of his bruises told her how serious the attack had been.

"Thank heavens for Tom! You must tell him how grateful I am."

"You can tell him yourself, just as soon as we leave for the coast. How soon can you be ready? Tomorrow? The following day?"

Anxiety knotted Hester's stomach. She had just arrived at Beckwith Manor, had not even had a moment to change her clothes. How could she leave tomorrow with so much unresolved? With Pamela and Dudley at odds, and Mary needing her in London?

St. Mars saw the hesitation on her face, and disappointment clouded his. He grasped her by the shoulders and stared piercingly into her eyes. "What? Why can you not go?"

The knowledge that she had wounded him hit her soundly in the heart. She shook her head. "It's nothing. I was just thinking of Pamela and Mary. I cannot help feeling guilty to leave them in so much turmoil."

The smile he gave her let her know that he understood her, but at the same time it begged her to think of him. "If I thought your staying here any longer would solve their problems, I might be willing to share you for a few days longer. But, my dear Mrs. Kean, it will not. You did not contrive the troubles in which they find themselves and it is not up to you to mend them."

He drew her into his arms again and pressed a kiss into her hair. "Whereas I, my dear, will be in the deepest sort of agony until you find it in your heart to live with me."

She could feel the beat of his heart against her breast. She knew he was correct. There was nothing she could really do for Pamela, and had not Mary proved how sensible she could be? Hester still feared that Mrs. Mayfield would force the girl into an unhappy match, but Mary might have enough strength to defy her. Even if Mrs. Mayfield managed to drag her to the altar, she was capable of refusing to pledge her troth. And if she did, nobody could make her accept a husband.

St. Mars held her away again to study her face, and she gave him a smile tinged with chagrin. "I am not as essential to them as my conceit has led me to believe."

"You are essential to me. So, if that is decided, when will you be ready to go?"

Things were moving so quickly. Hester had never had an impetuous nature. Nevertheless, she reflected no more than a second before saying, "The day after tomorrow. That will give me a chance to have a conversation with Dudley, and to pack the things I need."

St. Mars's evident happiness raised a bubble of elation inside her. "No need to take much. When we get to France, you can purchase all the clothes you want."

Running her mind over the things she had left behind in London, she looked at him in dismay. ""Oh, no! The fan you gave me is in my chamber at Hawkhurst House. How can I leave without it?"

He laughed. "My dearest simpleton! I shall buy you a dozen fans."

"But none will ever take the place of the first!" She sighed, feeling a pang. "If you insist on bullying me, however, I shall have to go without."

"Oh, I do," he said, kissing each of her hands in turn. "I plan to bully you mercilessly. You will never have a peaceful moment."

"Hester?" Mary's voice came from the hall. "Are you down here?"

St. Mars tightened his grip for one last instant. "I shall come for you very early, day after tomorrow, before anyone else is up."

With her heart leaping at the prospect, he released her hands. Hester moved past him to the door to answer Mary, whom she found making her way through the hall and nearly upon them.

"Oh, Hester! I cannot believe it. Sir Ralph, the murderer! And are you perfectly well?" She noticed "Sir Robert" behind Hester, and though a bit surprised, was not distracted from her cousin. She embraced Hester, who assured her that she had not been harmed.

"It was very frightening, but your brother and Sir Robert rescued me. I shall be eternally grateful to them both. But Pamela is the one we must attend to, for she will have to suffer all the consequences of Sir Ralph's wickedness."

She was glad to hear Mary evince compassion for her sister-in-law, who, she acknowledged, was not to blame.

After listening for a few moments, St. Mars excused himself, saying he had only come to see that Mrs. Kean had suffered no lasting ill effects. "I beg you will make my excuses to Mrs. Mayfield and send my wishes for her swift recovery. Tell her that I shall be leaving Coxwold shortly and do not expect to return."

"Will you not have to testify at Sir Ralph's trial?" Mary asked.

"No, I spoke to Mr. Mynchon about my desire to leave and he allowed that the testimony of your brother will be enough to convict Sir Ralph, who has now confessed at any rate. After Mrs. Kean made her statement, it was useless for him to lie, especially after he had shot your brother."

"Then you shall not be obliged to be a witness either, Hester?"

"No, thank God! The next assizes will not take place for months, and I should hate testifying." She gave an involuntary shudder, which made St. Mars glance at her in consternation. Recollecting her ordeal made her feel as if something could happen to steal her happiness again. Hoping not to infect St. Mars with her worries, she added for his benefit, "But we shall be able to forget all about it, once we are gone." She knew that Mary would think she was referring to their journey to London, but St. Mars would know what she meant.

With a smile that held a secret for her alone, he took her hand and kissed it, then bowed farewell to Mary before leaving them to make his way out of the house.

It pained Hester to see him go, even knowing that in two days, they would always be together. She wondered what preparations he would make for getting them to France. He had told her nothing of the details. She did not even know if Tom would go with them, but with Katy, Tom's wife, at St. Mars's house at Lambeth, she doubted it. This made her realize that the sacrifices she would make to leave with St. Mars would be small in comparison to his.

These thoughts passed quickly through her head, while Mary exclaimed again at her astonishment. She wanted to hear all the details of Hester's harrowing experience, so Hester sat down with her and talked, all the while feeling guilty for the hurt she would soon be causing her favourite cousin.

*B*esides, I now considered myself as bound by the Laws of Hospitality to a People who had treated me with so much Expence and Magnificence.

CHAPTER XX

Dudley returned home in time for dinner, while Pamela ate her meal on a tray in her bedchamber. Dudley was in the sunniest of humours now that Sir Ralph no longer held a knife to his throat. He was already making plans to expand his stable, hoping to breed a line of plate-winning horses. Hester said nothing to dampen his spirits, though the possibility that he would find himself bankrupt again made her cringe.

At the conclusion of their meal, she begged Dudley for a private conversation, which warily, he granted.

They retreated to the small downstairs parlour where she and St. Mars had met. Normally, a part of Pamela's domain rather than his, it still was the most comfortable room in which to chat.

Hester had contemplated speaking to Dudley about "Sir Robert's" bruises, for if he did not learn to control his temper, he might follow Sir Ralph to the gallows. But to speak of them would put his bristles up and she had a more important goal in mind, one that would take a great deal of persuasion.

"Well, here we are, Coz," he said, once they had seated themselves in two cushioned armchairs. "What was it you was wishing to say?"

Hester thanked him again for saving her. She complimented him on the courage it had taken to charge with Sir Ralph's loaded pistol aimed at him. The sincerity of her thanks eased his wariness and would make him more receptive to her requests, she hoped.

After he had basked in her gratitude for several minutes, she broached the real object of her talk. "I wished to speak to you of something while I still have the chance, since I will soon be leaving and you have plans that will take you to York and other places." She told him of her fears that he might find Yearsley Park was burdened with debt, basing her assumption on the fact that Sir Ralph had been willing to murder Mr. Fenwick for a relatively small parcel of land. "I do not suppose you will be able to discover the actual case until Sir Ralph's will is read, which will not occur for several months. But I know that Sir Ralph held a note on this estate, so it might behoove you to make enquiries before you expand your stable on the basis of expectations. I hope very much that I am wrong, and that the sale of the property will make you as rich as Croesus, but I beg you will be cautious until you know."

Her words had a sobering effect on him. He agreed that he should contact Sir Ralph's solicitor as soon as possible, but growled when she reminded him that Sir Ralph would spend some of his own money making himself comfortable in gaol.

"He don't deserve any comforts," Dudley declared, "not after he shot me and wanted to shoot you!"

Hester smiled. "I agree. Nevertheless, until he is convicted, he will still have control of his fortune. Perhaps Pamela can help you uncover the state of his affairs. If his debts do not reckon to an amount that should concern you, you can move ahead with your plans." She devoutly hoped that the sale of Sir Ralph's estate would cover all of Dudley's ambitions.

He was mulling over what she had said about Pamela. He gave Hester a shrewd look from beneath his brows. "What you're saying is that I ought to treat Pamela better, so she'll help me."

Hester gave him her frankest look. "It would be wise. It would also be kind. You could send Pamela to live in York—I believe it would be out of the question now for her to get a place at Court—but you would still need someone to keep house for you and to look after the children. If you and Pamela can arrive at a civil way of dealing with each other, you may both live to be grateful for your marriage."

Hester knew she was encroaching on Dudley's intimate affairs, but this would be the last time she would see him, and not only Dudley's and Pamela's happiness depended on their making the best of their marriage, but also the welfare of Hester's younger cousins. Speaking to him this way had been a gamble, but she could see Dudley turning her words over in his head and calculating the benefits of having a reasonably contented wife.

After he mused a bit longer, he shrugged. "Pam isn't too bad, I guess. She's a first-rate rider. Maybe she'll be more tolerable now that she won't have her father to tattle to."

"That's true," Hester agreed. "I had not thought of that."

"You have no idea," he said, "what a trial it's been, having that man watching over me. And knowing I had a spy in my own home!"

Hester nodded encouragingly. "I should be very surprised if Pamela refers to her father in any manner again."

Dudley was pleased to contemplate this improvement to his domestic felicity. Hester would have liked to suggest that he visit Pamela in her chamber to express some sympathy for her, but she knew she could only encourage matters to a point. Dudley and Pamela would have to work things out for themselves. If, as Dudley had suggested, his greatest problem with his wife had been that her loyalty had been to her father and never to him, then perhaps he would be kinder to her once that tie was severed.

They parted with a slight feeling of embarrassment, but also with ample goodwill.

Hester could not do anything more for Mary, a truth that made her sad. Since they shared a bedchamber, it would be difficult enough to pack a few belongings without revealing her plan to elope with St. Mars.

For that was what they were planning, she realized, as she climbed the stairs to her room. The thought almost shocked her but within a moment or two she was laughing. Somehow the use of that word made their adventure more real to her. The day after tomorrow had seemed like years away. She still could not quite believe that only one more sunrise stood between the life she had felt condemned to lead and her dream of being St. Mars's wife.

Whoever would have expected quiet, sober Hester Kean to elope with an outlaw? What would they think if they knew he was also the highwayman Blue Satan? She hoped that everyone she knew would be shocked and that they would enjoy gossiping about the scandal for several months. Mary, once she had recovered from her disappointment, would undoubtedly applaud Hester's daring. Hester's brother Jeremy—after he had read the letter she would write—would only wish for her happiness. Neither Isabella nor Harrowby would miss her much, but would keep on living for their own pleasure. Mrs. Mayfield would be furious to learn that her niece had fooled her and to lose her as a servant. This last idea gave Hester another reason to smile.

She needed to rest before returning to Pamela's bedside. It was not every day that one planned an elopement. She would use the time to organize her packing.

She spent the evening consoling Pamela again. Mary did her best to help. It was difficult to find a topic of conversation that would not depress Pamela, though. They dared not talk about Mary's removal to Hawkhurst House, for Pamela would dwell on the ambition she had had to wait at Court. Hester called an early end to the evening, saying that Pamela should rest, but her real reason was selfish. She could only comfort Pamela so much without dragging down her own spirits, and she did not want the anticipation of her happiness to be crushed.

In the morning, after breakfast, when Mary had gone out riding, Hester gathered two linen chemises, a night-shift, a freshly laundered cap, and the thinnest gown she could find and packed them in the portmanteau she had used on her journey north on the stage. She would be wearing a corset and hooped petticoat which would have to suffice as long as it took them to reach France. The chemises would give her a welcome change of underclothes, and, provided her gowns did not get too soiled, she hoped not to be a complete disgrace to St. Mars when they arrived at his estate. She left her hair and tooth brushes, as well as her small supply of tooth powder to be packed in the morning.

Her biggest concern was that her nervousness would give her away to Mary. She could not help feeling guilty about leaving the girl, and she was afraid her emotions would show.

As soon as she had gathered all she could take without weighing down St. Mars's horse too much, she put the portmanteau back into the chest, hoping to move it out quietly again after Mary had fallen asleep. It was going to be difficult enough to dress without waking her, especially as early as the sun rose, but already with autumn approaching, the hour of dawn was advancing.

With a few deep breaths to slow her racing pulse, she went to Pamela's chamber to resume entertaining her.

To distract herself as much as Pamela, she offered to read and managed to find among her uncle's old books, a short piece of writing by Mrs. Behn, entitled *Oroonoko, or the Royal Slave, a True Story.* Considering it, under the circumstances, more distracting than a collection of sermons, she had made a good start when a servant rushed into the room to announce the arrival of a stranger who insisted on speaking with Mrs. Kean.

"Who is it?" Pamela asked, sitting up abruptly.

"A Maister 'Enry. 'E says 'e's coom from London. And in a coach and four."

Hester jumped up in alarm. What could James Henry be doing here? Putting the book down on her chair, she started to leave the room.

Pamela was throwing off her covers. She told the servant, "Send my maid at once. I shall be down straightaway. Do not allow him to leave until I have spoken to him, Hester."

As concerned as she was about what James Henry's appearance could mean, Hester's thoughts had leapt to St. Mars. She must prevent James Henry from seeing him. She must find a way to warn him not to show himself at the house. He had not said he would visit her today. In fact, his message for Pamela had sounded like a final farewell, so perhaps she did not have to fear their encountering each other.

James Henry was St. Mars's half-brother. There had always existed an unhappy rivalry between them. After their father was murdered, James Henry, along with nearly everyone else, had suspected St. Mars of the crime. She had never heard James Henry say that he had altered his opinion, and she did not know if he would call the law down on his outlaw brother. Whether St. Mars had intended to come to Beckwith Manor or not, she would have to alert him.

But how would she manage to escape the house with James Henry in residence? Would he consider it his duty to ride after them once Hester's absence was discovered?

These thoughts spun round in her head as she flew from Pamela's chamber and hastened down the stairs. As soon as she reached the hall, where James Henry was waiting, she saw in his face that something terrible had occurred. He looked as if he had travelled without sleep. The dirt on his boots and clothes revealed that he had been riding very hard.

Hester bobbed the quickest of curtsies in response to his bow. She had not seen him since turning down his proposal of marriage. That memory was far from both their minds, however, when she asked what had brought him to Beckwith Manor.

Sympathy filled his eyes, and his tone was very grave. "I am come to take you and Mrs. Mary Mayfield back to London. I have hired a coach. My lord wishes you to make haste and come with me directly."

"Has something happened to Isabella?"

"No. I'm afraid it was Lord Rennington."

Hester felt her knees go weak. "Not poor Georgie," she breathed. Tears welled in her eyes.

"Yes. He was taken from us last week. He came down with the measles, and it was assumed he would recover. But then a second fever seized him, worse than the first."

A chill spread through Hester's veins, and she shivered. The sense of foreboding she had had descended over her like a cold rain.

James Henry went on, "The news reached his parents just a few days ago. My lady collapsed, and my lord is consumed with grief. Both wish for you to come. My lady's mother has been unable to console her. She says she needs you. Can you be ready to travel within the hour? We had best start as soon as possible. We have my lord's permission to stop as needed on the way."

Hester's heart was breaking. She had barely thought of Georgie since St. Mars had stunned her by coming into Yorkshire, but she had loved the child. She recalled the soft down of his hair and the feel of his tiny hands upon her face. He had learned to laugh just before they had left him in Kent. The notion of his suffering was more than she could take. And Isabella and Harrowby—they had learned to dote upon him, largely because she had encouraged them.

Anger built in her breast when she recalled the doctor's warning about putting him out to nurse. He had insisted that the child would be safer if his own mother nursed him, but Mrs. Mayfield had scoffed. None of her children had fallen ill when tended by a wet-nurse, so why should Isabella's baby, when nursing him would interfere with her pleasure?

"Shall I call a servant to you?" James Henry was bending over her, concern in his voice. "Someone should bring you a sip of brandy."

In a daze, Hester shook her head. "No, I thank you. I shall get ready." But she could not think of what to do. A languor had entered her limbs. She found it hard to move.

Somehow, she became aware of Pamela standing in the doorway, dressed and curious. When Hester fumbled for words to present James Henry and relate the reason for his coming, her voice caught on Georgie's name.

Pamela's hand flew to her lips, and she gasped.

James Henry explained that he had been sent to bring Hester and Mary back at once. While Hester stood, unable to move, he took charge, asking Pamela if she could send a servant to locate Mary and a maid to pack what the ladies needed for the journey. "Tell her to pack only a few essentials, as we shall stop on the road as few times as possible."

"You will leave today?" Dismay filled Pamela's voice.

"Yes. That is my lord's wish. He and his lady are prostrate with grief."

With her own sorrow so raw, Pamela responded with tears in her eyes. "Yes, of course. And I shall arrange for their other things to be sent to Hawkhurst House. Is that where they should be sent, Hester?"

Hester's mind was incapable of taking in Pamela's question. With more worried looks, James Henry answered for her, "Yes, please. That will do very well."

The next several minutes passed like a blur. Hester was made to drink a sip or two of brandy. Though her head still felt muddled—at times she was not very clear on what was occurring—she managed to follow James Henry's suggestion to walk to her chamber with the maid's help and to respond to the girl's questions when asked what she would like her to pack.

The maid exclaimed in surprise when she found the folded clothing in the portmanteau. Hester gave no response, but the recollection of the joy she had felt when packing it that morning thickened the painful lump in her throat. Her elopement with St. Mars had been nothing but a dream after all. How could she have thought that it was real?

Mary's hasty entrance into the chamber made Hester glance towards the door. The girl's eyes were large. She stared at Hester as if afraid to witness her grief then crossed the room to hold her in a silent embrace. Hester's throat hurt so much that she could not swallow.

Somehow between Mary and the maid, Hester's bag was readied and she found herself downstairs. The door of the hired carriage was open. She hesitated before ascending the low step. James Henry had taken her hand to help her into the coach, but she knew there was something she had forgotten.

From out of a mist, she turned to say goodbye to Pamela, who had followed them outdoors. As they embraced, Hester said, "Could you send word to Sir Robert that I shall not be here for his visit tomorrow? Please give him my sincere regrets and explain what has taken me away."

Surprised, Pamela nevertheless promised to deliver her message. She gazed at Hester as if fearing that she might break.

"Say, also, that I shall hope to renew our acquaintance in London."

As she allowed James Henry to assist her into the coach, she prayed that Pamela would keep her promise and that St. Mars would understand.

THE END

AUTHOR'S NOTE

I am often asked about the usage of Mrs. as a title for Hester Kean and other single women. In the early 18th century, the convention was to address all ladies as "mistress." In Restoration plays, this is abbreviated as Mrs. To be perfectly correct, in English there should be no period after Mrs, but for a mostly American audience, I have employed the American punctuation. Another generation would pass before "miss" became a title of respect for unmarried females.

My apologies to the real holders of the livings at Coxwold and Hawnby. An author has to make decisions about whether to make up place names, but these two villages are so charming they deserved to have their names used. This meant that I had to give my fictional characters positions that real people once held. I know nothing of the 18th century clergymen of either parish, nor of the innkeeper for that matter, so I suppose I owe him my apologies, too. The "small timber-framed house" in Coxwold I referred to, later in the century, became the red-brick Shandy Hall occupied by Lawrence Sterne, author of *Tristom Shandy*.

Historical novelists strive to convey a perfect understanding of the periods in which they work, but most of us, I think, find this frustrating and futile. For example, one reads of a few women, even men, who believed in the equality of women as early as Restoration England, but the reality of most women was that they lived, worked, and married entirely at the will of the men in their lives. To give our female characters notions of equality strikes most readers as an anachronism. On the other hand, to make them too subservient annoys others. I try to strike a balance, taking into account that every age produces rebels and freethinkers as well as timid souls, whether oppressed by others, a dislike of conflict, or a simple lack of initiative.

The English in the early 18th century were still a very rural people. Even aristocrats spent a good portion of their year in the country.

While differences in rank were strictly observed, there was less rigidity in the rules of behaviour, familiarity, and politeness than would develop over the succeeding century, and many gentlemen and ladies never went to Court. Regional differences in dialect and custom were greater than I could ever portray without losing my readers completely, even if I could get it right. So, I deal with this by trying to give just a taste.

The late 17th and early 18th centuries made up a period in which some of the greatest houses in England were built. Most of the work on Castle Howard in Yorkshire, the backdrop for *Brideshead Revisited,* was accomplished between 1699 and 1714. Nunnington Hall and East Riddleston Hall, belonging to the National Trust, both of which I visited, were Tudor houses extensively rebuilt during these years. In 1716, the medieval manor house on the Studley estate burned. Its new owner, John Aislabie, influenced by Queen Anne's gardeners, George London and Henry Wise, turned his attention to creating a magnificent garden. Over the next five decades, he and his son William created England's greatest water garden, Fountains Abbey & Studley Royal. My story was, in part, inspired by the ambition of these landowners.

No visitor to England should miss seeing one of its abbey ruins. While Fountains is the most spectacular, the less-visited Byland Abbey gives a greater sense of the solitude experienced by the monks. All these places show how powerful and far-reaching the Catholic Church was and are a stark reminder of the beauty destroyed by Henry VIII.

In *Acts of Faith,* I wanted to explore the history of religious discrimination in Great Britain, especially against Roman Catholics, which lasted for centuries. I have been careful to qualify Catholics as adherents of the Roman Church, because members of the Church of England, like all Anglicans, still recite the Nicene Creed swearing belief in "one holy catholic and apostolic Church."

By 1716, the laws concerning Dissenters of the Protestant variety—as long as they were Trinitarians, not Unitarians—had been relaxed. Although they were still required to take the oaths of Allegiance and Supremacy and to renounce papacy, and forbidden to hold public office or teach at universities, as long as they registered their places of worship, did not meet in private homes, and kept the doors of their meeting houses unbolted, under the Act of Toleration (William and Mary,1688) they were allowed to practice their religion. In the American colonies these Nonconformists, who had been encouraged to emigrate from England, found even greater freedom.

On the other hand, Roman Catholics were considered a threat to national security, what today would be called a "fifth column." The reason for this is best illustrated by a quote from William Blackstone's *Commentaries on the Laws of England (1765)*:

As to papists, what has been said of the Protestant dissenters would hold equally strong for a general toleration of them; provided their separation was founded only upon difference of opinion in religion, and their principles did not also extend to a subversion of the civil government. If once they could be brought to renounce the supremacy of the pope, they might quietly enjoy their seven sacraments, their purgatory, and auricular confession; their worship of relics and images; nay even their transubstantiation. But while they acknowledge a foreign power, superior to the sovereignty of the kingdom, they cannot complain if the laws of that kingdom will not treat them upon the footing of good subjects.

— *Bl. Comm. IV, c.4 ss. iii.2, p. *54*

The Pretender's refusal to renounce his Roman Catholic faith cemented the Jacobite cause with a papal conspiracy once and for all in Protestant minds.

Few of my Catholic friends today seem aware of the severity of the laws against their faith in the 18th century. As I learned about them, I read of the lengths Catholics would go to hide their religious observances, conceal their property from tax collectors, and live their secret lives. One of these practices struck me immediately as a good motive for murder, providing the mystery plot for this novel.

The prejudice against Catholics, and the consequent legal restrictions, have disappeared slowly over the past three hundred years. While measures of relief have been enacted throughout the centuries, a Roman Catholic may still not sit on the throne of the United Kingdom. Only in 2013, with the passage of the Succession to the Crown Act, were heirs to the British throne given permission to marry a Roman Catholic.

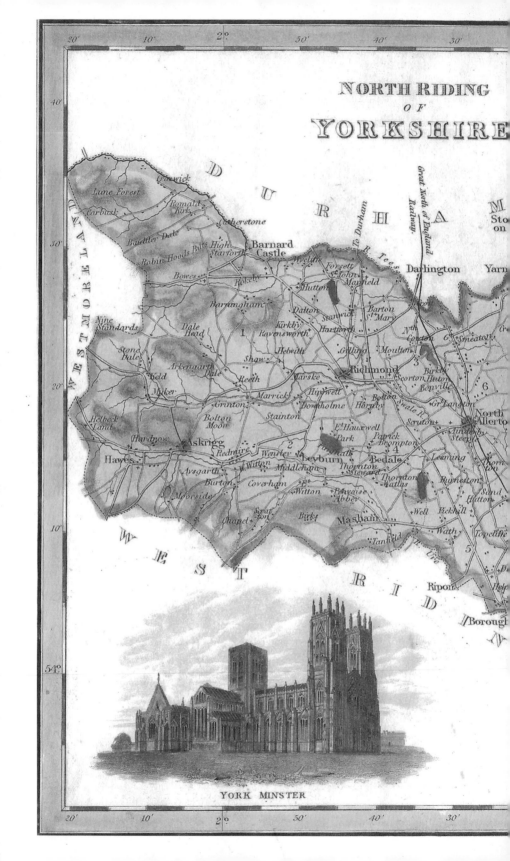

NORTH RIDING
OF
YORKSHIRE

DURHAM

WESTMORELAND

Carwick
Lune Forest
Romald Kirk
Carbusk
Catherstone
Buddler Dale
Robin Hoods Butts   High Starforth   Barnard Castle
Bowes   Rokeby   Wycliffe   Forcett   St John   Mayfield
Hutton
Barningham   Dalton   Stanwick   Barton St Mary
Nine Standards   Dale Head   1   Kirkby Ravensworth   Hartford   Nth Cowton   Smeaton
Stone Dale   Helwith   Gilling   Moulton   3   Birkby
Arkengarth Dale   Shaw   Richmond   Scorton Hutton   Bopville
Field   Reeth   Marske   Hipswell   Bolton   Gr Langton   6
Muker   Grinton   Marrick   Downholme   Hornby   Swale R   Scruton   North Allerto
Helbeck Land   Bolton Moor   Stainton   Et Hauxwell   Tindersby Steer
Hardraw   Askrigg   Redmire   Wensley   Leyburn   Park   Patrick Brompton   4   Leeming   Thorn on
Hawes   Aysgarth   W Witton   Middleham   Bedale   Thornton Steward   Burneston   Sand Hutton
Burton   Coverham   Et Witton   Jarvaise Abbey   Thornton Watlas   Well   Pickhill   Topcliffe
Moorside   Chapel Fort   Birks   Masham   Tanfield   R Ure   Wath   5
WEST   RIDING   Ripon   Boroug

DALE
Field
Great North of England Railway
To Durham
R Tees
Darlington   Yarn
Stockton
M

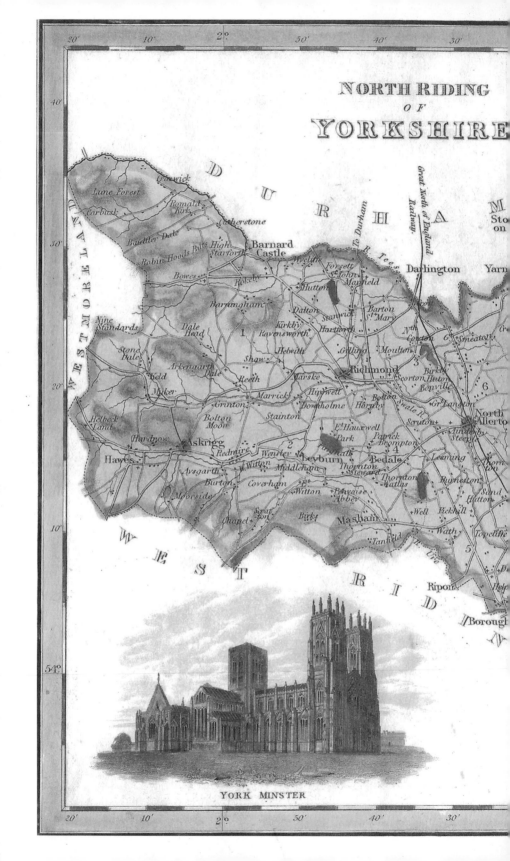

YORK MINSTER